MORE PRAISE FOR

SOME ENCHANTED SEASON

"I loved this story."
—*The Philadelphia Inquirer*

"A four-hanky book, not to be missed."
—*The Orlando Sentinel*

"This uplifting tale is for everyone who
believes in love."
—*Publishers Weekly*

"Intense emotion and riveting drama are the
hallmarks of Marilyn Pappano's work."
—*Romantic Times*

"A gripping novel [with] wonderfully drawn
characters. Pappano is truly an exceptional story-
teller . . . one of romance's finest authors."
—CompuServe *Romance Reviews*

"The story evokes deep emotions and
profound feelings. Riveting."
—*Rendezvous*

BANTAM BOOKS BY MARILYN PAPPANO

Some Enchanted Season

Father To Be

FATHER TO BE

Marilyn Pappano

BANTAM BOOKS

New York Toronto London Sydney Auckland

FATHER TO BE

A Bantam Book / September 1999

ISBN 0-553-57985-1

Published simultaneously in the United States and Canada

Bantam Books are published by Bantam Books, a division of Random
House, Inc. Its trademark, consisting of the words "Bantam Books" and the
portrayal of a rooster, is Registered in U.S. Patent and Trademark Office and
in other countries. Marca Registrada. Bantam Books, 1540 Broadway, New
York, New York 10036.

PRINTED IN THE UNITED STATES OF AMERICA

OPM   10   9   8   7   6   5   4   3   2   1

FATHER
TO BE

Chapter One

I T WAS FIVE-THIRTY ON A FRIDAY AFTERNOON when Caleb Brown walked into the grocery store two blocks off Main Street. Though he would have preferred to come earlier so he could get home before dark, circumstances chose the time. It was the end of the week, the beginning of the month, payday, and people were just leaving work and stopping on their way home to do their weekly shopping. The store was too busy for anyone to pay attention to one twelve-year-old kid whose parents were probably around somewhere.

He walked through the produce section as if looking for his mom, then took a turn onto the canned food aisle. The only shoppers there were at the other end and had their backs to him. They didn't see him sweep a half dozen cans of green beans off the shelf and into his backpack. On the next row, no one saw the bags of rice disappear either, or the macaroni, the peanut butter, canned tuna, and two loaves of store-brand bread.

Acting as normally as he could, he slung the full pack

over his shoulder by one strap and started toward the front of the store. This was always the hard part—walking past the clerks without making them suspicious. He was sure that if they ever really looked at him, they'd know he was a thief, and so he stared at the floor and hunched his shoulders and tried hard not to make anyone notice him. He must have gotten pretty good at it, because he hadn't been caught yet, but his hands got sweaty and his chest felt like someone was squeezing it tight. He was always afraid that each time would be the time something would go wrong.

Sure enough, it was.

He was almost even with the cash register in the express lane, maybe fifteen feet from the door, when a yank on his backpack jerked him to a stop. He tried to pull free but managed only to twist around enough to see that it was a big man in shirt-sleeves who'd grabbed him and was holding on tight.

"Where do you think you're going?"

Caleb tried to act innocent, but with his face burning hot, he knew it wasn't going to work. "Out to the c-car to—to wait for my mom," he bluffed, but his voice was high, like a girl's, and he couldn't look the man in the eye. "She's—she's getting groceries, and she said I can wait in the car."

"Your mother's in the store getting groceries," the man repeated as if he didn't believe him. "Tell me her name, and I'll have the clerk page her. She can come up to the desk and we'll straighten this out."

"Her—her name . . ." His gaze darting side to side, Caleb looked for a way out. If the guy would ease up just a little, he could slide out of the backpack and run, but the grip was so tight, it was cutting off the blood to his arm.

"What's wrong, boy? You forget your mother's name?" Looking disgusted, the man turned to the customer service desk and the woman working there. "Call the police, Eileen. Tell 'em we've got a shoplifter over here."

A sick feeling rushed up from Caleb's gut. He couldn't let them arrest him. Even if they didn't put him in jail, they'd hold him awhile, and they wouldn't just let him walk out by himself. They'd want to talk to his mom or dad, and then they'd find out everything. He couldn't let that happen. He'd *promised*.

"L-look, you got the stuff. I didn't t-take nothin'. Just let me go and I won't come back, I swear."

"Yeah, right. This isn't the first time you've stolen from us. Why do you think I've been watching you?"

"You can't call the police!" Caleb shouted and jerked, desperate to get loose. Surprised, the guy pushed him against the counter, forcing his face down until the cold glass was against his cheek, but he still tried to squirm free—until he heard a voice.

"Uncle Nathan, I know that boy. What is that man doing to him?"

Caleb went still, closed his eyes, and wished he could die. Of all the people in the whole stupid town of Bethlehem, New York, *she* was the one he didn't want to see, not now, not like this. He thought he'd been embarrassed when the guy grabbed him, but that was nothing compared to this. This was a hundred times worse. This was pure humiliation.

He heard footsteps as they came closer, heard a man speak. "Bill, what's the problem?"

"I caught this kid stealing, Nathan—and it's not the first time. He's trying to carry my store off one bag at a time."

"Why don't you let him up? He's not going anywhere, are you, son?"

Caleb didn't *want* to be let up. He didn't want to stand there, humiliated, in front of *her*. But Bill let him go and took his backpack at the same time, and he had no choice except to straighten up from the counter. He didn't have to look at her though. Instead, he stared at the floor, hot and sick and scared enough to cry.

"What's your name?" Nathan asked, but Caleb just stared harder at the floor.

When he didn't answer, *she* did. "It's Caleb Brown. He's in my class at school . . . sometimes."

"Caleb, I'm Nathan Bishop. This is Bill Mitchell, and you already know Alanna."

Nathan offered his hand, but Caleb didn't take it because then she'd see how badly his own hand was shaking. She'd know he was scared, and that would make her feel even sorrier for him. He didn't need anyone's pity, most of all hers, and so he just kept on staring at the floor.

Nathan didn't seem to mind. He turned away and started talking to the store guy about what was in the backpack, but Alanna kept looking at Caleb. What would he see if he looked back? Pity? Shock? Scorn? Would she still talk to him now that she knew he was a thief? Would she tell her friends, who'd always made fun of him anyway?

He didn't know, and he didn't care.

He *didn't*.

The sounds of the automatic doors opening drew his gaze. The two men were paying no attention to him. If he could get a good head start, he could outrun both of them and make his way through the alleys and back streets to the road that led home. Once he got outside town, they would never find him. They wouldn't even know where to look.

With his muscles tight, his jaw clenched, he moved an inch closer to the door. When neither man noticed, he took another step, bigger this time, and was about to take off, when Nathan Bishop took hold of his collar and pulled him back.

"Have the clerk ring it up," he was saying to Bill, "and I'll pay for it, then Alanna and I will give him a ride home. I'll have a talk with his parents."

Panic made Caleb look at Alanna's uncle for the first time. And he realized just how bad his luck was.

Nathan Bishop was a cop.

There was a loud rushing in Caleb's ears as he tried to think what to do. There was no way he could let a cop take him home. He'd take one look around and know something was bad wrong, and he'd call the welfare people and the sheriff and whoever else.

But there was no way to get loose either. Even when Nathan paid for the food, he pulled the money out with his left hand and kept a tight grip on Caleb with his right.

"Thanks for handling this, Nathan," the store guy said as they started toward the door.

Caleb considered dragging his feet, or grabbing hold of the rail that separated the in door from the out, or tearing off his shirt, but instead he let the cop pull him outside and across the parking lot to his truck—the black and white one with the light bar and the seven-pointed star on the door. Surely he would let go of him there, just for a minute, and then Caleb could run like hell. He knew some places to hide.

But Nathan didn't let him go. He unlocked and opened the passenger door, pushed the seat forward, and sort of helped, sort of pushed Caleb into the backseat. Then Alanna got in the front and Nathan got behind the wheel, and he was trapped with no way to escape.

Trapped. Like a scared animal.

There were people in town who thought his whole family wasn't much better than animals—people who laughed at him and his brothers and sister because their clothes were shabby and didn't fit, and they weren't clean and were poor and the little kids were hungry most of the time. Alanna had never been like those people, but now that she knew he was a thief, she might be. She hadn't even said a word to him so far. She'd talked *about* him, but not *to* him, like maybe she was ashamed to know him.

Hell, he wouldn't have answered her if she had spoken to him.

"Which way, Caleb?" Nathan asked.

He answered in his angriest, most sullen voice. "Take Tenth Street east out of town."

No one said anything as they drove. The cop didn't ask what he was doing in town by himself and did his parents know he was shoplifting from the grocery store, and why was he doing that anyway? Alanna didn't mention the last month of school that he'd missed or the end-of-the-year picnic at City Park or what she was doing for summer vacation. As for Caleb, he had no time for conversation. He had plans to make.

By the time they reached the crossroads near old Mr. Hayes's place, he'd come up with the best chance he was likely to get. As soon as the cop passed the mailboxes clumped together on the far side of the road, he spoke up. "Hey, that's our mailbox back there. Can I get our mail?"

Nathan was giving him a distrusting look in the rear-view mirror, but he stopped, shifted into reverse, and backed up.

"Don't get too close. Ours is the one falling over backward. You can't reach it from the car. I'll have to get out." It really was their mailbox, and looked it. It had been beaten in and hammered back out too many times to count. The bottom of the post had rotted away, and it tilted so far that only the barbed wire fence kept it from falling down. The lid was broken off, and when it rained, the mail inside would get soaked, if there ever was any.

There hadn't been for more months than he could remember.

Nathan came to a stop in the middle of the road, and Caleb scooted onto the edge of the seat. The backpack with the groceries was on the opposite floorboard, but he couldn't reach for it, couldn't risk getting seen. His nerves were tingling, his hands getting sweaty, as he prepared to make his big break.

Then Nathan looked at him. "Sit back, Caleb. Alanna? Do you mind?"

"Of course not."

Caleb waited until she circled the truck, then he dove through the open door. He hit the ground hard, rolled, and came up on his feet, then vaulted the fence and headed into the woods. The trees grew heavy, and their branches scraped his skin and tore at his shirt, but he didn't slow down. He heard shouts behind him—Alanna calling his name, the cop yelling at her to wait in the truck—then the sounds of pursuit, and he ran faster, blindly crashing through the undergrowth.

Stinging sweat dripped into his eyes, and he wiped them with his shirt-sleeve. His side was beginning to ache and his breaths were labored when he saw the fallen tree ahead. He couldn't go under it, and with all the brush along the sides, he couldn't go around. That left only over. He hit it at a run, the bark biting into his hands as he scrambled for a hold. He thought he'd found one, when abruptly he went sailing over the tree. He landed on the other side, then something dropped on top of him and pinned him there.

"Why'd you run, Caleb?" Nathan Bishop demanded.

With one side of his face pressed into the dirt, Caleb muttered, "You figure it out."

"I'd say it's because you're scared to go home—scared to let your folks know you got caught stealing. But even if you'd gotten away from me tonight, I would have shown up tomorrow. They still would have known." He breathed in a couple of times, deep and loud. "If I let you up, will you promise not to run off again?"

"No," Caleb replied, but he let go anyway. Caleb sat up and wiped dirt from his face.

"Lilah Brown is your mother, isn't she?"

"I don't have a mother." Not since she'd walked out two years before, when she'd gotten tired of being poor and never having money to spend on pretty things. She'd found a man who didn't mind buying pretty things, and she'd left her family behind. She didn't want them, and they didn't want her.

"So you live with your father. It must be hard for him, taking care of the farm and you kids all by himself."

Gritting his teeth, Caleb fingered a new hole in his shirt and said nothing.

"With him working so hard, he wouldn't be happy to find out you'd been caught stealing, would he? Unless maybe he put you up to it. Was that it? He figured they'd go easier on a kid than on him?"

"My dad doesn't steal!"

"So you're afraid of what he'll do when he finds out that you do. Will he punish you? Beat you? Hurt you?"

"*No!* Of course he won't! He *loves* us! Don't say he doesn't!"

"It has nothing to do with love, Caleb. Some people hurt their kids without meaning to. They love them. They just don't know how to deal with them."

"Not my dad! He'd never hurt us—never! He loves us and takes real good care of us!"

"Then why are you stealing food?"

Caleb slumped against the tree trunk. The shadows were getting deeper. Before long it would be dark. Maybe then he'd stand a better chance of getting away. But he didn't know these woods, and he didn't like the dark. Bad things happened in the dark—like his dad leaving.

"Is your father at home waiting for you, Caleb?"

"Yes," Caleb lied. "He'll be worried."

"Then let's get you home so he doesn't have to worry."

Caleb didn't get up, and neither did the cop. He was looking at Caleb real hard, as if he could see everything, and his voice when he started talking again was soft, pitying, because he'd already figured out the truth. "Your father isn't home, is he, Caleb? He left, like your mom did."

"*No!* He's coming back. He said he would, and he always does what he said."

"How long has he been gone?"

Caleb stared at the ground, wishing a hole would open up and transport him away from there. Sometimes it seemed like that was what had happened to their dad. He'd just disappeared.

"Caleb? How long?"

He wanted to lie, but it wouldn't work. Now that the cop believed his dad was gone, nothing would change his mind except seeing him, and there wasn't much chance of that happening. "I don't know." But he knew exactly— thirty-nine days. Somehow that sounded better than nearly six weeks or a month and a half.

"Come on." Nathan stood up and pulled Caleb up too, then held on to his arm as they started back toward the road. They hadn't gone far at all. In just a few minutes they were back at the truck, where Alanna was watching anxiously from the front seat.

"Where do you live?"

Caleb nudged gravel with his foot.

"You can tell me, Caleb, or the sheriff's department. It's your choice."

The cop was wrong. He didn't have any more choices. They'd run out when the store guy had grabbed him.

He gestured grudgingly down the road. "It's that way. Turn left at the first road and go all the way to the end."

Nathan put him in the backseat again, then pulled away from the mailboxes. Caleb stared out the side window. Thirty-nine days. That was all it had taken for him to screw up—to disappoint his father and put his family in danger. Less than six weeks. Not even a month and a half.

Just thirty-nine lousy days.

S INCE MOVING TO BETHLEHEM EIGHTEEN MONTHS earlier, J. D. Grayson had developed a rhythm to his life. Monday through Friday he kept regular office hours, though the office varied from a shabby space at the hospital to an empty classroom at school to an unused storeroom at the nursing home. Evenings and weekends he worked on the house he was building outside town. Saturday mornings he had breakfast at Harry's Diner, and Sunday mornings, like most other folks in town, he attended church. Interspersed in his schedule were daily five-mile runs, frequent visits with friends, occasional dates, and rare overnight liaisons. It was a comfortable life—more comfortable than he'd had any right to expect—and one he'd needed badly when he'd come to Bethlehem. One he wasn't eager to shake up in any way.

But apparently someone else had other ideas.

He'd barely made it to the bottom of the church steps after the Sunday morning service, when a woman approached. She was pretty, slender, not too tall. She wore a shapeless white dress that reached almost to the ground and an earnest expression that only young children and innocents could pull off. She managed. Her long hair was tied back, and her hands were clasped around the handle of an oversize attaché case. "Dr. Grayson? Can I have a moment of your time?"

The Winchester sisters had invited him for dinner, as they did every Sunday, and he'd rather not keep them waiting, but he could spare a few minutes. In Bethlehem a person always made time for someone who needed it. That was one of the reasons he'd moved there. "Sure," he said, gesturing to a stone bench nearby. "I have a few minutes."

She seated herself on the bench, opened the attaché, and rummaged inside for a business card. "It's a generic card—I don't have my own yet—but you can call me Noelle."

The card was familiar—raised black ink on white stock, the state seal, the social services address at the courthouse. That office had been closed down since before he'd moved to town, and all of Bethlehem's social service needs had been handled out of Howland. Apparently, that was changing.

He tucked the card into his pocket. "What can I do for you, Noelle?"

Once again she rummaged inside the case, this time pulling out four five-by-seven-inch photographs and arranging them on the bench. Kids, he could see from where he stood. Kids in trouble. A knot began forming in his stomach.

"These are the Brown children—Caleb, Jacob, Noah, and Gracie. She's five." Earnestness gave way briefly to a smile as she gazed at the last photo. "They live a few miles east of town—or, at least, they did. Their mother left them about two years ago, and their father disappeared six weeks ago. They've been on their own since then."

J.D. slid his hands into his pockets and refused to look at the photographs. It was a beautiful Sunday afternoon. The temperature was comfortable, the sun was shining, and after dinner with the Winchester sisters, he was going to hang eighteen sets of cabinets in the kitchen of his new house. It promised to be a relaxing, productive day, as Sundays should be, and he didn't want to spoil it with conversation about kids whose parents had thrown them away.

But he was a psychiatrist. He listened to a lot of conversations he didn't want to hear. He heard things that should never be imagined, dealt with the aftermath of things that should never be done. He'd *lived* the aftermath. If he couldn't handle it, then he should find a new job.

"Where are the kids now?" he asked, careful to keep his voice even, his tone strictly professional.

"They were taken into custody Friday night. They're at Bethlehem Memorial for physicals and observation."

"And you want *my* observations."

She looked startled. "Oh, no, Dr. Grayson, not at all— at least, not just yet. The children are fine. They're ready to be placed in their foster home."

The relief he felt shamed him. Tomorrow he could deal with unwanted, abandoned kids, but not today. Not on one of his regular put-J.D.-back-together days.

"Then, what do you want from me?"

Her forehead wrinkled, as if she were puzzled that he hadn't figured it out yet. "Why, we want you to provide that foster home."

Surely he hadn't heard right. There was so much more to assigning a child to a foster home than this. There were interviews to conduct, investigations to begin, home visits to attend to. All the preliminary work on prospective volunteers completed, so they would be approved and ready when a situation arose. *He* was certainly not one of those volunteers. Hell, as a psychiatrist, *he* would be the last person he'd approve for it.

"Look, I've worked with social services enough to know that this *isn't* how you do business. People have to volunteer for this. They have to undergo a thorough investigation. You can't just choose someone and dump the kids on him."

His argument didn't faze her at all. "You're right, Dr. Grayson. This isn't how we normally do business. But this is a special case. And we're talking a short-term arrangement—a few weeks, not more than a month. That's all."

"I'm sorry. I can't help you."

That didn't faze her either. "Not me, Dr. Grayson. The children."

She gestured to the photographs, and this time he couldn't help but look and notice details. The anger in the oldest boy's eyes. The other boys' fear. The girl's old-beyond-her-years solemnity. Good-looking kids whom nobody wanted. Rejected by their mother, then their father. Destined for a bleak future and probably children of their own to neglect and abandon, who would then face the same future or worse. A vicious cycle . . . unless someone stopped it now. He knew it could be done with the right home, the right parents. But his wasn't the home, and he certainly wasn't the parent.

"You know nothing about me."

"To the contrary. I took the liberty of making a few inquiries. You don't have an arrest record. You're not in debt. You have an excellent work record. The hospital administrator says you're a brilliant psychiatrist. Even the nurses adore you. Your landlady calls you an ideal tenant. You don't drink. You don't drive recklessly. You're reliable, trustworthy, and you're in church every Sunday morning—though the pastor says he wouldn't mind seeing you a few other times when the doors are open." She took a deep breath, then smiled gently. "For now that's all we need to know."

For now. Did that mean *later* there would be a more extensive background check? *Later* they might delve into all the nooks and crannies of his past?

He shook his head. "I'm a single man with a full-time

job. I can't do justice to four children with my work schedule."

"In a town like Bethlehem, you'll have no trouble finding neighbors to help out. And we don't discriminate against single parents, Dr. Grayson. Your marital status has nothing whatsoever to do with your parenting ability."

Oh, but it did, J.D. thought bleakly. More than this naive social worker could imagine.

"I'm a man," he tried again. "That little girl"—Gracie, five, old beyond her years—"needs a woman. A mother."

"She needs *you*. Trust me on this." Noelle's words hung between them, soft, reassuring. "Just a few weeks, Dr. Grayson—that's all I'm asking of you. The authorities are trying to track down a relative who might be able to take the children. If that fails, then we'll look for a permanent placement."

A few weeks. She made it sound so easy, but if there was one thing kids weren't, it was easy. They were trouble, frustration, and love, all wrapped together in one untidy package. They brought out the best in a man—and sometimes the worst. They could love you, hate you, break your heart.

The Brown kids had already had their hearts broken, had already been abandoned twice. They deserved better than that, deserved an adult they could trust, someone they could count on to be there for them anytime, all the time.

He wasn't that person. He'd already proved it. If he tried and failed again, he could do the same damage times four, and that was too big a risk to take.

"They're good children," Noelle said quietly. "I won't deny that they have some problems. You understand the issues of abandonment better than I. You can help them deal with those issues better than anyone."

His gaze strayed to the photos again, to Caleb in particular. The boy stared fiercely at the camera, as if daring anyone to come too close. He was angry, bitter, and, no matter how well he hid it, frightened. He needed stability in his life—a safe home, a parent to lean on, a chance to grow up before having the burdens of the world dumped on his thin shoulders. He needed to be average—just another kid living a normal life with loving parents. *Not* just another statistic.

Noelle was right about one thing. Professionally, he could help the kids. There hadn't been any call for his specialty since moving to Bethlehem—abuse, neglect, and abandonment simply didn't happen there the way it did in big cities—but he hadn't lost his touch. He'd simply lost his taste for it. These days he preferred patients who were less needy, whose problems were minor in the scheme of things. Patients who hadn't suffered unspeakable horrors, whose heartbreak and sorrow didn't reach right inside him and take up residence. These days he preferred safe patients, and while Caleb, Jacob, Noah, and Gracie Brown might be safe to J.D. the shrink, they presented a definite danger to J.D. the man.

"Have you tried the Thomases? Alex and Melissa love kids."

Noelle gave no sign of hearing the desperation in his voice. "Alex Thomas is the children's court appointed attorney. He can't also be their foster father. He agrees that you're the best choice."

"What about the McKinneys? Maggie and Ross have plenty of room for four kids, and she would be home with them all day. Or what about—"

"They need *you,* Dr. Grayson."

He turned away to face the church. Reverend Howard was locking the heavy doors while his wife and son waited at the car. Everyone else had gone home with their families or with friends. No one had to be alone in Bethlehem on Sunday unless it was by choice. Someone was always ready to offer a welcome.

"This town has given you a lot," Noelle said quietly.

That was true. It had saved his sanity, if not his life. It had given him a place to heal and the acceptance and love to do it. But the process wasn't finished yet, and taking in those kids—especially Caleb—wouldn't help it along.

Neither would turning his back on them.

He felt a gentle touch on his sleeve, heard Noelle's voice directly behind him. "It's not easy to place four children together. You know that. You also know how devastating it can be to children in their situation to be separated. We can't take those children away from Caleb, or take Caleb away from them. They couldn't bear it."

He fixed his gaze on the cross atop the church. "I have only two bedrooms," he said flatly, "and one of them is an office."

"The children are adaptable. They won't mind sharing their space with a desk and a few books."

That wasn't the point, he wanted to protest. *He* minded sharing his office space with four kids.

But that wasn't the point either. He rarely used the office, rarely had a case that required after-hours work. The point was, he didn't want these kids—this responsibility, this danger—but he felt he should take them.

Felt. God, how long had it been since he'd really, truly felt anything?

Two years, three months, one week, four days, and fifteen hours, give or take a few minutes. Not that he was counting.

He tried one last objection. "Don't you have any qualms at all about placing a five-year-girl with a single man?"

"Not with you and not with three brothers who fiercely protect her." A heavy pause. "I've always thought it unfair that men are automatically suspect when it comes to children, for no reason other than their gender. Surely you don't believe a five-year-old boy is safer with the average woman than a five-year-old girl is with the average man?"

No, he didn't. He knew too well that abusers came in both genders.

The sinking feeling in his stomach warned him that he was about to betray himself. He was about to open his mouth and make a decision he couldn't back away from. No matter how much he wanted *not* to make that decision, he couldn't stop it. It was beyond his control.

He turned to look at her. "All right," he agreed stiffly. "I'll take them. But only for a few weeks. No more than a month."

A brilliant smile lit her face. "Thank you, Dr. Grayson. You won't regret this. Well, from time to time you probably will, but not in the long run." She gathered the photographs and returned them to her attaché. "Judge McKechnie has agreed to give us a few minutes of his afternoon to get the formalities out of the way, then we'll pick up the children and get them settled in at your place. Shall we go?"

She started walking before she stopped talking. J.D. watched her with a scowl. "You were awfully sure of yourself, weren't you?" he muttered, too low, he thought, for her to hear.

She turned at the end of the sidewalk and smiled again. "No, Dr. Grayson. I was sure of *you*—sure you would do the right thing. And I was right, wasn't I?"

That, he admitted grimly as he joined her, remained to be seen.

•   •   •

Her eyes gritty from too many miles, Kelsey Malone gave a sigh of relief when she passed the road sign proclaiming that her destination was only five miles ahead. It had been a long journey from New York City to Bethlehem, one she'd anticipated ever since the Department of Family Assistance, formerly the Department of Social Services, had announced that it was reopening an office there. After much consideration—taking stock of her life, which was less than she'd hoped it would be—she'd put in for the job and gotten it.

There hadn't even been any competition. Not many people wanted to live in small, remote towns that needed their services only a few days a week. But a town where people treated their children like the gifts they were—a town a good six hours from the city—fitted Kelsey's current definition of perfect. Now she was almost there, just minutes from her new home, new office, and new life.

As the road wound down into the valley, the highway became Main Street and cut straight through the heart of town. The quaint shops, the grassy square, the kids skipping out of an ice cream shop with their parents close behind, all combined to stir deep within her a yearning for a place she'd never known, a life she'd never lived. The town was small-town America at its best.

There was no motel in Bethlehem, just a gracious old inn that exceeded her budget, so she'd rented an apartment sight unseen. She'd shipped her belongings from the city and arranged to meet the manager at three o'clock to trade the key for her deposit and first month's rent. Unfortunately, it was only a few minutes after two. She'd grabbed a burger at the last gas-up, so she settled on a tour of the town to pass the time.

Her friends had acted as if she were moving to the wilds, had wondered how she would survive without all the big-city conveniences. She'd reminded them that there *was* life outside the city—electricity, telephones, even computers—and a leisurely drive through the streets that made up Bethlehem's downtown proved her right. There was a movie theater, restaurants, a grocery store, a computer-cum-electronics store, and a bookstore—everything she needed to survive. She passed several clothing stores, doctors', dentists', and lawyers' offices, craft shops, hair salons, and gift shops—the icing on the cake.

Big-city conveniences combined with the ease of small-town living. On top of that, Bethlehem was definitely one of the prettiest places she'd seen in a long time. Oh, yes, she could live here and love it. Life could be perfect here.

She pulled into a parking space in front of the first pay phone she noticed, took out her brand-new calling card, and dialed her parents' home number. In the middle of a summer Sunday afternoon, her father was probably relaxing with a beer in front of the TV while her mother finished cleanup from the family dinner. For most Sundays in her life, Kelsey had been there to help with the cleanup. It gave her a lump in her throat to think that that family tradition was a thing of the past now—at least, for her.

When Kathleen Malone answered the phone, Kelsey heard the sounds of water running in the background. Without even closing her eyes, she could easily summon a picture of her mother, still wearing her church dress with Grandma Kelly's ruffled bib apron covering most of it, washing dishes in the sink while the nearby dishwasher served as draining rack. "Hi, Mom, it's me," she said, expending extra effort to make certain her voice sounded cheerful.

"Kelsey! Did you get there safely? Is everything all right? Let me dry my hands so I can get your phone number before I forget. We missed you today at dinner. The table seemed awfully emp—"

"Mom, I'm fine. I don't have a phone yet—I'll get that

taken care of tomorrow—so you can keep washing dishes."

"Well? What's it like? The town, I mean. Is it everything you'd hoped for?"

"It's pretty, Mom. It's old, but it's very charming. It sits in a valley with mountains all around, and it's really lovely. You'd like it."

"Was it worth moving halfway across the state for?"

Kelsey sighed softly. To say her parents weren't happy about her moving was a slight understatement. She understood their concern. She was their only daughter, and they worried about her. There would be a lot less to worry about with her living in Bethlehem, she'd tried to tell them—shorter hours, a safer environment, less crime, less stress—but they hadn't been convinced. They wouldn't stop worrying until she was married, staying home, and having babies, and preferably living only a few blocks away, like her brother, Sean.

"It's not so far, Mom," she said patiently. "You can come visit any weekend, and I can come home from time to time."

"You can't come for Sunday dinner. You can't come to your cousin Angela's baby shower this Friday. Of course"—honesty forced Kathleen to acknowledge this—"not being too fond of Angela, you would have found some way to get out of that even if you were here."

"Yes, I would have," Kelsey agreed with a laugh.

"So tell me all about your apartment."

"I haven't seen it yet. I just got into town not ten minutes ago."

"I can't believe you signed a lease on a place without seeing it first. It could be a dump. It could be on the wrong side of town. It might not even exist. The man could have taken your money and left the state."

"Mom, I don't think Bethlehem *has* a wrong side of

town. I'm not sure they have any dumps either." All the houses she'd caught a glimpse of in her back-and-forth tour of downtown were neatly maintained, not unlike the houses surrounding her parents' place. "I haven't signed anything, and no one's taken my money. I offered to send the manager a check for the deposit, and he said it wasn't necessary, that we could take care of it when I got here." A town with so few child welfare problems that it needed only a part-time social worker, and an apartment manager willing to do business with a stranger based on nothing more than a verbal handshake—two strong suggestions that she was in for a nice change of pace.

"Well, I hope you haven't been taken," Kathleen said stubbornly. "And remember, honey, nothing's permanent. If you find that you've made a mistake, you can always come back home."

"I'll keep that in mind. I'd better get going. I gave you both my home and office addresses, didn't I?"

"Yes, I've got them."

"And I'll call you this week with the phone numbers. Give Dad a hug for me and tell him I love him." She swallowed hard. "I love you, Mom."

"I love you too. And I really do hope you'll be happy there, even if I haven't acted like it. It's just that we've gotten used to having you nearby. We'd hoped to have you here always."

"I know. But it's not so far. Think about coming for a visit, will you?" She hesitated only a moment. "I'll talk to you later, Mom."

"You be careful." It was Kathleen's standard farewell, whether on the phone or in person, and all her life Kelsey had heeded the advice. It was part of the reason she'd wound up in Bethlehem.

After hanging up, she turned toward the car and realized that the courthouse was down the block. Since she still had time to blow before her three o'clock appointment, she drove the short distance to take a look at her new office. She could see what she had and what she needed before tomorrow's trip to Howland to meet with her new supervisor.

Most of the spaces in the courthouse parking lot were empty. The cars there, she assumed, belonged to the police officers and sheriff's deputies whose departments filled the first floor. Ignoring the elevator, she climbed broad stairs to the second floor, where city and county offices shared space with courtrooms, and followed an arrow to the third floor, where her own office was tucked among a dozen others.

The frosted glass in the door had been recently painted with the department name. She tried the knob and the door opened with a creak. The reception area was small and about as elegantly decorated as she'd expected—pale green walls, industrial carpet, beige metal desk, and orange plastic chairs. The sole door in the opposite wall led into her office, also pale green, beige, and orange. Two windows looked out on the street, but the view was blocked by the four tall file cabinets lined up across the wall. Once she squeezed behind the desk and leaned way back in her chair, she found she could see a wedge of the street below.

"An office with a view," she murmured with a grin as she propped her feet on the scarred desk-mat. What more could she ask for?

She turned her attention to unpacking the box she'd brought up from the car. Her degrees came out first, a bachelor's and a master's, then the personal stuff—a box of tissues, a makeup kit for emergency touch-ups, a bottle of aspirin, a bottle of antacid. There were a couple of silk plants that looked real, a duplicate of her home address book, and a few family photographs.

The last item in the box was also a photo, framed, its

colors faded with age. It was a yearbook picture, enlarged to five by seven inches—a pretty fifteen-year-old girl who hadn't lived to see sixteen. She and Steph had been born only three days apart, had lived only two houses apart. They'd grown up together and had been best friends forever. Steph was the reason Kelsey did what she did—Steph, and a need for atonement. For absolution.

She stroked a fingertip across the frame, then positioned it on a corner of her desk. Every time she looked up, she would see the picture and remember. She would work a little longer, try a little harder.

With a glance at her watch she decided it was time to go. When she was outside in the sun once more, she paused for a moment. The fragrance of flowers drifted over from the square, along with the sounds of children playing while parents watched from park benches. It was such a lovely, peaceful scene, with no loud music causing the very ground to vibrate, no shouts or arguments, no traffic backed up in the street.

She closed her eyes, breathing in deeply of clean air, peace, calm. The tension seeped from her neck and shoulders, drained out of her fingertips, and fell away. The sensation made her smile as she headed for the parking lot, but the smile faded as she neared her car.

She'd parked beside a mud-splattered truck. Now a man stood behind both vehicles, hands in his pockets, staring at her car as if she'd committed some unforgivable offense. Too much the city girl to succumb to Bethlehem's charms too quickly, she approached him with caution. "Excuse me. Can I help you?"

His gaze swung to her, but he didn't speak. She wouldn't swear he even saw her.

"You're staring at my car. I didn't bang your truck. I didn't get near it."

He blinked but still said nothing.

She took a step back toward the courthouse and the police officers inside. "Is something wrong?"

Abruptly, as if a spell had been broken, he drew a ragged breath, then expelled it with a harsh laugh. "Nothing that a good shrink couldn't take care of. Unfortunately, I'm the only one in town."

Before she could think how to respond to that, he pulled his keys from his pocket, climbed into the truck, and drove away.

Great. In her business she worked closely with psychiatrists, psychologists, and therapists of every kind. That was not an auspicious introduction to the only psychiatrist in town.

The directions the apartment manager had given her were easy to follow and took her to the other side of town. For the price he'd quoted, she didn't expect a lot, so she wasn't disappointed. She had nine hundred clean square feet plus a narrow porch in a fifties-era building that held its own shabby charm.

The boxes she'd shipped were stacked in the living room, surrounded by furniture the manager had tossed in for only a few bucks more a month, which was about what it was worth. The sofa was hideous, the dining table wobbled precariously, and the mismatched bedroom furniture bore the nicks and scars of a well-used life. The mattress was too soft, the kitchen sink had a permanent rust stain, and only the colorblind could truly appreciate the pink and lime tile in the bathroom.

"Home, sweet home," she said with a sigh.

She once again began unpacking. She didn't have much to show for thirty-five years of living—a few cartons of kitchen things. Two wardrobe boxes with clothes and shoes stuffed in the bottom. A television, VCR, and compact stereo. Fifteen small, heavy cartons of books, two filled with knickknacks, and one with photographs. Her entire life wouldn't fill the back of a ten-cubic-foot moving truck. It didn't even fill her *life*. She had room for so much more.

Maybe in Bethlehem she would find it.

Chapter Two

FTER LEAVING THE COURTHOUSE, J.D. HAD driven to the hospital, where Noelle introduced him to the kids. It hadn't been the warmest reception he'd ever received, but it wasn't the coldest either. He'd been met with far more contempt and distrust than all four Browns combined could muster.

Now, as he fastened his seat belt, he checked the kids in back. They were buckled in, their hands folded in their laps, their expressions somber. Beside him, Caleb was staring mutinously out the window.

"Fasten your seat belt," J.D. said. When the request brought no response at all, he went on. "We'll sit here until you do. I'm in no hurry." He folded his hands over the steering wheel, where he could keep a discreet eye on his watch. The second hand was beginning its third revolution when, with a great sigh, Caleb jerked the seat belt across his lap and snapped the ends together.

They'd gone a half dozen blocks when the boy spoke for the first time. "Our father's coming back."

For whose benefit was his fierce conviction? The kids'? J.D.'s? Or his own?

"Good," J.D. replied. "Sometime this week we'll go out to your house and leave him a note with my address and phone number. That way he'll know where to find you."

"You could just take us home and leave us there. The welfare people don't have to know."

"I can't do that, Caleb. You know that. The state put you in my custody. That means I'm legally responsible for you."

"We don't need to be in anyone's custody! We did just fine on our own!"

"Living without electricity or running water? Missing school? Stealing food and going hungry? You call that doing just fine?" J.D. glanced at him and noted the tight jaw, the clenched fists. "I hate to break this to you, Caleb, but that's no way to live. It's certainly no way for them to live."

Caleb glanced in the backseat, then stared out the side window again. His brothers and sister were his soft spot. For six weeks he'd devoted his every waking minute to taking care of them. It wasn't a job he would relinquish easily to J.D. or anyone but his father. He was convinced that Ezra Brown would return any day, but the authorities doubted he would show his face in town again. Taking care of four kids and a broken-down farm had apparently become more than he could handle, or wanted to handle, and he'd thrown in the towel and headed off to find himself an easier life. The sheriff was convinced of it. J.D. had seen it happen often enough to believe it.

Caleb had faith. But how could he *not* believe when the only other explanation was that the one person in the world who'd loved them no longer wanted them? If he lost faith in his father, he would lose faith in himself.

"I rent a garage apartment a few blocks up ahead," J.D. announced to no one in particular. No one showed any sign of hearing him. "It's not very big. I'll have to move some furniture out and see about getting some beds for you guys. Two of you can share the extra bedroom, and the other two will have to make do with the sofa bed. It's pretty comfortable, considering."

Silence. He might as well have been alone in the truck.

"There are some kids in the neighborhood. You probably know them from school. We'll have to have some rules regarding when you can go out and where you can go. When I'm at work, you'll have to stay with a baby-sitter." J.D. heard Caleb snort. "I don't know who yet. I'll have to take a couple of days off until we get all that straightened out."

More silence. He turned onto Sixth Street, then made a sharp turn into Mrs. Larrabee's driveway. The garage sat at the back of the property, a two-story structure stained the same deep red as the house. He parked near the bottom of the white steps that made a straight shot to his door. "This is it," he said as he shut off the engine. "We're home."

Caleb gave him a look of pure scorn but didn't correct him. Gracie did. "This isn't our home," she whispered. "I want to go to *our* home, please."

J.D. twisted in the seat to face her. "This is your home—for a while, Gracie."

She looked out the window, then back at him. Her brown eyes filled with tears, and her lower lip trembled. "No, thank you," she murmured in that fragile, little-girl-lost voice. "We'll go to *our* home."

"I can't take you there," J.D. said, and she burst into tears. Feeling incredibly out of his element, he climbed out of the truck. "Come on. Let's grab your bags and I'll show you around."

He meant *bags* literally. Their clothing—all that was fit

to bring, Noelle had murmured when the nurses handed it over—was packed in paper grocery bags, one for each child. There wasn't a full bag in the bunch.

While he retrieved the sacks from the cargo area, the kids climbed out of the truck. Though she was too big for him to carry comfortably, Caleb lifted Gracie onto one hip, then gestured toward J.D. with a curt nod. The other boys responded immediately, taking the bags from him, then returning to their brother's side. Four against one.

This wasn't going to be easy. But kids weren't easy, remember? And they *were* kids—frightened, abandoned kids. He was not only an adult, but an adult recognized at one time as among the nation's experts on frightened, abandoned children. He could handle them.

Maybe.

He went up the stairs first. They didn't follow even after he'd unlocked the door, then made a point of waiting for them—not until Caleb gave an almost imperceptible nod.

The apartment was partitioned into a living room, dining room, kitchen, two bedrooms, and one bath. The floors were wood, the walls a pale yellow that was soothing to the spirit. The furniture was mostly antiques, and none of it his. He'd left his furniture behind in Chicago for the new owner of the house. He'd taken nothing but his medical texts, two suitcases of clothes, and one box of mementoes—photographs, mostly, along with a few letters and souvenirs.

He closed the door behind Caleb, then went into the first room. "This is the kitchen. Glasses are in this cabinet." Looking at the younger kids, he made a mental note to move the glasses to a lower shelf and to stock up on some unbreakables. "The wastebasket's under the sink. Help yourself to whatever you want, and bring your dishes back when you're finished."

He opened the refrigerator and grimaced. He needed to

stock up on food too. He would ask them about their favorite foods, but he didn't think he'd get any answers, not with Caleb glaring at him like that. So he would learn by trial and error—the way most parents learned.

He continued the tour. "Dining room. Living room. My bedroom. Bathroom. Your bedroom—as soon as I get this stuff moved out." The photographs would go in his room, the books to his office at the hospital, and he would ask Mrs. Larrabee to store the furniture in the garage. Since she no longer drove, she'd gotten rid of her car, so space shouldn't be a problem. Then he'd have to get beds and a dresser, sheets, pillows, blankets, towels. And clothes. And books or toys or something to amuse them. What amused kids these days?

Not him, he acknowledged as he turned to find all four of them staring at him as if he were from an alien planet. "Which two of you want this room, and which two get the sofa?"

Caleb let Gracie slide to the floor but kept his hands protectively—possessively—on her shoulders. "We only need one room."

That was fine with him. He could get two sets of bunk beds, squeeze a dresser in, and the furniture problem would be solved. One down, a million or two to go. "Have you had lunch?"

No one answered.

"Are you hungry?"

Still no answer.

"Do you want to watch TV?"

That sparked interest in three pairs of brown eyes, but Caleb quelled it with one look. "We don't want to do anything but go home."

"You are home."

Mimicking his even, taut tone, Caleb said, "This will never be home."

J.D. drew a deep breath. "Come on out in the living room—"

"We'll stay here."

J.D. thought of all the things he wanted to remove from the room, and Caleb's hostility heightened. "Don't worry," he said sarcastically. "We won't touch anything and get it dirty. We'll just sit over there in the corner out of the way."

"Caleb—" The ringing of the telephone interrupted, which was fine with J.D. because he didn't have a clue what he was about to say. Giving the kid an exasperated look, he left the office and grabbed the bedroom phone on the third ring.

The voice on the other end belonged to Holly McBride, owner of the McBride Inn, former lover, and his best friend. "There's an ugly rumor going around town that you agreed to act as foster parent to those four kids Nathan found living alone. Is it true?"

"News sure travels fast," he said dryly. "We haven't been home fifteen minutes. Where'd you hear it?"

"I have my sources. Have you taken leave of your senses, J.D.?"

"I'm here with four kids between the ages of five and twelve. What do you think?"

Her chuckle made him feel better in spite of everything. "I think you're a sucker for anyone who needs you. You always have been."

Cradling the receiver between his ear and shoulder, he rubbed his temples with unsteady hands. His voice wasn't very steady either. "Not always, but I try."

"Need anything?"

"My head examined."

"What's that saying? Physician, heal thyself. Anything else?"

"You could come baby-sit while I go to the store."

Holly burst into unrestrained laughter. "Yeah, right. Do you need anything that doesn't involve me being left alone with small humans?"

"I need groceries, bunk beds, and a clue as to what the hell I've gotten myself into."

"I can help with the first two. You'll have to get your clue yourself. See you soon."

He hung up and listened for sounds from the room next door. There were none.

He wondered what they were doing, wondered what *he* was doing. He *should* be tracking down the all-too-persuasive Noelle and giving those kids back to her. She wouldn't have any problem placing them elsewhere. Bethlehem was full of kind people with generous hearts. She hadn't even considered anyone else because she'd known what Holly and everyone else in town knew—that he was a sucker for other people's troubles. For her he'd been an easy way to get rid of the kids.

But he didn't reach for the phone, and when he rose from the bed, it wasn't with the intention of taking the kids anywhere. Instead, he changed into shorts and a T-shirt, then went next door to start the process of giving them a place of their own.

They were sitting on the floor in the corner of the office, just as Caleb had said they would. Gracie leaned against him on one side, Noah and Jacob on the other, and all of them watched him. Children so young shouldn't know such distrust, but it was a sad fact that every day adults gave kids good reason to not trust. If the Brown children had simply been abandoned, then they'd gotten off easy.

But they didn't look as if they'd ever had anything easy.

He began clearing the room. The kids watched his every move, but they said nothing. He was painfully aware of

their scrutiny, but he said nothing either, until he ran out
of boxes and sprawled in the desk chair.

"So, guys, what should I get at the grocery store? You
like chicken? Spaghetti? Hamburgers? Ice cream?"

Gracie's and Noah's eyes lit up, but neither of them
spoke. They waited for a cue from Caleb, and he didn't
give it.

"Those aren't your favorites, huh? I know. I bet you
like liver and spinach and brussels sprouts. No problem.
That's what we'll have for dinner tonight."

"Oh, no, we love sketti and ice cream," Gracie blurted
out, then darted an anxious look at Caleb before clapping
her hands over her mouth and burrowing closer to him.

That was a start, J.D. thought. Now, if he could just get
a word out of Noah or Jacob . . . "What about you,
Noah? Do you like spaghetti?"

The boy stared, wide-eyed and tight-jawed.

"What flavor ice cream do you like? Vanilla? Rocky
Road? Praline sundae? You have a favorite, Jacob?"

Jacob's response mirrored his brother's. J.D. would have
given up even if the doorbell hadn't rung at that moment.

Holly stood on the porch, grocery bags in her arms.
Balanced on top of them was a brown paper sack from
Harry's Diner, and wafting from it was the tantalizing
aroma of one of Harry's deluxe cheeseburgers. "Since you
never made it to the Winchesters' house, I brought you
some lunch. And Miss Agatha and Miss Corinna will be
over soon with enough food to feed you guys for a few
days, so I just picked up necessities. Oh, and Sebastian
Knight is bringing over two sets of bunk beds from his
shop, and Emilie's got linens, and Shelley Walker's gathering some toys from the church." She peered past him.
"Where are they?"

"In the bedroom, sitting in the corner."

"You're making them sit in the corner? What kind of father are you, J.D.?"

Ignoring the pain her careless remark sparked, he unwrapped the burger and ate while she put away the groceries. "I'm not *making* them do anything. They're being difficult."

"Of course they're being difficult. It's part of the job description." All signs of teasing disappeared. "I have to tell you, J.D., this surprises me, even for you. I just can't imagine you fostering four children. What made you agree?"

He glanced toward the hall to make sure they were still alone, then shrugged. "I opened my mouth to say no—not only no, but hell no—and the wrong words came out."

"So subconsciously you wanted to say yes."

He scowled at her. "Don't analyze me, Holly. Subconsciously, I wanted to say no. Consciously, I wanted to say no. Every way possible, I wanted to say no."

"So why'd you say yes?"

He dragged his fingers through his hair. "Damned if I know."

DOWN THE HALL CALEB EASED BACK AROUND the corner. He'd known the shrink hadn't wanted them, had known the welfare lady had lied when she said he did. She'd told them he liked kids, that he was good with them. But Caleb knew he didn't like *them*. He didn't want them in his house, didn't want them touching his things.

So why had he taken them? Because the state was paying him? Nah, he was a doctor. He didn't need their money. Because he felt sorry for them? Because no one else wanted them and, being a shrink, he felt obligated?

Caleb didn't want to be anyone's obligation except his father's.

He went back into the office, and Gracie curled up beside him. "Was it Daddy?"

"No." He'd known it wouldn't be. Their luck wasn't that good.

"Who was it?"

He scowled at Noah. "Nobody you know. Some woman."

"What did she want?"

"I don't know what she wanted," he snapped. "It sure wasn't us."

Noah's eyes filled with tears, and so did Gracie's. Even Jacob looked like he might bust out crying too, and Jacob hardly ever cried. Caleb felt like he might cry himself, with his throat all tight and his stomach hurting. "Look, I'm sorry, but you gotta quit asking me questions I can't answer."

Gracie crawled into his lap and wrapped her arms around his neck. "I want my daddy," she sobbed. "When is he comin' back?"

"Like that one. I don't know, Gracie. I don't know when he'll be back."

"The police don't think he's comin' back," Jacob whispered as if it hurt too much to say the words out loud.

"That's 'cause they don't know him. He'll be back. He promised." Caleb had been telling the kids that for forty-one days, and they had always believed him, because their dad didn't lie and he didn't lie. But they'd heard the sheriff's deputies talking at the hospital yesterday—had heard them say that their dad had taken off and left them, just like their mother had, and *she'd* never come back. Now they wondered.

Not Caleb. Their dad *would* be back. He believed that. He *had* to believe it.

Noah sniffed and wiped his eyes. "It's a nice house, isn't it, Caleb? Nicer'n anything I ever seen."

"Maybe. But there's nothing wrong with our house."

"Our house don't smell like this," Noah pointed out.

"And it's not cool like this," Jacob added.

"It don't have a television."

"Or a 'frigerator that works."

"Or rugs on the floor."

"Or nice furniture."

"Or all this—"

Caleb glared at both boys and harshly repeated his last words. "There's nothing wrong with our house." That made them both be quiet, at least for a minute, and when they started again, at least it was about something else.

"Do you really think he'll make us eat liver?" Noah made a face like he already had the taste of it in his mouth. "I don't like liver . . . do I?"

"You'll learn to like it." Not that the shrink would make them eat it. He would serve spaghetti and ice cream, trying to suck up to them and make them like him and think he liked them too. He might fool the younger kids, but Caleb knew better.

"Liver is yucky," Gracie said with a giggle before Caleb shushed her. The shrink and his girlfriend were coming down the hall, probably to make sure they hadn't gotten into anything.

The woman came in first, her eyes widening when she saw them. "They really are sitting in the corner," she murmured, like they couldn't hear. "I thought you were kidding."

"I don't kid," the shrink said, which made him a liar, because he'd been kidding about dinner. "Guys, this is Holly McBride. She's responsible for all the junk food in the kitchen."

"Hey, in my house, ice cream, cookies, and chocolate

are a vital part of my diet." She came to them, her hand
stuck out. "You must be Caleb. It's nice to meet you."

Her hand looked pale, soft, with long, red fingernails.
She looked like somebody who never did real work and
dressed like it too—like someone with money. In his experience, people with money, or at least their kids, didn't
care much for people without. She was probably just acting nice to impress the shrink. Caleb wasn't interested in
impressing anybody, so he sat still, his arms around Gracie,
and just looked at her.

After a moment she pulled her hand back. "So, Jacob,
Noah, Gracie, want some ice cream?"

When Gracie started to nod, Caleb squeezed her. She
gave him a disappointed look, then shook her head.

"Aw, come on. We have strawberry, chocolate chip,
orange sherbet, and cappuccino chocolate. I even got
some cones."

This time all three kids looked hopefully at Caleb. It
made him mad that the stupid shrink's stupid friend made
him look like the bad guy for not telling them okay, but he
couldn't give in. He couldn't lose control. *He* was family,
not the shrink. *He* was the one their father had put in
charge.

"Let them have some ice cream," the shrink said,
sounding pissed. "You can help me move the desk while
they eat."

He still would have said no if Gracie hadn't sighed and
sagged back against him, as if she knew the offer was too
good to be true. She didn't expect treats, not anymore. It
was such a little thing. Any kid should get an ice cream
cone sometime.

Lifting her to her feet, he nudged her toward the
woman. "Go on. Get your ice cream."

"Us too?" Noah asked anxiously.

"Go on."

Once the kids and the woman were gone from the room, the shrink said, "That wasn't so hard, was it?"

"I didn't give in 'cause of you."

"I know."

"I'll never do anything 'cause of you. We don't need you, and we don't want you in all the same ways you don't want us."

The doctor gave him a long, steady look that made Caleb uncomfortable, as if he were seeing things Caleb didn't want him to see. Finally, he said, "You heard me talking to Holly, didn't you? I'm sorry about that."

"It don't matter. *You* don't matter. All that matters is taking care of Gracie and Noah and Jacob until our father comes back."

"And you, Caleb. You matter."

Yeah, right, like he believed the shrink believed that. The guy was a liar and couldn't be trusted. The kids might forget that, but *he* never would.

MORNINGS WERE THE HARDEST TIME FOR J.D.—those few minutes between being asleep and awake, when dreams were particularly vivid and sorrow was particularly harsh. Normally, some part of his subconscious ended the dreams as soon as they started and forced him to awaken completely, but Monday morning he stayed there in better times, better places, for every second he could. When he came awake, it was reluctantly, with a great raw pain that tingled through him.

He put off opening his eyes until the throbbing subsided, until he thought he could bear finding himself alone in his bed, alone in his existence, hundreds of miles from Chicago, where he belonged, hundreds of days from the life he'd destroyed. Finally, with a fortifying breath, he opened his eyes and saw the textured ceiling, the pale yellow walls empty of photographs, the furniture that meant nothing to him. He'd never shared this bed with anyone important, had never known satisfaction or peace there, had never let it be anything more than a utilitarian place where he slept.

Most mornings the instant he was awake, he jumped from bed, dressed in running clothes, and, after downing a cup of caffeine, ran a hard five miles. The exertion helped clear the dreams and memories from his mind. The fatigue helped keep them from returning until the next morning.

But this morning he didn't jump from bed and he didn't give more than a regretful thought to his running shoes in the closet, because this morning he wasn't alone. There were four kids asleep in the next room, and he hadn't thought ahead to make arrangements for a baby-sitter while he ran, which left him trapped.

He'd had a steady stream of company the previous day, bringing everything he could possibly need to take care of the kids—except the patience, know-how, and desire. It hadn't been so bad with people coming in and out, but eventually everyone had gone home and he'd been left alone with the kids. Dinner had been awkward. Bath time had been difficult, and bedtime— He'd given up, kept his distance, and watched from the doorway while Caleb tucked the kids in. He'd gone to his room, thinking one half of one day down. Fifteen or twenty or thirty to go.

What a damned depressing thought to fall asleep to.

Slowly, he sat up, rubbing his eyes, then the ache that had settled in his temples. Last night he'd called the hospital administrator and told him he wouldn't be in for a few days. Today he needed to take the kids shopping, get those cartons of books moved from the hallway to the hospital, set up a baby-sitting schedule, spend time with the kids. But first, he needed aspirin, a shower, and coffee.

The aspirin made a difference, and the shower and coffee helped. It was seven-thirty by the time he made it into the kitchen to fix breakfast. Most mornings he stopped at the diner on his way to wherever he was going and enjoyed Harry's cooking, Maeve's coffee, and the company of half the folks in town. This morning he would more or less duplicate the experience at home, he thought as he prepared sausage, eggs, and potatoes. He was fairly pleased with the results when he was done.

He walked into the guest room and flipped on the overhead light. "Come on and get up, kids. It's time for breakfast."

Gracie sat up first, hair standing on end, and yawned. She looked extraordinarily cranky. Caleb was next, throwing back the covers and sliding from the bunk above her to the floor. He greeted J.D. with a scowl as fierce as any he'd managed yesterday. "What do you want?"

J.D. bit back the impulse to suggest politely that Caleb ask the question again with a substantial improvement in his tone. The time would come for a firm hand with the boy, but not just yet. "Breakfast is ready. Noah, Jacob, come on."

The other two boys slowly rolled out of bed, and they all huddled together on or beside Gracie's bed.

"Get dressed, comb your hair, and come and eat," J.D. said as he turned away. "Make it quick, before the food gets cold."

Back in the kitchen, he sat down at the head of the table to wait.

They silently filed into the room, and with quick gestures Caleb directed each of them where to sit. Grasping the edge of a place mat, he pulled his own food around until he was opposite J.D., placing himself also at the head. Gracie was on his right, Jacob and Noah on his left, with their chairs squeezed together to leave extra space between them and J.D.

J.D. started to eat. After a moment he replaced the fork and fixed his gaze on the children, all sitting with their hands in their laps. "Do you usually say grace before you eat?"

"I'm Grace," Gracie piped up before Caleb motioned her to be quiet.

"Grace is also another word meaning prayer," J.D. explained. "A lot of people pray before they eat."

None of them made any response.

"Noah? What's wrong?"

The boy ducked his head until his chin rested on his chest. The instant J.D. looked at Jacob, he mimicked the action. That brought him to Caleb. "Well?"

"We don't like eggs."

"So don't eat them." J.D. turned his attention back to his own breakfast.

"We don't like sausage either."

His fingers tightening around the fork, J.D. took a slow, deep breath. "So don't eat it. And don't tell me you don't like potatoes. You ate them last night at dinner."

Caleb waited a beat, then said, "We don't like potatoes with all that crap in 'em."

"All that crap" was bits of onion and pepper and melted cheese, and it was a pretty good knockoff of Harry's famous hash-brown-potato casserole. But the issue here wasn't what *he* liked. It was what *they* liked.

He stood up and began gathering their dishes. "Let me guess. You don't like orange juice either, do you?"

The only response was Caleb's mocking smile.

J.D. dumped their plates in the kitchen sink. "Do you like oatmeal?" Caleb shrugged noncommittally. "Fine. Four bowls of oatmeal coming up."

Making instant oatmeal was easy enough. Five minutes later he was back in his seat and picked up his fork. Once more all four kids sat there, hands in laps, staring at their breakfast as if he'd served them shoe leather. "What?" he asked sharply.

It was Caleb, of course, who answered. "There's stuff in it."

"It's strawberry-flavored oatmeal. Those are little pieces of strawberry."

"Oatmeal's not supposed to have stuff in it."

"If oatmeal doesn't have stuff in it, it tastes like wet newspaper."

Noah picked up his spoon, poked around in the bowl for a moment, then let the spoon fall with a clang. "I don't think I'm hungry," he said with a mournful look that shouted the opposite.

J.D. took a breath for patience, then forced himself to say calmly, "All right. What do you want for breakfast?"

There was a long, tense silence, with the younger kids looking to Caleb. When he didn't speak up, Gracie ventured her own answer. "Ice cream?"

J.D. got four cartons of ice cream from the freezer, then dropped them in the middle of the table along with four big spoons. "Go to it," he said stiffly before returning to the kitchen. They were diving for the spoons the instant he was out of sight.

His own appetite gone, he did the dishes and fixed himself a fresh cup of coffee. Leaning against the counter, he stared out the window, wishing he were anywhere but in this apartment with those kids.

He felt incompetent. Granted, it had been a long time since he'd dealt with kids on any but the most superficial basis, a long time since he'd borne any responsibility for a child's well-being. Once he'd been very good at handling them. Given time, he might be good at it again.

He just didn't *want* to be good at it again.

But the issue wasn't what he wanted. In a moment of

insanity he'd agreed to provide a temporary home to the kids, and that was what he would do. He would give them what they needed, and in time they would give *him* what *he* needed.

They would get out of his life.

Chapter Three

KELSEY'S MEETING WITH HER NEW BOSS IN Howland had gone extraordinarily well. Mary Therese Carpenter was plump, motherly, and had a mind like a steel trap. She had great people skills and better instincts, and she swore Kelsey was going to love everything about Bethlehem. She'd given Kelsey enough files to fill at least one cabinet and had sketched out the details of her first case—four children found living alone after their parents' abandonment. Her priority was to visit them at the hospital and find out exactly what she could do for them.

"Oh, they're not here, dear," she was told by the old lady at the information desk.

She blinked. "What do you mean, they're not here?"

"Why, they're with Dr. J.D."

"And he is . . . ?"

"J. D. Grayson. Our psychiatrist."

Yesterday in the parking lot—big man, summer suit, befuddled look. Nothing wrong with him that a good shrink couldn't take care of. What exactly had he meant by that? she now wondered. "And where can I find Dr. Grayson?"

The woman checked her clipboard. "At home, I imagine. He didn't come in today. I don't believe he's coming in tomorrow either."

Kelsey was bewildered. The children she was supposed to interview and place had been taken home by the staff psychiatrist on his days off. *Why?* If he was counseling them, surely that was best done in a controlled environment. If he and his wife were providing emergency care to the children, it should have been cleared through her office and noted in her files. Hoping she had somehow misunderstood, she said, "He took the Brown children to his home?"

"Why, of course."

"Why 'of course'?"

"Well, honey, what did you expect him to do? He can't have custody of them *here*."

"Custody?" She drew a deep breath and forced an unsteady smile in what she was sure was a dismal attempt to look unshaken. "There must be some mistake here. The Brown children are currently in the custody of the state. No placement's been made yet. My department has to make recommendations and there has to be a hearing with a family court judge. Dr. Grayson can't simply take them, even if he is the only psychiatrist in town."

The volunteer finally lost her rosy smile. "But Dr. J.D.—a judge did—I think you'd better speak to our administrator."

When she reached for the phone, Kelsey stopped her. "Right now I really need to speak to Dr. Grayson. If you could give me his home address . . ."

"Well, now, I don't know . . ."

Another volunteer, young with the kind of long, silky

brown hair that Kelsey had always envied, interrupted.
"I'm sure it's all right. Everyone in town knows where
J.D. lives. It's on Sixth Street. Turn left out of the parking
lot, go down to Sixth, turn right, and it's behind the first
house on the right."

Kelsey curled her fingers around her briefcase handle
and left the building. This was amazing. She'd seen such
carelessness on occasion back home, when overworked
hospital staff lost track of who had a right to whom, but
she hadn't expected it here in Bethlehem.

Maybe it was part of the small-town charm. Maybe Dr.
Grayson had believed the kids would be better off waiting
for her in the comfort of his home rather than in the
sterile confines of a hospital. Maybe, in a small town
where everyone knew everyone else, that seemed a reasonable choice.

But it wasn't. The moment they were taken into custody, those children had become wards of the state. No
one had the right to just claim them, not even an apparently well-liked psychiatrist.

The volunteer's directions took Kelsey straight to the
doctor's home, a garage apartment behind the corner
house. Interesting quarters for a psychiatrist, she thought
as she climbed the stairs to the door. It suggested rental,
bachelor, temporariness. Was there no Mrs. Grayson? And
if there wasn't, didn't that make his taking four young kids
home with him on his days off just a little more curious?

When her sharp rap was answered, she immediately recognized the man from the parking lot yesterday, though a
rumpled version. Instead of a suit, he wore faded denim
shorts with more than their share of rips and a T-shirt with
permanent stains, and his hair stood on end. On the positive side, he didn't look befuddled but handsome—six-
feet-plus, blond hair, blue eyes, square jaw. How had she
missed noticing that yesterday?

Oh, and one other thing—he didn't appear to recognize her at all.

"J. D. Grayson? I'm Kelsey Malone, Department of Family Assistance." She offered him a business card, then a handshake. She expected a so-so grip and softness. She got restrained power and calluses—and not of the golf club or tennis racquet variety. "Can I come in?"

He stepped back and allowed her entrance into an apartment that was large, beautifully decorated, and scrupulously clean if she discounted the two dozen cartons of books stacked just inside. The combined fragrances of wood polish and fresh flowers perfumed the air, and the sound of a television was muted in the background.

She shifted her attention back to the doctor. "I understand you have the Brown children here."

"Of course I do. Where else would I have them?"

She ignored his testiness. "Can I see them?"

He gestured down the hall, and she followed the television sounds into the living room, where four children sprawled together on the sofa. Four pairs of identical brown eyes subjected her to a scrutiny as thorough as she gave them, then dismissed her as unimportant—meaning not their parent—and turned back to the television.

They looked as good as could be expected for four children who'd lived on their own for six weeks—a testament to the oldest boy's determination. According to their records, they were relatively healthy, though undernourished, and they hadn't suffered any apparent harm in their unauthorized time with the doctor. Still, he shouldn't have taken them. Though his intentions had no doubt been good, it was still against the rules.

When it came to protecting the children in her care, Kelsey was a stickler for following the rules.

She shifted her attention back to J. D. Grayson. "Is there someplace we can talk?"

"Down here." He led the way to a room that had hastily been converted into sleeping space, with nothing on the walls and a small collection of toys and children's books on the shelves. A dresser didn't quite cover the deep indentations in the rug where a larger piece—a desk, perhaps—had recently stood, and a few unfaded patches on the wall showed where photographs had been removed.

She turned in a slow circle between two sets of unmade bunk beds. The lower left bed was obviously the little girl's—Gracie's—with its pink sheets and lace-edged candy-striped spread. The bunk above hers sported a football theme, while race cars and cartoon characters roared across the other two. "This room is a bit small for four children."

"No one seemed to listen yesterday when I said I didn't have room," he said dryly as he leaned against the dresser. "What is it you want, Ms. Malone?"

She gestured toward the door. "Can we close that?"

"I'd rather not. Caleb has a habit of listening around corners. A closed door might be more temptation than he can resist."

And J.D. was standing where he could see if anyone so much as stepped into the hallway. She acknowledged the wisdom of his strategy. "I came to pick up the children."

"You what?"

"I assume you meant well, Dr. Grayson, but you can't just take them."

He was staring at her as if she'd begun speaking an alien language. "*I* meant well? Hey, lady, this was *not* my idea. You people came to me. You *asked* me to take them."

"There seems to be some misunderstanding here. This is my case, and I couldn't possibly have asked you—"

He waved one hand impatiently. "Not you. The other one."

"The other what?"

"The other social worker. Jeez, don't you people talk to each other?"

Feeling off balance again, Kelsey took a deep, calming breath. "What other social worker?"

"The one who came to me yesterday and asked me to take the kids—no, not asked, insisted. She said they needed me, said no one else would do. She even got Judge McKechnie to show up in court on a Sunday afternoon to sign an order for temporary custody. What's her name . . . Noelle. That was it."

"Noelle who?"

"I don't remember. You should know. It's your office."

"I admit I'm new here, Dr. Grayson, but I just met all the employees in the office this morning, and there's no one by the name of Noelle."

For a long time he stared at her. Once he opened his mouth as if to argue, then shut it again. Then, combing his fingers through his hair, he did argue. "You must be mistaken."

She shook her head. "There are only four of us. Two intake personnel named Dan and Lisa and two caseworkers—Mary Therese and me. There's not a Noelle in the bunch."

"But she gave me a card." He left the room, and an instant later she heard the slamming of drawers next door. In another instant he returned and handed her a business card. It was the standard card someone who was new to an office would have until she got her own cards printed— exactly the same as the one Kelsey had just given him.

"This doesn't prove anything."

He left the room again, then returned with a handful of official forms. "She gave me these."

None of the signatures on the custody papers were neatly formed, but she could make out Grayson's scrawl, and the judge's. She recognized Noelle's first name only because she could match the swoops and loops to the letters she knew to look for. The last name was nothing but a scribble.

Seeing that she remained unconvinced, Grayson tugged at his hair again. "She gave me the kids. The sheriff's department didn't question her. The hospital didn't. The judge didn't."

"Apparently, someone should have." Kelsey laid her briefcase on the top bunk, placed the papers and business card inside, then snapped the case shut again. "We'll have to get this straightened out, the sooner the better. Do you want to take the children with us, or is there someone trustworthy who can watch them while we're gone?"

His gaze narrowed dangerously at her use of the word *trustworthy*. He seemed to take it as a personal insult. "I'll ask Mrs. Larrabee to watch them," he said coldly, quietly. "She's my landlady, widow of the former mayor, a member of the hospital board of directors and the school board, a grandmother of eleven, and current or past president of every charitable organization in the county. She's quite trustworthy."

He walked to the door, then waited pointedly for her to leave. She returned to the living room, where the children once again subjected her to those long, flat looks. With a faint smile she sat down in an easy chair. "Hi. I'm Kelsey. I'm the social worker assigned to your case. Which one of you is Caleb?"

No one answered.

"Jacob? Noah?"

Still no response.

She smiled at the girl. "Well, I know you're Gracie. Gosh, you're pretty."

No smile, no blush, no shyly ducking her head.

Kelsey moved to sit on the coffee table directly in front of them. As one, they moved into a tighter huddle, shrinking away from her. "Look, kids, I know this is tough. You got along okay without any adults for the last six weeks, and you don't understand why things can't just go on the way they were. Unfortunately, they can't. Kids need grown-ups. You need your dad. But since he's not here, we're going to watch over you for him."

"He's coming back," the oldest boy said sharply.

Maybe, maybe not. Kelsey didn't know the percentage of parents who abandoned their children, then later returned for them, though she was sure some study somewhere had narrowed it to an educated guess. She did know in her experience that it didn't happen often enough. But maybe Ezra Brown was the exception to the rule. After all, he'd stuck it out two years longer than his wife had. According to the sheriff's report, he'd told the kids he was going to look for work and would return as soon as possible. Maybe he'd meant to keep that promise. Maybe something had happened to stop him from keeping it.

Or maybe it had merely been empty words.

"I understand you live in the country on a farm. I've never seen a farm before. I grew up in New York City. Have you ever been there?"

The oldest boy—Caleb, if she remembered correctly— rolled his eyes disgustedly, making her chuckle. "Feel free to point out a dumb question whenever I ask one. I do manage from time to time. So what do you guys like to do with your summers? Do you swim? Play baseball? Go fishing?"

No response. Not even a flicker of interest.

"When I was a kid, I went to the library a lot. And sometimes my mom would take us to the park, and for one week every summer, we would go to the beach. Have you ever seen the ocean?"

"That's a dumb question," the second oldest boy—Jacob, she thought—announced. Caleb scowled at him, and he protested in his defense. "She *said* to point out dumb questions, and that's a dumb question. We never been anywhere. How would we go to the ocean?"

"Shut up," Caleb hissed, and Jacob obeyed.

So Caleb was the key. If he ever relaxed and opened up, so would the others, but as long as he kept his guard up, reaching the kids in any way was going to be a slow, delicate job. She hoped Bethlehem was home to foster parents who were up to the job.

Before she could try again, Dr. Grayson came in. He'd changed into jeans and a less disreputable shirt and combed his hair—though she suspected that before their business was concluded, it would be standing on end all over again. He walked past them without a word, reaching the front door just as a knock sounded. When he returned, the eminently trustworthy Mrs. Larrabee was with him. With her round body and snowy white hair, all she needed was a red dress and spectacles to make a perfect Mrs. Santa Claus.

Dr. Grayson made the introductions, gave the kids a warning to behave, then fixed a less than friendly look on Kelsey. "Shall we go?"

She followed him outside and down the steps. Near the bottom he called over his shoulder, "We'll take my truck."

The look he gave her dared her to refuse—which, of course, was her first impulse, and second. The truck was caked with mud. It sat high off the ground. There was no running board to give her a step up, and her skirt was too narrow by far for the challenge ahead. But they could begin unraveling this mess on their way to the sheriff's department, and the sooner it was unraveled, the sooner she could get down to the business of helping those kids.

She covered her reluctance with what she hoped was a dazzling smile. "Thanks for the offer. You don't know how much I appreciate it."

He looked at her, her skirt, then the truck, and grinned an ill-tempered sort of grin. "Oh, I think I can guess."

Then he walked around the vehicle and left her to struggle in on her own.

J.D. WATCHED AS MS. MALONE MANEUVERED HER way onto the seat. She had to pull her skirt about four inches beyond decent, revealing a length of nice, tightly muscled thigh, then shimmied it back into place. With a huff she fastened her seat belt, settled her briefcase across her lap, and gave him a look that pretended composure. "We can go anytime, Doctor."

"You can call me J.D. Everyone else in town does." He started the engine, backed around her car into the side yard, then headed down the drive. "Where are we going?"

"To the sheriff's department. I want to talk to the deputy who took the children into custody."

"That would be Max Davis. I doubt he's on duty yet."

"Is Bethlehem so small that everyone knows everyone else's schedule?"

"Max works three to eleven. That means he won't be in yet. But, yes, Bethlehem *is* that small. Does that bother you?"

She showed no interest in the neighborhood they were passing through but watched him instead. "Why would it bother me?"

"Some people find small-town life stifling. There are no secrets here." Save one or two.

Her smile was humorless and made him wonder. "Every place has secrets, Dr. Grayson. Tell me about the children."

He considered correcting her use of his name, then shrugged it off. Bethlehem was a friendly town, and stiff, unyielding people didn't do well there. Ms. Malone would learn to loosen up, or she wouldn't last long. "Are you interested in my professional opinion or my temporary guardian opinion?"

"Either."

"I think they're in pretty good shape considering what they've been through. They're frightened and hurt, and Caleb's angry. He takes his role as big-brother-in-charge very seriously. He'll resent anyone who might come between them."

"Why did you take them?"

Annoyance tightened the muscles in his neck and made his voice sharp. "I told you, Noelle asked—"

"Why did you agree?"

He knew the sort of answer she expected. Though a few bad ones occasionally slipped through the approval process, the majority of people who became foster parents had admirable reasons for doing so. They loved kids. They wanted to help. They felt their lives had been blessed and wanted to pass on the blessing to someone else. They believed they could make a difference.

He loved kids—from a distance. He wanted to help— again, from a distance. His life had been blessed—until he'd screwed it up. And he *knew* he could make a difference.

He also knew that that difference could be good or bad. He could help, but he could also hurt. He could make one life better, but he could just as easily destroy another, and the guilt from that could destroy him.

So why had he agreed to take the kids? The only answer he could offer was the same one he'd given Holly yesterday. *Damned if I know.* Somehow, he didn't think Ms. Malone would like it any more than he did.

Fortunately, the courthouse was just ahead. Waving at a cop on his way out to patrol, J.D. turned into the parking lot and found a space. "We'll have to ask Sheriff Ingles to call Max in. He lives a couple of blocks away. It shouldn't take long."

The sheriff's department wasn't busy. It rarely was. The dispatcher looked up from her magazine long enough to wave them into the sheriff's office, where Ingles set aside the schedule he was working on and got to his feet. "J.D., ma'am. What can I do for you?"

After J.D. explained their reason for coming to see him, the sheriff shook his head with a chuckle. "Impersonating a social worker. Now, there's something you don't see too often. Me, if I were going to impersonate someone, it'd be a millionaire. No offense, Kelsey."

"None taken, Sheriff," she said dryly.

"Actually, though, there was no harm done. You couldn't ask for a better placement for those kids than J.D. here. He's an upright citizen, a doctor, and a shrink to boot. Everybody likes him."

J.D. felt her gaze on him, and he gave her a smug grin. Her only response was to look away.

Ingles went on. "I can understand your curiosity about who this Noelle is. Pretty little thing, wasn't she, J.D.? And she sure seemed to know what she was doing. But since everything worked out fine in the long run, it's not like it's really a big deal."

"It *is* a big deal, Sheriff," Kelsey disagreed. "We can't have some stranger going around choosing foster parents for wards of the state. Our job is to protect these children. We have rules, regulations, and procedures for just that reason. You should know that." Sending an accusing glare J.D.'s way, she added, "*You* should know that."

He did know. When a child was removed from his home, the caseworker made an emergency placement, usually for a few days, with one of the agency's preapproved foster parents. During that time a petition was filed with the court for temporary placement—again with a preapproved foster parent. Later, if it became necessary to terminate the parental rights, the caseworker sought a permanent home for the child.

They didn't just go out, pick a likely candidate—or, in his case, an unlikely one—and say "Here, take this kid."

But Noelle had done just that. And he'd taken the kids. And now Ms. Malone wanted them back.

Lucky for her, he had no problem with giving them back.

"We don't get a whole lot of foster care placements in Bethlehem," the sheriff said mildly. "That's one reason we don't have a social worker here."

"Well, as of this morning, that's changed."

The intercom buzzed, and the dispatcher announced Max's arrival just as he came through the door. The deputy greeted his boss and J.D., then gave Kelsey an appreciative look that made J.D. take another look. Since opening his door to her, he'd been too annoyed or dismayed to notice much beyond the great legs, but now he saw what Max had seen in five seconds—Kelsey Malone was an attractive woman. Her suit was too severe, her attitude too stiff, but the rest of the package—curly brown hair semi-tamed in a bun, hazel eyes, full lips with a lush cupid's bow, delicately shaped jaw—more than made up for the rest.

She asked Max for his version of events, and after taking a seat, he began. Friday evening he'd gotten a call from Nathan Bishop about four abandoned children. Before going out to the Brown place, he'd called Mary Therese Carpenter, who had met them there. She'd ordered the kids taken into custody, they'd packed their belongings, and he had transported them to the hospital.

"What did Mary Therese tell you before she left?" Kelsey asked.

"She said someone would be in touch regarding the

disposition of the kids. Then Noelle showed up Saturday afternoon, asked for a criminal history check on J.D. She said he would be taking the kids."

"Did she say Mary Therese had sent her?"

Max thought it over. "I don't think so. She said . . . she said she'd been assigned the Brown children and wanted to get them placed as quickly as possible. With J.D."

"Had you ever met her before?" He shook his head, and she directed the same question to the sheriff, then J.D. When he added his no to theirs, she shook her head too. "So a total stranger showed up and told you—a deputy, a sheriff, and a psychiatrist—that she was with the Department of Family Assistance. She offered no proof beyond a business card that didn't even have her name on it, and you took her word for it. Not only that, but you gave her four children to do with as she pleased. Do I have it straight?"

Though she didn't come right out and call them all incompetent idiots, she might as well have. It was clear she thought it. J.D. couldn't even take offense because she was right. They had been incredibly careless with the kids, and the result could have been disastrous.

He reached for the phone. "Good point, Ms. Malone. Sheriff, do you have Social Services' number over there in Howland?"

"What are you doing?" Kelsey asked as he dialed.

"A total stranger has come in here, telling us she's from the Department of Family Assistance. She has no proof beyond a business card that doesn't even have her name on it, and she wants to take four children who are legally in my custody." He offered her a cool smile. "I'm checking you out, Ms. Malone."

Of course she did check out. Mary Therese Carpenter described her from the top of her unruly hair all the way down to the no-nonsense flats on her feet. She ended with a question of her own. "Is there a problem, J.D.?"

"Not at all," he lied. "I just wanted to be sure she is who she says. You can't be too careful these days." He hung up, then sprawled back in the chair. "So you're legit. Now what?"

"Now we do things the *right* way. Deputy Davis, thank you for coming in. Sheriff, I would appreciate it if your department would locate this Noelle. I'm sure *my* department would like to investigate further. And, Dr. Grayson, would you please call Mrs. Larrabee and ask her to pack the children's things. I'll pick them up when I go back to get my car." With a nod, she left the office.

So it was that easy, J.D. thought. A little upheaval, a little rearranging of his life, and now, in less than twenty-four hours, it was over. All he had to do was give the kids to her, restore his office to its former order, and he was home free.

For some reason, he didn't feel as if he'd just been given his freedom.

He got to his feet and strode out to the lobby, where Ms. Malone was waiting for the elevator doors to open. She gave him the slightest of glances before stepping inside. "You've already called Mrs. Larrabee? Good. Then you can go on. I'll find a way over to get my car."

He followed her into the elevator, waited until the doors closed, then faced her. "What do you mean, we'll do things the *right* way?"

"Exactly what I said. I'll go over the parents on our list, find a temporary placement for the children, and—"

"They've been placed. With me."

"But you're not on our preapproved list."

The annoyance in his voice was mild compared to what he was feeling. "I've been approved by the whole damn town. Doesn't that count for something?"

"You don't even want them."

He wished he could deny it, but the situation was more complicated than wanting or not wanting. He wasn't even sure that what he wanted mattered. What did matter was that he could help the kids. They needed him. And while he didn't exactly want them, he might not mind having them.

She fixed a challenging look on him. "Can't deny it, can you?"

Scowling, J.D. followed her to her office. It was small, drab, and depressing—to match certain aspects of the job, he thought as he seated himself in a vinyl chair.

She squeezed behind the desk. "You can go home, Dr. Grayson, and get the children ready for me to pick up."

"I don't think so. *I* have legal custody."

"The state has custody, Dr. Grayson. You're just a temporary guardian, and that will end as soon as I find another home for them." She grabbed a stack of files, opened the top one, reached for the phone, and began dialing.

J.D. stared at a water stain on the wall. Why wasn't he doing what she suggested—going home, packing their ragged clothes in paper sacks, and reclaiming his office, his home, and his life for himself? Why didn't he just make an appointment to see the kids at some time in the future and forget about them for now? The kids wouldn't care this early in the game. It wasn't as if they'd formed any sort of bond with him. Hell, Caleb would be happy to get away from him.

It was exactly what he should do.

So why was he waiting?

Her first call was fruitless. So was the second. She began muttering to herself after the third.

"Is the state going to give you a receptionist?" he asked idly as she started to dial the next number on her list.

"They gave me an answering machine."

"A big-budget operation, huh? Since it's just you, you should move a couple of these file cabinets into the other office. Get 'em out of the window and get some light in here."

"I have plenty of light." She tapped a fingernail on the desk while listening to the steady ring at the other end of the line.

He leaned forward to see the list of preapproved foster parents, reading upside down. "If you're calling the Taylors, they're on vacation—went to California to visit her mother, with a stop in Montana to see her dad. They won't be back for a week."

She started to dial number five.

"I'd think twice about the Howards. They're great people, but they've got a son."

Her index finger hovered above the keypad. "And that's a problem because . . . ?"

"Ever see *The Bad Seed*?"

She disconnected and gave him another of those challenging looks. "And whom would you recommend, Dr. Grayson?"

Rising to his feet, he leaned across the desk and smelled musty papers, dust, and a faint hint of perfume. "This couple's moved. This one's divorced. He doesn't see his own kids, and I think the Brown kids would be more of a burden than she can handle right now. The Thomases are out because he's the kids' court appointed lawyer." For one reason or another, he legitimately eliminated every other name.

She gave him a smile that was all smirk. "And, conveniently, that leaves only you, who isn't on the list at all."

"I *am* the best psychiatrist in town."

"The *only* one."

"I was the best psychiatrist in Chicago." He said it

mildly, without arrogance. He didn't need arrogance when it was true.

"Then why did you come here?"

For an instant the air in the room grew heavier, damn near impossible to breathe, and faraway screams—his own—echoed in his ears. But his hands didn't knot into fists, his expression didn't change at all, and his voice sounded normal when he gave the lie he'd put together before he'd ever left the city. "I like small-town living. I wanted a slower pace, to know my neighbors, to have time for the things that are important. I wanted less crime, smaller crowds, and less traffic. Do you know that at the height of rush hour, you can get anywhere in Bethlehem in less than six minutes?"

"I didn't know that." She was good at that dry, sarcasm-laced delivery. It both annoyed and amused him. "But back to the problem at hand, Dr. Grayson."

"The only problem seems to be you, Ms. Malone."

Kelsey wanted to grind her teeth, to throw something, to let out one great, frustrated scream. She felt stupid even trying to explain, but try she did. "I cannot leave those children with you. You've had no background investigation. There's been no interview. Your house is too small. You have a full-time job. You can't be available for the children whenever they need you. You're not married. We know nothing—"

The rest of the words fled her brain as she opened a single manila folder. It contained all the initial documentation a caseworker could expect to find on a prospective foster parent.

And the name on the tab was J. D. Grayson.

How was that possible? She had thumbed through these files in Mary Therese's office and there'd been no file on Dr. Grayson. But here it was, in black and white—financial records, job history, confirmation of no criminal record from the sheriff's department. He'd been born in Philadelphia, raised in Boston, and graduated from Harvard, and no one had a negative thing to say about him. Not the hospital administrator, the chief of staff, various hospital and school staff members, the school superintendent, his pastor, or his neighbors.

"What is it?" he asked. When she didn't answer, he pulled the folder from her hands and flipped through the pages. "It's a background check. You heard the deputy say Noelle asked for a criminal history. It's logical to assume she was also looking at everything else."

"If she was a social worker."

His gesture was impatient. "The fact that you don't know her doesn't mean she isn't. You said yourself you were new. You just got into town—when?"

"Yesterday."

"And you were in the office yesterday afternoon? Jeez, don't you have a life?" Without giving her a chance to respond, he went on. "Maybe she used to work for Mary Therese and filled in this weekend as a favor. Maybe she works in some other social services office and was in Bethlehem on a visit. Maybe—"

He ran out of *maybes* because one of his two suggestions was most likely correct, Kelsey acknowledged with a sinking feeling. After all, what was the alternative? That someone was impersonating a social worker? That someone playing a convoluted game of let's pretend knew exactly what was needed to get those children placed in a home? Noelle had done everything Kelsey would have done—except start with the preapproved parents before moving on to someone else. She'd conducted all the right interviews, asked all the right questions, gotten all the right background information.

And she hadn't benefitted personally. It wasn't as if

she'd tried to take the kids herself. She'd simply seen to it that they were placed in a proper home as quickly as possible, which would have been Kelsey's own goal. And, judging by all the personal endorsements in Dr. Grayson's file, she'd made a good choice.

She *must* have some sort of official connection to the department, and Kelsey was simply unaware of it. If not notified by somebody in the system, how had she even known about the Brown children? Without the proper credentials, how could she have gotten all that confidential information on Dr. Grayson? And—most compelling— without *some* connection, how had her file gotten into Kelsey's box?

J.D. held the last page out for her to see. Two typed lines recommended approval of J. D. Grayson as a foster parent and bore the signature of Noelle last-name-illegible. Underneath it were the initials of a supervisory caseworker, MTC. Mary Therese Carpenter.

Heat flooded her face as she cleared her throat and fixed her gaze somewhere around his jaw. "I—I'm sorry, Dr. Grayson. It was my understanding that the children hadn't been placed yet, and when I heard that you had taken them home with you, I—I—"

"Overreacted," he supplied helpfully.

She ran one finger around the tight collar of her blouse. "Yes. When Mary Therese went over the case with me this morning, I assumed she had told me everything. I didn't see this file. I didn't know she had approved . . . I'm sorry."

He brushed her apology off with a shrug. "So what do we do now?"

Needing a moment to shift from embarrassment to business, she straightened the pages in the folder, closed it, then took a pen and pad from a drawer. "The, uh, the question of child care wasn't addressed in the records. What are your hours at the hospital?"

He leaned back, looking totally relaxed. "I usually go in around nine and I rarely work past five or on weekends. Most of that time is at the hospital, though I spend about ten hours a week at the nursing home, and during the school year I put in ten hours or so a week in the schools—sometimes more, sometimes less."

"You didn't get to be one of the best psychiatrists in Chicago by quitting at five and taking weekends off."

"*The* best," he stressed. "You're right. I didn't. That's one more reason I like Bethlehem."

"What do you intend to do with the children while you're working?"

"Mrs. Larrabee will keep them part of the time. So will Miss Agatha and Miss Corinna." He watched as she made notes. "That's Agatha Winchester and Corinna Winchester Humphries. They're sisters—retired schoolteachers—and the grandes dames of Bethlehem."

"Three elderly women? Couldn't you find someone younger?"

He studied her so long that she was barely able to contain the urge to squirm in her seat. When he finally spoke, his voice was calm, soothing—like a psychiatrist addressing a patient. "You really ought to do something about these prejudices of yours, Ms. Malone. If you'd like to make an appointment, perhaps I could help."

"I'm not prejudiced!" she declared hotly.

"You've already made it clear that the fact that I'm not married is a strike against my parenting abilities in your eyes. Now you think I should choose a baby-sitter based on age rather than experience, willingness, and capacity for caring?"

"That's not what I—" Drawing a breath, she made an effort to calm herself. "I didn't mean it that way. It's just that young children are a handful. My concern is that they might overwhelm an elderly caregiver."

"Grandmothers have been taking care of grandchildren since the beginning of time," he pointed out flatly. "Besides, if you'd ever met the Winchester sisters, you wouldn't refer to them as elderly. Their daily routine could overwhelm you and me both."

She straightened her shoulders and carefully said, "I would like to meet them."

"I'd like to introduce you. We'll stop by their house on the way home. Anything else?"

She stared at the notes she'd made on the pad. "What about emergencies? I assume you get called out in the middle of the night."

"On occasion. There are plenty of people I can call if it happens."

"Such as?"

He rolled his eyes in exasperation. "Mrs. Larrabee. The Winchesters. Holly McBride—she owns the McBride Inn and is about a tenth-generation resident of Bethlehem. Emilie and Nathan Bishop—he's the police officer who found the kids. Mitch and Shelley Walker—he's the chief of police. Alex and Melissa Thomas—he's the kids' court appointed lawyer and she owns the plant nursery. Leanne Watson, who has the baby shop in town. Denise and Don Allen, the kindergarten teacher and football coach who live next door. Amy—"

Kelsey raised both hands in surrender. "All right. Enough. One last thing." She cleared her throat again. "Are you involved in a relationship right now?"

Grayson's scowl held steady, then in a heartbeat it transformed into a broad grin. "Why? Are you interested?"

Her face flamed again. She chose to ignore his question and concentrate instead on her own. "If you *are* in a relationship, you must understand that you can't, ah, bring someone into the house to, ah—"

"No sleepovers. I understand."

"Good." She added her notes to his file, then folded her hands on top. "I think that takes care of everything for now. I'll be making some home visits. You'll know when I show up at your door. For now you're free to go."

He made no move to stand.

"Do you have any questions?"

"Just one. You left your car at my house. Do you plan to walk back to get it, or would you like a ride?"

She sighed heavily. It seemed there was no end to her mistakes today. "I would appreciate a ride if you don't mind."

"If I minded, I wouldn't have offered." They were on their way out the door, when he added, "You really need to lighten up, Ms. Malone. You're not in the big city anymore."

This was what she'd wanted, she reminded herself—small-town life. Making a difference. Making a connection.

So far it seemed all she'd made were mistakes.

It was a silent ride back to the garage apartment. Halfway there, J.D. pulled to the side of the street and gestured toward the corner house. "That's the Winchester place. The sisters live there together."

The house looked like something out of a storybook, with a big veranda, fish-scale shingles, gingerbread, and soft colors. There was a swing at one end of the veranda, a glider in the shade of a spreading oak, and flowers blooming everywhere. It was a homey, welcoming place, the sort that she'd sometimes dreamed of in her fifth-floor walkup.

"Can we meet them?"

"If they were home, their car would be in the driveway.

They're probably at the hospital—they do volunteer work there—or maybe at the library for story hour. We'll set something up later." As he pulled away from the curb, he asked, "Have you found a place yet?"

Back in the city, she'd rarely engaged in personal conversation with therapists or foster parents. With the therapists it had been all business. With parents she'd known practically every intimate detail of their lives, while they'd known her only as Ms. Malone the social worker. But she wasn't in the city anymore.

"I have an apartment on the other side of town."

"Did you get the pink and green bathroom or the red and yellow?" At her questioning look, he grinned. "There's only one apartment complex on the other side of town. I lived there for about a month before Mrs. Larrabee offered me the garage apartment. Maybe once I've moved out, she'll give you a shot at it."

"When are you moving?"

"As soon as my house is finished."

"Which will be . . . ?"

"Not as soon as it would have been before I agreed to take the kids. I'm building the place myself. I usually spend my evenings and weekends working out there."

That explained the calluses on his palms. An eminent psychiatrist who was building his own house while caring for four children who weren't his own. J. D. Grayson was proving to be an interesting man.

He turned the corner into his driveway, then parked beside her car. "Do you want to come up and talk to the kids again?"

"No, thanks. I'll stop in soon for the first home visit." She paused. "About our misunderstanding . . . I really am sorry, Dr. Grayson. I don't usually make mistakes."

"Everyone makes mistakes."

Simple words, presumably meant to reassure her. Somehow they didn't. "In my job I can't afford many mistakes. It won't happen again." It was a promise to herself more than to him—a promise she would do her best to keep.

Chapter Four

J.D. WATCHED KELSEY DRIVE AWAY, THEN SLOWLY, reluctantly, turned toward the house. He could think of a hundred places he would rather go than inside, a hundred things he'd rather do than face those kids. With Mrs. Larrabee, they were certainly in more capable hands than his own. They wouldn't miss his presence for a few more hours.

But when he moved, it wasn't toward his truck and escape. No, he walked to the bottom of the stairs, climbed up one step at a time—the way he'd learned to live again. The way he would learn to live with these kids. One step at a time.

The apartment was quiet. With four kids inside, he found the silence unnatural. Uncomfortable.

They remained where they'd been when he'd left them, sprawled together on the sofa in front of the television. Mrs. Larrabee sat in the easy chair near the window, using the afternoon light to do her needlework. When she saw him, she smiled, removed the half-glasses that had slipped to the tip of her nose, and tucked her work into its tote before joining him in the hallway.

"Is everything all right?" she asked quietly. "Was the social worker satisfied? Is she leaving the children with you?"

He glanced over her head and caught Caleb's scowl. "Yes, she is." Though why in the world he'd wanted her to was beyond him.

Obviously, Mrs. Larrabee didn't share his misgivings. "Wonderful. I have no doubt you'll give them exactly what they need. I'll run along now. If you need anything, just give me a call. Children, I'll see you later."

The offered no response but merely watched her go.

What was he supposed to do now? Sit with them while they watched their sixth or eighth hour of the Disney Channel? Retreat to his room? No doubt, that would make them happy, but it wouldn't go far toward resolving anything.

He studied them a moment longer, taking in the solemn stares, the shaggy hair, the worn clothes. He knew that they were clean and so were their clothes, but they still looked like urchins. They still looked shabby. So doing something about that was as good a place to start as any.

"Turn off the TV," he said, pulling his keys from his pocket, "and let's go shopping."

None of them moved. He pushed the off button, then waited expectantly.

"I never been shopping," Noah murmured softly, then shrank back against the cushions.

It was the first time J.D. had heard him speak in more than twenty-four hours. J.D. summoned a faint smile for him. "Then it's time you went. Come on. Let's go."

When Gracie would have risen from the sofa, Caleb tightened his hold on her. He signaled the other two with a look to stay where they were. "Shoppin' for what?"

"Clothes."

"We have clothes."

"New clothes."

Gracie's eyes lit up, and there was a hint of interest in Noah's. Jacob took his cue from Caleb, who said, "We don't need new clothes."

J.D. kept his tone level and friendly even as he sent a warning glance Caleb's way. "You seem to have misunderstood, Caleb. I'm not making a request. I'm telling you what we'll be doing for the next hour or two. Get up and let's go."

Caleb didn't move. The other kids looked from him to J.D. and back again. If Caleb refused, there was no question they would also refuse, leaving J.D. with no choice but to back down.

And backing down, he was sure, would be a mistake. But what would be the alternative? Fortunately, he didn't have to look for one. After a moment, with all the hostility he could manage, Caleb gave in. "Fine. Let's go."

There were only a few clothing stores in Bethlehem, all of them located on two adjoining blocks. What were the chances, J.D. wondered sourly, that Caleb wouldn't find anything he liked?

J.D. herded the kids into the nearest shop, where Mandy Lewis, daughter of one of his fellow doctors, was working for the summer. Somehow hearing the bell over the door in spite of the discordant racket coming from the radio under the counter, she lowered the volume, spit out the gum she'd been popping, and greeted them with a bright smile. "Hi, Dr. J.D. What can I do for you?"

"We need new wardrobes—shorts, T-shirts, underwear, whatever they need for the summer. And something for church."

"I never been to church," Noah murmured.

"Well, it's never too late to start," Mandy replied. "At

least, that's what my grandfather the minister says. Why don't you two"—she held out her hands to Gracie and Noah—"come with me, and I'll help you get started while Dr. J.D. takes care of your brothers."

Noah looked to Caleb for permission. Gracie, her attention caught by a rack of pretty dresses, felt no such need. She immediately placed her hand in Mandy's and headed for the dresses. Only then did Noah grab the girl's other hand and follow.

J.D. considered coming up with an excuse for leaving all four kids in Mandy's care. The courthouse was nearby. He could check in with the sheriff's department and see if there'd been any progress in the last hour or so in the search for Ezra Brown. He could cross the hall to the police department and shoot the breeze with his friends there. Or he could go to the third floor and unnerve Kelsey Malone a bit more.

His grin faded. No use considering could-dos. What he *would* do was admit—at least to himself—that he was once again out of his element and try his best in spite of it.

As he looked around, his gaze settled on a display of denim shorts. Since that was his own summer uniform when he wasn't working, he headed that way. "Jacob, what size do you wear?"

With a bewildered expression the boy looked at Caleb, then shrugged. He probably wore hand-me-downs from his brother, whose own clothes appeared to be hand-me-downs from their father.

J.D. picked out a variety of sizes, then handed them to Jacob. "The dressing room's over there. Try those on until you find a pair that fits." After taking a breath for patience, he turned to Caleb. "What about you?"

"I got clothes."

"You need more."

"Don't want any."

"You need some for church."

"I'm not goin' to church."

"Yes, you are. Sunday morning. We don't go to the same church as Mandy, but you'll know some people there. Mr. Montero, the principal at your school. Miss Smith—she was your teacher last year, wasn't she? Oh, and Alanna Dalton. Her family goes there too."

Caleb's face turned red at the mention of Alanna's name. "I'm not goin' to church, and I'm not buyin' new clothes, and I'm not takin' *anything* from *you*."

Out of sight behind the stacks of shorts, J.D.'s fingers curled into a fist. For one brief moment he considered letting Caleb have his way, letting him continue to live in ragged old clothes that fitted badly and gave other kids reason to tease or feel sorry for him. But that would be the easy way out, the coward's way out. It would mean giving in to a twelve-year-old, and he wasn't quite ready to do that.

"You're getting new clothes for church," he said in an even voice. "You will show respect by dressing appropriately when you're there. The rest of the time, I don't care if you wear rags out of the trash." But others would, and because they would, eventually so would Caleb. "So you can pick out stuff you like, or I can pick it out for you. It's your choice."

Anger made Caleb's dark eyes even darker and sharpened the ever-present hostility as he slowly, noisily, breathed to control his emotions. Off to the side, the dressing room door squeaked as Jacob pushed it open, and back in one corner, Gracie made a delighted sound. "I'm pretty!" she exclaimed, and Mandy replied, "Of course you're pretty," as if there'd never been any question of it. J.D. didn't take his eyes off Caleb, who returned his stare for a moment before finally selecting a pair of shorts.

"You can make me get them," he said quietly. "But you can't make me wear them."

J.D. shrugged as if it made no difference to him, then turned his back to check on Jacob. A moment later Caleb pushed past him and a moment after that the dressing room door slammed shut. The sigh he released wasn't one of relief, J.D. told himself. There would be plenty more standoffs to come. He hadn't won anything yet.

By the time they left the store an hour later, that morning's headache was back and he'd made a dent in his bank balance, but the kids had clothes. Gracie and Noah had wanted to wear one of their new outfits home, but Caleb had insisted they put on their old clothes. Their *own* clothes, he'd called them.

They couldn't separate the kids, Noelle had insisted yesterday. The younger ones needed Caleb and he needed them. J.D. couldn't help but wonder if in this case separation might be the best thing.

They went to the shoe store down the block. It took another hour—faced with so many choices, Gracie had found it difficult to decide—but at last they returned to the truck.

"What're you gonna buy us now?" Caleb asked snidely.

"Food. Then we're going home." There he was going to swallow a bottle of aspirin and another of antacid, put a wet cloth over his eyes and plugs in his ears, and not move until the following morning.

They drove the few blocks to the grocery store. As they turned into the parking lot, Caleb's palms got damp, and as they pulled into a parking space, his face grew warm. He didn't want to go in there, had sworn he'd never come back. Now, only a couple of days later, here he was.

But he wasn't going in.

Grayson turned off the engine and opened his door. In back the kids were leaning against Caleb's seat, ready to climb out. He looked at them over his shoulder before saying, as if it were no big deal, "We'll wait here."

Grayson didn't believe him. "Yeah, right. Come on—all of you."

Arguing wouldn't do any good. Caleb knew that. He'd argued with just about every adult he'd met in the last few days and none of them even listened to him. They all thought he was just some dumb kid who couldn't possibly have anything important to say. Maybe he was a dumb kid—hadn't he been held back once in school? And hadn't he gotten caught by the cops? But he knew what he wanted, and what he wanted most of all just then was not to go back in that store.

"Let's go, Caleb," the doctor said, sounding pissed. "Now."

Clenching his jaw, Caleb shoved the door open, stood back while the kids jumped out, then dragged his feet to the door. Inside, he took a quick look around. The checkers were busy ringing up customers, and the desk at the other end, where the man had pushed him down, was empty. Maybe he wasn't workin' today. Maybe nobody who was workin' that night was there now—at least, nobody who'd remember him.

He was so busy convincing himself of that that he almost ran into Gracie when she stopped all of a sudden. Noah joined her, and, with their eyes open wide and their mouths too, they looked around them. They'd never been in a grocery store before. Their mother, before she ran off, liked to come to town by herself so she could look in all the stores and pretend she wasn't poor and didn't have a husband and four kids waiting at home. Their dad had always come alone too, and Caleb, when he'd come to steal, sure couldn't let the kids tag along.

"Is all this place filled with food?" Gracie asked in a hushed voice.

Grayson answered, "Food, paper stuff, cleaning and bath stuff. Want to ride in the shopping cart?"

She looked at the cart, nodded, and raised her arms. Before he could pick her up though, Caleb pushed between them and *he* picked her up. He set her inside the cart, then Noah too. Giving Grayson a smug look, he began pushing them away.

"What kind of fruit do you guys like?" Grayson asked, sticking close to Caleb. "Want some bananas?"

No one said anything, but he got a bunch anyway and gave them to Noah to hold. Noah looked like he might peel one and eat it right there.

"What about apples? Oranges? Strawberries?"

The thought of strawberries made Caleb's mouth water. Strawberries were his most favorite food in the whole world, but he didn't say so.

Grayson put two big baskets of berries in the foldout seat of the cart, handed Gracie and Noah bags of apples, oranges, grapes, and carrots. Caleb stared at the berries, wishing they weren't so close he could smell them. Hell, he wished they weren't in the cart at all. He wasn't takin' nothin' from the shrink, remember? Just a place to live and three meals a day. No new clothes, no new shoes, no special treats like strawberries.

They sure smelled good though.

Grayson went to the cereal aisle next. "What kind of cereal do you like?"

Nobody answered. They acted like they didn't hear him.

"Noah? What do you like for breakfast?"

Nervous, Noah shrugged. "We don't never eat breakfast."

"At my house you do. You want to try some super-sugar-frosted wheaty bits? Mini-chocolate-chip-cookie-o's? Honey-raisin-cinnamon-nut bran?"

Noah hesitantly nodded. Yes to all of 'em, Caleb thought with satisfaction. It was a stupid question anyway. What little kid *wouldn't* want to try all of 'em? Now stupid Grayson had to buy 'em all, and it would cost a lot. 'Course, he didn't care. It wasn't like he was spending his own money. The lady from the state would give it all back to him.

Grayson put six big boxes in the cart, then pulled it to another aisle for throwaway cups, napkins, and bathroom tissue. He got two gallons of milk and a loaf of some fancy bread, then finally they went to check out.

Always when he left the store, Caleb felt guilty, as though he had to sneak past the checkout without anybody seeing him. He felt guilty now, even though he'd done nothing wrong, even though nobody was likely to even look twice at him since he was with the doctor. Still, his face felt hot, his hands were getting sweaty all over again, and he wished he were anyplace in the world besides right there. The only thing that could possibly be worse was seeing Alanna or the man—

The voice he dreaded interrupted his thoughts. "Afternoon, J.D. I thought I caught a glimpse of you back there, but I wasn't expecting to see you with kids, so I assumed it was someone else. You have company?"

"In a manner of speaking," Grayson said. As he began unloading the cart, Caleb kept his head down. The man, busy ringing up boxes of cereal, might not even notice him. But then the stupid doctor was introducing them.

"—Noah and Gracie, and this is Jacob and that's—" Grayson looked straight at Caleb and stopped talking because he knew. He knew why Caleb hadn't wanted to come into the store, knew he was embarrassed and afraid, and he felt sorry for him.

For that Caleb hated him.

"Caleb and I have met," Bill said. He looked at Caleb as

if he didn't trust him, making the boy's face burn hotter. Caleb stared at the toe of his ragged shoe until finally Grayson said, "Let's go."

Nobody said anything till they got the bags loaded in the back of the truck and the kids had climbed in the backseat.

Then Grayson said, "You don't have anything to be ashamed of, Caleb. Yes, stealing is wrong, but you had a good reason—"

Caleb slammed the passenger door, cutting off his words.

At home Grayson tried once more. He came into the house last, carrying the bags with Gracie's clothes. Caleb stopped him at the bedroom door.

"I know it wasn't comfortable going back in the store so soon, but it will be easier—"

Caleb took the bags, then, just like he did back at the store, he closed the door in J.D.'s face.

O N Tuesday morning J.D., taking care to make no sound, went to the guest room, where the door was propped open. Two nights in a row, after the kids had gone to bed, he'd turned out the lights and closed the door. Two mornings he'd awakened to find the door open and the hall light on. He wondered which of the kids was afraid of the dark. The natural assumption would be Gracie, who was youngest, or Noah, who was smallest, but J.D. knew better than to make assumptions about kids.

They slept soundly, looking so innocent and sweet. When they woke up, the younger three would still appear innocent and sweet, maybe even more so, as they clung to their big brother/protector, but Caleb awake and alert was neither. What he mostly was was difficult. Obstructive. Angry.

And he was well within his rights to be all that and more, J.D. kept reminding himself.

From the kitchen came the faint aroma of coffee, drawing him in that direction. The timer-controlled coffeemaker was his best gift ever to himself, giving him coffee on demand to make him feel human and in control. He *needed* to feel in control. He filled a mug, then took it, his shoes, and his socks out onto the steps. The pale gray sky was showing pink off to the east, and there were lights on in houses up and down the street. The dawn air was cool, sweet, and the neighborhood was quiet. It was a peaceful time of day.

By the time he'd finished his coffee and laced up his shoes, Mrs. Larrabee's back door had opened. His landlady made her way across the damp grass to his steps, offering a cheery smile when she saw him sitting there.

"I admire your energy so early in the morning," she said in greeting.

"I admire your good humor."

"Are the children still in bed?"

"Yes, ma'am. Thanks for coming over."

"I can drink my coffee in your kitchen as well as in my own. Go on now. Stretch your legs. Have a good time."

She went inside and he headed down the steps. After a series of stretches, he trotted down the driveway and to the street, where he turned right. He'd been running—in one way or another, he thought cynically—more years than he cared to count. Sometimes he loved it, sometimes he didn't. Sometimes he couldn't bear having nothing to do but think. Sometimes he found himself the worst company in the world—the last person he wanted to spend time with, the very last person he wanted to be.

Today was one of the better days, with things to think about besides himself, his mistakes, his failures. There were the kids. It was difficult to reach the younger kids with

Caleb exerting such control. Maybe if he got them around other kids . . . Alanna Dalton knew Caleb from school, and the younger Daltons, Josie and Brendan, were near the younger Browns' ages. If they could spend some time together, maybe Caleb could ease his rigid control just a little. Maybe he could be a kid again for a while.

J.D. was approaching Main Street, planning to turn right. But the sight of a familiar figure turning off Main onto Sixth and jogging away from him changed his plans.

She wore bright red shorts and a royal blue tank, a pleasant change from the brown suit of the day before. Her curly hair was pulled into a ponytail that bounced with every step she took, and her legs . . . He sucked in his breath in a low whistle. No denying it, she had great legs.

He thought about catching up to her and about staying fifteen yards behind her. Both ideas had their merits— talking to her versus watching her. Learning more about her or just admiring the obvious.

The decision was taken from him when she reached City Park, turned onto the paved path, and slowed her pace, leaving him no choice but to join her. Once he did, she returned to her original pace. They'd passed the ice rink and the picnic tables before she finally spoke. "You know, I usually run alone."

"You're alone. I just happen to be going in the same direction."

"I noticed. In the city, following a woman jogger is a good way to get yourself in trouble."

"What kind of trouble? What did you carry for protection? Pepper spray?"

"That's illegal in New York."

"Like that stops anyone," he scoffed. "Besides, we're not in the city. One of these days you'll become so much a part of Bethlehem that you'll almost forget you came from someplace else. Your years in the city will seem like nothing more than a distant nightmare."

"Is that how you think of your years in Chicago? As a nightmare?"

It was an innocent question, one he'd inadvertently set himself up for. Knowing that didn't stop it from stinging though. It didn't ease the sudden queasiness in his stomach or the sick taste in his mouth. "What years in Chicago?" he asked with forced lightness that sounded phony. "My life began when I came to Bethlehem."

Maybe she recognized the phoniness, maybe not. Either way, she gave him a long look and fell silent until they'd rounded the playground, when she changed the subject. "You never answered my question yesterday."

"You asked a lot of questions, and I answered every one. 'Can I come in? Can I see the kids? Is there someplace we could talk? Can we close that door?'"

"Why did you agree to take the children?"

Fixing his gaze on the path ahead, he listened to the sound of their footsteps, hitting the pavement in unison. As the sun climbed higher, the sky lightened and the temperature began to edge up. Sweat trickled down his spine and left damp spots on his shirt. He was uncomfortable, but it was a pleasant discomfort.

"I'm waiting, Dr. Grayson."

Rather than try to explain what he didn't entirely understand himself, he answered flippantly. "Noelle was persuasive."

She responded dryly. "So you're susceptible to pretty little things. What a surprise."

For a long time he hadn't been susceptible to anything except self-pity, self-loathing, grief. Bethlehem—and the people he'd met there, the acceptance he'd found there— had changed that. "I'm a man. I like pretty women. So shoot me. But I didn't take custody of four kids simply because a beautiful woman asked me to. And I didn't give them up simply because another beautiful woman told me to."

The look she gave him was long, steady, and unimpressed. "Am I supposed to be flattered?"

"When I flatter you, Ms. Malone, you won't have to ask for confirmation. I was merely stating the obvious. Besides, *you* were the one who brought looks into the conversation."

After a moment she grudgingly said, "I suppose you can call me Kelsey."

"I suppose I would anyway, with or without your permission." Then he grinned. "I don't suppose you're going to call me J.D."

"Who's with the kids?"

"Is that a new habit? Ignoring comments you don't want to respond to?"

"Surely you didn't leave them home alone."

"Because it's very rude. You really should break it before it's too late."

She scowled at him, her hazel eyes narrowing. "Giving unsolicited advice is also rude. Who is with the kids?"

"Mrs. Larrabee. If I'd left them alone, don't you think I would have run the other way when I saw you instead of following you?"

"Why did you follow me?"

"Uh, this is my regular route? I didn't want to run with the sun in my eyes?" A quick glance showed that she didn't buy either answer. Why should she, when it was so obvious? Gorgeous legs, six miles long, were an enticement no right-minded man would turn his back on.

"I ran this route yesterday and didn't see you, and the sun wasn't up high enough when you started to even clear the trees."

"Maybe I'm just being neighborly."

"Huh." Clearly unimpressed, she gestured toward the long, low building up ahead. "This is it for me—back where I started."

He turned into the parking lot with her, passed a half-dozen cars, and stopped at the end of the cracked sidewalk that led to number three. "Hey, I used to live in number three."

"What a coincidence." She bent over, hands to the ground in a long stretch that pulled her clothes snug. It was an interesting sight from the front—the long line of her neck, her back exposed where her tank top dipped down, the muscles clearly defined in her legs and arms. How much more interesting it would be from behind, J.D. suspected, but if he walked around her to confirm that suspicion, no doubt she would stand up immediately.

"You have any plans for tonight?"

She straightened, unfolding her spine one vertebra at a time, raising her arms high above her head. When finally she looked at him, her face was flushed, her hair mussed, her tank top still clinging like a second skin. His heart rate should be slowing, his body cooling now that he'd stopped moving, but it wasn't. If anything, his pulse might have increased a few beats and his temperature climbed a few degrees.

"Why do you want to know?" She sounded aloof, wary, as if he might be asking for nefarious reasons, which was ridiculous. Not that he couldn't think of a few wicked deeds he'd like to do with her if she were merely a woman, but she wasn't *merely* anything. She was a social worker first and foremost—the social worker assigned to him and the kids. As long as that professional association existed, anything personal was totally off limits.

"I thought I'd call Miss Corinna and Miss Agatha, ask if we could stop by their house this evening. You can see for yourself that they're nowhere near too old to take care of the kids."

"All right. You can call the office and let me know." She pulled a key from her shorts pockets and climbed the steps of her small porch without so much as a good-bye.

"What? No invitation inside to see what you've done with the place?" he teased. "No 'Thanks for the company, I enjoyed the run'? The least you could do is offer me a drink of water."

"Would you like a drink of water, Dr. Grayson?" She gestured to the right as she opened the door. "The hose is right there."

"You're a hard woman, Ms. Malone." Though she looked incredibly, womanly soft. "That's okay. We'll work on your manners. Bethlehem will teach you to be gracious in no time."

Her smile came slowly, unwillingly. "Would you like to come in and see what I've done to the place? How about a glass of water?"

"No, thanks. I've got a few more miles to go."

"Thanks for the company. I enjoyed the run—even though I normally do run alone."

He began jogging in place, warming muscles that had started to cool. "Hey, you never did tell me. What did you use for protection in the city?"

"My neighbor's dog—a big, mean, man-hating Rottweiler." This time her smile was wickedly amused. "See you later, Dr. Grayson."

KELSEY STOOD IN FRONT OF HER OPEN CLOSET doors, staring at the clothes hanging inside. She'd come back from a visit to Alex Thomas's law office that afternoon to find a message from J. D. Grayson that he'd arranged a six P.M. meeting between her and the Winches-

ter sisters—a dinner meeting, no less. Though it was unusual—in eleven years she'd never been invited to dinner
by a client's baby-sitter—she could handle dinner with
strangers.

But could she handle dinner with the client?

J.D. had been on her mind so much of the day that
she'd even stopped thinking of him as Dr. Grayson. She
had watched from the door that morning until he was out
of sight, had thought about inviting him inside into her
personal space. She'd considered the fact that her space
had been his first—that he'd cooked in her kitchen, showered in her bathroom, maybe even slept in her bed. She'd
wondered why he wasn't married and what he'd given up
in Chicago to come to Bethlehem and if he was as remarkable as he seemed.

Thinking, considering, and wondering were all right, as
long as that was all she did. She wanted a relationship
somewhere down the line, once she was completely settled
in and had had a chance to meet some men, but absolutely
not with a client, and probably not with a psychiatrist.
Their fields were too similar, their work too involved.

With a sigh she reached for the navy jacket that matched
the skirt she was wearing, then put it back, stripped off her
blouse and skirt, and pulled on a dress instead. It was soft,
summery, with a scooped neck, short sleeves, and a hem
that fell almost to her ankles. The print was pale yellow
flowers on a muted aqua background, and she tied her hair
back with a matching yellow ribbon. The overall effect
was much more casual, much more pleasing than her usual
conservative suits and shirtwaists.

And it was just for her. She wasn't looking to impress
anyone.

After dumping the contents of her purse into a straw
handbag, she locked up and headed for the Winchester
house. It was exactly six o'clock when she parked out

front. There were kids playing in the yard—the younger three Browns, plus two she didn't recognize. Caleb sat at one end of a glider by a tree, pointedly ignoring the pretty girl at the other end.

Kelsey stopped on the sidewalk to watch the kids for a minute, long enough to catch the attention of one of their playmates. The girl slid to a stop in front of her, pushed her blond hair back from her face, and stuck out her hand. "Hi. I'm Josie Dalton. Who're you?"

"Kelsey Malone."

They shook hands, then Josie bluntly asked, "Are you the welfare lady?"

"I'm a social worker. I work for the Department of Family Assistance."

"You're here 'cause of them and not us, aren't you?" She gestured to the Browns with an outflung hand. "'Cause the welfare lady with the orange hair an' the judge said we can stay with Aunt Emilie and Uncle Nathan till our mama's well enough to take care of us herself, even if it is a long, long ti—"

The girl on the glider had gotten up, walked over, and slipped her hand over Josie's mouth. "You talk too much, Josie."

Josie wriggled free. "I do not. Miss Agatha says I talk just the right amount," she said indignantly before running off to play.

"Just the right amount for three kids," the girl murmured. "Hi. I'm Alanna Dalton."

"I'm pleased to meet you, Alanna." Kelsey lowered her voice. "Are you a friend of Caleb's?"

Alanna glanced over her shoulder at him, then shrugged. "Sort of. At least, I was until I saw him when he got caught . . . you know. Stealing." She whispered the last word. "I don't think he wants to be friends anymore."

She looked hurt—another female learning the power of

males, Kelsey thought. She smiled gently at the girl. "I think he's embarrassed about that, and probably a little frightened by being taken from his home. He needs a friend though. Maybe if you give him a little time . . . An awful lot has changed in his life, you know."

"I know," Alanna said solemnly, and Kelsey thought she probably did. After all, she was living with her aunt and uncle instead of her parents.

"Dr. J.D. and the rest of the grown-ups are inside. You can just go on in."

"Thank you." Kelsey went to the top of the steps, then turned back to watch a moment longer. Alanna didn't return to the glider and Caleb. Instead, she picked up Gracie and swung her around in circles, making her giggle delightedly, until they both collapsed to the ground.

Smiling, Kelsey turned to ring the doorbell, only to find that the door was open and J.D. was standing there. "This is a pleasant surprise," he said through the screen door.

"I *was* invited."

"Actually, I was referring to the dress. For once you don't look like you raided a prison matron's closet."

Her mouth dropped open, and she stared at him. "I beg your pardon."

"Oh, you don't have to beg—not for that. You have to admit, that brown suit you had on yesterday and that navy blue thing today are—"

"Professional," she interrupted.

"Severe."

"Conservative."

"Lacking in style."

"Simple."

"Plain. Ugly enough to scare the kids."

She gave him a narrow-eyed scowl. "I bet you wear shorts to work, and shoes without socks, and you probably don't even own a suit."

His grin was supremely smug. "I own *two* suits—one for summer and one for winter. You saw me in one Sunday."

She'd thought he didn't remember their brief encounter in the courthouse parking lot Sunday afternoon. He'd certainly given no sign of it on Monday. "You weren't wearing a tie."

"I took it off before I was tempted to hang myself with it." He offered another of those grins, so arrogant that part of her itched to slap it away while part of her wanted only to smile in response. The smile was winning out, when a woman appeared beside him.

"J.D., don't keep our guest waiting on the porch. Heavens, what kind of host are you?" She was slender, white-haired, with a warm welcome in her smile and her voice. "You have to forgive the boy. Sometimes he forgets his manners. You must be Kelsey. We've been waiting all day to meet you. Come in, dear. Let me introduce you around."

This time the smugness was all hers as she slipped past J.D. and let the older woman guide her into the living room, where the others waited. Her escort was Corinna Humphries. Her sister, Agatha Winchester, was plump, also white-haired, and almost overwhelmingly friendly. The other guests for the evening were the Daltons' aunt and uncle, Emilie and Nathan Bishop. He was the police officer, Kelsey recalled, who had brought Caleb's family to her department's attention, and she mentioned this.

He shifted the baby he held to his other shoulder. The nieces and nephew outside bore a strong resemblance to their aunt, but the baby—Michael—looked just like his father. "It's a tough situation," he replied, and the sisters murmured their agreement.

"Why, if it was work he was looking for, Ezra Brown could have found it right here in town," Agatha declared. "All he had to do was let someone know he was in need."

"Did you know Mr. Brown?" Kelsey asked.

"Only to say hello to," Agatha replied. "He and his family moved in out there . . . oh, six or seven years ago. They pretty much kept to themselves—didn't come to church, take part in any of the holiday festivities, or send the children to school very regularly. That's how Caleb wound up in Alanna's class. He should be a year ahead of her, you know, but he got held back."

Kelsey made a mental note to check Caleb's school records, to identify his deficiencies and get him whatever help he might need. In the easy chair across from her, J.D. looked as if he were making the same note.

Corinna picked up where her sister left off. "We occasionally bumped into Mrs. Brown at the store. She was never particularly friendly. She always seemed rather distracted. Then suddenly we began seeing Mr. Brown. Later we heard that she had gone away."

"Actually, we heard that she had run off with another man."

Corinna frowned severely at Agatha. "That's gossip."

"It's information, and Kelsey's looking for information, aren't you, dear?"

Holding back a smile, Kelsey nodded. "You said Mr. Brown could have found work here in town. Are there jobs readily available?"

"Not many," Emilie replied. "But Bethlehem takes care of its own. Somebody would have *found* a job for him."

"Maybe he was too proud to admit that he needed help."

"Or maybe looking for work was just the excuse he gave the kids for leaving," J.D. said flatly.

"It *wasn't* an excuse."

Everyone's gazes shifted toward the door, where Caleb stood, his face white with anger, his thin body shaking.

J.D. grimaced, then took a deep breath as he stood up and walked toward the boy. "Caleb—"

"My dad's coming back. He said he would."

"I hope he does."

"Of course you do. Then you won't be stuck with us anymore."

"I'm not stuck with you. If I didn't want you—"

"Liar."

There was a moment of heavy silence. It seemed that even the kids outside had gone silent. Then J.D. reached out one hand. "Caleb—"

The instant his fingers made contact, Caleb spun around and darted away, the screen door banging behind him. Kelsey went to stand beside J.D.

"Not one word," he muttered in warning. It wasn't necessary. She didn't have a word to offer.

Alanna appeared on the other side of the screen. "I'll talk to him," she offered anxiously. When Kelsey nodded, she raced down the steps and across the yard.

"Welcome to the world of foster parenting," Kelsey murmured. "It's a tough job, but someone's got to do it."

J.D. scowled at her before turning away, leaving her alone at the door.

Chapter Five

CALEB WAS HALFWAY DOWN THE BLOCK BY the time Alanna caught up with him. He was walking too fast, but she could keep up if she skipped along. She waited for him to say something, but when he didn't, she did. "Where are you going?"

He didn't answer. He just shoved his hands in his pockets, hunched his shoulders, and walked faster.

"You might as well go back. You don't have anyplace to go except Dr. J.D.'s or Miss Corinna's."

He started across Fifth Street even though there was a car coming. Alanna waited until it passed, then ran to catch up with him. "You can't just keep being angry and running away, Caleb. Everybody's sorry that your daddy left, but—"

He wheeled around and shouted right in her face, "He didn't *leave*! He went to find work, and he's coming back, and I'll be angry if I want! I'll do whatever the hell I want!"

She took a step back, her eyes wide, her heart thumping. If she yelled like that, or used bad words like that, Aunt Emilie would . . . Well, she didn't know what Emilie would do. Be angry, she supposed—or, worse, disappointed. Just like *she* was disappointed in Caleb. "I know how you feel," she said timidly.

"You don't know *nothin'*."

"I live with my aunt and uncle. Do you think that's just for fun? Because I *want* to?"

For a long time he stared at her, then slowly he started walking again. This time she could keep up easier. At the corner he turned right, and she followed. They were passing their principal's house when he asked as if he didn't really want to know, "Where's your parents?"

"My dad left when I was a baby. I don't even remember him."

"What about your mom?"

"She's in Boston."

"Why aren't you with her?"

She sneaked a look at him. He was staring at the ground, as though he had to see exactly where he was walking or something bad might happen. After taking a deep breath, she told him something she'd never told anyone before. Not that a lot of people in town didn't know, but *she'd* never told. "My mom's an alcoholic and a drug addict. She's been in rehab a bunch of times, and in jail. She doesn't want us—at least, not as much as she wants to have fun."

The words made her stomach hurt. Sometimes it was easier to not think about her mother, to pretend that it was just her, the kids, and Aunt Emilie and Uncle Nathan. Sometimes—the sad times—she couldn't help but think about her mom and wonder why she didn't love them more. What could they do to make her want them?

Aunt Emilie said they couldn't *make* Berry do anything.

She said it wasn't their fault. They hadn't made their mom drink and use drugs, and they couldn't make her stop. Dr. J.D. said she had to want to change, had to want it for herself, or it would never happen. Alanna didn't understand why she couldn't want it for *them*. Why couldn't she love them more than she loved the alcohol and drugs?

"My dad *wants* us," Caleb insisted. "Our mother doesn't, but that don't matter, 'cause he does. He wants us a lot."

"Where did your mother go?"

"I don't know. I don't care."

She wondered if he really didn't care. No matter how mad she got at her mother for not wanting them she still loved her and worried about her. She didn't believe there could ever be a time when she didn't care. Maybe Caleb was just lying to hide his hurt that his mom had left them.

"Don't you have any other family?"

"I don't know."

"You've got to have grandparents, or maybe aunts or uncles or cousins. Don't you remember anybody?"

As they turned right at the next corner, he shook his head.

"Didn't your mom and dad ever talk about anybody?"

He shook his head again.

"Didn't they have any pictures or letters or an address book?"

"There's a box of pictures. I found 'em when my dad didn't come home. But it doesn't matter. I don't know the people in 'em."

"But maybe they're clues. Maybe Uncle Nathan could find out who they are. He's a good cop. He can find anybody. Let's ask Dr. J.D. to take us out to your house to get the pictures—"

"I'm not asking him anything." Caleb sounded mad again and hateful. It made Alanna lose hope and made her sad too, 'cause she liked Dr. J.D. He was one of her most favorite grown-ups in all of Bethlehem.

They turned toward Miss Corinna's house and walked in silence until she saw Uncle Nathan and Dr. J.D. standing in the yard, talking. Stubbornly, she said, "Well, *I'll* ask him if you're afraid to."

"I'm *not* afraid! I *hate* him! He's stupid and mean and he doesn't like us and I don't like him and I don't like *you*." Shoving his hands into his pockets, he stomped off to the glider, dragged it around to the other side of the tree, and sat down hard enough to make the metal clang.

Tears filling her eyes, Alanna followed him. Even though she stood right in front of him, he wouldn't look at her, but she didn't care. "You know what, Caleb Brown? I don't like you either. I just feel sorry for you."

He looked up then, but she ran for the house, slamming the screen door behind her, racing upstairs to the canopied bed, where she slept when she stayed over. She knew someone would check on her—Aunt Emilie or Uncle Nathan, maybe Dr. J.D. or one of the sisters. She wasn't expecting Josie.

Her younger sister crawled into bed behind her, leaning on one elbow, patting Alanna's shoulder with her free hand. "Caleb Brown's trouble. Aunt Emilie said so."

Alanna sniffled. "She said *troubled*, Josie. There's a difference. Someone who's trouble is always causing problems. Someone who's troubled already has a lot of problems."

"Then Caleb's both. But I like the others. I could beat up Jacob. I could beat up Noah with only one hand. He's only one year younger than me, but he's *little*. But I won't hurt 'em. They're kinda nice kids." Josie leaned over, her eyes gleaming. "You and me together could beat up Caleb. Want to?"

"We're not going to beat up anyone." Alanna rolled

onto her back, and Josie snuggled closer, using Alanna's shoulder for a pillow. "We've got to be nice to them."

" 'Cause their mama and daddy 'bandoned them?"

"Because Aunt Emilie taught us to be nice to everyone."

"You wasn't nice. You told Caleb you don't like him."

Alanna's face got hot. "I shouldn't have said it. And I didn't mean it."

"I don't know why not. There's an awful lot there to not like. Even his own mama and daddy don't like—"

"Don't say that! It's not true!"

"But they left 'em."

"Our mama left us, but it didn't have anything to do with not liking us, did it?"

Josie glared at her. "Mama loves us!"

"Well, Caleb's mama loves him too—or, at least, his daddy does. He's gonna come back."

"And our mama's gonna come back someday. She's gonna come to Bethlehem, and we're all gonna live together—just you and me and her and Brendan and Mikey and Aunt Emilie and Uncle Nathan. Boy, that's a lot of people for our house. Maybe we can borrow the house across the street—you know, the one where we used to live. Or maybe we can build a house up on the mountain like Dr. J.D.'s doing. Maybe we could be neighbors with him and—" Josie twisted around to look at her. "Hey, are you done being about ready to cry? 'Cause if you are, dinner's ready. If you aren't, Aunt Emilie's gonna come up."

"I'm done," Alanna said. Later, when she had to apologize to Caleb, she might start all over again, but she was all right.

For now.

•   •   •

CALEB SPRAWLED IN THE GLIDER, STARING AT the street, where cars passed once in a while, and wished he were home. He wished he were anywhere but there, wished he didn't even exist. He'd never been as miserable as he was then, and it was all Grayson's fault. If he hadn't said Caleb's dad had lied, Caleb never would have had to prove him wrong and he wouldn't have gone for that walk and Alanna wouldn't have gone with him and she wouldn't have said what she did.

I don't like you either. I just feel sorry for you. Of course, he'd said he didn't like her first, but he'd just been mad. He didn't mean it. *She* did. He'd always known anyway that she was nice to him only 'cause she felt sorry for him. But it was different knowing something in your gut and being told so flat out to your face. Like knowing Grayson really didn't want them. Knowing Alanna only pitied him.

Well, he didn't need either one of them. He'd gotten along just fine without them. They could both go to hell. He didn't care.

Behind him the screen door opened and closed. Someone had come out once to tell everyone dinner was ready, and again to ask him if he was going to eat. He hoped this was ol' dumb Alanna going home with her family, or dumb Grayson come to make them walk to his house. But it was one of the old ladies—Miss Agatha—and she sat down at the other end of the glider. She set a plate between them, then sighed. "Look at the weeds in that flower bed. Sometimes I think all my hard work and fertilizer does them more good than my flowers."

The food on the plate smelled good enough to make his mouth water. There was a thick slice of turkey, some mashed potatoes and gravy, a piece of bread with butter and honey, and some green beans. Lunch—soup and sandwiches—seemed a long time ago. His growling stomach said it was past time for supper, but he didn't reach for the food. He'd been hungrier than this before. He could wait.

"I understand your father is a farmer. Is making things grow in your blood?"

He stared hard at the flowers so he wouldn't see the plate beside him. "I had a vegetable garden."

"Really? What did you grow?"

"Tomatoes. Zucchini. Beans." The green beans on the plate were cut in slanted pieces and seasoned with butter and pepper and little pieces of bacon. His dad had taught him how to cook them like that, with chunks of new potatoes that he brought home from the store.

"Ah, zucchini. Plant one zucchini, feed the nation." She laughed, then scooted the plate closer to him. "These beans are out of last year's garden. What do you think?"

He swallowed hard, then rubbed his stomach as it growled again. While she waited, he picked up the fork, speared one bean, and chewed it. "It's fine."

"Oh, you can't tell from one little piece of one bean. Try a couple. Get a taste for them."

He let himself be coaxed only because he was hungry and she wasn't Grayson or Alanna or the welfare lady. When the green beans were gone, he started on the potatoes, then the bread, then polished off the turkey.

Miss Agatha didn't say anything about him finally eating. Instead, she pointed toward the flower beds. "Perhaps on the days you're over here, you could help an old woman with her garden."

"We don't need to stay over here."

"No, you probably don't. You appear quite capable. But it'll be good for you to have a break from all your responsibilities."

"I don't *need* a break."

"Of course you do. Everyone needs a break at times." Was that what she thought his dad was doing? "My dad's not taking a break," he said stiffly. "He's got a job, and he's working really hard to save the money to bring us there to live. He probably has to work every day, even weekends, so he can save money quicker and come back sooner. He'll take a day off real soon and come get us."

She gave him a look that said maybe she believed what he said, but her question said she didn't. "If that's the case, Caleb, why hasn't he called?"

"We don't have no telephone. What do you expect him to do—call some stranger and say, 'Hey, go tell my kids that I left alone that this is where I am and this is when I'll be back'?"

"Couldn't he write you a letter?"

"He could, but we don't never get no mail. We don't even check the mailbox." They didn't get any bills, not since the electric was shut off months ago for not paying, and it wasn't like his mother was ever gonna write.

But what if his father did write? What if he knew that was the only way to get in touch with them without letting the cops know they were living alone? What if there was a letter out there in the mailbox right now, if their dad was somewhere waiting to hear from them before he came to get them?

Excited over the possibility, he jumped to his feet. He needed to tell the kids, but then they'd want to go with him and would slow him down. Better that he wait until he had their dad's letters in his hand before he surprised them. "Tell—" Tell who what? Shaking his head, he said, "Thanks for dinner," then took off down the sidewalk. Miss Agatha called his name twice, but he didn't look back. He just ran faster.

•   •   •

"I'M SO SORRY, J.D.," MISS AGATHA SAID AS SHE rummaged in her handbag for the car keys. "I was trying to point out that his father could have contacted him if he'd really wanted to. I certainly never intended to give him false encouragement."

"It's all right, Miss Agatha. Caleb hears what he wants to hear." She held out the keys, and J.D. all but snatched them from her hand. "The other kids—"

"We'll take care of them. You go on now and find the boy."

He was halfway to the driveway when Kelsey caught up with him. "I'll go with you."

"I'd rather you didn't. It's not as if he's lost or run away. He knows exactly where he's going. So do we."

"But—"

"You put the kids in my care. Now let me care for them." He stopped beside the car and she almost ran into him. "Trust me on this, Ms. Malone. I can handle it."

She looked prepared to argue, but he didn't give her a chance. He got into the car, started the engine, and backed into the street. With the hasty directions Nathan had given him, added to all the looking he'd done before buying his land outside of town, he knew exactly where to find the bank of mailboxes Caleb was headed for. With any luck he would spot him on the way. If somehow he missed the boy, he would wait at the mailboxes.

He chose his route based on the direction Caleb had run off. Though he kept a sharp lookout, it was the mailboxes he saw first. Maybe Caleb had taken the shortest path as the crow flew, cutting across fields or through woods.

He drove past the boxes, looking for a place wide enough to turn around the Winchesters' full-size car. When he came to a narrow road a few hundred yards down, he remembered the rest of Nathan's directions. *In case he goes to his house, it's the first road on the left after the mailboxes, all the way to the end.*

All the way was only another half mile. The rutted lane ended in a clearing with fallen fences, a ramshackle barn, and a dilapidated house. So this was where Ezra Brown, devoted father, had left his children to fend for themselves—on a broken-down farm in a shack not fit for animals. Oh, yeah, he was devoted, all right, to himself and to his own needs, and the hell with his kids.

Keeping his anger under tight control, J.D. turned around and returned to the county road. He pulled to the side a few yards before the mailboxes, shut off the engine, and waited.

The night was still, the breezes cool through the open windows. Darkness was settling, shadows deepening. He thought about the hall light and the open bedroom door at home and wondered if Caleb's willingness to come out here alone meant he wasn't the one who was afraid of the dark, or if it was merely proof of his desperate need to believe in his father.

He thought about the boy's anger back there at Miss Agatha's house when he had once again gotten caught saying something he shouldn't have said, and he wondered if that was bad luck, timing, or something else. He wouldn't hurt Caleb for the world, but Caleb was so hard to warm up to, so hard to show patience to. Was that because he was the oldest, the least cute, the least cuddly, as well as the most hostile and belligerent?

Or because he reminded J.D. of someone else? Another boy, two years older, also hostile, belligerent, also eager to see the last of J.D. in his life. Trey had good reason though. J.D. had damn near destroyed his life.

He was trying to help save Caleb's.

For one painful moment he closed his eyes and let Trey's image form in his mind. Dark hair, dark eyes, tall—

a good-looking kid with all the advantages in the world, and yet, through no fault of his own, his life had fallen apart. Maybe someday he would get it put back together. Maybe someday someone would undo the damage that had been done. But it wouldn't be J.D. Trey had already paid enough for *his* mistakes.

J.D. could never pay enough. No matter what he did with the rest of his life, no matter how many people he helped, it would never be enough to make up for the ones he'd hurt.

Opening his eyes, he forced a deep breath in spite of the pain in his chest. He unclenched his fingers from the steering wheel, commanded the muscles in his jaw to relax, twisted his head to ease the tension in his neck. There had been a time when the guilt had almost destroyed him, a time when the grief had almost finished the process, but somehow he had survived. He had come to Bethlehem and made a new life for himself, made a new man of himself. But he could never let himself forget.

Carried on the breeze were sounds of movement in the woods to his right. J.D. studied the darkness, searching for the source, then suddenly Caleb was there, slipping between strands of barbed wire, eagerly approaching the battered mailbox. He grabbed out a handful of mail—junk, it appeared. Sale ads, catalogues, and flyers. Frantically, he sorted through it, discarding each piece on the ground, then jerking it up and looking again.

After the third check, he grabbed hold of the box, raised it above his head, rotted post and all, then slammed it to the ground. He kicked it, then with a great frustrated cry, heaved it over the fence and into the woods. When metal connected with rock, a clang rang out, seeming to reverberate through the air, through the car, through Caleb's body as he sank to his knees in the dirt.

J.D. felt sick. They *need* you, Dr. Grayson, Noelle had

told him, but she'd been wrong. Caleb needed help, he needed love, he needed somebody who wasn't capable of finishing the destruction his parents had started. He needed— God, he needed more than J.D. could ever give.

But at that moment he was all the boy had. It wasn't much, but just maybe it was better than nothing.

He got out of the car and was only a few feet away when finally Caleb heard him. He jerked back and looked up at J.D. with such hatred. His question was little more than a snarl. "Did you take them?"

"Take what?"

"The letters from my father."

"There aren't any letters, Caleb."

"I don't believe you!"

Unmindful of the dirt, J.D. sat down nearby. "Why would I lie?"

"Because that's what you do. You're a liar."

"No. If I had letters from your father telling where he is, I would put you in the car, I would get your brothers and Gracie, and I would take you to him." And that was the truth. He could give Ezra Brown enough money to buy his loyalty to his children for the next thirteen years until they were all grown and needed a parent less than they did now. He would much rather do that than try to fulfill that parental need himself.

Caleb flung a handful of dirt into the air. "He *didn't* abandon us."

"Yes, Caleb, he did." J.D. spoke harshly, earning a sharp look from the boy. "Whatever his reasons, he *did* abandon you. He left, and he didn't come back."

"He *will* come back!"

"It's been a long time, Caleb. Maybe he will come back, I don't know. But you can't spend your days waiting for it to happen. You've got to get on with your life.

You've got to make sure there's something left for him to come back to."

Caleb's gaze narrowed as it focused on him. Though J.D. couldn't read his expression in the dark, he felt the scorn in it. "I *hate* you."

"You're allowed that. You're allowed to be angry and hurt—"

"I'm *not* hurt!" But in spite of his strong words, his voice quavered and he sounded as if he might cry at any minute.

J.D. wondered if he had ever cried, if he'd taken five minutes from caring for the younger kids to sneak off someplace private and sob out his fears. He doubted it. It might do him a world of good if he would. J.D. was a big believer in the healing power of tears. God knows, he'd cried plenty himself.

Caleb drew a couple of ragged breaths, sniffled once, and wiped his sleeve across his face, then said stubbornly, steadily, "My dad would never leave us. If you knew him, you wouldn't say he would."

"So tell me about him. Help me to know him."

Moment after moment ticked by while Caleb considered—or ignored—the request. An owl hooted in the woods. Way off in the distance a gunshot echoed. A plane passed overhead, carrying some lucky soul to someplace else, then finally he spoke. "He *loves* us."

When nothing else came, J.D. said, "Most fathers do love their children. There's nothing in the world my father wouldn't do for me." He would even help with this if J.D. called and said, Come to Bethlehem, Dad. *I need you.* He would be gentle and patient with the kids. He would never say anything hurtful for anyone to overhear. No matter how much they frustrated or disappointed him, he would never let them know.

He had never let J.D. know.

"He never finished school, but he done all right for himself."

J.D. thought of the house down the road. Whose definition of *all right* did it fit? Caleb's? Or Ezra's?

"He taught me to hunt, and he read to us every night. He believed in the Bible, but he didn't have much use for church. Said it was nothin' but a bunch of busybodies."

"It must have been hard for him after your mom left."

The few moments of peace fled. "No, it wasn't! It wasn't different at all. All he had to do was take care of the farm. We pretty much took care of ourselves."

Meaning Caleb took care of them. No wonder he seemed older than his years. He'd been raising himself and his siblings for two years. He'd shouldered more responsibility by the age of twelve than many men faced in a lifetime.

He stood up and brushed the dirt from his jeans. "I've got to get home," he said with a scowl. "It's almost the kids' bedtime."

J.D. stood too and followed him to the car. On the way back into town, he tried to think of something to say, something to do. He came up empty on the first, but did think of something they needed to do. Instead of turning onto Fourth Street, he followed Main downtown, where he pulled into a parking space in front of dimly lit buildings closed for the day. "Come on."

Caleb looked perplexed, but he followed.

The post office lobby was quiet. Lights shone on the wall of boxes with their numbers painted in gold flourishes, and another light illuminated the display rack of forms bolted to a scarred oak table. He found a change of address form, made sure the pen chained to the table worked, then set both in front of Caleb. He looked at the form, then at J.D., then fiddled with the pen.

J.D. understood his reluctance to fill it out. Now that

the family's mailbox was gone, he could always have an excuse to explain the lack of mail from his father. But if he turned in a change of address, directing their mail to J.D.'s house, and no letters came, then there was no excuse. Just a painful truth.

Looking reluctant and frightened, he finally began writing. Any other foster parent in the county could have reassured him—hugged him, sympathized with his fears, made him understand that he was doing the right thing. If he'd been any other kid in the county, J.D. probably would have done all those things. But he wasn't any other parent and Caleb wasn't any other kid, and so he did nothing but stand and watch.

They returned to the Winchester house. Emilie Bishop had taken her kids home, but Nathan waited on the porch with Kelsey, the sisters, and the younger Browns. The kids ran to Caleb as J.D. returned the keys to Miss Agatha. "Thanks for the dinner. We're going home now."

Of course, it wasn't that easy. Kelsey followed him to the sidewalk. "Is everything okay?"

"Not particularly. I take it I failed my first test as a foster parent."

"No, not really."

He smiled faintly. "Your enthusiasm for my abilities overwhelms me, Ms. Malone. It's been a long day, and it's past the kids' bedtime. Can we continue this later?"

"Sure."

He continued walking, but she didn't. Once they reached the corner, he glanced back, but she was gone.

It was only another block to his apartment, but Caleb was already carrying Gracie and Noah was dragging his feet. J.D. scooped him up, only to have Caleb glare at him. "He don't need you to carry him."

"He's tired, and you can't carry both of them."

"Yes, I can. Give him to me." Caleb shifted Gracie to one hip, then reached out for Noah.

"This is ridiculous," J.D. protested even as Noah reached for his brother. It was a silly sight—thin Caleb struggling to carry two kids who together probably weighed as much as he did. They were far too heavy a burden for him to carry, but carry them he would, for as long as they wanted, as long as they needed.

"Let's skip their baths tonight," J.D. said as he unlocked the apartment door. "We'll put them to bed—"

"*I'll* put them to bed." Caleb's sharp look said what his words didn't. *Your help isn't needed or wanted.*

J.D. stood back, leaving Caleb room to shepherd the kids inside and to the bedroom. A moment later he followed, but he stayed in the hallway, where he could see without being seen. As efficiently as any mother, Caleb got the kids undressed, into their pajamas, and into bed, then he sat on the edge of Gracie's bed while she murmured a prayer.

"Now I lay me down to sleep. I pray the Lord my soul to keep. I don't like that part about dying 'fore I wake, so I'm leaving it out." She stopped for a big yawn. "God bless Caleb and Jacob and Noah and Gracie—that's me. And God bless our daddy wherever he is, 'cause we love him very much and we miss him."

As all four kids said amen, J.D. moved away from the door and into his room. Ezra Brown may not have finished school. He may have been poor and pretty much a failure at everything, but he had four kids who loved him dearly. By anyone's definition, he'd done all right for himself.

KELSEY SAT AT HER DESK AND GAVE A QUIET sigh. It was Thursday afternoon. Her work week was almost over, and her office was almost organized. One more day here, and next Monday she would report to the Howland office and find out what other duties Mary Therese had to keep her busy.

Today's work wasn't quite finished though. She owed J. D. Grayson the first of several home visits. It was five o'clock, and he said he usually left the hospital then. She would give him time to pick up the kids from whoever was watching them that day and get home, and then she would drop in. In the meantime she could just sit here and relax or run by the drugstore to pick up a few things or maybe even go by the apartment and change—

A scowl wrinkled her forehead. There was nothing wrong with the way she was dressed. Her ivory shirtwaist and khaki jacket were perfectly suitable for anything she might do, from court appearances to home visits, from church to dinner out. She'd dressed for her job in exactly the same way for twelve years, and no one had ever complained before. J.D. had just been trying to get under her skin . . . and he'd succeeded. What woman wanted to be told by an attractive man that her clothes were ugly?

Oh, hell, they *were* ugly. There was no dress code for this job. She could find clothes that were both professional and pretty. Other women managed.

Grabbing her handbag and briefcase, she locked up and headed home. She wasn't dressing to impress, she reminded herself as she traded plain and ugly for another summery dress. But if her office clothes were severe enough to put off a grown man, didn't it stand to reason that they could have the same effect on young kids? The Brown kids already viewed her as someone to distrust. Anything that made her appear more approachable could only be good.

This time she left her panty hose behind and her hair down. There wasn't much she could do with it anyway. She'd always wished for straight, sleek hair in some fabu-

lously rich shade, but she'd become resigned to long, unruly curls in brown—not blond-streaked brown or red-
highlighted brown, but just plain brown.

It was five-twenty when she left the apartment. By five
twenty-five she was pulling into J.D.'s driveway. The pleasures of small-town traffic, she acknowledged with a satisfied sigh.

At the top of the stairs she was lifting her hand to
knock, when the door opened. Gracie and Noah gave her
wide-eyed looks, then he croaked, "Caleb! The welfare
lady's here!"

Caleb and Jacob came around the corner from the
kitchen, followed by J.D. He looked more relaxed than the
last time she'd seen him, though she wasn't sure that meant
things were going better between him and Caleb. Judging
from the boy's glower, she'd say they weren't—unless, of
course, that glower was meant for her.

"Am I interrupting something?" she asked, gesturing
toward Jacob's quilt and Caleb's ice chest.

It was J.D. who answered. "We're having a picnic supper out at the house. I've got to get back to work, or it'll
never get done. I take it you're here to make sure I'm not
using the kids as slave labor or shackling them to their beds
at night."

"Are you?"

He stepped back and gestured down the hall. "Take a
look."

She opened the screen door, and all four kids silently
moved aside to allow her entry. Dirty dishes were stacked
on the kitchen counter, and toys and game pieces were
strewn across the living room. A stack of kids' books had
fallen off the coffee table, and down the hall a pile of
clothing had accumulated on the floor outside the laundry
room. In the guest room the beds were made—sort of—
with the spreads tossed carelessly across each bunk. New

clothes hung in the closet, and a few more toys and books helped fill the empty shelves.

Though the place was by no means slovenly, it was a change from the immaculate condition on her first visit, and she was happy to see it. It appeared the kids were gradually settling in. Instead of huddling together on the couch in front of the television, they were starting to act as if they lived there and weren't merely visiting against their will.

Turning back to find them watching her, she smiled. "I can come back another time. I'm holding you up."

The kids took her words as permission to go. They started out the door, then turned back when J.D. spoke. "You want to go with us?"

Her first impulse was to say no. Going on a picnic with them wasn't her preferred method of inquiry. But what could it hurt? Weren't the two primary purposes of her visit to make certain the children weren't living in unfit conditions and to evaluate their interaction with their guardian? She already knew the living conditions were more than adequate, and she could study their interaction as well at the new house as she could here.

"What do you say, kids? Do you mind if I tag along?"

The younger three looked immediately to Caleb, who stared mutinously at the floor. After an awkward moment Gracie ventured a timid response. "I don't mind." A look from Caleb robbed her of her courage, though, and made her seek cover behind Noah, who was a head shorter and every bit as timid.

"Thank you, Gracie," Kelsey said somberly. "I'd like to come."

"You'll have to take your car," J.D. said as they filed outside and down the stairs. "My truck seats only five."

"That's not a problem. Jacob, why don't you ride with me?"

Panic flared in the boy's eyes, and he shot a look at his older brother, but Kelsey gave Caleb no chance to intervene. She slid her arm around Jacob's shoulders and steered him to her car.

"I see you have new clothes," she remarked as she followed J.D. At least, three of them did. Caleb's clothes, she'd noticed, were old, faded, and ill-fitting.

"Uh-huh."

"And some pretty neat shoes."

"Uh-huh."

"Where did you get them?"

He fixed his gaze anxiously on the truck. "The—the man. He took us to the store and bought us stuff."

She thought back to Tuesday night and how the Dalton kids had addressed J.D. "You mean Dr. J.D.?"

"Yeah. Him."

"What do you think of him?"

"Caleb says he don't like us so we don't like him neither."

Up ahead J.D. turned onto a paved secondary road. Kelsey slowed to follow, then glanced at Jacob again. "Everyone knows what Caleb thinks. I want to know what *you* think."

"He—he's—Caleb says he's a liar."

"Has he lied to you?"

He nodded vigorously.

"About what?"

The moment of animation faded, and he stared, bottom lip out, into the distance. "I don't know. But Caleb says—"

"Jacob, don't you have an opinion of your own? Isn't there anything Caleb likes that you don't like?"

As the road grew narrower, pavement gave way to gravel and ruts. He leaned as far forward as the seat belt would allow and watched the road, bracing himself well in advance of each jarring bounce. "He likes school an' I don't. He likes zucchini. And living in our house all alone. And sleeping with a light on. Not that he's scared," he hastened to add. "He's not scared of nothin'. He just likes being able to see when he wakes up in the middle of the night. We couldn't at our house 'cause we didn't have no 'lectricity."

"And it's all right with you that Caleb likes those things and you don't. So don't you think it would be all right if you liked something—or someone—Caleb didn't? Like Dr. J.D.?"

"I s'pose. Ya know, he's got good food. And a TV that gets more channels than I ever seen. Did you know you can watch baseball every day?"

"Do you like baseball?"

"Uh-huh."

"What position do you play?"

"I never played." Predicting her next question, he shrugged. "The kids at school never let me play, and we never had no money for a ball and bat of our own. But I know about it. My teacher—once she got me a book from the library, and I read the whole thing. And I seen some games on TV every day this week. And I know all the rules. Ask me somethin'."

Kelsey was still stuck on his careless comment that the kids at school had refused to let him play their games. She needed a moment to think of a question. "How many outs in an inning?"

Jacob gave a disbelieving shake of his head. "That's an easy one. Three. And there's nine innings. Don't you know any questions harder than that?"

"Sorry, Jacob. I'm not a big baseball fan myself." She hesitated, then suggested, "Maybe you should ask Dr. J.D. about signing you up to play this summer." She figured

J.D. would agree, but that wasn't the point. Getting Jacob to ask something of him was.

But a glance at the boy's face didn't make the prospects look good. He didn't consider the possibility for even a moment, but shook his head. "He'd just say no. 'Sides, no one would want me on their team. I never even throwed a ball before."

"I bet Dr. J.D.'s thrown more than a few. He would probably be happy to give you some pointers."

Shaking his head again, Jacob settled back in his seat as they turned onto an even narrower lane that ended abruptly in a clearing with a nearly finished house. "Wow. Look at that."

The house was perfectly suited to its setting. The logs that created sturdy walls, the fieldstone that supported their weight and lent shape to the fireplace, the wood planks of the wraparound porch, and the cedar shakes that covered the roof—all of it came from the land and worked to blend right back into it. Tall windows supported the illusion, allowing a person to stand in front and look right through the house to the forest and mountains in back.

She parked beside the truck, climbed out, and walked to the far edge of the clearing to get a better look. The position afforded her a better view of the house as well as its owner, who walked to the back of the truck, lifted the window, lowered the tailgate, and began pulling out supplies. Of its own will her gaze shifted from beautiful house to snug-fitting jeans, from tall, arched windows to broad shoulders, from the serene welcome of *home* to the faintly dangerous aura of *man*.

Wow, indeed.

Chapter Six

A FTER LOOKING TOO LONG, THOUGH NOT nearly long enough, Kelsey joined J.D. at his truck. "You have great taste."

"I know." His tone was smug, his grin friendly. "But thanks for noticing."

"You did all this yourself?"

"Hey, I'm good, but even I'm not *that* good. I cleared the site and gathered most of the stone, but I had help with everything else. I'm doing all the finish work inside myself."

Why? she wondered as he instructed the kids to help unload food and tools from the truck. Why would a very successful, top-dollar psychiatrist spend what must have been months doing hard physical work that any laborer with a strong back could have done? In her business she'd met a lot of doctors, and she'd never known one who would even consider such a job. Giving up a lucrative practice was surprise enough, but cutting down trees? Hauling rock? *Why?*

When he looked at her, she realized she'd spoken the last word aloud. She shrugged. "You have to admit it would probably surprise the hell out of your colleagues back in Chicago or your classmates at Harvard."

"Probably."

"So why did you do it? Why *are* you doing it? Why not just hire someone to handle it for you?"

His shrug appeared every bit as casual as her own had been. But she sensed a layer of tension underneath. "I need the exercise."

"You run miles every day." She'd caught a glimpse of him during her runs both the previous morning and that morning. She'd even been a bit disappointed that he hadn't changed his route to join her. No, *not* disappointed. Just curious why he hadn't.

"I like working with my hands."

"You're a doctor. Become a surgeon."

"Too much stress in surgery. If I make a mistake here, I redo it or I live with a crooked cabinet or a door that sticks. Make a mistake in the OR, and someone could die." He shrugged again. This time the casualness was more real. "Take that stuff around back," he called to the kids. "We'll eat on the deck."

The deck was multileveled and stretched completely across the back of the house. There was a stone barbecue at one end, a rough-hewn table at the other, and built-in benches all around. Kelsey helped Noah and Gracie spread the quilt while J.D. laid out the food on the table.

She was hungry, she realized as her stomach growled. If she'd gone home, she would have eaten a microwave dinner in front of the television without much appetite. This, even though it was business, was so much more appealing. There were turkey sandwiches on homemade wheat bread, potato salad, chopped veggies and dip, and huge oatmeal raisin cookies for dessert.

The kids took their plates to the quilt. Kelsey sat on the bench across the table from J.D. "Jacob says you have good food. He's right."

"I can't take credit for this. All I provided was the soda. The Winchester sisters had the rest waiting when I picked up the kids after work. Besides"—with a glance toward the kids, he lowered his voice—"Jacob's definition of good food is anything that's plentiful. They're collecting a stash in their closet."

Kelsey didn't find that unusual. Kids who'd gone hungry had a tendency to squirrel away food in the hope of preventing a recurrence. She'd known foster parents who'd found food hidden in dresser drawers and underneath bedclothes. The well-meaning parents removed the food when they found it. The smart ones left it. Sooner or later the kids would realize that there would always be enough, and they would quit hoarding it.

But it still broke her heart every time she heard about it.

"Other than that, how's it going?"

"The younger kids are adjusting. They're particularly good with those three elderly baby-sitters you were opposed to. Of course, Mrs. Larrabee and the Winchesters are particularly good with kids."

She ignored his reminder of her objection. "What about Caleb?"

"He watches over the kids or keeps to himself during the day. When we get home, he checks the mail for a letter from his father, doesn't find one, and sulks the rest of the evening. Any luck in locating some relatives?"

"I stopped by Sheriff Ingles's office this afternoon. About all they know is that the Browns moved around quite a bit before settling here. If either Ezra or Lilah Brown is working now, it's not being reported under their social security numbers, which means they could be taking payment in cash, using a different identity, or not working at all."

"Have they checked—" J.D. looked at the kids again, and a deeply regretful look came over his features before he returned his gaze to her. "Are they checking any unidentified bodies that turned up over the last six or seven weeks?"

"Yes, they are. So far there's been nothing."

"Wouldn't that be the good news/bad news from hell? 'Hey, kids, guess what? Your father didn't abandon you. He really did intend to come back. Unfortunately, he can't because he's dead.' "

Which would be worse? Kelsey wondered. Living with the fear that their father had walked out on them and the constant hope that he might return, or knowing he could never return but that he'd loved them and never would have abandoned them voluntarily?

"Well, that was a grim enough conversation. Let's lighten up a bit. Now that you've been here a few days, what do you think of Bethlehem?"

"It's a nice town."

"Uh-huh." His tone was leading, his expression bordering on amused. "Finding everything you need?"

"Everything," she said firmly, though it wasn't exactly true. She'd discovered from experience that the only places in town open after nine P.M. were the police and sheriff's departments and the hospital. Most shops closed at five or six, the video store at seven. The grocery store didn't carry her favorite brands of a dozen or more items, and the selection of what they did have was limited, to say the least. Worst of all, while in the throes of egg foo yung withdrawal, she'd discovered that the nearest Chinese takeout was forty-five miles away in Howland.

But those were the tradeoffs for the slower pace, the lower crime rate, the reduced stress, and it was a fair enough trade. She could learn to live without her favorite bottled water or the specialty frozen yogurt to die for. She could even learn to have egg foo yung cravings only on the days she was working in Howland.

"You don't miss all the stores and choices you had in the city?"

The smile she gave him was saccharine. "Not at all. I can find everything I need right here."

"Have you met many people?"

She took a deep breath that smelled of pine, sawdust, and clean, fresh air. "I met Alex Thomas, and his wife brought me a welcome-to-Bethlehem bouquet that was gorgeous."

"Alex and Melissa are good people. They're an important part of the town."

That was what she wanted to be—a good person who was important to those around her, and not just because of her job but because she belonged. Because she'd found a place that wanted her as much as she needed it.

"I also met Mitch Walker and most of his officers." The chief of police was a kind man with pictures of his kids on his desk and a soft spot in his heart for everyone in his town. He was a good person too, and so were the Bishops, the Winchesters, Mrs. Larrabee, and J.D. They were all important to Bethlehem.

"Drop a hint to the Winchesters, and they'll give a big party and invite the whole town for you to meet."

"Is that what you did?"

"Yeah. They called it Christmas."

"You moved here at Christmas?"

"Where better to spend that particular holiday than this particular town?"

"It seems a strange time to leave your old home for a new one. Did you have family in Chicago?"

He twirled a carrot in dip, as if coating it thoroughly

was of utmost importance, then bit off the end with a loud crunch. "No. When my mother died, my father moved from Boston back to Philadelphia, where they were from."

"And that's it? No brothers or sisters? No nieces and nephews to spoil?"

"Nope. I was an only child."

"Have you ever been married?"

"Once."

"What happened?"

"It ended a long time ago." Crumpling his paper plate with enough force to snap the plastic fork inside, he stood up. "Why don't you talk to the kids while I get started working?"

She watched him go inside, moving smoothly in spite of the tension that hummed through him. So his marriage was a sore point. Had it been that bad, or so good he hadn't wanted it to end? Had the emotional and financial costs of the divorce been too high? Did he consider the marriage a mistake he wished he hadn't made, or was the divorce a regret he hadn't yet made peace with?

She could find out under the guise of doing her job, but the idea felt too sneaky. He'd already been approved as a foster parent. Noelle had already conducted his background investigation, and Mary Therese had already signed off on it. Without a legitimate reason to request more information, asking would smack of pure nosiness or, worse, personal interest.

She would like to pretend that she had no personal interest in J. D. Grayson, but it wouldn't be true. He was handsome, charming, great with people. He was intelligent, supportive, an emotional rock, and obviously fond of children. In short, he appeared to be everything most single women were looking for in a man.

Appeared being the operative word. There was more to

J. D. Grayson than met the eye, more, she suspected, than even his closest friends in Bethlehem knew.

Which didn't matter much, because he was also off limits—*way* off limits as long as the Brown children were in his care.

After depositing her dishes in the trash bag he'd brought, she descended the stairs to the lower deck and stood at the rail looking out. This would be a wonderfully healing place to sit on a quiet evening as dusk settled. She could watch the light fade from the sky and the wild creatures who passed by on their way from one place to another. She could listen to the nighttime birdsongs and the creek that was just out of sight and literally feel the tension ease out of her body. This place could put her mind at rest.

Was that just coincidence, or the hotshot psychiatrist at work?

"Hi."

Gracie had caught her unaware, creeping quietly onto the bench that supported the rail and stopping a half dozen feet away. Kelsey smiled at her. "Hi yourself."

The girl leaned against the railing and held her cookie in both hands while she took a bite. With crumbs trickling from her mouth, she asked, "Are you gonna put my daddy in jail?"

It wasn't the first time Kelsey had been asked that question, but it never failed to surprise her. The loyalty innocent children could display toward the parents who abused and abandoned them was amazing. "That's not my job, Gracie. My job is to make sure that you and your brothers are taken care of, that you have a nice, clean place to live, clothes to wear, and food to eat."

"I got a blanket with pink and white stripes. And a bed all to myself. And I got a new dress. And new shoes, see?" She stuck out one foot with its lavender sneaker.

"And you've got food. That cookie's almost bigger than you."

"I helped make it. Miss Agatha said I'm a good baker. Want a bite?" She thrust the cookie out, but Kelsey shook her head with a smile.

"Just a bite? Kiddo, I'm getting a whole cookie all my own." Kelsey sat down on the bench, her elbows resting on the rail, her feet crossed at the ankles. "What do you think of Dr. J.D., Gracie?"

"Caleb says—"

"You know what? I want to hear what *Gracie* says."

Putting her cookie aside, Gracie sat down and tried to mimic Kelsey's position, but her arms didn't reach the railing. Instead, she sat cross-legged and munched a moment longer. "He's kinda nice for a bad man," she said at last.

"A bad— Who told you—" Caleb, of course. "Dr. J.D.'s not a bad man, Gracie. He's a very good man, like your father. Your daddy would be happy to know that he's taking care of you."

Gracie tilted her head to study her. "Do you know my daddy?"

"No."

"Do you know my mama?"

"No, I don't."

"Me too. She left when I was free, and Caleb won't tell us nothin' about her. But my daddy used to tell us stories. He said she was a good mama, and she wanted to stay with us but she *had* to go away."

Truth or fiction? Kelsey wondered. Had Ezra Brown made an effort to present them with the mother he wished they'd had? Or was there more to Lilah Brown's leaving than anyone knew?

"Sometimes I miss havin' a mama," Gracie continued, her voice soft and wistful. "Miss Agatha and Miss C'rinna and Miss Bee . . . They're kinda like grandmamas, and they're nice and all, 'cause we never had one of them neither, but I'd like to have a mama. The man, he don't got no wife. If we had to live with someone 'sides our daddy, I wish it was someone with a wife. And maybe a little girl for me to play with. And a puppy. Miss C'rinna's neighbor lady has a big puppy named Buddy that she lets play with us, and he snuggles with me when he sleeps and I like that. Ya think that man would let us have a puppy?"

"I don't know, Gracie. You'd have to ask him."

The girl gave her an appealing smile. "Maybe *you* could ask for us. Maybe you could tell 'im the welfare people says we need a puppy."

"I'm sorry. I can't do that. But you can talk to him. He'll listen, but," she warned, "he might say no."

The smile disappeared with a huff. "I know. 'Cause he's mean and don't really like kids."

"Gracie," Kelsey chided.

"Well, Caleb says." Swiftly, she changed the subject. "Hey, can we go inside?"

Because she wanted to go inside too, Kelsey was quick to agree. "Sure. Come on." She stood up and extended her hand. After several silent moments Gracie took it, her fingers curling tightly around Kelsey's. Her hand was warm and sticky and heartachingly small. Kelsey wanted to sweep her up into her arms, wanted to swear on her own life that Gracie would always be safe and protected, that she would never be hurt again.

She didn't, of course. Instead, she cleared her throat and offered a husky invitation. "What do you say, kiddo? Let's give ourselves the grand tour."

•   •   •

J.D. MANEUVERED THE LAST CABINET FROM ITS box. Cabinets filled the center of the kitchen and trailed into the dining room, box after box of unpainted pine. He could have asked for help in hanging them, and enough friends would have shown up to finish the job in one evening, but one part of him liked the idea of doing it all by himself. The part that had worked all day, though, wished for a helper to screw the supports into the studs while he held them steady.

The subfloor creaked, drawing his gaze to the open French door. Kelsey and Gracie stood just inside, the woman's hands on the girl's shoulders, both in their sundresses, both with their unruly brown hair, creating too pretty a picture. Why did she try to hide behind ugly clothes and do up those great curls in a matronly bun? Why go out of her way to be plain when she was so lovely? Was she afraid of drawing a man's attention? Too late, because she sure had his, at least until he slowly, deliberately, and just a little reluctantly turned it back to the cabinet he was manhandling into the dining room.

"Can we take a look around?" Kelsey asked.

"Be my guest."

They wandered off, talking about the rooms and their functions, picking out their favorite features. It'd been a long time since he'd heard the distant softness of a woman's voice in his house. Then he'd taken it for granted—the sound of Carol Ann on the phone, visiting with friends or chatting with the housekeeper. It had been comforting background noise, reminding him that he wasn't alone, that she was there, taking care of everything, waiting patiently for her share of his time. He hadn't given her enough of it, of course. He'd been too busy becoming respected, renowned, *the* authority in his field. He'd paid for his neglect. *She* had paid for his ambition.

Footsteps clumped up the stairs then down the hall and

around each room. There were three bedrooms up there, two too many for a man who lived alone. But maybe someday he would have company. His father would visit, if he ever got the place finished, and maybe—

Swallowing hard, he cut the thought off right there. There were limits to how much of the past he could endure in one evening, and with Kelsey's question about marriage, he'd already surpassed them. Better to think about something else, *anything* else.

He leveled the cabinet, tossed a handful of screws inside, then reached for the drill where he'd left it on the ladder paint tray. He'd misjudged the distance, though, and could barely brush the cord with his fingertips.

"Looks like you could use a little help." Kelsey laid the drill in his palm, then came closer. "Need an extra hand?"

"No, thanks." But it was a lie. He needed a couple extra hands, just not hers.

"I wasn't planning to offer my own. I was going to walk to the door and call Caleb."

"I can manage. Where's Gracie?"

"Lounging in the bathtub upstairs. It's a great bathtub."

It was, he acknowledged as he drilled the first screw into the stud. Oversized, marble, set in a corner, and looking out on the best view on the place. Any lounging *he* did would likely be on the deck, but he'd included the tub on the off chance that someday . . .

What? He'd get married again? Maybe, but he wasn't at the point yet where he could imagine it. Married or not, he wouldn't be celibate. Maybe he would get involved with some woman who would appreciate the luxury. Someone who would look incredibly enticing wet and naked. Someone with long hair and longer legs and a wicked smile. Someone—ah, hell, why ignore the obvious? Someone like Kelsey.

And if *she* was lounging in his bathtub, he thought with

a wry smile, it was a sure bet he wouldn't be on the deck out back. At the very least he'd be in the room, watching her. At the very most he'd join her and—

Taking a deep breath, he put the brakes on that line of thought.

"It's a great house," she remarked, standing close enough that he could see the floral print of her dress from the corner of his eye, could smell the faint fragrance of her perfume. "How long have you been working on it?"

"I bought the property in March of last year. It's been slow going." But therapeutic. Chopping down trees, digging out stumps, and hauling rock had saved his life. It had kept him too busy to think, had left him too tired to dream. By the time the actual construction had begun, he'd been in better shape both physically and mentally than he'd been in years.

He'd been able to cope. And though that didn't sound like much, he knew from experience that it was the most precious gift in the world.

After checking the level of the cabinet one last time, he began searching for the next one. It was a double unit and heavy enough to make his muscles strain until Kelsey gave it a boost.

"Are you going to stain or paint?" she asked, bracing it while he dug more screws out of the box.

"Paint. White."

"What about the walls?"

"Dark green. White and green tile floor, serpentine marble countertops, white tile backsplash with an ivy pattern."

"Sounds lovely. Who made all those choices for you?"

"You don't think I could come up with a plan like that myself?" He grinned. "You're right. I would've given all the trim a light oak stain and painted all the walls white. Holly's in charge of decorating."

"Who is Holly?"

"McBride. She owns the inn in town." It was the most basic answer to her question, but Holly was so much more. He'd met her at a party given by the Winchesters right after he moved to town. They'd spent that night together, and a fair number of others. Before long he'd become convinced that he'd found something extraordinary, and as it turned out, he had, but not what he'd thought. She couldn't be what he needed—namely, Carol Ann—and the best sex in the world couldn't give her what she wanted, and so they'd become friends. She was the best friend he'd ever had.

"Is she . . . special?" Kelsey's cheeks when he glanced at her were tinged pink, as if she'd asked a most intimate question. Exactly how intimate did she mean to get? Did she want to know if he'd dated Holly? Had sex with her? Intended to share this house with her?

"I like to think that all of us are special in one way or another." He watched her nose wrinkle in scorn at his pat answer, and chuckled. Then his humor fled. "You know, Ms. Malone, I'm never quite sure when we're having a conversation and when you're conducting an interview."

"Funny. I don't always know whether I'm talking to a client or a psychiatrist."

"Or an interesting man. You forgot that one."

"Or a smug, arrogant—"

He interrupted her with a tsk-ing sound. "Don't forget. There are children around."

"Speaking of children . . ." Releasing the cabinet, she went into the front hallway. "Gracie?"

There was a moment of silence, then a soft "What?"

"What are you doing?"

Another silence, another faint answer. "Nothin'."

J.D. went to join Kelsey in the hall. "Come on down, Gracie," he called.

After a moment, dispirited footsteps came from the direction of the guest rooms, and a moment later a bedraggled Gracie, on the verge of tears, appeared at the top of the stairs. Her clothes were wet, her hair stuck to her face, and her words were barely audible. "It *wasn't* my fault."

She looked so pitiful that J.D. choked back a laugh, earning himself a glare from Kelsey. "What happened?" she asked calmly, motioning for the child to come down the stairs.

"I went to see if the other room had a great big tub too, but it don't, but it's big enough for me, and so I climbed in. I was just playing. I didn't mean to turn the knob, but my foot slipped and water came out and got my new dress all wet, and when I tried to jump up and get away, it got my new shoes wet too, and now it's all ruined."

Kelsey looked to him for an answer. He rose to her unspoken challenge. "Nothing's ruined, Gracie. You just got your bath a little earlier than you expected. Why don't you hang your dress over the railing out back to dry?"

Gracie looked horrified. "And be *naked*? No *way*!"

J.D. ran his fingers through his hair. He didn't keep extra clothes in his truck, and if Kelsey had an extra shirt in her car, she wasn't offering. There was the quilt on the deck, but it was much too warm to wrap up in. Short of giving her his own shirt—

Abruptly, he strode down the hall to his office, where he'd been caulking the woodwork the previous weekend. The best thing for wiping away excess caulk, according to his experts, was a damp piece of old, soft T-shirt. He'd cleaned out his closet when he'd started the job, and a few shirts, fortunately, were still in one piece. He shook one out, sending enough dust into the air to make him sneeze, then delivered it to Gracie in the hall.

"That's a lot of modesty for someone who lets one brother give her a bath every night while she shares the tub with another," he murmured as she raced through the house to the deck.

Kelsey gave him a sidelong look. "But her brothers are family. You're not."

It was a simple observation, one he might have made himself if someone else had said the same thing, and it was true. So why did it sting just a little?

Nah, he'd merely imagined it. The truth couldn't hurt unless he seriously wanted a different truth, and in this case he didn't. He wanted to help the kids, would especially like to help them settle into a permanent home, but he absolutely did *not* want that home to be with him. He didn't want to be any more to them than he was just then—someone temporarily in their lives who, he hoped, did them some good, whom they would forget soon after he was gone.

Returning to the kitchen, he positioned the next cabinet, then began securing it. "You know, I'm not getting much accomplished here tonight."

"Don't blame me. I'm not distracting you."

Wasn't she? She'd asked him the marriage question and made him think about Carol Ann. She'd made him notice how pretty she was by doing nothing more than walking into the room, and she'd put in his head the image—the very erotic image—of her, him, and that bathtub upstairs. For a man who hadn't been in a relationship for a very long time, he'd say that was pretty damn distracting.

"Why don't you put Caleb to work?"

"I don't need his help."

"Actually, I wasn't thinking about what you need."

He glanced at her and saw that she was looking outside. Gracie was sitting on a bench, her knees drawn to her chest, her entire body except her head enveloped in his shirt, and giggling at the conversation between Jacob and Noah. Caleb stood a few yards away, staring into the woods. His rounded shoulders made him look vulnerable, while the set of his jaw gave him an angry air.

"He doesn't want to work with me."

"Or maybe you don't want to work with him."

Maybe. He made the admission silently, because it shamed him. Truth was, he didn't particularly like Caleb. He felt sorry for him. He was angry for him. He wanted to help him, *needed* to help him. But he didn't like him. Caleb was too difficult, too wounded, too powerful a reminder of the damage adults could do the children who depended on them.

He was too powerful a reminder of the damage J.D. had done Trey, and somewhere deep inside J.D. found it possible to hold that against him.

What incredibly mature reasoning for an adult and a psychiatrist.

He glared at Kelsey on his way to the door. It was a few degrees cooler outside, the air about a hundred times sweeter. "Caleb." Even from across the deck he saw the kid stiffen. "Do you mind helping me in here?"

Moment stretched into moment, and Caleb didn't move. Neither did the other kids. Just when J.D. was ready to give up and throw Kelsey an I-told-you-so smirk, Caleb slowly turned. "With what?"

"Hanging cabinets."

His usual scowl intensified. "I don't know how."

"I didn't either until someone showed me."

He wanted to refuse, J.D. could see that. Instead, he left the railing and, with halting steps, approached the door. When he was ten feet away, J.D. went back inside to locate the next cabinet unit and considered the boy's agreement. Why hadn't he said no? It wasn't likely he was looking to get on J.D.'s good side. Was he just so accustomed to doing what adults told him? So responsible it didn't occur to him to turn down a request?

Or was he tiring of his own anger and hostility? Did he, somewhere deep inside, want more peace, more emotional comfort, in his life?

Whatever the explanation, J.D. wasn't going to worry over it. He was simply going to take advantage of it.

THERE WAS NOTHING WRONG WITH CHANGING her route.

Kelsey repeated the words in her head, keeping silent rhythm with the sound of her shoes on the pavement. She was living in a new town, and what better way to familiarize herself with it than on foot? That was all she was doing. Honest.

But she was already familiar with this block of Sixth Street, the devil in her pointed out unnecessarily. The fact that she'd missed catching even a glimpse of J.D. in her first four and a half miles couldn't possibly have influenced her decision, could it? She couldn't possibly be so . . .

Normal? Typical? Female? Simple fact—it wasn't unusual for a woman to go a little out of her way to see an attractive man. Besides, she needed to burn off the calories from the two giant-size cookies she'd scarfed down last night with Gracie and the boys. A few extra miles were called for. And if they happened to take her past that attractive man's house . . .

There was a car pulled to the curb at the end of his driveway, a flashy, expensive sports car that apparently belonged to the woman beside it. Standing next to her, wearing his running clothes but looking as if he'd just rolled out of bed, was J.D.

Kelsey felt like a teenager seeing the boy she had a crush on making eyes at the head cheerleader whose favorite pastime was making Kelsey miserable. A flush swept through her, and her stomach did a flip or two. She wished she could make a U-turn in the middle of the street and head back the way she'd come, but they'd already spotted her. If she avoided them now, they would wonder why, and J.D., damn his smug arrogance, would probably figure it out.

He pushed away from the car as she drew nearer and stepped into her path. "Are you following me? And don't tell me this is your regular route or you didn't want the sun in your eyes."

She eased to a stop, bent forward in a stretch, then straightened. "Nope. And I'm not being neighborly either."

Up close, the woman reminded her even more of a cheerleader. She was gorgeous. Her outfit was of better quality than Kelsey could dream of affording, her short, sassy hairstyle couldn't have suited her better, and her colors were perfect—from the auburn hair to the peaches-and-cream complexion to the rich salmon of her clothes.

And here Kelsey was in a sports bra, an old tank top, faded shorts, and shoes that were due for replacement, dripping sweat from head to toe, with her plain brown uncontrollable hair even more out of control than usual.

"Kelsey Malone, meet Holly McBride," J.D. said with a grin. "Kelsey's our new social worker. Holly provides warm beds and good food to strangers in town."

Holly rolled her eyes at him. "You're so amusing, J.D. Kelsey, I own the inn in town."

Damn, even her voice was perfect—husky, low-pitched. Kelsey was breathing too hard to even make hers work right.

Holly looked her up and down, then asked in a puzzled tone, "You do this every day? On purpose?"

"I like running." Kelsey gulped a deep breath, then pulled the bottom of her shirt up high enough to wipe her face. "I've got to do something to stay in shape."

The smile that crossed the other woman's face was, of course, flawless. "Oh, honey, there are better ways to do that. Trust me." She placed her hand on J.D.'s arm—long nails, neatly manicured, polished. Kelsey wanted to hide her short, uneven, unpainted nails behind her back. "J.D., thanks for your time. I appreciate it. Kelsey, nice meeting you."

When Holly drove off, she gave them a smile and a wave. Kelsey felt the most incredible urge to screw up her face and stick out her tongue. Luckily, she stifled it, because when she looked away from the car, J.D. was watching her.

"So that's Holly. You can add one more to your list of people you've met."

"Huh. Well, see you." She started jogging, but he accompanied her.

"Holly caught me when I was leaving for my run this morning, so I'll run with you for a while."

"What'd she have, some kind of fashion emergency? Broken nail trauma? Shortage-of-admirers distress?" A quick glance showed that he was looking at her—worse, that he was grinning.

"That's pretty snide coming from an advance-degreed, state-licensed, certified do-gooder," he teased. "Holly's vain, I admit—so does she—but she's not shallow." He turned serious. "She's going through some tough times. She has a few unresolved issues with her dying mother, her husband's having an affair, and their oldest daughter wants various, rather delicate portions of her anatomy pierced to match her boyfriend, Slash."

For an instant an awful remorse swept over Kelsey. She *never* said nasty things about people she didn't know, and the one time she'd given in to the temptation, the poor woman was going through enough traumas for—

Then she caught the twitch of the grin J.D. was trying

to suppress and realized she'd been had. "You . . . *you!*" She gave a shriek of pure frustration. "There's no boy-friend named Slash, is there? And no daughter, no hus-band, and probably no mother, because women like that aren't born. They're *created* by fashion designers and hair colorists and plastic surgeons. You are *twisted*, Dr. Gray-son."

"Oh, but you make it so much fun."

She scowled at him, then picked up her speed until she was running flat out. He easily caught up with her and stayed by her side as she covered the last two blocks to the town square in record time. There she collapsed on the first bench she saw, bending over so her head was between her knees, dragging deep, sweet breaths of air into her bursting lungs.

He paced back and forth, then finally stopped directly in front of her. "Is that the best you can do? That's not even a fast jog." She looked up at him, sucked in desper-ately needed air, and he pushed her head back down. "Breathe."

"Need I remind you that you're at least six inches taller than me?" A gasp for air. "Your legs are proportionately longer, which means your stride is longer." Another gasp. "And I've already run over five miles this morning, while that was your first half-mile and—"

"And, gee, you're a girl too. That gives one of us an unfair advantage." He crouched in front of her and her gaze, blurred with sweat, slowly moved up from top-of-the-line gel-cushioned shoes to muscular calves to long, defined thighs to— Abruptly, she closed her eyes. Even so, she felt the air stir as he leaned closer and lowered his voice to an intimate level. "I'm just not sure which one."

Before she could respond, a call came from the nearest sidewalk. "Is everything okay there, J.D.?"

"Everything's fine, Mayor." His voice was a shade too

jovial, his amusement way too obvious. "She's just not in as good shape as she thought."

Slowly, Kelsey sat up and glared at him. "You are too smug and obnoxious for words. I am in outstanding shape."

He subjected her to the same sort of scrutiny she'd started on him. "Your shape looks fine to me. And I'm not sure my legs are that much longer. Yours are pretty damn long, and pretty damn nice, and, you know, Holly's right. There *are* better ways to get all sweaty and hot."

Seething, she considered how satisfying it would be to wipe that insufferable grin off his face. Instead, she settled for maintaining whatever dignity she had left. She stood up, forcing him to move back so quickly that he lost his balance and sprawled the few inches to the ground.

"Hey, where're you going?" J.D. called good-naturedly.

"Home. To shower. To work." Turning back, she smiled smugly. "And then to buy a big, mean, man-hating Rottweiler of my own. To keep the riffraff away."

She walked the next few blocks to cool down, then decided there was no reason to get all sweaty again and kept a slow, steady pace the rest of the way home. There she kept to her word—showered, dressed, and left again for the office. She stopped at Harry's Diner for coffee and a biscuit and egg sandwich to go, then settled behind her desk.

By eleven, annoyed by the hint of a view that she couldn't see and tired of squeezing between her desk and the wall every time she needed something, she'd set her work aside and determined to follow J.D.'s advice. At least, one part of it. She was going to move the file cabinets and open her office to the view.

The empty cabinets weren't heavy, merely unwieldy. She got the two of them into the outer office, then tackled one that actually held files. It didn't budge. She could call downstairs and get a couple of volunteers from the sheriff's or police departments, or she could remove the drawers and try again. She opted for removing the drawers, then tilting, walking, and scooting the cabinet across the vinyl floor.

"You know, there's this great invention to handle heavy jobs like that. It's called men."

Shoving her hair out of her face, Kelsey looked at her unexpected guest. More than four hours into the workday hadn't ruffled Holly McBride's appearance one bit. A shower, a chignon, and a suit hadn't improved her own that much.

She offered the woman a smile, hoping the insincerity behind it didn't shine through. "I thought about that, but I see no reason to ask someone else to do a job I can do perfectly well."

"Except those big, strong, masculine someone-elses would have been finished a long time ago. You've been at this awhile, haven't you?"

So it showed. "What can I do for you, Ms. McBride?"

"Well, for starters, you can call me Holly. I came to invite you to lunch."

And what was on the menu? Roasted social worker?

"You do eat, don't you? Real food, I mean. Not sprouts and yogurt and health-nut stuff."

"I eat," Kelsey said evenly. "Sugar and butter and everything." And if she didn't run faithfully, her hips showed it. Not that she would ever admit that to Ms. Perfect.

"I have a table at the best restaurant in town, and I should know. I own it." Holly smiled, a more genuine smile than that morning's. "Come on. I'm making a friendly gesture. Bethlehem is renowned for its friendly gestures."

"I don't think so. Not today. I'm awfully busy."

Holly studied her for a moment, then shrugged, but instead of leaving, she came farther into the room. Laying her leather bag on the desk, she moved to the opposite side of the file cabinet. "Where are we going with this?"

"Into that corner." Kelsey gestured behind her. "You don't have to help."

"I don't mind. It'll give us a chance to talk."

But they didn't talk until the second cabinet was in place and the drawers back where they belonged. Holly looked at the stained depressions left on the vinyl tile, then shook her head. "Those marks are permanent. But at least you can see out. Now all you need is a little paint, some new furniture, a better floor." She tugged on the cord dangling in one window and venetian blinds jerked down, showering dust over the room. "And blinds that have been cleaned within the last twenty years. Sorry. So . . . what has J.D. told you about me that makes you reluctant to share a meal with me?"

"Actually, nothing. Other than giving you credit for his kitchen plans, he's avoided the subject."

"Then let me set the record straight. When he first came to town, we were . . . involved. It didn't work out, and we've been friends ever since. *Just* friends. He's a great guy, but he's not *my* guy."

That was hunger, not relief, that made Kelsey's stomach flip-flop. And even if it were relief, it was professional in nature, because without a woman to claim his time, he'd have more to give the kids.

Yeah, right.

Holly sat down behind the desk and swiveled around to face her. "So . . . why do you think he avoided the subject? An affair that ended nearly eighteen months ago couldn't possibly have any effect on his suitability to foster those kids, could it?"

"Not in this case, no."

"Hmm. Then maybe his reason was personal. Maybe he thought it might have an effect on his suitability to court the new social worker in town."

Kelsey wanted to scoff, but all she managed was a blush and a stammer. "Oh, please. That's not— He's not—" Breaking off, she swallowed hard. "There's nothing between us. It would be inappropriate. He's a client, I'm a professional. We're *both* professionals."

Delighted laughter filled the room. "Oh, you're so young and so innocent. We're going to get along just fine. Come to lunch with us."

Feeling as if she'd lost a battle and was about to concede the war, Kelsey sank into an orange chair. "Who is 'us?' "

"Lock up and I'll tell you on the way."

It was a short drive—in Bethlehem, what wasn't?—to the McBride Inn. Kelsey fell in love with it right away, from the long, narrow lane that led to the main entrance to the gorgeous gardens to the welcoming feel inside. It was a wonderful place, one where even she—of the nine-hundred-square-feet, ratty furniture, and pink and lime bathroom—felt right at home.

A table of women awaited them. She'd already met Emilie Bishop and Melissa Thomas. Maggie McKinney lived catercorner from the Winchester sisters and was owner of Buddy, Gracie's naptime friend, and Shelley Walker was Chief Walker's wife and mother of the three kids whose photos dominated his desk. They were obviously close friends, and they welcomed her as if they'd known her forever. They talked that way too.

They were polishing off a sinfully rich dessert when Shelley groaned. "Now I won't even be able to make it to my car on my own. You'll have to open the door and wheel me out."

Holly pointed her fork at Kelsey. "This one can help you burn off the calories. She *runs*. Every day."

Four dubious gazes turned Kelsey's way.

"With J.D."

Strike dubious. Insert intrigued.

"I don't run *with* him," Kelsey protested. "We just happened to be going the same direction a couple of times."

"Uh-huh." Unfazed, Holly continued. "He showed her the new house."

"Is that a big deal?"

"Yes," the others answered in unison, then Emilie added, "*We* haven't seen it, except Holly."

"I showed up to do a home visit. They were going out there, and he invited me along. It was business." Kelsey stacked her silverware on her plate, pushed it away, then folded her napkin neatly into quarters. When she looked up, everyone was watching her.

"I went by this morning to talk to him," Holly announced. "He insisted on talking outside, by the street. He wouldn't invite me in, and he even turned down breakfast at Harry's."

"J.D. *never* turns down breakfast at Harry's," Maggie said solemnly.

"It was like he was watching for someone, and sure enough, before long, there came Kelsey. He alerted on her like a fox on a hound."

"Excuse me?" Kelsey turned a look that was equal parts insult and wry humor on Holly. "I know I didn't look my greatest—you try running five miles before seven A.M.— but you're comparing me to a *hound*?"

When the laughter settled, Holly squeezed her hand. "Maybe I should have turned that around. You're the fox, *he's* the hound. And for running five miles, you looked pretty good." Then she returned to her discourse. "She thinks it's all business, that they're strictly one professional dealing with another. She thinks there's nothing between them but work. *I* think our search might be over."

Kelsey had to ask the question, though she dreaded it, dreaded the answer even more. "What search?"

It was Melissa who replied. "We've been trying to marry J.D. off ever since he moved here. When he and Holly started dating, we thought we might have killed two birds with one stone, but that fell through. Lately he hasn't shown much interest in anyone. But if he's turning down breakfast at Harry's . . ."

"Jeez, what are you guys?" Kelsey asked. "The official matchmakers of Bethlehem?"

"Actually, no." Emilie's voice was soft, her accent faded-southern. "That title belongs to Miss Agatha and Miss Corinna. We just help out where we can."

They'd had their fun, Kelsey decided. Now it was time to set them straight. "Okay, Cupid's little helpers, listen up. I am a social worker. Dr. Grayson"—she ignored their snickers at her use of his title—"is a psychiatrist. He's also the foster parent of four children assigned to my care. We are working together. To some extent we will always be working together. Having a personal relationship with him right now would be severely frowned upon by my bosses. It would be inappropriate. It would be unwise."

Holly snorted. "Oh, please . . . if appropriateness and wisdom had anything to do with romance, Emilie never would have fallen in love with a cop when there were felony warrants out for her arrest. And Maggie certainly wouldn't have fallen in love with her husband while in the process of divorcing him."

Felony warrants? Blond, lovely, southern-belle Emilie, whose smile at that moment was so pretty and innocent? Kelsey made a mental note to read the records on the Bishops and the Daltons that were in her files. Too bad she didn't have a similar file that would explain Maggie's wicked grin.

"And *I* would not fall for every handsome face that crosses the county line," Holly continued. "Speaking of handsome faces, Maggie, when is Tom Flynn coming back to town?"

"I don't know. I'll tell Ross he needs him." For Kelsey's sake, Maggie elaborated. "Tom Flynn is my husband's lawyer. He's a ruthless, arrogant, reasonably attractive, and incredibly ambitious son of a bitch who has caught our Holly's eye. Unfortunately, when Ross moved the corporate headquarters here, Tom elected to stay in Buffalo."

"That's okay," Holly said carelessly. "He still has to put in an appearance from time to time. I'll hook him one of these days, and then I'll reel him in *real* slow. Who knows? He just might be a keeper." Then she grinned lasciviously. "Or I might just have my fun, toss him back, and set my sights on the next catch."

Hers was an attitude Kelsey wouldn't mind sharing. She wished that were her nature—lots of men, lots of affairs, and lots of fun, and *then* Mr. Right, kids, house, and responsibilities. But unless her change of locale had also brought her a change of character, that wasn't the way she worked. She didn't have affairs. She had relationships, hopes, dreams, and, ultimately, disappointments. She went into every romance thinking that this guy might be the one, even though she'd thought the same thing about every guy before and been wrong every time. With the last one she had been *so* wrong that she'd wound up moving six hours away.

Well, not entirely because of him. But not having to see him, deal with him, or even hear his name had been a sweet incentive.

"Ladies, this has been fun," she said with a sigh, "but

I've got to get back to work. If I could trouble someone for a ride . . ."

"I'm going that way," Shelley volunteered.

"We do this every Friday, Kelsey," Emilie said. "Same time, same table, same fascinating company. Mark it on your calendar."

"Thanks. I will." And she meant it. After all, this was what she'd come to Bethlehem for—friendship. A sense of community. A sense of belonging.

Not romance. Certainly not with J. D. Grayson.

Chapter Seven

FORTY-SIX DAYS.

That was the first thought that came into Caleb's head when he awakened Saturday morning. Forty-six days since their father had kissed them all good-bye and driven away from the farm in his old truck. Forty-six days since he'd given his promise that he would be back just as soon as he could. Forty-six chances to keep that promise.

So far, forty-five broken promises.

Nobody believed he was coming back, not Grayson or the cops or the welfare lady, not Mrs. Larrabee or Miss Agatha or Miss Corinna. Sometimes not even Jacob, Noah, or Gracie believed it. Only Caleb always believed.

Did that mean he had more faith than the others?

Or that he was dumber?

After forty-five disappointments, he didn't know.

He lay on his back and listened to the noises down the hall. The shrink was in the shower, which meant he was back from his run. He always came back in a good mood, but it didn't last. Not that he ever got mad and yelled at them or anythin' like that. It was just the look he got on his face when he saw Caleb. Gracie didn't get it, and neither did Noah or Jacob, but Caleb always did. It was a look of dislike.

Well, he didn't care if Grayson liked him or not. In fact, he liked knowing that the shrink didn't. He'd be glad to see the last of the shrink.

The water in the bathroom shut off, and a minute later the door opened. A couple of minutes after that, Grayson stuck his head in their room. Caleb lay still, pretending to be asleep.

"Come on, wake up, kids. It's time to be up and about. We're going to Harry's for breakfast, and then we're heading out to the house."

"Who's Harry?" Gracie mumbled from below.

"He owns the café downtown."

That made her wake up completely, and Noah too. "You're taking us to eat in a restaurant?" She asked as if he'd just offered something special.

Noah sounded that way too. "We never been in a restaurant before."

Until last week, the children had eaten at one of two places—at school or at home. At school Jacob and Noah got free breakfasts and lunches. Caleb could have gotten 'em too, but he'd rather go hungry than let the kids who made fun of him see him eating for free.

"Nope, we never have." That was Jacob, sitting up now in the other top bunk. Through slitted eyes Caleb saw him prepare to jump to the floor, but Grayson stopped him.

"Don't do that. You could hurt yourself. Use the ladder." He grabbed hold of Caleb's covers and pulled them back. "Come on, Caleb. Quit playing possum and get up."

Below, Gracie giggled. "Caleb's not a possum."

"It's a figure of speech, Gracie," the shrink explained. "It means pretending to be asleep or dead."

"Maybe he's really asleep," she suggested.

"If he's really asleep, then he won't mind if I tuck him in and give him a kiss, will he?"

Gracie giggled again, and Noah did too as Grayson began pulling the covers back. When he got too close, Caleb's eyes snapped open. Grayson was wearing that I-really-don't-like-you look. He was trying to hide it, but Caleb recognized it.

Grayson took a few steps back. "I thought you were awake. Get up and get dressed so we can go."

"I'm not hungry."

"Then you can sit and watch us eat."

"I'm not gonna work for you today. You can't make me. I'm not your slave."

"I didn't say a word about you working today. But you are going to the house with me, and you're going to stay there while I work. Get moving." He turned away to start making Jacob's bed.

Caleb jumped to the floor, landing with as loud a clatter as he could manage. For a minute Grayson got all still and stiff, but he didn't turn around, didn't say a word. He just went back to making the bed.

Obviously, he wasn't as worried about Caleb hurting himself as he was about Jacob.

They took turns in the bathroom, brushing their teeth, combing their hair, then got dressed. The kids put on new clothes, then went to the living room. Caleb stared into his open dresser drawer. He didn't have any clothes there, at least, none of his own. They were all in the laundry, waiting to be washed. If he went anywhere today, he'd have to wear either dirty clothes or the clothes the shrink bought him.

Picking up a pair of shorts that still had the price tag on

it, he rubbed the denim, then sniffed the new-clothes smell. Like the kids, he'd never had any new clothes all his own that he could remember. Even though he'd swore he wouldn't wear them 'cause they came from *him,* they'd sure felt good when he'd tried them on in the store. He'd looked real different too. Nobody who didn't know him would look at him in those clothes and figure his family was poor.

He curled his fingers around the price tag and yanked it off, then thrust his legs into the shorts. Just this one time, it would be all right to wear these.

Just this one time he could look like every other kid in town, even if everybody knew he wasn't.

When he went into the living room, the others were all waiting. Grayson looked at him as if he wanted to say something about the clothes, but he didn't. He just jangled his keys and said, "Let's go."

Caleb had seen Harry's Diner plenty of times, but he'd never been inside. There'd never been enough money, not even when his dad was around. Not even when his mother was there. The shrink had lots of money. He didn't work nearly as hard as Caleb's dad did, but he got paid a whole lot more. It wasn't fair.

But Caleb quit thinking life was fair a long time ago.

Everybody in the café said hello to the shrink. There was even a booth with a cup of coffee waiting for him. It wasn't big enough for all five of them though, so he moved the coffee to a bigger one, a round one in the corner.

"Mornin', J.D." The waitress set down a stack of menus, pulled a pencil from her hair and a pad from her pocket, then smiled. "My, my, what a good-looking bunch you are. I'm Maeve, and I'm pleased to make your acquaintance."

Reluctantly, Caleb shook hands with her and mumbled his name. The other kids did the same.

"Three handsome young men and the prettiest girl I've seen in a long time," she said, still wearing that big smile. "J.D., you are a lucky man."

Yeah, right, Caleb thought with a scowl.

"What can I get for you? Let's start with you, Gracie."

"Do you have pancakes?"

"Yes, ma'am, we do. The best pancakes in town."

"I want free, please." Gracie held up four fingers, and Caleb folded one down.

"It's *three,* not *free,*" he corrected her in a hushed voice.

She gave him her stubborn look. "I like free. Free pancakes, please."

Maeve turned her smile on him. "What about you, Caleb? What would you like?"

He'd told Grayson he wasn't hungry, and he'd meant not to eat to prove it. But the smells coming from the kitchen were too good, and he wasn't sure he could sit there and watch them eat without his mouth watering. But he also wasn't sure he could back down in front of the shrink. If he ate now, Grayson would know he'd lied and he would get that look again.

"Well, honey?" the waitress asked.

Across the table, Grayson spoke. "Caleb isn't sure he has an appetite this morning. Why don't you see if Harry's got anything back there to tempt him, Maeve?"

"I'll bring you the special, Caleb," she said with a grin and a wink. "It'll put some meat on your bones for sure."

Noah ordered pancakes and bacon, and Gracie asked for bacon too. Jacob ordered eggs and toast, and Gracie asked for toast too. When Grayson ordered the special with ham, she opened her mouth to call after the waitress, but he stopped her with a raised hand. "No, you cannot have ham too. If you eat everything you ordered, it'll take all four of us to carry you out."

"Gracie's a little piggy," Jacob teased, until Caleb poked him.

"I'm not a pig," she argued. "What I don't eat, I can take home for later. You know, for if we need it."

Now it was her turn to get poked. The food in the closet was a secret, for emergencies. If Grayson knew, he'd take it all away and they wouldn't have anythin' when they needed it.

"You're not going to need it, Gracie," the shrink said. "No matter what happens, you're always going to have enough food."

She shook her head sadly. "We been hungry before."

"But you won't be again. I promise."

Shaking her head again, she snuggled closer to Caleb. "Our daddy promised to come back and get us, but he didn't. Caleb promised to take care of us and not let nobody find us, and we got finded. And our mama promised she would love us forever, but Noah and me, we don't even remember what she looked like."

Everyone who'd made her a promise had let her down, including Caleb. It made him feel empty inside. He'd done his best, but it wasn't good enough. Like his dad's best hadn't been enough either.

Grayson signaled the waitress, who came over with her arms full of plates. "Maeve, would Harry let me run a tab here?"

"Well, we don't normally do that, but . . ." She grinned. "Anything for you, Doc. You want this morning's check put on a tab?"

"No, this one's not for me. If any of the kids ever comes in here wanting a meal, give them whatever they want and put it on my tab." He looked across the table. "Do you understand what that means, Gracie?"

She shook her head.

"It means that anytime you're hungry, you can come here and Maeve will feed you."

Her eyes opened wide. "For free?"

"For free."

"For how long?"

"Forever. I promise."

She fell for it. So did Noah, and maybe even Jacob. Caleb didn't. He knew Grayson was a liar, knew it was just a trick. If any one of them came here asking for food after they'd moved out of his house, they might get it, 'cause Maeve seemed like a real nice woman, but the shrink wouldn't be paying for it. Once they'd moved out of his house, he would forget that they'd ever existed, and he would forget about his promise.

And they would forget him too. Caleb swore they would.

SUNDAY MORNING'S CHURCH SERVICE WAS WELL under way when Kelsey slipped into the last pew. Attending church was no longer a routine part of her life, though it had been when she was growing up. Every Sunday she and Steph had shared a pew directly behind their parents. They'd gone to the same Sunday school class, had both sung alto in the choir, and had passed notes and played silent games during long, uninspired sermons.

Then Steph had died. Kelsey attended her funeral, but she hadn't set foot inside a church for a regular service since. Yet here she was today, in panty hose and heels on a warm Sunday morning, and she wasn't even sure why. She should be home cleaning the apartment or maybe taking a lovely drive through the countryside. She could be reading the book on her night table or window shopping at all those quaint little shops downtown. She belonged any-where but here, doing anything but this.

Partway through the sermon she slipped out again. She hoped no one had seen her, but if someone had, she could always say she'd been paged. In her job that could—and did—happen at all hours of the day, and no one, with the possible exception of J.D., was likely to call her on it.

Lying about church. Kathleen Malone would be ashamed that the thought had even occurred to her daughter, and mortified that she might actually follow through. She'd raised Kelsey better than that, but while her faith had remained strong, Kelsey's had waned. Of course, her mother hadn't seen the things Kelsey had seen, hadn't lived with the guilt that haunted her every day.

Please, God, make sure she never would.

She had cleared the heavy carved doors and was on her way down the steps, when a young woman greeted her. Her face was vaguely familiar, although no name came to mind. Then Kelsey remembered where they'd met—at the hospital her first day on the job. The woman was the younger of the two volunteers she'd spoken with, the one with the straight hair that made her own curls look more disorderly than ever. Instead of her volunteer's lavender lab coat, today she wore a sleeveless dress in vibrant red, and her hair was done up in a soft style that exposed her neck.

"Sometimes the Reverend Howard does go on," the woman said, "but he usually doesn't send the parishioners flying from the church. You must be in a hurry to get where you're going. And where would that be on a beautiful day like today?"

Kelsey opened her mouth, but the lie wouldn't come. Maybe Kathleen had raised her even better than she'd realized. Sighing, she shook her head. "Nowhere."

"Ah. So maybe you weren't in a hurry to get some-where—rather, in a hurry to leave somewhere." She smiled warmly. "You're the new social worker. Kelsey, isn't it?"

Kelsey nodded.

"How do you like Bethlehem? It's a wonderful place, isn't it?"

"Yes, it is. I'm going to be very happy here."

"Going to be? So you're not now?"

"I'm perfectly happy." Most of the time.

"You're meeting people? Making friends?"

"Yes. Everyone's been very nice."

"I'm sure they have. Bethlehem's a community in the true sense of the word. They believe in sharing the Christmas spirit year-round."

The woman sat down on a concrete bench and patted it in invitation. Kelsey wanted to say *No, thanks, I'm in a hurry, remember?* But somehow that seemed rude. Though was it any ruder than a stranger demanding her time? her devil asked. Still, she didn't want to be rude on the church steps on a Sunday morning. With a glance at her watch she sank onto the sun-warmed bench. She could spare a few minutes and still be on the other side of town when the church service ended.

"Are you a regular here?" she asked, wondering why the woman wasn't inside with the faithful.

"Oh, I can be found here virtually anytime," the woman said with a laugh. "Whether the doors are open or not. I understand you come from New York City. Why such a big change?"

"I wanted to work someplace where I could really make a difference."

"Don't you think you were making a difference in the city? Surely there were people you helped, children you protected, lives you saved."

Kelsey gazed up, her attention drawn to a stained glass window of Jesus with children drawn around. She *had* done some good in the city, but she'd had failures too. She'd been to too many trials, too many funerals. In a small town, she figured, she stood a better chance, with less bureaucracy, more caring neighbors, a community looking out for its own.

Without waiting for a response, the woman went on. "How are the Brown children?"

"As well as can be expected, under the circumstances. They're in a good home."

"Oh, the best. J.D. is exactly what they need. You couldn't ask for a better father for those children."

She'd done just that, Kelsey remembered. How odd that of the whole long list of preapproved foster parents, there'd been no one else to take the kids. Even in the city, with its much bigger problems, she'd never failed to find a temporary placement. "Everyone certainly sings his praises," she remarked dryly.

The look the woman gave her was steady and one hundred percent assured, as if she knew these things for a carved-in-stone fact. "He's a good man. Those children couldn't find anyone better." Then she smiled. "*You* won't find anyone better."

Ah, so she was another of Bethlehem's unofficial matchmakers. Was there a single soul in town who didn't see them as a perfect couple? Was there no one else who understood the concepts of impropriety or unprofessional behavior? Not that it really mattered. As long as she and J.D. understood and kept their distance.

Something easier said than done, she feared.

From the cupola above, the church bell tolled and the woman popped to her feet. "Ah, the service is over and the doors will be opening." She smiled brightly as both heavy doors were pushed back and propped open. "It's been a pleasure talking to you, Kelsey. If there's ever anything you need from me, I'm always around. Just give me a call."

Calculating her chances at getting away unnoticed now that the parishioners were spilling out, Kelsey needed a moment to process the last comment. "Give you a call? I don't even know your—" Turning, she saw that she was talking to herself.

Ducking her head, she started for her car, parked in the shade of an old oak down the street. She wasn't even halfway there, when just the voice she hadn't wanted to hear spoke from a few feet behind.

"Well, well, I thought I felt the church walls tremble. I assumed it was just the aftershock from getting Caleb and Gracie through the doors earlier."

Kelsey drew a deep breath, pasted on a smile, then turned and looked up. "I'm not such a sinner that God would be shocked to see me."

"Just seriously surprised, huh?" J.D. stopped too, and he shoved his hands into his pockets.

She let her gaze slide over him, from head to toe and back again, making note of his fine creamy-hued suit, the blindingly white shirt, the richly patterned silk tie. "You told me you had one summer suit and one for winter. This is *not* the same summer suit you were wearing last Sunday. You lied."

"I didn't lie. I do have one summer and one winter suit. I also have other summer and winter suits." He grinned. "I wasn't aware you were so interested in my wardrobe. Let me ditch the kids for a while, and I'll give you a tour of my closet."

She resisted the smile that tugged at her lips. "I believe I'll pass. Where are the kids?"

He gestured toward the crowd gathered in front of the church. "Jacob and Noah are talking to Josie Dalton. Caleb is ignoring Alanna Dalton, and Gracie is probably behind a bush somewhere stripping down to her skivvies."

"And be *naked*?" She mimicked Gracie's scandalized tone of Thursday night. "Surely not."

"You haven't seen her church dress. Picture the frilliest, fanciest dress ever seen outside a kiddie beauty pageant, complete with stockings and dress shoes. She *wailed* while Caleb was dressing her."

Kelsey smiled. "Why didn't you just let her wear one of her sundresses?"

"They're dirty. Everything's dirty except her old clothes." The amusement faded from his voice. "Having new clothes all her own has been quite a novelty for her. She changes as much as three times a day."

Just a few days earlier Kelsey had been envying Holly McBride's clothes. While she couldn't afford designer garments like that, at least she'd always had her own clothes. She found it difficult to imagine that Gracie could reach the age of five without ever having a single new garment bought specifically for her, though she knew that it happened all too often.

"You know, we normally give vouchers to cover the cost of new clothes," she remarked.

He shrugged as if the money were of no consequence. For a hot-shot psychiatrist with no obligations besides himself, maybe it wasn't. "Why did you come late and skip out early on the service? Did the reverend's sermon hit too close to home?"

Frankly she couldn't remember what the sermon was about. She'd been too lost in the past to listen. "I'm not much of a churchgoer," she admitted.

"But you believe in God."

"Most of the time." As his look shifted from teasing to serious interest, she gestured impatiently. "I believe there's a God who created the universe and everything in it and is watching over us all. I just don't believe he pays very close attention sometimes."

"Why? Because prayers go unanswered? Bad things happen?"

She gave a stubborn shake of her head, refusing to reply. As a rule, she didn't discuss her faith with anyone, and she certainly wasn't going to discuss it with J.D. in his hotshot-psychiatrist persona. "You'd better gather the children and go."

"Come and have lunch with us."

"No, thanks."

"It'll be the best lunch you've had since coming to Bethlehem."

"Oh, so you're going to the Winchesters'."

"Yes, ma'am. They outdo themselves for Sunday dinner." He caught her hand and tugged, but she didn't move. "Come on, Kelsey. Don't make me beg. It's not a pretty sight."

But it would definitely be an interesting one, she thought as she freed her hand. "Learn some manners, Dr. Grayson. When a woman says no, she means no. And when someone is kind enough to invite you *and* your four wards to dinner, you don't drag along other guests."

He turned away from her, but she didn't think for an instant that he was giving up. Instead, he scanned the crowd, then called in a voice guaranteed to draw everyone's attention their way, "Miss Agatha! Do you care if Kelsey comes to dinner?"

"Why, of course not, J.D. You know better than that. Kelsey dear, we'd love to have you. I would have invited you myself if I'd known you were here."

With a blush warming her face Kelsey closed her eyes for a moment and sarcastically muttered, "Thank you, J.D." When she opened her eyes again, she found him staring at her. "What?" she asked grumpily.

"That's the first time you've called me by my name."

She opened her mouth to disagree, to point out that she'd been calling him that for days now, but it wasn't exactly true. While in her thoughts he was J.D., in person she'd called him Dr. Grayson or nothing at all.

"You're warming up to me, aren't you? You must be, 'cause your little cheeks are turning pink."

Kelsey rolled her eyes. "You are the most arrogant, smuggest, most frustrating person I've ever met."

"Thanks," he said solemnly. "I like you too." He hooked his arm through hers and forced her to start walking with him. "Leave your car here and come to the Winchesters' for dinner, and then we'll stop by your apartment so you can change clothes and you can spend the afternoon out at the house with us."

She gave in because it was easier than arguing. Because she had nothing planned for the rest of the day but a phone call to her mother after a solitary lunch. Because it was too lovely a day to spend alone.

Not because she really, truly wanted to go.

"I thought your truck seated only five."

"Gracie's already informed me that she's riding with the Winchesters. *They* bought the hated dress, but *I* get the blame for making her wear it."

"But my car . . . I shouldn't just leave it on the street."

He gave her an exaggeratedly patient look. "This is Bethlehem, Kelsey. On these streets you're more likely to come back and find it washed and waxed than vandalized."

They stopped beside his truck, and he called the boys, instructing them to climb in back. Jacob and Noah obeyed. Caleb announced with a scowl that he was going with Gracie, and together they watched him climb into the Winchesters' car.

"Any more arguments?"

Kelsey glanced at J.D. "I guess not."

"Then get in the truck, please. And do me a favor." Lowering his voice so the boys couldn't hear, he said with a lascivious grin, "Pull your skirt up real high like you did last time."

"I don't think so." Last time her skirt had fitted so snugly that she'd had no other choice. This time she gathered the long, full folds and climbed into the seat without revealing anything more than her ankles. She smiled smugly. "Shall we go, Dr. Grayson?"

J.D. SAT CROSS-LEGGED ON THE DECK, HIS EYES closed, the sun warm on his skin. It was the middle of the afternoon, and there wasn't a single sound that didn't belong in his world. No televisions or stereos blaring, no cars driving past, no airplanes flying overhead. Just the birds, the wind, the water. The quiet of nature, along with the absence of man-made intrusions, soothed him, made him feel almost whole. He wasn't there yet, might never be completely there, but he was better. He was making progress.

"What does J.D. stand for?"

For a moment he considered the voice. It should be an intrusion, unwelcome and out of place. But this voice didn't feel as if it didn't belong. Like the birds, the wind, and the water, it seemed a very part of this place. Natural. Right.

"Just Delightful," he replied. His own voice felt natural too. For a long time it hadn't. He'd looked in the mirror without recognizing his own face, heard his own voice and wondered whom it belonged to. For many long, difficult months, everything about him had seemed all wrong, especially the fact that he was alive. That had been the biggest wrong of all.

Beside him Kelsey snorted. "Puh-leeze. John David?"

"Just and Divine."

"James Douglas?"

"Jaded Do-gooder."

"Joshua Dylan? Jerry Dean?" A pause, then . . . "Are you?"

He'd never been corrupt or degenerate, but in the word's second meaning . . . Fatigued, exhausted, worn out. Oh, yeah, he'd been that for a very long time.

Opening his eyes, he stretched out to face her and leaned on one elbow. "Are those your best guesses? What about Jasper Derwood? Jebediah Demetrius. Julius DeWitt."

She was watching him with a look that said she was still stuck on *Jaded Do-gooder,* but she let herself be distracted. "I bet it's something simple, like Jack Daniel."

"Nope, but I once was acquainted with a Jack Daniel's." Ignoring the tension seeping through his muscles, he went on. "Would you believe my father's name was Jay and my mother's name was Dee?"

"Nope."

"I didn't think so. Where'd you get a name like Kelsey?"

"My mother thought it had a good Irish ring to it. I looked it up in a baby book once. It said it was Norse or Scandinavian, neither of which I am."

"But you are Irish."

She smiled faintly. "Kelsey Colleen Malone, only daughter of Patrick Ryan Malone and Mary Kathleen Malone and only sister of Sean Kieran Malone."

"So tell me, Kelsey Colleen. How did a good Irish girl come to have her doubts about God?"

An uneasy look crept across her face, and her movements as she got to her feet and dusted her clothes were jerky. "It's a long story, and you came here to work, not listen to long, sad stories."

He gazed at her, from sneakers up mile-long legs to denim shorts, over a snug T-shirt advertising a 10K run, finally reaching her face, in shadow because the sun was at her back. "I generally get paid well to listen to sad stories," he said quietly. "I'm offering to hear yours for free."

"It's not that sad. It's not really anything at all except boring." She started toward the house. "Come on. Break time's over. Let's get back to work."

J.D. watched until he couldn't see her anymore, then slowly got to his feet. They *had* come to work, just the two of them. Jacob and Noah had wanted to play with Josie and the Walker kids, Gracie had insisted on baking with the Winchester sisters, and Caleb had refused to leave the others for anything as insignificant as the work on this house. He was afraid someone else might exert some influence on them while he was gone, might in some small way start to usurp his position as the most important person in their lives. And he was right to be afraid, because it *was* happening, so slowly it was hardly noticeable but happening just the same.

He had expected Kelsey to back out too, but when he'd given her the opportunity, she hadn't grabbed it. That fact pleased him more than he could say. They'd finished the last of the kitchen cabinets before taking their break and would be moving on to the cabinets in the office. No doubt she was in there, waiting, pretending their conversation hadn't gotten the least bit serious. But that was all right. He knew how to coax people into talking when they didn't want to. And if they absolutely refused, he also knew how to patiently wait until they were ready.

She was in the office, sitting on the unfinished window seat, work gloves on, feet tapping out a rhythm on the subfloor. When he walked in, she stood up, stretched, and moved to the nearest cabinet, helping him shift it into place.

"So you have a brother. Is he older or younger?"

"Younger."

"Is he married? Does he have kids?"

"Married, no kids."

"What about your folks? What do they do?"

"My father is a partner with his brothers in a little business their grandfather started. My mother oversees everyone else's business."

"Including yours?"

"Of course. What good Irish mother doesn't try to run her children's lives?" As she moved, a strand of hair fell away from the band that secured her ponytail. He thought about working it back into place, then about removing the band and letting it all fall free—long, heavy, wildly curling around her shoulders, his hands, his body.

He cleared his throat, but it did nothing to clear the image from his mind or the sudden heat from his body. Giving the cabinet an overzealous push, he smashed his finger between it and the wall and muttered a curse, then forced his attention back to the conversation. "What does your mother think of your moving here?"

"She thinks I've moved to the other side of the world." Her level gaze settled on him as he examined his already-swelling finger. "I bet when you did your surgical rotation, you cut yourself with your own scalpel, didn't you?"

"No, I didn't," he retorted, but didn't allow her to change the subject. "She's not so wrong, is she? Bethlehem and New York City are in two different universes."

"They're not so different."

"Hey, don't forget, I came here from Chicago. I know the differences firsthand. What do you miss most so far?"

She tilted her head to one side to consider. "My favorite bookstore. I used to go to this wonderful huge store that spread over three floors and had every book I'd ever wanted and a coffee bar that sold the most delicious frozen cappuccino, and there were big comfy chairs for reading and dozens of aisles for browsing. What about you? What do you miss most about Chicago?"

He didn't need even a second to consider it. The things he missed most were people, people he had loved. People to whom he'd had obligations and duties, whom he had failed so thoroughly. People who were now lost to him forever. "I'm over missing anything," he said, feeling guilty for the lie. "In the beginning I think I missed the restaurants most. I like Greek food and sushi and Thai. Trying to get those now gives new meaning to going out for dinner." Deliberately he turned the conversation back to her. "What was your mother's problem with you moving here?"

"She likes having the family nearby. I'm probably the first one in three generations to move farther than an hour away. Most of my relatives live within five miles of each other. They like being close enough to have Sunday dinners and go to church together. The men work on each other's cars and watch the big games on TV, and the women give each other advice, visit every day, and take turns baby-sitting all the kids." She smiled faintly. "That's Mom's biggest fear, I think. That I'll fall in love, get married, and raise her grandbabies out here, where she won't be able to spoil them every day."

Now, that was a powerful image—Kelsey, in love, pregnant, surrounded by sassy little girls with curly brown hair and hazel eyes. But that was all that formed. There was no lucky man in the picture. Whoever he might be, J.D. hoped he stayed away long enough to give *him* a chance with her first. It wouldn't take long, because whatever she needed, he couldn't give. Carol Ann and Trey were the proof. All he was good for these days was affairs—short, sweet, and, in the end, unsatisfying, because for so long he'd had so much more.

Until he'd destroyed it.

"Why did you describe yourself as a jaded do-gooder?"

He scowled at her as he began shimming the cabinet to level it. "It was a joke, Kelsey. You know, humor?"

"Is that why you left Chicago?"

"I told you why I left Chicago." The scowl was starting to feel more real as he screwed the braces into the studs.

"Yeah, I know, small-town living, neighbors, slower pace, less traffic. Were you burned out? Is that why you left?"

He'd been burned out for so long that the ashes were cold. He'd had no heat, no passion, no life, and very little reason for living. In the end he'd lost even that.

Getting to his feet, he set the drill down, then faced her. "Who's asking?"

"I don't under—"

He made a sweeping gesture that encompassed her entire person. "Friend or social worker?"

It took her a while to answer, and he wasn't sure he could trust the answer when she gave it. "Friend."

He held her gaze for a long time, wondering how well Kelsey, attractive woman and, yes, friend, could separate from Ms. Malone, dedicated social worker. Not very, he suspected. Anything Kelsey learned, Ms. Malone would use. For that reason he redirected the conversation. "Friend? Really? I'm flattered."

"Against my better judgment," she said dryly.

"I knew you couldn't resist my charm."

"Is that what you call it?"

When he started past her to get the next unit, she stopped him with a hand on his arm. His skin was damp with sweat, gritty with dust, but that didn't lessen the impact of her touch. It didn't stop his throat from going dry, his temperature from climbing higher, or his voice from turning thick and husky. "What do you say we shoot for something beyond friendship?"

She very delicately removed her hand, as if she'd grabbed hold of danger and was now trying to retreat without losing her fingers. "We can't— You know—" The breath she took was audible, strengthening. "Funny."

"Actually . . ." J.D. drew his own noisy breath. "I haven't been more serious in a long time." Two years, three months, two weeks, and four days.

She moved away, all the way across the room, and stared out the window. "Why don't we back up a bit and pretend these last few minutes of conversation never happened? I won't ask you about Chicago, and you won't ask me—"

"For more than you want to give?"

Slowly, she faced him. "For more than I *can* give."

Interesting distinction, and a bit of an ego stroke to ease the— What exactly was it he felt? Disappointment? Regret? Loss?

He went back to work, but after installing enough cabinets to accommodate everything he owned twice over, the job was pretty routine. It left him plenty of time to think, to wonder about that distinction, to try to identify that emotion.

For dealing with others' emotions every day in his work, he'd become pretty detached from his own. For so long he'd been dead inside. Even now, compared to the man he'd been ten years before, he was an emotional cripple. He'd learned to function, to act normally, to make jokes and make friends while keeping everyone—keeping life—at a safe distance. As fond as he was of his neighbors, as much as he genuinely loved some of them, not one had slipped inside the defenses he used to keep himself intact.

The Browns were the first kids who'd threatened to breach those defenses. Kelsey was the first woman.

But with the Browns, he felt threatened. With Kelsey, he just felt tempted. Because he knew nothing riskier than an affair would come of it? Because when it came down to letting her in—if she ever wanted in—his carefully reconstructed instincts for self-preservation would save him?

Or was it possible that instead of part of the destruction, she could be part of the healing?

It was a seductive thought—that one day he might be healed, healthy, and whole, the man he used to be, capable of great good, great feeling, wholehearted commitment. And that Kelsey could be part of the process or the reward at the end . . . That could be the most seductive thought of all.

Or she could be none of that, nothing more than she was at this moment. A friend. She could be as totally unavailable to him as she seemed to think, which could be another reason he was tempted by her, he admitted. It was easier to resist temptation that had a snowball's chance in hell of coming to fruition.

So why was she unavailable? Why was a relationship with him not more than she *wanted* to give, but more than she *could*?

The first choice was obvious. She was in love with someone else. Why not? She was a beautiful woman, and few beautiful women made it to their mid-thirties without at least one serious relationship. It was hard to imagine the fool who would leave her or let her go, but he knew men like that existed. Hell, he *was* a man like that. Hadn't he lost Carol Ann?

Using his best nonjudgmental, soothing psychiatrist voice, he asked, "Have you ever been married?"

Her look was wary. So was her voice. "No."

"Ever been in love?"

"Once." She lifted the corner of the cabinet so he could shim it, then drew her shirt-sleeve across her forehead to dry the sweat. "I was twelve. He sat across from me in social studies. His family moved over Thanksgiving break and I never saw him again. It broke my heart."

"What about later? Once you were out of braces and pigtails? There must have been someone."

A faint flush tinged her cheeks, and she hedged when she answered. "I don't exactly meet a lot of great guys in my line of work. Fathers losing custody of their children. Foster fathers, usually married, taking custody of those children. Cops, lawyers, mental health professionals." Her tone put the last bunch in the same group with the first.

J.D. tilted his head to study her. Obviously, there was something she wasn't telling him, someone she wasn't willing to discuss at the moment. He considered pressing the issue, then decided it could be done later. Just then he let her direct him off on a tangent designed to keep her secret. "You don't like cops and lawyers?"

"I like some of them just fine, but I wouldn't want to date any of them."

"Why not?"

"Because of what I do, and what they do."

"That doesn't have to be a negative. A cop, lawyer, or therapist would have some insight into your work and vice versa. It could make things easier, give you common ground to build on."

"You would advise two people in difficult professions to try to build a relationship based on their similar difficulties?" She snorted. "It's a good thing you didn't go into marriage counseling, Dr. Grayson. You would have failed."

"I certainly failed at my own."

The words came out a low murmur and hung in the air between them. He hadn't intended to voice the thought aloud, hadn't intended ever to tell her anything more about his marriage than she already knew, which was more than anyone else in Bethlehem knew. Other than a few unimportant facts—that he'd been a prominent psychiatrist in Chicago and that his degrees were from Boston University and Harvard—his past was a secret from everyone else in town. His successes and failures were private, and he meant to keep them that way.

"What happened?" Her voice was as nonjudgmental and soothing as his best, the voice in which she might question an abused child or counsel a grieving parent. It reminded him that some aspects of her job weren't very different from his. She knew how to coax people into talking and how to wait patiently if they weren't ready.

In this case she needed the patience of Job, because he would never be ready to fully, truthfully, unflinchingly answer her simple question.

He faced her, the distance between them about two arm's lengths. If she reached out, and so did he, they could touch. They could connect, maybe just for a while, maybe for always. Or they could stand there, arms at their sides, and never take that risk.

"We're friends, right?" he asked, his tone curiously brittle. "We've established that."

She nodded.

"And you don't want, won't let yourself want more than that, right?"

This time her nod was slower, less sure.

"Then what happened with my marriage is none of your business. It's very personal, and I don't discuss very personal business with just friends. All right?"

If she took offense at his bluntness, she hid it. But there was no denying the chill that settled over the room, though whether it came from him or her, he couldn't say. It took away his pleasure in the day, turned work that he had always enjoyed into a chore that he no longer wanted to do. Grimly, he unplugged the drill, then started closing the windows.

"We've done enough here," he said shortly. "We'd better get back to town."

For a moment she looked as if she might protest, and he wanted her to, wanted her to say something, anything, that he might respond to, that might get them back on comfortable footing. She didn't though. She simply nodded once, then walked out. A moment later he heard the front door close. A moment after that came the thud of the truck's door.

He finished closing the kitchen windows, then stepped onto the deck. The sunlight, the wind, and the sounds of the water encouraged him to stand still, to close his eyes and breathe deeply. There had been long periods when he'd forgotten to breathe, when he'd been too rushed, too distressed, too driven. It was amazing what the simple act could accomplish, how it could release the tension and ease the anxiety. He should try it more often, especially when Kelsey was around.

Or maybe he should just make sure she wasn't around.

His responding smile was thin and humorless. He knew himself better than any man ever should. Soul-searching, for him, was one of the greater hazards of the psychiatric profession. He would be kidding himself if he thought there was any chance he would keep his distance from Kelsey, and he'd made a point of not kidding himself—for the last few years, at least. Down that path lay danger.

Kelsey waited in the truck, seat belt on, fingers tapping impatiently against the glass. Down that path lay danger too, he acknowledged with a grin.

But some dangers a man just had to face.

Chapter Eight

"I 'VE NEVER SEEN HIM DRESSED NICE BEFORE. You know, he's really kinda cute."

Alanna was spending her Sunday afternoon on the front steps of her house with her best friend beside her. They were supposed to be talking about the slumber party they were having the next weekend, but she'd spent most of her time watching Caleb, across the street in Miss Corinna's front yard. Now she finally looked away from him and gave Susan Walker what she hoped was a good imitation of what Miss Agatha called her chastening look. "How a person dresses doesn't have anything to do with whether he's cute."

Susan blew a bubble with her pink gum, then made it pop loudly. "Maybe not. Maybe he was cute before. The way he acted at school, who could tell? He was always so mean and hateful."

"He was never hateful to me," Alanna remarked, resting her arms on her knees, her chin in her hands. But that wasn't really true. Caleb had been mean to everybody.

After all, if he didn't care what the kids said, then what they said couldn't hurt him. At least, that was what he'd pretended.

But some of the things the kids said *had* hurt him, had hurt his pride—and pride, she'd overheard the teacher say once, was all Caleb had. He had too much of it as far as she could tell. He didn't like anybody, didn't trust anybody, and didn't want anybody around.

Especially her, because last week she'd hurt his feelings. She'd tried to apologize on the way to Sunday school that morning, but he'd walked away from her, and when she'd followed, he'd gone out the side door. He'd spent the whole Sunday-school time sitting outside on a bench, looking like he hated the whole world, including—and maybe most especially—her. At dinner, when Dr. J.D. had asked him how class was, he'd said fine, and then he'd glared at her as though daring her to tell the truth.

She hadn't. But that hadn't made him stop glaring.

She sighed heavily, and Susan looked at her. "Whatsa-matter?"

"Nothing."

Susan kept looking at her, then got real serious. "You hear from your mother?"

Alanna shook her head.

"Are you worried about her? You don't think she's—" Susan stopped herself and looked away quickly, but Alanna knew what she'd been about to say. *You don't think she's in trouble or dead or anything, do you?* She'd asked it before. So had their other friends, and a couple of times Alanna had asked Aunt Emilie or Uncle Nathan the same thing. They'd tried to reassure her, but there wasn't much they could say. Lots of times drug addicts and alcoholics and women who went home with strange men died. Unless her mama straightened up once and for all, *she* could die. Alanna had understood that since she was five years old.

No, she wasn't worrying about anything important like that. She was just wondering if Caleb would ever quit being mad at her. But she couldn't tell Susan that. Her best friend in the whole world didn't know she had a crush on Caleb, a silly little one, the kind Susan had every week on a different boy. It was her own private secret.

He sat across the street in the glider under Miss Corinna's tree. Brendan and Gracie were inside helping the sisters bake bread, and Josie and his brothers were playing around him, but Caleb had a book open and hardly ever looked up from it. She wondered if he was really reading. A couple of times the teacher had asked him to read out loud in class—she made everyone do it—and he'd had a hard time. He'd missed easy words, and some of the kids had snickered.

Alanna had trouble reading too when she'd first come to Bethlehem, but Miss Agatha and Miss Corinna had helped her. Now she read better than anyone else in her class. Maybe they were helping him too. Still, she wished he'd put the book down and look their way once in a while.

"Lannie and Caleb, sittin' in a tree, k-i-s-s-i-n-g," Susan sang near her ear.

Alanna's face turned red, and she poked her elbow into Susan. "Be quiet."

"Well, it's the only thing I said that got through to you. You're so busy looking at him like he's your boyfriend that you're not even listening to me. Do you like him?"

"Susan . . ."

"*Do* you? Tell me. I won't tell anyone, cross my heart and hope to die. *Do* you?"

Alanna looked at him, then looked at Susan, gave a great sigh, and nodded.

Grabbing her arm, Susan squealed, "Oh, my gosh! I can't believe it. You've never liked *any* boy! Does he know? Have you told him? Does he like you too? Has he *kissed* you?" Then suddenly all the excitement disappeared and her voice dropped to a whisper. "Do your aunt and uncle know?"

"I don't know. I don't guess so. Why?"

"Because he's, well, Lannie, he's Caleb Brown. He's not . . . not . . ."

Alanna's excitement disappeared too. She scrambled to her feet and stared down at Susan. "Not what?"

Susan stood up too and brushed the seat of her shorts. "He's . . . him and his brothers and sister, they're not like us."

"Like us how?"

"Well, they don't live in a nice house. And they don't come to school all the time. And they don't have any money. And they look hungry. My aunt Francine says they're not respectable. She says if ever a saying was tailor-made for a family, the saying is poor white trash and the family is the Browns. She says—"

"It's not Caleb's fault that they're poor or that his mama ran off or his daddy disappeared. *We* were poor when we came here. We were homeless, and Aunt Emilie had only seventy-six dollars to get us home to Georgia, and she was getting ready to turn herself in to the police so we wouldn't have to sleep in the car and freeze to death in the blizzard, when she found the house and the key and the firewood! Did your aunt Francine say *we* were poor white trash too? Did she say *we* weren't respectable, that you shouldn't be friends with *me* 'cause we weren't like you?"

"No, but that was different. You were just broke for a while 'cause your aunt lost her job. The Browns have always been poor and always will be, and Aunt Francine says that's 'cause they're trash."

"Your aunt Francine is *stupid*, and *you're* stupid for listening to her!"

"I am not stupid! I'm as smart as you are, smarter even! *I* didn't have to have someone help me learn to read in the fourth grade!"

Alanna shoved her hands into her pockets. "You can go home now," she said angrily. "I don't want to be friends with you today."

"Well, maybe I don't want to be friends with you at all!" Susan stomped across the yard to the sidewalk, then turned back. "Why don't you go and be friends with ol' dumb Caleb? The two of you can be dumb together!"

Alanna watched her go. Part of her wanted to yell at her to come back, to say she was sorry and did too want to be friends. Part of her wanted to yell, "Good riddance!" at Susan's back. And part of her just wanted to pout.

When Susan turned the corner, Alanna crossed the street, then went up the driveway on the other side. She climbed the steps at the end of the porch and walked all the way to the other end, then leaned over the rail, watching as her shadow stretched out over the grass.

She was sorry she'd been mean. Susan was her best friend in the whole world. When they'd first come to Bethlehem, she'd been scared to leave the house and even more scared to go to school, but on her very first day Susan had walked up to her and said they would be best friends and, sure enough, they were. She'd needed a best friend more than almost anything, and now she'd told her she was stupid and Susan had called her dumb and all because of Caleb, who probably thought she was dumb too. Now she'd have to come up with another apology, when she still hadn't gotten Caleb to take his, and she just wished—

"Who lives here?"

Looking between the spindles, she saw an upside-down version of Caleb at the other end of the porch. Slowly, she straightened, then turned to face him. "Nobody."

He stopped about in the middle and leaned against the rail. She leaned against it where she stood. "When we first came here, we sort of borrowed the house, but after a while we got caught and had to move out. We lived with the sisters for a while, then Aunt Emilie married Uncle Nathan and we moved into his house."

"How do you borrow a house?"

"We just sort of took it. Aunt Emilie was desperate for a place to stay 'cause there was a blizzard, and the house was just sitting here all empty, and she prayed that it was all right for us to use it just for a little while and just like that she found the key. It was a miracle."

He snorted. "Lots of people hide keys to their houses where they can be found. That's not a miracle. It's dumb."

"It was too a miracle, because we got to stay here and Aunt Emilie met Uncle Nathan and they fell in love and got married and she didn't have to go to prison for kidnapping us and we didn't have to go to foster homes. Instead, we have a real family."

"You can't have a real family without your mother or father."

"Yes, you can. We're a real family. And maybe if your dad doesn't come back, you'll get to be a real family with someone else too."

The mocking look disappeared from his face, and he got very serious. "My dad's coming back for us."

She wanted to pretend she believed him, but she had more experience with a parent leaving than he did.

"You don't believe me, do you?"

She inched closer to him, finally stopping when there was only one section of porch railing between them. "Sometimes kids are just more than parents can handle. It doesn't mean they don't love us. It just means there are other things going on."

He snorted again. "That sounds like *him* talking."

"Dr. J.D.'s a smart man. He knows practically everything about why people do what they do." After a moment she asked hopefully, "Don't you like him a little better now?"

"No. I hate him, and he hates me."

"No, he doesn't."

"Yes, he does. I've seen the way he looks at me."

"How?" She'd known Dr. J.D. practically since he came to Bethlehem. He liked kids better than any other grown-up she'd met. He was always nice to them and listened to them as if what they had to say was important.

"Like he wishes I was gone. Like just looking at me makes him kinda mad."

She shook her head hard enough to make her hair swing. "You're wrong. Dr. J.D. likes everybody, and everybody likes him back. You just want him not to like you so you don't have to like him."

Caleb shook his head too, convinced he was right. She walked back to the end of the porch, stared out into the yard, and took a deep breath. "For whatever it's worth, Caleb—"

A creak at the other end made her spin around. He was crossing the driveway, walking fast, as though he needed to get back to Miss Agatha's right away. She watched until he disappeared around the hedge, then sadly finished her sentence. "I like you." For whatever it was worth, which apparently was nothing.

A S THEY BEGAN THEIR NINTH FULL DAY TOgether, J.D. realized they'd fallen into a fairly regular routine. Mrs. Larrabee stayed with the kids while he ran; he returned to shower, then woke them. While they got dressed, he headed for the kitchen, where he cooked breakfast, but only for himself. All the kids required was bowls, spoons, and glasses, a pitcher of milk, and however many boxes of cereal the pantry held. By the time breakfast was done, they had a few seconds for last-minute details, like shoes and anything they wanted to take to the baby-sitter's with them, and then he was off to work. Off to feeling like his old self again.

Tuesday morning, though, the routine got interrupted. He'd just sat down at the table with his breakfast—fried ham drizzled with maple syrup and Harry's hash brown casserole—when Gracie looked at his plate. "Them 'tatoes smell good, Dr. J.D.," she said, taking an extra deep breath for effect.

He stilled in the act of reaching for the salt and looked at her. "What did you say?"

"Them 'tatoes smell good."

Dr. J.D. She'd added that. For nine full days and half of another she'd avoided calling him anything but *the man,* and that only when she thought he couldn't hear. He wouldn't even have bet that she *knew* his name, certainly never would have thought that she'd use it. But she had, and so naturally that it hadn't even registered with her.

But it had with Caleb. At the opposite end of the table he was scowling so hard that milk sloshed from the spoonful of cereal he was gripping in midair.

J.D. decided that paying any more attention to the moment wouldn't be a good idea, so instead he focused on what Gracie considered to be the important part of her comment. "You want some of this, Gracie?"

Wearing a broad grin, she nodded. As he pushed his chair back from the table, Noah looked up anxiously. "I ain't never had 'tatoes like that before."

"I'll get you a plate too, Noah. Jacob? Caleb?"

His mouth full of chocolate-flavored cereal, Jacob shook his head. Caleb simply glared.

J.D. served one plate to each of the two kids. Gracie

pronounced them the "goodest" potatoes she'd ever had except for French fries. Noah inhaled them, then returned to his cereal.

It was a small step forward, J.D. reminded himself as they ate in relative silence. With kids like these, success came only in small steps, and every one was sweet.

As soon as breakfast was finished, they all carried their dishes into the kitchen. "Get your shoes on and grab your things," he directed as he rinsed the dishes, then stacked them on the counter. "We've got to be out of here in five minutes."

Gracie ran to get her favorite storybook so Miss Agatha could read it to her for the dozenth time. Jacob got a book of his own, a history of baseball, picked up when Mrs. Larrabee had taken them to the library the day before, and Noah went searching for his shoes.

Caleb waited sullenly by the front door. J.D. had done laundry over the weekend, so Caleb was back to wearing his own shabby clothes. Each of the last two mornings when he'd come from their room, his hostile expression had dared J.D. to comment on the clothes. He hadn't. There were so many more important things for them to fight about.

"My shoe comed untied," Noah announced as he came down the hall, dangling his tennis shoe by the laces.

J.D. and Caleb turned at the same time. "Let me see—" J.D. broke off as Caleb said loudly, "I'll tie it for you."

Noah looked from one to the other, bit his lip, then eased into the kitchen and brought the offending shoe to J.D. Muttering something better left unheard, Caleb went outside. The door slammed behind him.

J.D. lifted the boy onto the counter, then slid the shoe onto his foot. "Do you know how to tie your shoes, Noah?"

He shook his head.

"Does Caleb do it for you?"

"He did once."

"Who does it the rest of the time?"

It was Jacob who answered. "Mostly he just wiggles his foot in and out so's they don't have to be untied."

"Remind me this evening, and I'll teach you how to tie them." He finished a neat bow, then asked, "How's that?"

Noah examined it, compared it to the rather ragged bow on the other shoe, then, with a grin, nodded his approval. J.D. lifted him to the floor, and he ran to the front door. There, though, he turned back. "Thanks, Dr. J.D."

Something suspiciously close to a lump filled J.D.'s throat. "You're welcome, Noah."

And for the first time in nine full days and half of another, he knew without a doubt that he meant it.

KELSEY WAS TYPING A REPORT AT HER DESK ON Tuesday morning, when a knock sounded at the open door. Looking up, all she saw was a brown paper bag dangling from two long, tanned fingers.

"Are you going to throw something, or is it safe to come inside?"

At the sound of J.D.'s voice, she was tempted to smile. She didn't though. "That depends. What's in the bag?"

"Chicken salad on a croissant, with Harry's prize-winning potato salad on the side."

She considered it a moment. As conciliatory gestures went, this one was pretty good. She loved chicken salad and buttery, flaky croissants, and it *was* lunchtime. And she hadn't seen J.D. since Sunday. She hated to admit that she'd missed him, but there it was—the truth, in all its ugly, worrisome shame.

"Can I come in?"

"Would you settle for just leaving the bag on the desk out there and closing the door on your way out?"

"Nope."

"I didn't think so. All right. Come on in."

The bag disappeared. When he came through the door a moment later, his hands were empty. The fact hardly registered, though, because she was busy appreciating the sight. He wore pleated trousers in a buttery caramel shade with a white shirt and suspenders. He looked incredibly preppy, handsome, and quite possibly more appealing than she could resist.

"What's wrong? Cat got your tongue?"

She swallowed hard. "Where's my lunch?"

"It has strings attached."

"What strings?"

"Just one, actually. Shut off your computer and come out here."

She hesitated, then obeyed. By the time she'd circled her desk, he'd retreated to the outer office. By the time she got to the door, he was out of sight. So was the bag, but a piece of fuzzy twine tied in a bow swayed gently from the knob. She got her keys, locked up, then tugged the end of the string. It led her into the hall and down the stairs, across the lobby and out the door. Gathering it loosely in one hand, she followed it across the grass, into the square, and to a park bench, where the other end was attached to the brown paper bag. A matching bag, along with two sodas, sat alongside, and J.D. was waiting.

She seated herself primly at the other end of the bench and removed the sandwich from the bag before giving him a sidelong look. "Not a bad apology."

"It's not an apology. It's a bribe. I always make apologies in person."

"Always," she repeated. "Do you make a lot of them?"

"Actually, no. I generally try not to say or do anything

that requires one. If you use the words too often, they become meaningless, then when you really, really need them, they're not worth much."

"Do you ever really, really need them?" she asked, then immediately raised one hand. "I'm sor— Don't answer that." After all, weren't her prying questions what had brought them to this point?

He took a bite of his own sandwich before glancing her way. His features were carefully schooled to show no emotion. Still, she caught a hint of deep regret in his eyes. "It's okay. Yes, sometimes I have a lot to apologize for."

"But Sunday's not one of those times."

"I brought up the subject of my marriage," he disagreed. "I can't blame you for asking a question about it."

"And you can't blame yourself for not wanting to answer it." Some things—certain dreams, certain disappointments—were best kept to oneself. Others were meant to be shared with only the dearest of friends. She certainly couldn't claim that status with J.D. Even the simple title of friend was stretching it, considering that she hardly knew the man.

No matter how much she would like to know him better.

"No one else in town even knows I was married," he remarked as he tossed a piece of bread to the birds gathered under a nearby tree.

Kelsey wasn't sure whether his trusting her with his personal history made her feel honored or frightened. Before she decided, she asked, "So why did you tell me?"

"Because you asked."

She smiled. So much for honored or frightened. Truth was, she was just plain nosy. "How are the kids?"

"Fine."

"Are they adjusting?"

"Gracie and Noah actually called me by my name this

morning. That was a first. And when Noah needed help tying his shoe, he came to me instead of to Caleb."

"Foster parenting is made up of small victories." She took a bite of salad, savoring the sweet tang of the dressing. "How is Caleb?"

J.D.'s expression took on a troubled edge. "Caleb is Caleb. He's still angry, still hostile, still insisting his father's coming back."

The older the child, the more difficult the situation. She'd learned that early in her career. It wasn't a hard-and-fast rule, but it held true often enough. "Are you able to talk to him?"

"I've got nothing to say that he wants to hear."

"Do you say it anyway?"

"Sometimes. Sometimes I just let him be."

She stabbed the last bite of potato with her fork but didn't lift it to her mouth. "Maybe he should see the family counselor over in Howland."

"No."

"I'm not questioning your ability to deal with him. It's just—"

"Caleb and I will handle our problems."

Our problems. Meaning there was more to the situation than simply a twelve-year-old child acting out because of his parents' abandonment. Keeping her voice carefully neutral, she said, "I understand Caleb's problem with you. What is your problem with him?"

He pinched off pieces of sandwich to throw to the birds. She thought he was planning to ignore her question, but when the food was gone, he dusted his hands, then faced her. "He reminds me of someone . . . someone I wasn't able to help. Someone I did more harm than good."

"I find that difficult to imagine," she said. "You were the best psychiatrist in Chicago."

"How would you classify yourself as a social worker?"

"I'm good."

"Just good? Or very good? Dedicated. Committed."

She shrugged.

"But you've had failures, haven't you? You've determined that a child has lied, or that a home is safe. You've left a child in the custody of a parent who swore on her own life that she wasn't the one abusing him. You've investigated and weighed the evidence and made decisions that are generally for the best, but once in a while they've been horribly, painfully wrong and some child has paid for it. You've made a few mistakes."

"Yes," she admitted in a whisper. She'd made some mistakes, and she had paid for them. She'd been taken in by some of the best liars in the business, had gone with evidence that supported one conclusion when in reality the other was correct.

"Trey was my mistake," J.D. said quietly.

"Only one?" Her voice was shaky. She took a deep breath to steady it. "You should count yourself lucky."

"Lucky?"

"Is he alive?"

"Yes."

"And well?"

"Relatively. Considering."

"And he's the only one. You're very lucky."

They fell silent, and she wondered how they could engage in such bleak conversation on such a gorgeous summer day. The sky was pure blue, with hardly a cloud to be seen. The air was warm and heavy with the perfume of flowers growing nearby. Even the buzz of bees working around the flowers couldn't detract from the sweet perfection of the afternoon, and yet there they sat, talking about failures and mistakes.

But maybe this was the best time to discuss such things,

under a bright warm sun, with no shadows to hide in, no darkness to lie in.

"How do you deal with it?"

She tidied up, stuffing all the trash into one bag, depositing it into a can near the sidewalk. When she returned, she didn't sit down but instead leaned against the closest tree. "The first time, I turned in my resignation. How could I continue to make life-and-death decisions when a child lay in the hospital because of me?"

"But it wasn't because of you."

"That's what my supervisor said. I wasn't the mother who worked out her anger and frustration by punching her child. I wasn't the father who lied to protect his wife. I wasn't the grandmother who supported the lies because she didn't want the authorities coming around."

"But?"

Of course there was a *but*. There always was. "I *was* the one who chose not to remove that child from his home. Who chose to leave him in the care of the mother who hit him and the father who let her."

"Obviously, you didn't quit. How did you deal with it the next time?"

"I wrote it off." Her laughter was harsh and painful. "God, that sounds so cold. I looked at all the times I'd done good and the two times I'd screwed up, and I decided that one outweighed the other and I rationalized the screwup away. I'm not perfect. I'm only human. I'm bound to make mistakes. I'll try harder and be smarter and maybe, please, God, it won't happen again." After a moment she finally asked, "How did you deal with failing Trey?"

His smile was thin and mocking. "I came to Bethlehem."

"And did it help?"

"It saved my life."

"So . . . if you fix things with Caleb, then somehow that'll make up for not being able to fix things with Trey."

J.D. gazed past her to Main Street. There was the usual midday traffic. People were going about their business— shopping, running errands, going to lunch. Their lives were, for the most part, normal, well-adjusted. They knew everything about their neighbors, and their neighbors knew everything about them. They had no secrets, and their troubles were the usual sort—unruly children, financial binds, difficulties at work, or a rough spot in the marriage.

He envied them.

Kelsey was waiting for an answer, and he gave the one she expected. "Yeah. Dealing with Caleb could help with Trey." But it was a lie. All the successes in the world could never make up for failing Trey. He would take that burden to his grave.

"Well," he said, inhaling, then exhaling loudly. "Isn't this captivating lunchtime conversation?"

"Now you know why I don't date people in similar professions. Over dinner we'd wind up talking about how the court system protects the criminals and punishes the victims, we could spend the evening debating mandatory sentences and the death penalty, and before bed we could compare war stories from the trenches."

He gave her a long, slow look, from her hair, which had been semi-tamed in an intricate braid, to the bold floral print of her dress, down to bare legs and sandals, then murmured, "Honey, if we were going to bed together, war stories would be the last thing on my mind."

She started to speak but thought better of it, then turned away. When she turned back, her fingers were working nervously together. "Do you feel—" She coughed, cleared her throat. "Do you think you've made any progress at all with . . . with . . ."

"Caleb," he supplied, and she nodded. "It's hard to say. Why don't you come over for dinner this evening and see for yourself?"

"I can't."

"Do you have other plans?"

"N-no, but . . ."

But she didn't think going to his house was a good idea, even when they were chaperoned by four kids. Her unstated objection said that she was at least aware of the possibilities. That he wasn't the only one who saw some potential or felt some interest. Now, if he could just figure out why she was so determined to ignore the potential . . .

"You could call it a home visit," he said evenly.

"Home visits aren't scheduled in advance. If you're expecting me, then you'll be prepared. I can't observe you in your usual routine."

"Then surprise me sometime. You know where to find me."

She nodded, then glanced at her watch. "I guess I'd better get back to the office. I've got an appointment at the nursing home this afternoon, and I need to finish that report before I go."

"What a coincidence. I'll be over there this afternoon too. Page me when you get there and I'll give you the nickel tour. Trust me. It's worth it."

She started back to the courthouse. At the park entrance she turned again. "Hey, J.D.? Thanks for the lunch. I enjoyed it."

For a time he remained where he was, seeking the energy, the desire, to get up and cross the street to his truck. But all he really wanted to do was sit there and absorb everything around him. He wanted to soak up the sun, breathe, relax, recoup. He wanted to stay until he became a part of the bench, a part of the park, unnoticed by the people passing by.

But he had obligations. They were expecting him at the nursing home. He had few truly troubled patients there but saw mostly people who wanted to talk, who were grateful that he was willing to listen. They would be disappointed if anything less than a bona fide emergency kept him away. J.D.-doesn't-feel-like-it-today didn't qualify.

He had to make a stop at the McKinney house first. As he pulled up out front, he noticed one of the Winchester sisters with a half dozen kids in their front yard. Seeing Maggie McKinney's dog, Buddy, over there too, he pulled across the intersection and parked.

Miss Agatha and Caleb were weeding the flower bed while Jacob, Josie, and the older Walker kids tossed a Frisbee back and forth. J.D. ducked an errant toss as he crossed the grass. "Afternoon, Miss Agatha, kids."

Miss Agatha shaded her eyes underneath the brim of an enormous straw hat. "Why, J.D., what brings you by so early? Ah, you're here for Buddy, aren't you?"

"Yes, ma'am." He watched the kids for a minute, then asked, "Is Noah inside with Miss Corinna?"

"Yes. They're making lemonade, I believe. Just go on in."

J.D. did just that, ignoring Caleb's glare as he climbed the steps to the door. The house was darker, cooler, and filled with sweet fragrances that whispered *home* even though he'd never lived in a home that smelled quite the same way. His mother had been a notoriously bad cook, so the only food aromas that lingered around his childhood home had been scorched and bitter. Because of Carol Ann's myriad allergies, the house they'd shared had smelled antiseptically clean. Even his own place, with the fresh flowers Mrs. Larrabee provided every few days, lacked the combination of aromas that he found so welcoming.

He wondered if he would find them in Kelsey's place.

At the rate things were going, he might never get invited into Kelsey's place to find out.

Miss Corinna was in the kitchen with Noah and Gracie. The older woman greeted him with a smile, then said, "You can pour the sugar in a little faster than that, Noah."

Noah sat on the counter, his bottom lip sucked in between his teeth, balancing a cup of sugar on the rim of a pitcher. Gracie was stirring the lemonade inside with a long wooden spoon.

"How are you, J.D.?"

He accepted Miss Corinna's hug and kissed her cheek. "I'm fine." It was his standard answer. Sometimes it was even true. "I came to pick up Buddy and to see if I could borrow Noah for a while."

Startled, the boy dropped the sugar, cup, and all into the lemonade, making it splash. He looked wide-eyed from J.D. to the pitcher to Miss Corinna, then his lower lip began to tremble.

"It's ruined!" Gracie said.

"Of course it's not," Miss Corinna disagreed.

"But he dropped the cup inside."

"And the cup was clean, wasn't it?"

"But he *touched* it."

"And his hands are clean, aren't they? Remember? You both washed up before we started. It's not ruined at all, children." Miss Corinna fished out the cup, scraped the remaining sugar into the pitcher, then laid the cup in the sink.

"What for do you want Noah?" Gracie asked.

"Buddy and I are going over to the nursing home. I thought Noah might like to keep Buddy company."

"Why?" she asked, her gaze narrowing. Though there

was a strong family resemblance between all four kids, when she frowned, she looked uncannily—uncomfortably, for J.D.—like Caleb.

"Because Buddy needs someone to hold on to his leash and make sure he doesn't get into trouble."

"I can do that," she said boldly. "Buddy likes me."

"I'm sure he does. But I think Noah can do it too. What do you say, Noah?"

The boy looked from him to Miss Corinna, who nodded. Turning back to J.D., he mimicked the solemn nod, then held out his arms to be lifted from the counter.

Gracie jumped to the floor and ran to the front door, flinging it open. "Caleb, Caleb, the man's takin' Noah to the home!"

J.D. rolled his eyes. He and Noah were in the dining room, when abruptly the boy wheeled around and headed back to the kitchen. "Miss C'rinna, will you save some lemonade for me? Please?"

"I will, Noah. Have a good time."

J.D. made it as far as the top porch step before Caleb blocked his path. "Where're you takin' him?"

"To the nursing home."

"Why? He don't need nursin'."

"He's going to visit some patients with Buddy and me."

"Will you bring him back?" Gracie asked.

"Oh, puh-leeze," Josie said with dramatic gestures. "Of course he'll come back! Don't you know nothin'? A nursing home is a place for old people who can't live by theirselves anymore. Little boys don't stay there. My Sunday-school class goes and visits every month, and no one's ever tried to keep any of us."

"So why're you takin' *him*?" Caleb demanded. "Why not Jacob? Or Gracie?"

"Or, hey, I could take you," J.D. said, not proud of the faint sarcasm in his voice. "But today I want to take Noah.

I'm the guardian, Caleb. That means I'm the boss. And *that* means I don't have to answer to you. Come on, Noah."

He slowly moved ahead, forcing Caleb to step aside. Noah eased past quickly, then went to claim Buddy's leash from Miss Agatha. The Lab was almost as tall as Noah and was probably double his weight, but he was well trained. He walked sedately at the boy's side to the truck, jumped into the backseat, then sat down, head regally high, and gazed out the window.

As they circled the block, Noah stared silently out the side window. He was the quietest, the shyest of the four kids. He did what Caleb told him to do and played with his siblings or kept to himself. He rarely voiced an opinion or made any requests. He was a timid little shadow, devoting his energy to going unnoticed.

"You like lemonade, Noah?" J.D. asked.

His response was the merest bob of his head.

"You like Buddy?"

Another nod, this one slightly more emphatic.

"Have you ever had a pet?"

He was silent for more than a block before murmuring, "Once. His name was Blackie. He was a stray. He didn't stay 'cause we couldn't feed him, so he found another little boy to live with. Do you think our mama and daddy found some other little kids to live with?"

J.D. swallowed hard. "I don't know, Noah."

"Caleb says our mama didn't like kids so she wouldn't live with no other kids. But our daddy loved us. He singed us songs at night." He hummed a few bars. "Maybe he's singin' to some other little boy right now."

"I don't think so, Noah. I think your daddy—" Where did he draw the line between reassurance and well-intentioned lies? How much harm could he do if he promised Noah that his daddy was trying to make a home for him, that he was coming back for him as soon as he could, and it never happened? Who was at fault if he promised Noah that his father hadn't made a new family or a new life for himself someplace else and in reality he had? "I think your daddy will try very hard to keep the promises he made you."

"It's been a long time," Noah whispered to his reflection in the window. "Sometimes I can't 'member . . . Is Caleb going away?"

"No."

"Maybe he will. First Mama had to go, then Daddy. Maybe Caleb will too, and then Jacob, and then I'll have to go, and Gracie will be all alone. We'll all be all alone."

"No, Noah. You can live the rest of your life in Bethlehem if you want. You won't ever have to go anywhere."

The boy didn't turn to look at him, but instead whispered once more to the window, "We'll all be all alone."

J.D. was relieved to see the nursing home ahead. He parked out front, then circled the truck to help Noah and Buddy out. "Buddy comes here every week to visit," he explained, crouching in front of the boy. "All you have to do is hold his leash and follow him around. If he tries to take something that isn't his, tell him no, and if someone wants him to sit so they can pet him, say, 'Sit, Buddy.' "

The Lab hastily obeyed.

"Good boy." He scratched behind the dog's ear. "Are you ready?"

Noah wrapped the red leash around his hand. "Are there sick people in there?"

"A few. Mostly they're just old people."

"Do they like seeing Buddy?"

"Sure. Don't you?"

He nodded but didn't look reassured. "I don't know no old people."

"They're just people, Noah. They're somebody's grandmas and grandpas."

"I don't got none of them."

"They're like Miss Agatha and Miss Corinna."

A look of relief swept over his features. "Oh. Well, that's okay."

They walked up the sidewalk and through the double doors. J.D. checked in at the front desk, then he and Noah took Buddy to the first of the bedridden patients, who always saw the dog ahead of the others. Initially, Noah hung back, his head ducked, his shoulders hunched, his whole body somehow compressed, as if he might render himself invisible. After a time, though, he answered one question, then asked one of his own, then gradually eased right up to the bed. By the time J.D. was paged over the intercom, he felt confident enough to leave Noah in Buddy's and the patients' care.

Kelsey was waiting at the front desk, her expression equally perplexed and thoughtful. "When did all this come about?" she asked with an encompassing gesture.

"About eighteen months ago."

"And you came to town . . . ?"

"About eighteen months ago." He grinned. "What do you think?"

She looked around the lobby, and so did he. Nothing in the decor suggested *institution*. One wall was painted with a folk art mural of mountains, forest, and towns, and another provided the canvas for a life-size tree whose limbs stretched across the cloud-spotted, blue-sky ceiling. The furniture was upholstered, with plenty of pillows and throws, and the coffee tables, bookcases, and lamps wouldn't look out of place in anyone's home. The birds were a little noisy, he admitted, when they all got to chirping at once, but the splash of water in the corner fountain helped mute the racket.

"It beats beige walls and orange plastic chairs," she remarked. "Though I think I could live without the cats." She gently nudged one away with her toe, but the cat wasn't so easily deterred. It chose to wind itself around her other ankle.

Start simply, work your way up, and be persistent. Smart creature.

"Maybe *you* could live without the cats, but some of our residents here couldn't. Going into a nursing home is hard enough for most folks, but when they have to leave behind the pets who have been the most faithful of their companions, it can break their hearts. Geriatric patients don't live long with a broken heart."

"So you have cats and birds and . . . ?"

"There's a rabbit in the dayroom and aquariums in the sun room, and though we don't have a resident dog, they get visits four or five times a week from neighborhood dogs." He gestured toward the main corridor on the other side of the desk, and they started that way. "We also have plants in every room, bird feeders outside the windows, and regular visits from kids' groups in town, and out back there's playground equipment and picnic tables."

"And what's the payoff for all this?"

"A death rate lower than the statewide average. A lower incidence of infection. A lower hospitalization rate. And we use less medication than most homes this size."

"Sounds good."

He screwed up his face as if struck a mortal blow. "Aw, come on, Ms. Malone, surely you can do better than that. How about, 'Wow, Dr. Grayson, I'm impressed!'?"

"You don't need me to be impressed. Everyone else fawns all over you."

"They do? What do they say?"

Shaking her head with good-humored dismay, she stepped inside the dining room. Like the lobby, it was decorated to look as if it belonged in any home. Well, any home that routinely served sixty meals three times a day. "I *am* impressed, Dr. Grayson."

"Good." He grinned again as he indicated the dining room with a sweeping gesture. "And what do you think of the home?"

"I was talking about the home," she said dryly.

"I could impress you too if you'd give me a chance."

"And how would you do that?"

"I'm very smart."

"And very smug."

"I run fast."

"Your legs are long."

"But I'd let you catch me."

"As if I'd try." She crossed the hallway to the look into the sun room, then continued down the corridor.

"Everyone adores me."

"Must be your incredibly modest nature."

As they reached the end of the hallway, where glass doors led into the backyard, he stepped in front of her to block her way. She drew up short only inches before colliding with him. "I'm a great catch," he murmured.

She started to take a breath, then apparently thought better of it. He didn't blame her. Every breath he took was heavy with the fragrance of aftershave and perfume, delicately mixed to create a new scent neither his nor hers but theirs—and thoroughly enticing. "Too bad my motto is No keepers," she said softly, breathlessly.

"Then maybe . . ." Though he knew he shouldn't, he raised his hand, slid a finger underneath a strand of hair that had escaped her braid, and tucked it behind her ear. "Maybe we should work on finding you a new motto."

She moistened her lips with the tip of her tongue. "Please, J.D."

"You don't have to say please."

"Please don't—"

"You *really* shouldn't say don't."

Her laughter was wobbly and unsteady as she backed away. "You are—"

He folded his arms across his chest to keep from reaching out to her again, then leaned against the wall. "Incredible? Amazing?"

"Insufferable. Impossible. Are you *sure* my office approved you to foster those kids?"

"You've got the papers, signed and approved."

As if the mention of papers jogged her memory, she glanced down at her briefcase, then back at him. "Mrs. Duncan."

He blinked, shifted mental gears. "Room 7B. Back to the central desk, turn right. I'll show you."

"I can find it."

"Then I'll follow you." And enjoy every step of the way, he thought as she retraced their path. Of course, for maximum enjoyment, he wished her long, full dress would be replaced by something shorter, snugger, and a little more revealing. But even with long and full, it was a view to be appreciated.

"Definitely impossible," she murmured as she passed elderly twin sisters with matching blue hair.

And she sounded as if she meant it.

Chapter Nine

O N SATURDAY THE CIRCUS CAME TO town.

Well, not exactly the circus. Carnival, Kelsey supposed, was a more appropriate description for the assemblage on the empty field behind the high school. She'd jogged by there early that morning and watched as burly men in sleeveless shirts that showed their tattoos set up the rides and booths. She'd even earned a whistle from a man with a dark and wicked smile. She'd stick to the safe, respectable type, thank you.

Ten hours later, as she walked through the gate and her gaze lit immediately on J.D., she faced an inescapable fact. Safe and respectable could, depending on its package, be far more dangerous than all the dark, wicked smiles in the world.

He was standing in front of a game booth with the kids. He wore shorts and a T-shirt, like the majority of the men present, and a Chicago Cubs cap pulled low over his eyes.

He looked like any other father out with his family. All that was missing was the mother.

Kelsey turned away, heading off down one side of the midway instead. She felt funny coming to a carnival alone. Everywhere she looked, she was surrounded by couples, families, friends, and there she was, by herself. But she had friends, and when she ran into them, they would invite her to join them.

Just as J.D. would have invited her to join *them*.

She stopped to watch a teenage boy trying to win a prize to impress a pretty teenage girl. The prize was small—a little pink bear—but his success earned him a kiss, and not the chaste peck on the cheek *she* would have given at that age. The pretty girl put a lip lock on the boy that brought catcalls from their friends nearby.

"Would you ever have dreamed of kissing a boy like that in public when you were her age?"

Kelsey turned to find Maggie McKinney and her husband standing beside her. "I wouldn't have dreamed of kissing a boy like that in private when I was her age," she replied.

"Me neither. Of course, at her age, I wasn't even allowed to date."

"Which probably explains why you were married just a couple years later," her husband added dryly. He extended his hand. "Ross McKinney."

"Kelsey Malone." They shook hands, then Ross immediately reclaimed his wife's hand.

"Are you enjoying the carnival?" Maggie asked.

"I just got here. Haven't even had a chance to sample the cotton candy."

"It's wonderful, but don't take my word for it. Try the candied apples too. And the sausage with sweet peppers. And the big pretzels."

"And don't forget the antacids," Ross added. "That's

where we're headed now—home to the antacids and to rest."

Maggie scowled at him. "I don't need to rest."

"Right. You walk funny for the hell of it."

"Jeez, you break a bone or two . . ."

"You broke your hip and your leg. It took you months to learn to walk again. You—"

Maggie laid her fingers over his mouth. "All right," she said softly. "Quit frowning like that, and I'll go home with you. Maybe I'll even give you a kiss that'll make that girl look like an amateur." Drawing her fingers back, she brushed her mouth across his. "Okay?"

Kelsey watched as his entire expression softened. When was the last time a man had looked at her like that? More accurately, had a man *ever* looked at her like that? She couldn't recall, which was a pretty good indication that the answer was no.

The McKinneys said their farewells, and Kelsey resumed her stroll, feeling more alone than before. What had she been thinking when she'd decided to come? Carnivals were *not* solitary pursuits. Eating junk food, people-watching, riding the rides—somewhere was an unwritten law that those activities required two or more participants. They just couldn't be done and enjoyed alone.

She was about to slink back to her car and go home, when Holly McBride called her name. She held up two sodas, then gestured toward the picnic tables off to one side.

"Are you here alone?" Kelsey asked as she sat down.

"No, but I might as well be." Holly skimmed her hand over hair that wouldn't dare muss. "Tom Flynn's in town. Ross McKinney's lawyer?"

Ruthless, arrogant, reasonably attractive. Kelsey remembered.

"I had to get Ross to practically order Tom to take the

afternoon off and come here with us, but ever since we got here, he's spent the whole time working. His pager's constantly going off, and if he's not on his cell phone, it's ringing, and get this. The man has his computer in the car so he can get faxes and e-mail. It's a *carnival*, for heaven's sake!"

"Dump him," Kelsey said flatly. "Trade him for someone with more potential."

"You're right. I should. But he's such a challenge." Holly gave a great, dramatic sigh, then her smile turned devilish. "J.D.'s here."

"I saw him."

"Doesn't he make a great family man? If, of course, a family's what you're looking for, which, of course, you are, aren't you?"

Kelsey fiddled with the paper she'd stripped from her straw, rolling it into a tiny ball before tossing it aside. "Tell me about Maggie and Ross."

"Oooh, changing the subject. How interesting." Holly took a long drink of her soda before dutifully beginning to speak. "Maggie and Ross were poor college students when they got married. But Ross was ambitious, like Tom, and driven, like Tom, and before anyone knew it, he had his own company and was worth millions, like Tom. The millions, at least. Not the company. Apparently Tom's quite happy working for Ross."

"So ruthless-arrogant-and-attractive is worth millions?" Kelsey's voice quavered a bit at the end. "I just advised you to dump a man who's worth *millions*?"

In all seriousness, Holly leaned forward. "It's not the money, honestly," she said, and Kelsey believed her. "He's just so . . ." Eyes wide, she shrugged, unable to finish the sentence. "Anyway, back to the McKinneys. Ross was obsessed with turning his millions into billions, and Maggie never saw him, and their marriage fell apart. She was leaving him one Christmas Eve in a blizzard, and she drove off the side of the mountain. She almost died. When she got out of rehab eleven months later, he agreed to live here with her while she got settled, and then they would divorce, and instead they fell in love all over again."

Romantic story. But part of Kelsey's mind was still focused on Tom Flynn. "Millions," she repeated. "If you decide to toss him back, could you toss him my way?"

"Tom's not your type," Holly said dismissively.

"What's not my type about handsome, powerful, and rich? And what *is* my type? A poor-as-a-churchmouse preacher? A barely-making-the-mortgage teacher?"

"Or maybe a comfortably well-off psychiatrist."

Kelsey groaned. "You know, I find it interesting that everyone's been eager to introduce me to people in Bethlehem, but I haven't yet met one other single man. Are there any, or is this some sort of matchmaking scam?"

"There's Dean Elliott. He's an artist, a little moody. Does these great sculptures that absolutely fascinate me, but I don't want to look too closely into the mind that creates them. And there's Sebastian Knight. Nice guy, a carpenter, lives out by J.D.'s new house, but I don't think he's ever gotten over his wife."

"She died?"

"Nah. She left him, just packed up and moved out. Didn't even kiss him or their little girl good-bye. Let's see, who else is single . . ." She tapped a nail against her lower lip while she thought, then suddenly smiled. "Well, well, look who's wandering back. Say, you look rather familiar. Your name wouldn't happen to be Tom, would it?"

Kelsey twisted on the bench to get a good look at the second richest man she'd ever been close to. He wasn't particularly handsome, but there was character in the hard lines of his face. Not necessarily *good* character, but character all the same.

A certain vulnerability flashed through his eyes when he looked at Holly, as if he didn't know what to do with her. As if he didn't trust what she might do to him. Kelsey would have been charmed if it didn't make her feel like the last unattached person in the whole entire world.

Holly didn't make introductions, but Kelsey understood. Better snatch what time she could get with the man before business called again.

She returned Holly's wave, then turned around to sit on the bench, the edge of the table warm against her back. She sipped her soda and watched the people passing by, occasionally responding to a greeting from someone she'd met. She was thinking once again of going home, when suddenly the bench shifted underneath her, and a tall figure slid in close.

"Hey, darlin'. I thought I recognized those legs."

That morning she'd thought he was dark and wicked— and he was even more so up close. He was the sort of man who would ride a Harley. His jeans were snug enough to leave little to the imagination, and his white T-shirt was stretched to the limits across his broad chest. He was the perfect bad boy for every bad girl—or wanna-be—in the free world.

And he didn't even make her heart beat fast. Didn't make her hot. Didn't make her search her memory for the sultriest, naughtiest come-on she'd ever heard.

Leaning forward, she made a show of looking at the few inches of her legs that showed beneath the hem of her long skirt. "Really? You recognize these legs? Describe them to me."

"They've got ankles, two of 'em. And knees. And thighs."

"You can see the ankles. That doesn't count."

He laughed and suddenly looked neither wicked nor bad. "You *are* the one who went jogging past here this morning though, aren't you? There can't be too many women in this little burg with hair like that."

"I do my best to keep it under control," she said dryly.

"Oh, no, darlin'. You should wear it down, wild and free, so a man can appreciate it."

"Uh-huh." She was about to glance away, when fifty pounds of warm, grubby kid launched itself against her.

"Mama, Mama, there you are! We been looking for you forever! You gotted lost!"

"Mama?" Dark and Wicked echoed.

"No, she's mistaken. I'm not." Kelsey maneuvered the wriggling child back far enough to get a look at her. "Gracie. What are you doing?"

Now the wicked smile was adorning a normally cherubic five-year-old face. "We been lookin' for you, and now we found you. See?" She flung her arm out, one finger pointing, and Kelsey followed it to their small audience: Caleb, Jacob, and Noah, all looking impressively solemn, and J.D., enjoying his joke entirely too much.

Dark and Wicked leaned closer. "Apparently one man's already appreciated you wild and free. Later, darlin'."

"Later," she murmured, watching him walk away with a purely dispassionate appreciation for the view. As she turned her attention back to the others, Gracie disentangled herself and returned to J.D., tilting her head far back so she could see his face.

"How was that?" she asked proudly. "See, I told you I could too pretend."

"You did, and you were right."

"So where's my cotton candy?"

J.D. pulled some bills from his pocket and offered them to Caleb. "Get everyone a soda and a snack, then meet us back here. Hold on to Gracie."

Caleb scowled but took the money with one hand, Gracie's hand with the other, and started in the opposite direction.

"Bribing a child with food. Surely an eminent psychiatrist should know better," Kelsey chided.

"This eminent psychiatrist knows to use what works, and with Gracie, food works." He sat down beside her, closer than Dark and Wicked had. "Besides, he wasn't your type."

His arm rested on the table behind her, close enough so she could feel the warmth, or was that just her imagination overheating?

Forcing her gaze away, she concentrated on the conversation. "You're the second person this evening who's tried to tell me what my type is. I find that incredible, since *I'm* not even certain what my type is."

"It isn't a guy like that."

"Apparently *he* disagreed with you."

"A guy like that picks up women everywhere he goes. If you're alive and breathing, you'll do."

"So you're saying his standards are so low that any woman can meet them. Gee, thanks, Doc. You work wonders for my ego."

He didn't look the least bit chagrined. "His standards are different because he's looking for something different—a few hours' fun, maybe even a whole night, and then he'll never see them again."

"And what are other men looking for? Or, more to the point, since you're the one discoursing here, what are *you* looking for?"

J.D. simply held her gaze while he considered the answer. A month ago, he thought, it would have been an easy one, pretty much the same as the tough guy, though on a longer-term basis. A few weeks, maybe even a few months, of pleasure before the woman realized she was giving more than she was getting. That the relationship wasn't going anywhere. That whatever he felt for her was superficial and shallow. A month ago he would have been satisfied with that.

Now he wouldn't be.

But maybe now he wouldn't have to be. Maybe he could have more.

"Is that such a difficult question?" Kelsey prompted.

"No, the question's not tough at all. The answer though . . ." He shrugged and blatantly changed the subject. "Have you ridden any of the rides?"

"I think I'm getting taken for a ride right now."

"Mrs. Larrabee is going to take the kids home at six and get them bathed, fed, and into bed. We'll ride the Ferris wheel then. You haven't lived until you've seen Bethlehem at night from the top of the Ferris wheel."

"I've seen Bethlehem from the top of the mountain," she pointed out, and he shrugged as if that didn't count. "Not with me." After a moment's silence he glanced at her. "What would you have done if Gracie hadn't interrupted? Would you have gone with him?"

"Who says he would have asked?"

His gaze slid from her hair, tied back with a scarf, over her dress—mossy green, long, and perfectly modest, yet exposing a good deal of smooth, soft skin. Her sandals were nothing more than a few delicate straps crisscrossing long, delicate feet, and she wore that fragrance again. "He would have asked," he replied, his voice huskier, his body warmer than they should have been. "Trust me. So what would you have answered?"

She gazed away. Her smile was barely formed, equal parts innocence, womanly satisfaction, and curiosity. Considering the possibilities? Savoring the fact that every woman's decadent fantasy had been about to offer the fantasy to her?

"I would have said yes and slipped away to heat up the night doing wild and depraved things best not spoken of in the light of day," she said in a dreamy voice.

J.D. swallowed hard, then did it again. Spoken of, hell. Kelsey, wild and depraved, was best not *thought* of in the light of day either.

Her voice returned to normal. "More likely I would thank him for the invitation, but, while I find him incredibly attractive, he really isn't my type."

"He wasn't *that* good-looking," he said with a scowl.

"I would worry if you thought he was. There's Mrs. Larrabee."

"And there are the kids." He gestured in the opposite direction, where Caleb was herding the kids toward them. He was patient with them, stopping to let them listen to a barker's spiel, keeping a close watch on them as people passed by. Something about him seemed so familiar—the way he stood, the way he tilted his head to watch the show. For one blessed moment J.D. didn't realize what it was. Then, with a pang, it hit him—Trey. *He* had stood that way, looking relaxed on the outside but filled with anger and resentment on the inside. He tilted his head like that, watching people and things he didn't quite trust through narrowed eyes like that.

The last few times they'd been together, he'd looked at J.D. like that.

Swallowing hard, he forced his attention away from them. The last thing he wanted just then was to be reminded of Trey. Those were memories he couldn't handle, not today, not with Caleb slowly heading this way.

"Have they had a good time?"

He listened to his own breathing, short and harsh, and made a conscious attempt to sound perfectly normal before answering. "I think so. They've eaten enough junk food to last a year, and they've ridden every ride at least twice and played every game more than twice. Jacob's pretty good at the pitching games. I told him I'd dig out my old mitt and practice with him, then see if we can still get him on a summer team." His grin was rusty and felt phony, but he didn't think she noticed. "I played in college. Does that impress you?"

"Do I look the type to be impressed by a jock?"

"You were impressed by a thug. Why not a jock?"

"Were you any good?"

"Sweetheart, I'm *very* good. Want me to show you?"

She rolled her eyes, then returned to the subject. "Is everything else all right with the kids?"

"We're holding our own. Since the visit to the nursing home on Tuesday, Noah's opened up a bit more, and both Jacob and Gracie were interested in tagging along next time. Until Caleb gave them one of his looks."

"You need to practice the divide-and-conquer theory," she said, her voice softening as the kids drew closer. "As long as Caleb exerts so much influence over them, they're going to be harder to reach. Separate them from him, though, and they'll be much easier to win over."

"And when that happens, Caleb's going to be more difficult than ever," J.D. muttered. He'd agreed with Noelle in the beginning that the children should be kept together, but now that they were adapting to their situation and to him, life would be easier all around if Caleb were placed elsewhere. Well, maybe not easier for Caleb. The kids had been the reason for everything he'd done for so long, he would find it difficult to let them go. He wouldn't know what to do without them, wouldn't know who to be.

"Hello, J.D., Kelsey." Mrs. Larrabee's pleased smile included them both. "I wondered if you had a date this evening. I have to say, I'm happy to see you do."

"Oh, it's not—" Before Kelsey could finish her correction, the kids descended on them. Gracie immediately demanded Mrs. Larrabee's attention to show off the yellow rabbit J.D. had won for her in the ring toss, and Noah sidled up between J.D.'s feet.

"Look. Blue." He stuck out his tongue to show that it matched the Sno-Kone he held. So did the drips on his shirt, his shorts, and his shoes. "I never had a—"

"Blue tongue before," J.D. said in unison with him. "Mrs. Larrabee, you want us to clean them up before you head off?"

"Oh, what's a little Sno-Kone and cotton candy in my car?" she asked carelessly. "What time is bedtime?"

"Eight-thirty," the younger three answered together.

"So it's baths, then dinner, then bed." Mrs. Larrabee gave J.D. a sly wink. "You can stay out as late as you'd like. The children are in good hands. Come along now, kids."

As soon as they were out of sight, Kelsey punched his shoulder. "You let her believe this is a date."

"I didn't let her believe anything. She just assumed it was." He rubbed his shoulder with exaggerated motions. "Hey, you've got a pretty good jab there."

"An assumption you didn't bother to correct, and my right hook is even better. Don't make me prove it."

"Well, you didn't make much of an effort to correct her yourself. Besides, look at the facts. It's Saturday night. You and I are alone. Together. We're going to have a little entertainment, a little dinner, and a little good night—"

"Handshake at the gate," she interrupted. "You didn't even ask me if I wanted to see the carnival with you."

"You're right. I didn't." He put some distance between them and asked seriously, "Kelsey, would you like to come to the carnival with me tonight?"

She pretended to consider it before grudgingly saying, "All right, but it's *not* a date."

He drew her to her feet, then stepped closer than the

situation called for. "Who are you trying to convince? Mrs. Larrabee, who's gone? Me? Or yourself?"

She gave him a startled look, then moved away without answering. Missing that instant of closeness, he turned to follow her.

They walked along the midway, stopping to talk with friends, sharing cotton candy, playing a game or two. She won an elephant. He won a stuffed 'gator that she promptly christened Al. After a while they went to the food court, where she got an Italian sausage and sweet peppers on a bun. In deference to the sweets he'd snacked on all afternoon, he chose a plain hot dog.

"What do you want to drink?"

She eyed the choices listed on a chalkboard beside the cash register. "Beer."

"Should I make that two?" the helpful clerk asked.

J.D. considered it. There was something incredibly satisfying about a beer at the end of a long, hot day. If he closed his eyes, he could almost taste it—cold, smooth, full-flavored. But he didn't close his eyes. "One beer, one lemonade."

"Are you not a drinker?" Kelsey asked as they carried paper plates and cups through a maze of tables and folding chairs to a distant, unoccupied table.

"You should know I'm not. It's in your files."

"I can get something else if you prefer. I mean, if this is a strong conviction of yours."

"I try not to make rules for other people to live by," he said as he slid into a chair. "Just because I don't drink doesn't mean others can't."

"Why don't you?"

He smiled faintly. "Make rules? Most people wouldn't follow them."

"Why don't you drink?"

"For a number of reasons. I'm on call pretty much all

the time. I never know when someone's going to need me, and I can't risk being impaired when they do." He shrugged. "I've worked too hard to get in shape. You're going to have to run about two miles to burn off the calories in that one cup."

She paused, cup halfway to her mouth, then offered her own shrug. "And how many miles will you have to do to burn off the sugar in that lemonade?"

"Point taken." He squirted a glob of mustard onto his hot dog, then took a bite. Away from the carnival, it was a quiet, peaceful evening without much traffic or anything going on. He'd spent many such Saturday nights at his house in the woods, sleeping bag spread out on the deck, no lights but the stars, no distractions.

Of course, distractions could be good or bad. When a man needed quiet to think or remember, distractions were a pain. When he didn't *want* to think or remember, they were a blessing.

He wasn't sure how he would classify the distractions tonight. If he were alone with Kelsey, with no carnival, no noise, no people, God only knows what might happen. And only God knows whether whatever happened would be good or bad. Whether it would heal or hurt. Whether he would regret it, or she would, or maybe both.

Or whether it would, just possibly, be a blessing.

"Jefferson Davis."

He shifted his attention back to her.

"Jefferson Davis," she repeated. "For J.D."

He shook his head.

"Jeremiah Darnell."

"Nope."

"Give me a hint."

"No way. That would be cheating. Why don't you look in your files?"

"I did. It says just J.D. If Noelle got your full name, she

didn't include it in her notes. And a hint's not cheating. Do you know how many names begin with *J* and *D*?"

"More than a few, I imagine. But you need only two."

"Two out of hundreds, maybe thousands," she scoffed. "It hardly seems fair when I've told you my full name, my brother's name, and even my parents' names."

"Yes, but you volunteered the information. I didn't ask."

"Why the big secret? Is it a really awful name?"

"Depends on your definition of awful, I suppose. My mother and father must have liked it. After all, they stuck me with it." He hesitated, then took her hand in his. "I think the more interesting question is why the big deal. Everyone in town has been perfectly content to call me J.D. You're the only one who cares what it stands for."

The instant his fingers had closed around hers, she'd become very still. Finally she took a careful breath and gently tugged. He didn't let go.

"I wouldn't exactly say I *care*," she said in a voice that was breathier, less substantial than usual. "It's just that your refusal to answer has aroused my curiosity."

There were other things he'd much rather be arousing, but he didn't say so. He didn't need to, judging by the flush that heated her cheeks and the insistence with which she pulled free.

She busied herself with cleaning up the remains of their meal, then gave him a too-bright smile. "Well . . . I'd better be getting home soon, so how about that Ferris wheel ride?"

They waited in line at the Ferris wheel, standing side by side, looking mostly in opposite directions. When their turn came, she stepped into the car first and slid to one side. Even so, mere inches separated them once he was seated.

"Did I mention that I really prefer to have solid ground under my feet at all times?" she asked conversationally.

The attendant closed and locked the safety bar, then signaled a second attendant to lower the next car.

"Do you realize it's a little late to bring that up?" J.D. teased as the car jerked into motion. "Are you afraid of heights?"

"No."

"Are you afraid of *me*?"

She gave him a long, long look, then tossed her head and turned away so he had to strain to hear her answer. "Maybe."

Good.

The car rocked gently as the wheel began spinning. The carnival below became a dizzying mix of trailing lights, sounds, and smells, intensifying as they swept down, diminishing as they climbed high again.

"Mr. Ferris was a bright man," Kelsey said, brushing back a strand of hair that had blown free. "It's really a simple design to have stayed popular for so long."

"Simple pleasures are the best."

"Such as?"

"Sitting on the deck at dusk. Sunday dinners at the Winchesters' house. Watching fireworks on the Fourth from City Park." He paused, and she turned to look at him. "Watching you."

She tried to smile, but her mouth refused to cooperate. Instead, she settled for looking away again.

After a moment of pleasantly edgy silence, he leaned close to her and pointed toward one of the booths. "There's your guy."

The man who'd come on to her had found someone more receptive, and they were sharing a very intimate kiss behind the ring toss booth.

"Imagine, that could be you."

Kelsey burst out laughing. "I don't think so. I don't kiss on first dates."

"He would have been sorely disappointed."

"Nah. If we hadn't been interrupted, we would've talked a few minutes more and he would've realized that I wasn't his type."

"Would *you* have been disappointed?"

"Nah. He's too easy."

Well, if there was one thing J.D. knew he wasn't, it was easy. He carried too much emotional baggage, had too much past and not enough future. Would that put her off? Or was she the sort who liked a challenge?

He didn't know the answer to either question, but he might enjoy finding out.

The ride ended. In silent agreement they turned toward the entrance. At the unmanned ticket booth Kelsey looked at her stuffed elephant as if she didn't remember where it came from, then offered it to him. "Why don't you give this to the kids?"

"Thanks." He crammed it under his left arm with the 'gator, then extended his hand. "I enjoyed it."

"Me too." With an endearingly awkward gesture she shook hands with him. "I'll see you around."

"I'm hard to avoid." He let her walk a few feet away before he caught up with her.

"What?"

"That was your good-night handshake at the gate. Now I'm going to walk you to your car."

"It's just over there. There are lights and people all around. You don't have to—"

"I want to."

That silenced her.

They cut between cars to the far side of the makeshift

lot. He waited while she unlocked the door, then tossed her purse inside. "Thanks," she said when she turned back to face him. "Now do we have to repeat the handshake again?"

"No. Now I get my kiss."

The car door was between them—probably a good thing, he acknowledged as he slid his fingers into her hair. He figured one good kiss was about all it would take to make him forget caution, common sense, his reputation, and hers. A little distance was a good thing.

But a little intimacy was better, and a whole lot of intimacy . . .

He took her mouth, coaxed her lips apart, then her teeth, and she made a soft little sound—part whimper, part moan, all erotic. She brought her hands to his shoulders, but she neither drew him near nor pushed him away. She simply held on. He understood the need. Hell, he shared it.

Moving on their own, his fingers found the scarf that secured her hair and worked loose the knot, pulled it away, let her hair fall free. He wound long, silky curls around his hands and restlessly, anxiously, moved closer, only to meet the barrier of the car door.

The metal and glass reminded him that they were standing in a field right outside the carnival, where every soul they knew could walk past at any moment. It reminded him all too clearly that there was no way she was going home with him that night, no way she was taking him home with her.

He freed his hands first, then ended the kiss, but he didn't step back. In the dim light he stared at her, and she stared back, her lips parted, her expression slightly stunned—and a lot turned on.

"I . . ." Her mouth moved, but the sound was negligible. She breathed deeply, then tried again. "I don't kiss on first dates."

"I know." He didn't resist the urge to brush one small kiss to her forehead before he started toward his truck. A safe distance away, he turned again and managed a grin far cockier than he felt. "But this wasn't a date. Remember?"

Chapter Ten

CALEB WAS SOMEWHERE BETWEEN SLEEP AND wakefulness, on the edge of a dream he didn't want to leave, a dream that he was home, lying in his own bed, listening to his dad out in the kitchen. Sometimes his dad worked late, even long after it was dark, and didn't eat supper until the kids were asleep. Nights when he wasn't too tired, Caleb would get out of bed and sit at the kitchen table with him. Sometimes they talked. Sometimes they didn't. Either way, they were still just about his most favorite times.

But the more awake part of his brain knew that he wasn't home, he wasn't in his own bed, and that wasn't his dad shuffling around out there. It was *him*, Grayson.

Giving up trying to hold on to the dream, he leaned over the side of the bed to see the clock. It wasn't even nine-thirty yet. Not much of a date, he thought scornfully. Maybe the welfare lady was too smart to fall for his lies. Probably not though. After all, hadn't she left them with him?

He rolled onto his back and stared up. Light came from the hall and through the window, throwing weird shadows across the ceiling. Some nights he tried to make out things, like they used to do with clouds, but late in the night there weren't any birds or animals or trains to be found. There were just shapes that sometimes moved and were a little bit scary.

Everything at night was a little bit scary.

Down the hall the television came on, turned loud enough for him to hear but too low to understand. Footsteps went to the bathroom, then back. After a few minutes they came again, this time right to the bedroom door. Long shadows that looked nothing like a man stretched across the ceiling, over Caleb's head to the wall behind him.

"Caleb?"

He closed his eyes, held his breath.

"You know, you're kind of old to have an eight-thirty bedtime. If you want to stay up awhile, you can. You can watch TV or read or here's a novel idea—we could talk."

His lungs burning, Caleb eased out a little air, then sucked in a bit more. Other than that he didn't even twitch a muscle.

"Or you can lie there, pretending to be asleep until you really do fall asleep. It's your choice."

At the sound of footsteps leaving, Caleb opened his eyes. The shadow was gone.

He didn't know if Grayson had really known he was awake or just guessed. He hoped he knew that Caleb would rather lie awake in the dark than spend even a minute with him. He hoped the shrink knew just exactly how much he didn't like him or trust him or want him around.

Even if he was bored lying awake in the dark.

Even if he did hate the dark.

Even if he did like the idea of having a different bedtime because he was the oldest and most grown up.

His stomach growled, and he rubbed one hand over it. Mrs. Larrabee had fixed soup and sandwiches after they had their baths, but everyone had been too tired and too full from all the carnival food to eat. She'd wrapped everything and put it in the refrigerator in case they got hungry later.

Down the hall the microwave dinged, and a moment later he smelled something tomatoey. Soup? The pizza left over from last night's dinner? His stomach growled louder, and his mouth began to water. He tried to ignore the hunger. He knew how to keep busy doing other things, to think hard about other things, but tonight he just couldn't make it work.

He slid out of bed, careful not to wake Gracie below. Just a sandwich, that was all he was getting. A sandwich and a glass of milk, and he'd eat at the table in the dining room. He wouldn't even have to look at the shrink, much less speak to him.

Only one light was on in the living room, that and the TV. Caleb looked from the corner of his eye as he passed and saw Grayson lying on the couch, pizza leftovers on a plate in front of him on the coffee table.

In the kitchen the light over the sink was on and was all he needed. He put a sandwich on a saucer, poured a glass of milk, and sat down at the table.

"You might as well come in and watch TV while you eat," the shrink said from around the corner.

He stubbornly remained where he was as he took a bite, chewed, and washed it down with milk.

"You had a good time at the carnival, didn't you? Not as good as you would have had if I weren't there, I know, but it was fun, wasn't it?"

Caleb ignored him and concentrated on eating.

"I saw Alanna Dalton there with her family."

Caleb's stomach got a pain in it. He'd seen Alanna too, had even said hi to her once. She'd said hi, then Susan Walker poked her and her face had gotten all red, and they'd run off together, whispering and giggling behind their hands. He'd felt like an idiot.

Alanna was so pretty, just like a doll his mother used to have. She left all of them behind, but she took the doll with her. Wasn't hard to figure out who she loved most.

He hated that doll almost as much as he hated his mother, but it *was* pretty and it did remind him of Alanna. It also reminded him that *he* was the unimportant one. He was the one who got left behind.

Suddenly the light over the dining table came on. The shrink stood there by the switch, watching him. "I see mention of Alanna made you get awfully quiet."

Because Grayson was the last person in the world he wanted to know what he thought about Alanna, he scowled as hard as he could and said, "I was already quiet."

The chair across the table scraped on the floor as the shrink sat down. "I think she likes you."

For just a second, hope made it hard to breathe, but just as quickly as it came, it went away. She didn't like him. She was nice to him sometimes because . . . Well, he didn't know why. Probably because her aunt made her be nice to everybody. But today she'd been embarrassed to talk to him, and she'd run off to make sure no one thought she might know him or anything.

"It's hard for kids when they like someone," the shrink said. "Especially girls Alanna's age. They're kind of silly sometimes, giggling with their girlfriends about it, getting embarrassed really easily."

So she was mean because she liked him. Hell, then his mother must have loved him a whole lot. Only his mother hadn't loved him at all. That stupid doll had meant more to her than all four of them and their dad put together. And Alanna was ashamed to talk to him when kids from school were around.

But that was okay. He didn't need his mother, and he sure didn't need Alanna. As long as he had the kids, that was all that mattered.

"What do you—"

A whine from down the hall made him stop. Gracie came from the bedroom, dragging her yellow rabbit behind by its ear, her hair sticking out all over, and she was whimpering. "I doan feel good."

Before Caleb could go to her, the shrink held his arms out and Gracie went right to him, climbing up on his lap. Caleb filled with anger and fear. He stomped around the table. "Give her to me."

Grayson ignored him. "What's wrong, Gracie?"

Caleb started to reach for her, but the shrink blocked him with his arm. The look on his face was full of warning.

Clenching his fists at his sides, Caleb repeated his words, angrier now, demanding, "Give her to me."

Gracie gave him an annoyed look. "Leave me alone, Caleb. Go 'way. I'm talkin' to Dr. J.D." Then, looking sweet and pitiful again, she said, "My stomach hurts *real bad*."

Grayson felt her forehead, then combed her hair back the way Caleb always did when she woke up crying in the middle of the night. But *he* had the right to do that. Grayson didn't.

"You know why your stomach hurts? Because your stomach's about this big"—he showed her with his hands—"and you've stuffed it with hot dogs and corn dogs and candied apples and—"

"And cotton candy and Sno-Kones." She started to giggle, then clamped her hand over her mouth and wailed, "I doan feel good! I think I'm gonna be——" Her eyes got real big and her face turned white, and all of a sudden she puked all over Grayson. It splattered his shirt and shorts and ran down his legs to the floor, and it made him turn white too.

Caleb backed off to where the smell wasn't so strong, then said as innocently as he could, "Gee, you probably feel better now, Gracie. I know I do. See you in the morning."

If Gracie had come to him, he'd have taken her straight to the bathroom just in case she did puke. But, no, she'd gone crying to *Dr. J.D.* instead, who was dumb enough to sit there, holding her on his lap when she was about to spill her guts. It was their own fault. Let them deal with it.

And he would try real hard to forget that Gracie *had* gone crying to Grayson. Just as Noah had the other day when his shoe needed tying, she'd chosen him over Caleb.

Please, God, don't let it happen again.

E VERY MONDAY FOR A HUNDRED AND EIGHTY-one years, the Ladies Auxiliary of the First Church of Bethlehem had met for lunch, fellowship, and community service. Winchesters had been active in the group from the beginning, and Corinna and Agatha were no exception. They'd done many good works over the years, shared thousands of tasty meals, and made friendships that had lasted a lifetime. Corinna's daughters and daughters-in-law and now one of her granddaughters were continuing the tradition, a fact that made her heart proud.

This particular Monday the group's makeup was not the usual, as many adults were on vacation and a large number of children, who were on summer holiday, attended. Corinna stood in the doorway that led from the kitchen to the dining hall and gazed across the crowd. The ladies, along with an occasional baby, filled the tables along one side of the hall. The children sat on the other side, creating their own small groups, with one notable exception.

Caleb sat at the near end of the long row, his lunch barely touched. Other children sat in the chairs on either side, but for all the attention they paid him, and vice versa, he might as well have been alone.

"He could break your heart, couldn't he?"

Corinna glanced up as Lucie Smith came from the kitchen with two cakes for the dessert table. Lucie taught fifth grade at the elementary school and had had both Caleb and Alanna in her class. "Yes," she agreed. "He certainly could."

"And, of course, it had to be that bunch who sat by him. That Kenny Howard . . ." She looked at Kenny's mother at the far end of the room, then shook her head. "That child shouldn't be allowed in public without a gag and restraints. You'd think the reverend and his wife would hold him to a higher standard of behavior, but no. They think their precious little darling can do no wrong."

Corinna smiled gently. "You know Fern lost several babies. The doctors told her she'd never have a child, and then Kenny came along. We can't fault them for doting on him."

"No, we can't," Lucie acknowledged, but she wasn't chastened for long. "But it's possible to dote on a child and teach him proper behavior at the same time. You did it with yours. Most people have managed with theirs. Don't the Howards realize they're doing that boy no favors? He's a bully pure and simple, and he's just going to get worse as he gets older unless someone sets limits for him."

Corinna couldn't argue that point with her. Kenny *was* a bully. Why, just last Christmas he'd given Josie Dalton a black eye. And for hitting a younger, smaller girl, his punishment had probably been something as insignificant as losing his computer privileges for a day or two. Hitting a girl never would have crossed *her* boys' minds, and if they had ever committed such an act, well, her Henry would have made sure they never forgot the consequences.

"How did Caleb behave in school?" she asked.

Lucie set the cakes, too heavy to hold for a lengthy conversation, on a nearby table. "About like that. Some of the kids openly made fun of him. Others kept their distance because he was different. He was defensive and wary and stayed away from just about everyone. Except Alanna. She tried to be friends with him, and, for the most part, he let her."

Corinna's gaze shifted to the other end of the table, where Alanna sat with her girlfriends. Corinna had overheard her directing Susan to sit by Caleb, but Kenny and his friends had beaten them to the seats. She wished Alanna had asked Caleb to join them, but she hadn't, and now he sat looking miserable and angry, a misfit who understood too well that he didn't belong.

"Well, I'd better get these cakes to the table over there before everyone stuffs themselves and I have to take them back home. I'd wind up eating them myself, and that's the *last* thing my hips need." Lucie reclaimed her cakes, and Corinna returned to the kitchen.

The church had bought a dishwasher a few years earlier, but she found it as easy to wash the dishes by hand in the double sinks. Besides, someone always came along to help, and she enjoyed the companionship.

The first someone to come along was Caleb. He scraped his leftovers off, then set the dishes on the counter beside her.

"Thank you, Caleb."

For a moment he simply stood there, endearingly awkward. Then he asked, "Can I help?"

"It's not necessary. But if you'd like to, I would enjoy your company. Would you rather wash or dry?"

"Wash."

She moved to the second sink and began rinsing the dishes. Beside her, Caleb went to work with the scrubber.

"You didn't have very pleasant company for lunch," she commented.

"I don't mind."

"With you boys being in the same grade and likely to be in the same class next year, it's a shame you're not friends."

"I don't like them, and they don't like me, so we're even. I just ignore 'em."

"That's probably the best thing you can do with people like that."

From the dining hall came the scraping of chairs and loud voices, followed by Lucie's command. "Hey, you guys scoot those chairs back up to the table so no one trips, then take your dishes in the kitchen."

"Aw, Miss Smith." That was Kenny's voice, and the first to chime in was his best friend, Garth. "That's what the girls are here for."

"Don't 'Aw, Miss Smith' me. Do it now." Lucie was using her best teacher's voice, Corinna noted with a smile. She and Agatha had both retired from teaching years earlier, but they still relied quite often on that voice, because it brought results.

With much grumbling the boys—Kenny and Garth, and their usual cohorts Tim, Rob, and Matt—shuffled into the kitchen. Corinna hoped Caleb would dry his hands and pretend to be merely visiting with her while she worked, but he didn't. With deliberate movements he added another stack of plates to the sink and began washing the top one.

"Look at Caleb," Kenny said with a snicker. "Doin'

dishes. What a dummy. Ever'one knows boys don't wash dishes. That's girls' work."

"Hope you don't get dishpan hands, Caleb," Garth mocked.

"Hey, we thought you was allergic to soap and water, you know, since you come to school dirty all the time." All the boys laughed, Kenny loudest of all.

"That is enough." Corinna stared down all five boys. "Bring your dishes over here, then get out of this kitchen."

The boys obeyed her one at a time, with Garth bringing up the end. "There's no room for my plate. Here, Caleb."

As Caleb turned to take the dish, Garth pretended to stumble and tipped the plate against Caleb's chest. Bits of everything he'd eaten clung to Caleb's shirt—potato salad, green beans, meat loaf, chocolate frosting, and strawberry-tinted whipped cream. "Oops," Garth said coldly. "I tripped."

"Hey, now you're dirty again, like you're used to," Kenny taunted. "*And* you got something to snack on later if you get hungry."

The other three boys backed away a few steps. Caleb stood stiffly, his face crimson, his thin body trembling. Corinna was so angry that she was practically shaking herself. Without bothering to dry her hands, she snatched Garth by the arm, then shook a finger at the other boys. "Get out of here right now. You and I are going to talk to your mother, Garth Nichols."

She shooed the other boys ahead of them and all but dragged Garth from the kitchen, passing Alanna just inside the door. The girl looked as if she might cry. A glance back at Caleb showed that he might, too, if he weren't too proud.

Corinna had a talk with Nora Nichols, who promptly went outside to deal with her son. Back in the kitchen she found Agatha fussing over Caleb, cleaning his shirt with a damp cloth while Alanna silently dried dishes.

"They're horrible children," Agatha said huffily. "Their parents spoil them rotten, never offer them any consistent discipline, and then wonder why they behave so badly."

"Let's just get back to work," Corinna said quietly. "Caleb, you needn't wash dishes if you don't want to."

His words were clipped, his voice tightly controlled. "My dad says except for havin' babies, there's no such thing as women's work and men's work. A person does what he has to do."

"Your dad is exactly right," Agatha agreed.

They worked in an uncomfortably quiet atmosphere until only one load of dishes remained on the counter. "Caleb, would you mind taking this trash bag outside?" Corinna asked as she tied the top into neat knots. "The garbage cans are out this door, down the steps, and around the corner to the left."

As soon as the door closed behind him, Alanna set a serving platter down with more force than necessary. "I *hate* Kenny and Garth."

"Hate what they did, dear, not them," Corinna counseled.

"What they did is just part of who they are. They're mean to everyone, but especially to kids who are . . . are . . ." She sputtered, trying to find the right word.

"Vulnerable."

"Yeah, that, and I hate them!"

While Agatha calmed Alanna, Corinna went to work on the last dishes. After a few minutes, though, she dried her hands. "I'll be right back. I'm just going to see what's taking Caleb so long."

•   •   •

J.D. WAS ON HIS WAY OUT OF THE OFFICE TO A staff meeting when the secretary flagged him down. "Yes, Miss Corinna, he's right here," she said into the phone cradled between her shoulder and ear. "Hang on one second."

He took the phone with a glance at his watch. Staff meetings at Bethlehem Memorial were pretty informal, but, barring emergencies, he generally tried to show up on time. Once this one was over, he was taking the rest of the afternoon off. He was planning to pick up dinner at Harry's and the kids at the Winchesters', then head out to the house for a good four or five hours of work. He might even decide, somewhere along the way, to invite Kelsey along.

"Miss Corinna, what can I do for you?" he asked with a smile. The smile faded as she spoke. When she finished, he said quietly, "I'll be over in a few minutes. Thanks for calling me." He handed the phone back to the secretary. "Call up to the meeting and tell them I'm not going to be able to make it today. I've got a problem with one of the kids."

"Hope it's not too serious," she called as he walked away.

It took only a few minutes to make the drive from the hospital to the church, not nearly enough time for J.D. to calm down. He parked in the back lot, took a few deep breaths, then walked around the corner to the kitchen door.

On one side of the room, surrounded by fussing women, was Kenny Howard. Miss Agatha, Miss Corinna, and Alanna stood in the middle, wearing identical troubled looks, and just inside the door, arms folded across his chest and by himself, stood Caleb.

Though he bore little physical resemblance to Trey, in that instant they could have been twins. Caleb wore the same anger, the same resentment, and the same bitter hatred as the image of Trey that haunted J.D. He saw Trey's features superimposed on Caleb's, heard Trey's anguished pleas for J.D. to stay away, felt the undeniable burden of his own guilt.

In that instant he knew Caleb had to go.

He stopped in front of the boy, who coldly met his gaze. They stared at each other for several moments, then J.D. looked away, after taking in the mussed hair, the cut lip, the T-shirt stained with food and blood.

Without saying a word he crossed the room, brushed Fern Howard aside, and pulled the bloody towel from Kenny's face. The boy's nose was puffy, but the swelling was no more than J.D. would expect from a solid punch. Pushing the towel back in place, next he removed the ice pack Nora Nichols was holding to Kenny's left eye. It was swollen too, and discoloring quickly, but it was no more impressive than the shiners Kenny had given other kids over the years.

"That boy shouldn't be here." Fern's voice was soft, but in the still room it carried easily. "I realize he's troubled and you're trying to help him, but—"

J.D. interrupted her. "You don't realize anything, Fern. Keep his head tilted back and put pressure on his nose, like this." Lifting the towel once again, he pressed his fingertips together just underneath the bridge of the boy's nose. "Keep using the ice pack on his eye. If he has any problems later—an increase in pain, the bleeding won't stop, headaches, whatever—take him to the emergency room. You"—he pointed to Caleb—"come with me."

Caleb pivoted around, pushed through the door, and let it slam behind him. By the time J.D. got outside, he was turning the corner ahead.

"Dr. J.D.!" Alanna caught up with him, grabbed his arm. "It wasn't Caleb's fault!"

"It wasn't Caleb's fault that his fist connected with Kenny's eye? That it almost broke Kenny's nose?"

"But Kenny started it! He's a horrible child, Miss Agatha said so! He deserved a black eye and a broken nose and a whole lot more!"

"Well, Lannie, unfortunately we can't go around giving people what we think they deserve." He turned her back toward the church. "Go back inside. We'll see you later."

He watched until she obeyed, then reluctantly went after Caleb. The boy, looking mutinous and not the least bit remorseful, waited beside the truck. Once they were both settled inside, instead of starting the engine, J.D. faced him. "What happened?"

Caleb stared straight ahead. "I hit him."

"I'd say that was fairly obvious. Why?"

He simply shook his head.

His silence sharpened the edge to J.D.'s voice. "You don't have an answer? You don't know why? You hit him for no reason?"

This time he offered no response at all.

J.D. breathed in deeply, seeking patience and trying to separate Trey and Caleb in his mind and in his emotions. When he was calmer, he tried again. "Alanna says it's not your fault. She says Kenny started it."

Caleb's eyes shifted just a bit toward J.D., then he caught himself and stared even harder at the stone wall in front of them.

"Of course that's no surprise. Kenny usually does start it. But you were wrong to finish it."

He expected the boy to protest, to defend himself, to tell him that he didn't know what the hell he was talking about, but Caleb didn't say a thing.

"You want to tell your side?"

Not a word.

With a sigh J.D. turned the key. They drove home in

silence. When they walked in the door, the phone was ringing. J.D. looked at the caller ID, then grimaced. "Get cleaned up, then go to your room."

Caleb walked as far as the hallway, then turned back. "I hate you." His voice was flat, dull, so empty of emotion that J.D. had no doubt he meant the words with every fiber of his being.

J.D. lifted the receiver. "You don't waste any time, do you, Ms. Malone? Of course, the Howards don't waste any time either, do they?"

"No. I just got off the phone with Reverend Howard. He was not happy with the way you and I are doing our jobs. Can I come over?"

"Nice of you to ask, considering you have that right, regardless of what I say."

She was silent for a moment. Trying to judge his mood? Lots of luck, because he wasn't sure himself exactly what he was feeling. He was angry—with Kenny for being such a brat, with Caleb for getting into trouble, with himself for not knowing how to handle it. Frustrated because he knew Caleb needed something right now—friendship, understanding, affection, support—that he couldn't give. Guilty because he'd taken responsibility for the boy when he could hardly bear to deal with him. Sick because he was failing. Again.

"If this is a bad time, I can come later," Kelsey said quietly.

"No. Now is fine." Maybe she could provide Caleb what he couldn't.

"I'll be there in a few minutes."

J.D. hung up and started down the hall. As he passed the bathroom, the door opened and Caleb stepped out, his hair wet and slicked back, his soiled clothes in a ball. J.D.'s gaze settled on his mouth, and he reached out to tilt his chin up. "Let me see."

Caleb grabbed his wrist with surprising strength for a skinny, underfed child. *"Don't touch me."*

J.D. forced another couple of deep breaths, then quietly commanded, "Let go of me, Caleb."

After a few moments, Caleb obeyed.

"Don't grab me again."

"Don't *ever* touch me again." Caleb eased past without making contact, threw his clothes through the open laundry room door, then went into the guest room, closing the door quietly behind him.

J.D. stared at the wall, still feeling the throb in his wrist. He didn't need another Trey in his life, couldn't survive another Trey, and he was going to tell Kelsey so as soon as she got there. He would be happy to keep the younger three kids, but Caleb had to go—for his own sake, but most especially for J.D.'s.

The peal of the doorbell made him flinch. Spinning around, he stalked down the hall, opened the door, then went into the kitchen without waiting for Kelsey. She came in, closed the door behind her, then watched as he searched the cabinets.

"Misplace something?" she asked.

He closed the last cabinet door, then leaned against the counter, arms folded across his chest, hands tucked flat so they couldn't knot into fists. "Just my common sense."

"I usually leave mine in the kitchen too, when I grab those bags of chocolate kisses or finish off a half-gallon of ice cream in one sitting." Her faint smile faded when he didn't respond to her teasing. "Where is Caleb?"

"In the guest room."

She started to walk away, then came back. "May I suggest something? You've had the kids for more than two weeks now. Don't you think you could refer to the room where they're sleeping as *their* room?"

He glared at her but said nothing.

"Gee, excuse me while I go talk to someone whose behavior is sure to be a little more adult," she said sarcastically as she turned away.

He wanted to call her back, to tell her that he couldn't keep Caleb any longer. To plead with her to pack the kid's clothes and take him away. To hold her until everything was all right again. But he stood where he was and listened to her footsteps, her knock on the door, her soft "Caleb, may I come in, please?" When the door opened, then closed, and the house became relatively silent again, he jerked open the refrigerator and grabbed a soda.

He *really* needed a drink.

KELSEY LOOKED AROUND THE BEDROOM, NOTICing the changes since the last time she'd been there. There were more books and games on the shelves, and posters hung on the walls. Two were cartoon characters, the third the teenage heartthrob from a recent hit movie. The posters had been prizes at one of the carnival game booths. She'd seen countless other kids carrying them Saturday.

When she stopped to study the movie poster, Caleb finally spoke. "Gracie's never seen any movies except on TV the last couple weeks, and she doesn't have any idea who that is, but the girls ahead of her made a big deal over him, so she wanted it too."

"I don't see as many movies as I used to. I'm not sure *I* know who he is." Kelsey turned toward his bunk. "There's a theater downtown. Maybe some Saturday afternoon we can all go to the movies." Back in the city, she and her single friends had had a regular dinner-and-movie night, since dates to provide the same were few and far between for most of them. She'd always liked that moment in the theater when the lights went down, the screen lit

up, and music swelled from the speakers. She had actually
thought about a solo dinner-and-movie night here, but the
theater's sole screen was home only to second-run family
features. Perfect for the Brown kids, not so perfect for a
single adult out alone.

"Maybe," Caleb muttered. He lay on his back, his bare
toes pointed toward the ceiling. All it would take was one
good growth spurt, and he'd be too big for the bed. But it
wasn't likely to happen in the next few weeks, and after
that he'd be living someplace else.

"Want to sit up and talk to me?"

"No."

"Okay." She laid her bag on the dresser, kicked off her
flats, then started climbing the ladder.

Caleb raised up on one elbow. "Hey, what are you
doing? You can't come up here."

"Why not? The beds seem sturdy enough." Grasping
the footboard, she rocked from side to side, but the bunks
were solid.

"Because you're a grown-up. Grown-ups don't climb
up on bunk beds. Just kids do."

"Oh, so that explains why you're shorter and look so
much younger than me." Gathering her skirt around her,
she eased onto the mattress. He scrambled to sit at the
other end, knees drawn to his chest. She stayed at her end,
legs dangling over the side. "I always wanted bunk beds
when I was a kid, but my mom was afraid I'd fall off the
top. That happened to my brother once at a friend's
house. He had to have sixteen stitches to sew up his head
where he hit his buddy's roller skates." She glanced at him.
"You worry about falling off?"

"No."

"What do you worry about besides your dad?"

He scowled and lowered his gaze. "Nothing."

"You worry about getting in trouble? Maybe getting teased a bit?"

"No."

"You know I got called about what happened at church." She looked at his lip. "I don't think you're going to be eating any lemons for a while. Are you all right?"

"Yeah," he muttered.

"Anything hurt besides your lip and your pride?"

"No."

"You want to tell me what happened? All I have is Kenny Howard's version, and from what I hear, he's not exactly reliable. You took the trash out for Miss Corinna and . . . ?"

He stared down at nothing while his fingers nervously worked against one another. Finally he blew out his breath. "Kenny and his friends was out there. They was mad 'cause Miss Corinna got Garth in trouble for dumping his lunch scraps on my shirt.

"I put the trash in the can and started to leave, but they wouldn't move. They were laughing and saying things, mostly Kenny, and finally I hit him." The look he gave her was so serious, it added ten years to his face. "I warned him first. I told him if he didn't move, I would move him. And he just laughed. So I did."

"You hit him."

"No. I shoved him. Then he hit me, and I hit him back. Twice. And then Miss Corinna came out." He fell silent, then, looking like a child again, asked, "Am I in trouble? Are you gonna arrest me?"

"No, you're not going to get arrested." She reached out to pat his knee and was somewhat surprised that he let her. "You know, Caleb, violence never solves anything. It's always better to walk away." But the words left a sour taste in her mouth because they weren't true. Sometimes violence *did* solve problems. Sometimes walking away was impossible. Still, she went on with the responsible-adult speech. "There are always going to be people like Kenny Howard around. You can't give every one of them bloody noses and black eyes. Your knuckles would get mighty sore if you did."

He glanced down at the reddened knuckles on his right hand and smiled faintly.

"You have to find another way of dealing with them. Right now it might be as simple as avoiding Kenny. Whenever he's around, find some friends and stay close to them. People like Kenny will leave you alone if your friends outnumber his."

"I don't have any friends."

The softly uttered words created a knot in her throat. "So make some. It's not so hard to do."

He looked as if he wanted to argue the point with her, but he didn't. Instead, his features settled into a scowl. "Is *he* gonna make me leave?"

"Leave?"

"And go live somewhere else."

The idea surprised her. J.D. had admitted that he had difficulty relating to Caleb, but he'd also indicated that he was determined to overcome that difficulty. There was no way he would turn his back on him now, particularly for so minor an infraction. "Of course not," she insisted, then thought to ask, "Did he say he was?"

"He didn't say much at all. He was more worried about Kenny than about me. He didn't even ask . . ." His voice trailed off from low to inaudible.

"Didn't even ask what, Caleb?"

He slid lower on the bed, his body twisted awkwardly, the pillow crumpled underneath his head. "He just walked in, looked at Kenny's nose and his eye, and talked to his mom, then pointed at me and said, 'You, come with me.' " He did a creditable imitation of J.D.'s deeper voice. "He didn't even ask if it hurt."

Kelsey climbed down from the bunk, then went to the other end, resting her arms on the mattress, her chin on her hands. "Does it hurt?"

"Yeah. Some. But not bad."

"You know, he's a doctor. He could probably tell it wasn't bad by looking."

"Maybe. But if it'd been Gracie or Noah or Jacob, he'd've asked. If it'd been Gracie or Noah or Jacob, he'd have stood up for 'em and not blamed 'em without finding out what happened. He blamed me. He hates me."

"No, Caleb, you're wrong."

"He does, but that's okay, 'cause I hate him too, and Miss Corinna says that's the best thing to do."

Kelsey was positive something had gotten lost in the translation there, but she didn't question him. She just rested her hand on his shoulder. "No one hates you, Caleb. You're just having a tough time right now. It'll get better, I promise."

"Not until my dad comes back. If he doesn't . . ." He turned onto his side, curled into the fetal position, then fixed his too-adult gaze on her. "Things'll *never* get better."

Chapter Eleven

KELSEY CLOSED THE BEDROOM DOOR, THEN went looking for J.D. She found him in the kitchen, staring out the window over the sink with a can of soda clutched in one hand.

She'd been both looking forward to and dreading seeing him since Saturday night's kiss. It had been so inappropriate . . . and so sweet. On Sunday she'd run a route where she'd never caught even a glimpse of him, had avoided any thought of attending church, and turned down an invitation from Miss Agatha for dinner. When restlessness had driven her to her car that afternoon, she'd deliberately headed in the opposite direction from his house.

Now she was here. On business. That was all that should be between them, all that she could allow between them.

But knowing that didn't stop her from wanting more.

"What happens now?" he asked without turning.

"Nothing," she replied, but he continued talking as if he didn't hear.

"You want to put him in a home where he can be more closely supervised? Because you won't get any argu—" He turned. "Nothing?"

"Well, actually, I thought I would recommend to Reverend and Mrs. Howard that they seek counseling for their son."

His expression was blank. "Counseling? For Kenny?"

"Apparently he's quite a problem."

"And you made that determination after fifteen minutes with Caleb?"

"No, actually I got it from you." At his puzzled look, she explained. "In my office, my first day on the job. I was looking for a placement for the kids and the Howards were on my list. You said you wouldn't recommend them because their son was 'the bad seed.' "

"So you believe this was all Kenny's fault."

"No, but I believe Kenny was the instigator. Frankly I think Caleb showed great restraint in stopping with a bloody nose and a black eye."

"He didn't stop. He was *stopped*. There's a difference."

"The point is Caleb had a problem, and he dealt with it. I wish you would do the same."

"What do you mean by that?"

She pushed her hands into the deep pockets of her dress, then curled her fingers tightly as she approached him. "Did you ask him even once if he was all right?"

J.D.'s face flushed crimson. "I tried to examine him. He wouldn't let me."

"When? At the church, in front of the others? Or in the truck or here at the house, where no one would see?"

He opened his mouth, then closed it again.

"Did you show any concern at all for him when you got

to the church? Or did you walk in and go straight to the other boy to examine *his* injuries?"

His voice was stiff, his tone icy, when he answered. "All Caleb had was a split lip."

"And all Kenny had was a bloody nose and a black eye. A bit more dramatic, perhaps, but no more serious and no more painful than a split lip." She sighed softly. "Did you even speak to him there? Did you ask, 'Caleb, are you all right? Are you hurt? What happened?' Or did you ignore him until you were sure the other kid was fine, then snap your fingers as if he were a servant and command him to leave with you?"

The color along J.D.'s cheeks heightened. He set the soda in the sink, then leaned against the counter, gripping the rounded edge with both hands. "You're right," he admitted. "I handled it all wrong. I'm a lousy parent. So place him with someone else."

"I'm not going to remove him from your care. I just think—" Breaking off, she studied him. *So place him with someone else.* That hadn't been offered as a flippant challenge, not with that uncharacteristically grim look in his eyes. It had been a request. A demand.

She took a breath to steady her voice, but it didn't work. "You want me to remove him from your care."

He shifted uncomfortably and refused to look at her. He didn't like what he was saying—she knew him well enough to realize that—but he was saying it anyway. "I think it would be best. He's not doing well here with me."

"Have you really given it a chance, given *him* a chance?"

"We've had more than two weeks. He wants nothing to do with me. He's angry with the world and he takes it out on me. He's difficult, obnoxious, and obstructive. I just think . . ." His voice faltered, softened, as if the words shamed him. "I think he'd be better off elsewhere."

Her stomach was queasy, and her hands were knotted so tightly in her pockets that her nails bit into her palms. "So that's it." Her own voice was heavy with disillusionment and dismay. "He gets into trouble one time, and because *you* can't forgive him for reminding you of your worst mistake, that's the only chance he gets from you. You're washing your hands of him."

J.D. said nothing in his defense.

For a time there was only silence between them, cold, angry, bitter silence. Then Kelsey drew a breath, straightened her shoulders, lifted her chin. "All right. I'll begin looking for a new home for all four children. I'll be in touch with you as soon as I find one." She walked to the door, then came back. "You know, J.D., you might have been a hotshot psychiatrist in Chicago, but from what I see, you're not much more than a coward here."

He didn't have anything to say to that either. He just stood where he was and watched her go.

She returned to her office but was too frustrated to concentrate. She made one home visit but caught herself making overly critical judgments about the care an eight-year-old was receiving from his obviously devoted grandmother. Deciding she was better off back in the office, she returned to start the paperwork that would remove the Brown kids from J.D.'s care, but the files she needed were in the cabinet and the drawer was stuck. Muttering curses, she gave it a great yank and succeeded far too well. The drawer glided free of the cabinet, and she tumbled to the floor. An instant later the drawer landed with a crash, scattering its contents across the room.

"Good heavens, what was that?"

"Are you all right?"

Though she'd never felt less like a smile, she pasted one on her face before she turned toward the door. Three curious faces peered in—the secretary from next door, the accountant from down the hall, and a vaguely familiar woman, probably someone she'd passed in the halls or shared an elevator with.

"I'm fine," she said, sweeping papers from her lap and rising to her knees. One hip throbbed with the movement, but other than that, everything appeared to be working. "My drawer got stuck, but I unstuck it."

The accountant's forehead wrinkled. "You really ought to get a file cabinet with stops on the drawers to keep that from happening."

Kelsey looked at the drawer with its releases on each side. "It has stops. I guess I somehow managed to unstop them. But everything's okay. Thanks for the concern."

The secretary and the accountant left. The other woman remained in the doorway. "You've got quite a mess here. I'd help you sort everything out, but I imagine your records are confidential."

"Yes, they are. Thanks anyway." She began gathering folders and papers into haphazard stacks. It would take hours to undo the damage, but, hey, she had hours. She had no place to go after work, nothing to do, no one to see. Her job was her life and was destined to remain so for a long time.

"You don't remember me, do you?" the woman asked. "We met at church Sunday before last. You were in a hurry to leave, and I was waiting outside."

"Oh, yes." The woman who thought J. D. Grayson was exactly what the Brown children needed, who'd sworn that Kelsey couldn't ask for a better father for them. A fat lot she knew, Kelsey thought before reminding herself to at least give an appearance of friendliness. "Do you work in the building?"

The woman's smile was lovely. It transformed a rather ordinary face into something extraordinary. "My work takes me everywhere, though Bethlehem's more or less my home base. How are the children?"

She gestured, and Kelsey looked down at the papers in her hands. Photographs of Gracie and Noah Brown were on top. "They're fine."

"I heard about the little problem at the church. I'm afraid some parents indulge their children entirely too much. Is Caleb all right?"

"He's fine. I saw him at Dr. Grayson's later."

"I hope J.D. understands that the boy did only what he thought was necessary."

"J.D. doesn't understand anything he doesn't want." Kelsey shook her head. "I'm sorry. I shouldn't have said that. I shouldn't be discussing this with you at all."

"You look as if you shouldn't be doing anything right now except perhaps rejuvenating somewhere. Tough day?"

Kelsey smiled wryly as she surveyed the disorder surrounding her. "Yes, and it doesn't look as if it's going to get better soon."

"Oh, it will. Tomorrow will be much better. Of course, you've got to get through the rest of today first. But your biggest problem will be resolved tomorrow. Trust me." She glanced at her watch. "I'd best be going. Take your time with this, and take a few deep breaths. Oh, and you might want to put some ice on that hip, or it's going to bruise." With a quick smile and a wave, she disappeared into the outer office.

Kelsey rubbed her right hip. How had the woman known? And how had she gotten away yet again without giving Kelsey a chance to ask her name? And what made her so sure that tomorrow would be so much better?

Logic, coincidence, and optimism. Simple explanations. Nothing more.

Getting to her feet, she tiptoed over stacks of papers to

the file cabinet, inserted the empty drawer, then gave it a tug. It opened smoothly, and the stops caught it two thirds of the way out. Second and third tests yielded the same results. Apparently, whatever had caused it to stick, then fly free of the tracks, had been fixed. She wouldn't face this problem again.

Now she just had to deal with the consequences, and then she would turn to the important job.

She would find a new home for the kids.

I T WAS THE MIDDLE OF THE NIGHT. THE KIDS WERE asleep, hell, the whole town was probably asleep. Only J.D. remained awake. Considering how edgy he felt, he might never sleep again.

He'd let Kelsey down and would soon let the kids down. Damn it, he wished people wouldn't depend on him, wished they wouldn't expect anything at all from him. He couldn't help disappointing them. It was just the way he was. He always let the important ones down.

But Kelsey would get over it. She would never look at him again the same way, would never let him kiss her again, but it wasn't going to break her heart or ruin her life.

Too bad he couldn't say the same about the kids—or himself.

He'd spent a good portion of the night trying to imagine giving them back. He'd tried to envision himself packing their clothes, books, and toys and carrying the bags to her car. Saying good-bye to Gracie, Noah, and Jacob. Looking Caleb in the eye and saying good-bye to him. Turning their room back into an office, with his desk instead of bunk beds, his things on the shelves instead of theirs, his pictures on the wall. Going to bed without the hall light on. Going for a run without getting Mrs. Larrabee to stay with them. Coming home from work to an empty house and dinner for one, followed by an evening alone.

No matter how he tried, he couldn't bring the images into focus.

When Noelle had asked him to take the kids, he'd agreed to more than simply housing and feeding them. He'd accepted obligations, responsibilities. He'd known there would be difficulties, Caleb being the chief one, and he'd said yes anyway. He couldn't back out now because the difficulties were more difficult than he'd wanted. He couldn't live with himself if he did.

After pacing the length of the apartment for the hundredth time, he stopped to pick up the cordless phone, punched the auto-dial number that would ring his father, then resumed pacing. It was late for a talk-some-sense-into-me call, but his dad wouldn't mind. He'd always been there for J.D., night or day.

The way no one was there for Caleb.

The *hello* came on the third ring, the voice strong and vital.

"Dad, it's me, J.D."

His father chuckled. "I may be old, but I'm not forgetful, not even in the middle of the night. I remember my only child's name. How are you, son?"

Parents asked their children that simple question all the time, and it was nothing more than that. A simple question with a simple answer. *How are you? I'm fine.* Or *Not too bad.* Or *I've been better.*

But when Bud Grayson asked, it wasn't so simple. Neither was the answer.

"I'm . . ." Relatively healthy. Slowly healing. Sometimes finding life worth living. All those answers were true. So was the one he gave. "I'm having some problems."

"What sort of problems?"

"I've got temporary custody of four kids whose parents abandoned them."

After a long silence, Bud's question came hesitantly. "Do you think that's wise?"

"No."

"Then, why . . . ?"

"I don't know. I felt . . . I don't know." It was the only explanation he offered. Pitiful as it was, it was enough for his dad. "They're good kids, Dad. They're smart and innocent and scared as hell. They'd break your heart."

"But have you forgotten, J.D.? Your heart's already been broken."

And that was the problem. The repairs he'd managed in the last two years and four months were still fragile. It wouldn't take much at all to undo all his hard work, to put him right back where he was when he'd come here. It wouldn't take any more than Caleb, keeping him or giving him up. Helping him or letting him down.

"Tell me about these kids, son."

He settled in the darkened living room by the window. "Gracie's the youngest. She's five. She's a pretty little girl, brown hair, brown eyes. Noah's six. He thinks leaving and being left are the most natural things in the world. He doesn't expect anyone to stick around."

And what would he think when Kelsey came to take them to a new home? Would he believe that just like their mother and their father, J.D. had abandoned them too?

The hell of it was, he'd be right.

"Jacob is eight. He's a big baseball fan. He's never played, though, because the kids at school wouldn't let him. He watches it on TV every chance he gets, and with cable, he gets *lots* of chances."

J.D. fell silent again, but this time it stretched on. Finally

Bud cleared his throat. "That's only three. What about the oldest one?"

Tension knotted the muscles in his jaw, his neck, his fingers. "His name is Caleb. He's twelve years old, and he hates me." *And sometimes I hate him too. I hate him for reminding me of Trey. For being wounded like Trey. For not being Trey.* And yet, for the same reasons, he felt obligated to him. He owed Caleb.

"Kids that age can be difficult," Bud said quietly.

Oh, yeah. And relating to them could be damn near impossible. And not trying could be even more impossible. And failing . . .

Neither he nor Caleb might ever recover.

"How long have you had these children?"

"Two weeks."

"And it took you this long to tell me. Were you afraid of what I might say?"

J.D. smiled in the dark. "I've made bigger mistakes and survived what you had to say. I'm not afraid this time."

"And that's what these kids are? A mistake?"

"No. They're the third hardest thing I've ever done." His father knew what the first and second hardest things were, so there was no need to explain.

"Nobody ever said being a parent was easy." Unexpectedly Bud chuckled. "The once-foremost psychiatric expert on kids should know that."

"I do know in theory. But in practice . . ."

"It's harder, isn't it? All that advice that seems so reasonable in your safe, secure doctor's office isn't reasonable at all when applied to living, breathing kids, especially kids who've been hurt." There was a creaking of bedsprings, then a barely hidden yawn. "I'll tell you what, son. Why don't I mosey on up to New York and give you a hand with these temporary grandchildren of mine?"

"You would do that?"

"I think the Tuesday-night bingo gang can get along just fine without me for a while."

"Quarters are a little cramped here," J.D. warned. "The only place left to sleep is the sofa."

"I've slept on sofas before." Another yawn. "I'll let you know when my plans are set. In the meantime, don't worry too much. Just treat those kids like the people they are. Like the gift they are."

Appreciating Caleb as a gift. That was even harder to imagine than giving him up. But he wanted to try—for his own sake, for Caleb's, for Trey's. "Thanks, Dad. I love you."

After a brief silence Bud said, "I love you too, son."

J.D. disconnected, tilted the phone so the light outside shone on the keypad, then punched in another number. It rang a few miles away, until the sixth ring was followed by a bang, a thud, then a sleepy voice murmuring "H'lo."

"You can forget about finding another placement for the kids."

"Wha— Who— J.D.?"

"I'm keeping the kids, all of them. So don't even think about trying to put them someplace else. Understand?"

In the silence that followed, it was all too easy to imagine Kelsey waking up, pushing her hair back from her face, stretching her arms high over her head. She cleared her throat, then said in a more normal, less sleepy-soft voice, "Okay, I'm awake. Now, what did you—"

"I'm keeping the kids."

"I don't think—"

"They were placed in my care, Kelsey. They need to stay there."

"At this point that's not your decision to make. I'm no longer convinced that living with you is in their best interest."

That hurt, though he had only himself to blame. He

pushed the ache away, though, and concentrated on his argument, his plea. "Don't do this, Kelsey. Don't fight me on this. You accused me this afternoon of giving Caleb only one chance before washing my hands of him. Don't do the same to me."

Silence came again, heavy and disapproving. So was her voice when she broke it. "Caleb can't be your salvation, J.D. You can't use him to absolve yourself of whatever guilt you feel for failing Trey. It's too heavy a burden to put on him. He'll pay too big a price if you fail again."

"That's not what I'm doing," he protested, then honesty forced him to add, "Not entirely. Caleb needs me." Noelle had been convinced of it. Somewhere deep inside, he believed it too. And somewhere deep inside he needed Caleb. For his own selfish reasons, he needed to help him, needed to undo the damage that had already been done.

"He needs someone who can look at him and see the frightened child he is. Not someone who sees only a real-life reminder of his biggest mistake."

"I can do that." J.D. rubbed the ache that had settled behind his eyes. "One more chance, Kelsey. That's all I'm asking for."

"One-more-chances are risky in this business. You know that."

"And you know I'd never do anything to hurt these kids."

"Your antagonism has already hurt Caleb." After a pause she sighed. "Have you gotten any sleep tonight?"

"No."

"Go to bed. We'll talk in the morning."

He wanted to protest but swallowed back the words. "All right. Should I come to your office, or do you want to come to mine?"

"Why don't you stop by mine? Nine o'clock?"

He agreed, and after a softly murmured good-bye the

line went dead. He made his way across the room through shadows and pale, thin light, then walked silently down the hallway to the last door. For a long time he simply stood there, watching the kids sleep, listening to the even tenor of their breathing. As his gaze settled on Caleb, he recalled one thing Noelle had told him two weeks before when he'd agreed to take them. *You won't regret this,* she'd promised, then honesty had forced her to add, *Well, from time to time you probably will, but not in the long run.*

Not in the long run.

He was counting on that. In fact, he was betting his and Caleb's futures on it.

God save them both.

K ELSEY SKIPPED HER MORNING RUN AND INSTEAD drove to Howland, where Mary Therese had agreed to meet her for breakfast. There was a coffee shop across the street from the concrete and glass building that housed their offices. They shared a booth for two in the middle.

She told her supervisor everything, then asked for advice. Instead, her boss turned the question back on her. "What do *you* want to do?"

"I don't know. The younger kids seem to have adapted well to J.D. Caleb . . ."

"Would probably have problems with any man whom he sees as trying to take his father's place."

Kelsey nodded in agreement.

"Do you think the children should be separated?"

Vehemently she shook her head. "I think that would be the worst thing that could happen to Caleb. He's devoted to those kids."

"So with any placement we make, the younger kids are going to adapt and Caleb's probably going to be hostile."

"But not every foster father is going to have J.D.'s baggage."

"I've known J. D. Grayson since he came to this area. I'd heard of him long before that. He's bright, capable, widely respected. If he says he can help Caleb, I have to believe he can." Mary Therese signaled the waitress for a refill of coffee, then added sugar and cream to the empty cup while waiting. "Everyone has baggage, Kelsey, and we all learn from our mistakes. J.D. believes he failed this patient Caleb reminds him of, so let's hope he'll use that experience to succeed with Caleb. If you hadn't made a few bad choices in your past, you wouldn't be so cautious about this choice. And if I hadn't trusted the wrong people a few times, I might not be so sure that J.D.'s the right one."

"And what if he's not? What if he does Caleb more harm than good? Do we give him another child to experiment on?"

Mary Therese held her gaze for a long time before softly saying, "If you honestly believe that he'll do *anything* to harm Caleb, then you need to remove those children from his care immediately. *Do* you believe that?"

Not in a million years. But did she believe J.D. could help Caleb? That he could put aside his past with Trey and achieve a different result with Caleb?

Maybe.

Mary Therese was right about one thing. Caleb was likely to resent *any* father figure in his life. He would be difficult, obnoxious, and obstructive with any man other than Ezra Brown, and J.D. was probably better equipped to deal with that fact than any other man in Bethlehem. As far as she knew, the only times his experience with Trey had negatively affected the way he'd treated Caleb had been purely subconscious. The first step in banishing subconscious behaviors was to become aware of them. Then they could be dealt with.

And, truthfully, what had he done that had been so bad? He hadn't shown Caleb any sympathy after being called away from work because the boy was in trouble. How many birth fathers would have handled the situation any differently? In fact, if she hadn't known about Trey, yesterday's incident would hardly merit discussion. If J.D. hadn't overreacted. If *she* hadn't overreacted.

If she hadn't been so disappointed.

"Kelsey?" Mary Therese prompted.

"I started out yesterday afternoon assuring J.D. that what had happened wasn't cause for removing the kids from his care. Then I spent the next eighteen hours convincing myself that it was." Her smile was thin, more of a grimace. "In reality, what happened had little to do with my decision. I based it on the fact that for a while, at least, he wanted to give them up."

Mary Therese laughed. "Honey, I promise you, there's not a parent out there who at moments hasn't wanted to give their kids to someone else. And those moments usually don't come when the kids are being perfect angels."

Kelsey put her fork down and pushed the plate away. "I should have told J.D. to cool down, take the evening to think it over, and if he still wanted to give them up this morning to call me. Instead, I acted like a brand-new caseworker dealing with her very first crisis. I'm sorry for bothering you."

"It's never a bother, hon, not when kids are involved. So . . . other than that, how's it going?"

"Fine. I like Bethlehem. I like the people."

"It's a great little town, a good place to raise a family." Mary Therese's smile took on a sly edge. "Met any guys yet?"

"A few," Kelsey lied. She didn't want to tell her boss

that J.D. was the only single man the town matchmakers thought she needed to meet. She certainly didn't want to tell her about that kiss Saturday night.

"Of course, you're getting well acquainted with the best one in the bunch. That J.D. is so fine—and sweet too. Too bad I'm married. Too bad *you're* his caseworker. Might as well hang a Hands Off sign around his neck." Mary Therese slid to her feet and picked up both checks. "I've got an early appointment this morning, so I've got to skedaddle. I'll see you later this week?"

Kelsey nodded. "Thanks for breakfast. And for the advice."

"I didn't give you any advice, hon. I just listened while you sorted it out for yourself. Be careful on the drive back home. And if you ever need to talk, just pick up the phone. I'm usually available."

After another nod Kelsey left the coffee shop. Though she knew it was always better to be safe than sorry when it came to the welfare of the children in her care, she did feel foolish for driving ninety miles round-trip to reach the same conclusions she would have found at home if she'd given herself the chance, and she felt like an idiot for overreacting to the whole situation.

It was J.D.'s fault. If he weren't so appealing and handsome, if he didn't tease and flirt with her, if he hadn't kissed her, she wouldn't have lost her perspective. She wouldn't have been so disappointed, and she would have known the proper way to handle it. It was *all* his fault.

But blaming him didn't make her feel better. Neither did seeing him when she stepped off the elevator on the third floor. He wore shorts and a T-shirt and looked more sexy than any man had the right to.

He also looked more serious than any man should.

"I'm sorry I'm late," she murmured as she unlocked the outer door, then the inner one. She set her briefcase on her desk, put her purse in the bottom drawer, then faced him. On the drive back from Howland, she'd thought of ways to ease into her decision, but now that it was time, the words just slipped out. "You want to keep the kids? They're yours."

"For how long?"

"If the authorities don't find a family member who wants them within the next few weeks, we'll have to make a permanent placement then."

He nodded, and the tension slowly seeped from his body. "You have a lot of power, Ms. Malone. On one whim you can take the kids away. On another you can give them back."

"I don't operate on whims," she said stiffly.

"I didn't mean—" He exhaled loudly. "Can I sit down?"

She nodded to the chair beside him, then slid into her own chair.

For the first time since they'd met, he seemed at a loss for words. He looked around the office, noticing that she'd taken his advice and moved the file cabinets, and he skimmed his gaze across the desk, looking, she thought, for something to talk about. He found it on the corner of her desk. "Who is that?"

It wasn't the first time she'd been asked about the photograph. Usually she just said a friend, and left it at that. If she wanted to leave it at that today, she knew J.D. would let her. But today, for the first time, she knew she would answer. Completely. "Stephanie. She was my best friend."

"Was?"

"She died soon after that picture was taken." She gazed at the picture, at the straight brown hair that Steph would have traded for her own curls, the brown eyes that were so solemn and sad, the smile that was a pale reminder of her real smile. By the time the photo was taken, she'd had nothing left in life to smile about. She'd had nothing, period. "Her family lived a few doors down from mine. We went to school together, to church, played together. We were inseparable. Until the year we turned fifteen."

"What happened then?" J.D.'s voice was soft, nonintrusive.

"Her parents were killed in an accident. She didn't have any family who could take her. My parents wanted to, but the state wouldn't let them. They placed her in a foster home." She cleared her throat, straightened in her chair, shifted her weight away from her bruised hip. They were delaying tactics, but they weren't important. J.D. in concerned mode was nothing if not patient. He would give her all the time in the world to go on.

Finally, drawing a breath, she did. "Before long, Steph started missing school. Her grades fell. She lost weight. Everyone said it was just grief, that she needed time, that she would adjust. But it wasn't grief."

J.D. knew where the story was headed. He'd heard it often enough in his Chicago practice, and he'd hated it every time. He wished he'd ignored the photo so Kelsey could be spared the telling. So he could be spared the listening. But he hadn't ignored it, and she wasn't sparing herself anything.

After a moment she picked up the frame, rubbing her fingers over the polished wood, her touch as gentle as if it were her friend she was touching, as tender as if she could soothe the girl's spirit. "Her foster father was molesting her. He had raped her the day after she moved in, and he continued to do so for months. She confided in the caseworker, but nothing was done. She tried to tell me, but . . . I wouldn't let her. It was more than I could deal with. She was my *best friend*. I couldn't handle knowing that that man was—" She closed her eyes, then swallowed hard. "I changed the subject, and she let me. Because I insisted, she pretended nothing was wrong. The next few times I saw her, it was like the old Steph was back. She was smiling. Happy."

And soon after, he thought regretfully, she was dead. She was smiling and happy because she'd reached the decision that she wouldn't go on living that way—betrayed, abused, unable to find help or even to confide in her best friend. She'd decided to end her life, to be with the parents who'd loved her and never hurt her, to leave the people who *had* hurt her, Kelsey included.

Her voice dropped to little more than a whisper. "She overdosed on pills belonging to her foster mother. And it turned out that hers wasn't the first accusation against this man. He had molested four other girls placed in his care. But it took her death to make them stop him."

"And that's why you became a social worker. Because you failed her. The system failed her. And you want to make sure it doesn't fail anyone else."

She nodded blankly.

"You were fifteen years old, Kelsey. What could you have done?"

"I could have told my mother, our teachers, our priest. I could have listened to her. Believed her. Sympathized with her."

"Those are great responses from an adult. And if you'd been an adult, you would have done all that and more. But you weren't. You were a child. You couldn't even imagine what she was going through."

"I could have tried. I could have—"

He shook his head. "She was your best friend, Kelsey. You loved her. If you could have done anything, you would have."

After a long while she returned the frame to its place, then faced him. "I don't want another Steph on my conscience. Sometimes I overreact. Yesterday was one of those times."

"Were you really going to take them away?"

"I came back here to start the paperwork. If fate hadn't intervened . . ." She shrugged.

"We don't believe in fate around here. We call those interventions miracles. Goes with the town name, you know."

"Well, whatever you call it, if the file drawer hadn't gotten stuck, then pulled out of the cabinet, scattering me and my files all over the room, I would have had the paperwork finished before the close of business yesterday. Instead, I spent hours getting everything back into the drawer and nursing the hip I bruised when I fell."

"I'm sorry," he said, then innocently asked, "Want me to look at it?"

Her cheeks turned pink, and she wriggled in the chair as if she couldn't sit still. "No, I don't. It's not a bad bruise."

"Actually, I meant the file drawer," he lied. "Maybe the stops somehow got jammed."

The pink turned red. "Oh. No. It's fine. It was just a freak accident."

"I'm not sure we believe in those around here either. Everything happens for a purpose." And what had been the purpose of yesterday's incident? To force him to acknowledge that he did want to keep those kids? To provide a means through which he and Caleb could get closer? Or to somehow separate him and Kelsey? Though there was only a desk between them, he felt as if they'd never been farther apart.

"Are you working today?" she asked, looking pointedly at his clothes. I bet you wear shorts to work, she'd accused when he'd told her her severe, drab-colored suits were ugly. The memory made him smile. So did the pretty summer dress she was wearing that day.

"Nope. I took the day off. I'm taking the kids out to the house. I'm trading a picnic and a swim at the creek for some help cleaning up before the carpet layers come. Care to pack your swimsuit and join us?"

She shook her head, making him wish her hair were down, loose and tumbling over her shoulders, instead of confined to that damned braid. "Unlike you rich doctors, I have to put in a full week to get my paycheck."

"You put in a full week and then some. It wouldn't hurt you to take a few hours off. Call it a home visit."

"That would be deceptive, Dr. Grayson, and I try very hard not to be deceptive."

"It would be a *visit* to my *home*. There's nothing deceptive there."

"Home visits are work."

"So spending the afternoon with me, with us, at the house would be pleasure?"

She smiled faintly. "I didn't say that. But I feel quite certain that the first caseworker who makes home visits in her swimsuit will also be the last."

"So you're turning me down."

"Regretfully, but yes."

"You don't look regretful." He stood up from the chair, feeling about five years younger than when he'd walked through the door. "By the way, my dad's coming for a visit. He's claiming my couch indefinitely."

The light in her eyes brightened. "Your dad? The man who helped your mother name you? Who knows what J.D. stands for?"

He grinned as he walked to the door. "Don't even think about trying to charm it out of him. He's been keeping my secret for ages. He's coming in tomorrow around five. Why don't you have dinner with us?"

"I don't want to intrude."

"You need to meet him. After all, he'll be spending time with the kids. Consider it work. Wednesday. My apartment at six."

She was still for a moment, weighing her professional need to meet his father against her personal desire to . . . what? Avoid him? Keep him at a distance? After a moment she nodded, and the muscles that J.D. hadn't even realized were tight eased and sent a fluttery, freeing sensation through him. "I'll be there at six," Kelsey said.

He nodded, too, and walked out. Halfway down the stairs, he stopped and took a deep breath. When he exhaled, it was shaky. So was he. He got to keep the kids awhile longer, and Kelsey was still willing to smile at him and tease with him. He'd won the battle.

Now, if he could just win the war.

Chapter Twelve

BUD GRAYSON HATED TO FLY, DIDN'T CARE for trains, and had cut back on his driving once his eyeglasses got thicker than a Coke-bottle bottom. That was why five o'clock Wednesday afternoon found J.D. and the kids downtown, waiting outside the restaurant that marked Bethlehem's bus stop. Caleb stood off to the side, hands shoved in his pockets, and Gracie and Jacob displayed great interest in the ants that marched in a weaving red line across the sidewalk. Noah was content to sit beside J.D. on the stone wall of the planter that fronted the restaurant.

"Where's the bus station?" Noah asked, swinging his feet so that the rubber soles of his shoes bounced off the rock.

"Right here."

"But where's the ticket seller? And the suitcase man?"

"You buy your ticket from the bus driver, and he stows your luggage."

"I wish he'd come by plane. Then we could've gone to

the airport to pick him up. We've never been to an airport before. Or I wish he'd come by train. We've never been to a train station before. Or—"

"Or maybe he could've come by spaceship," Caleb said sarcastically, "and then put you on it before it went back out in space."

Noah leaned around J.D. to give his brother a long, wary look, then resumed talking again. "This is your dad, right? I didn't know grown-up people had dads. Our daddy didn't. And our mama didn't neither. And Miss Agatha don't, and Miss C'rinna don't, and Mrs. Bee—"

Caleb sighed loudly. "Do you have to talk all the time? You're getting like Josie."

Noah's sigh was softer, sweeter. "I like Josie. She's funny, and she can beat up Gracie and Jacob and Lannie and prob'ly even Caleb and definitely me. And she's *real* smart. She knows where babies come from."

Before Caleb could respond to that, the bus came into sight at the end of Main Street. Noah scrambled up to stand on the wall, looking as excited as if it were his father arriving. He rested one small hand on J.D.'s shoulder. "What if he don't like us?"

"My dad likes everyone."

"But what if he don't like *us*? Then we can't be his . . . his . . ."

Caleb came a few steps closer. "We aren't his *anything*, Noah. We ain't nothin' to him. He's *his* family," he said with a jerk of his head at J.D. "Not ours."

The bus pulled to the curb, brakes squealing, and the door opened with a rush of air. Before turning his attention that way, J.D. scowled in the opposite direction. "Caleb, do me a favor. Shut up."

Bud was the only passenger getting off. He studied the kids, three lined up like little soldiers, one dragging the toe of his shoe across the sidewalk with his head ducked down, then said in greeting, "What a fine-looking bunch you are. You must be Gracie."

She smiled prettily and tossed her head.

"And Jacob."

"Yes, sir."

"And Noah?"

Noah tilted his head back and squinted to see into the sun. "Do you like us?"

"I like everybody."

"That's what *he* said. But do you like *us*?"

"I like you just fine, Noah." Bud mussed his hair, then turned to the outsider. "You must be Caleb."

"I must be," he drawled sarcastically.

"Be a good boy and get my bag from the driver." He didn't wait to see if Caleb obeyed but assumed he would— and he did. "J.D. You look well, son."

J.D. stepped up for his hug, holding him tight, for a fleeting moment feeling safe, the way he always had as a child. As long as his father had been there to hold him, nothing really bad could ever happen.

Too bad his father hadn't been with him in Chicago. The world would be a different place. *He* would be a different man.

Though sometimes he rather liked the man he'd become.

"It's good to see you, Dad. It's been a long time."

"You know, the same bus that brought me here from Pennsylvania could take you there to see me. Though I suppose you'd rather take the train or a plane or drive your fancy car. Where is it?"

The bus pulled away, and J.D. pointed to the truck across the street. The mud-spattered, battered off-road vehicle brought a broad grin to Bud's face. "Nice," he said, reaching for Noah's hand as they prepared to cross the street. "Very nice."

The kids doubled up in the backseat for the ride home. The apartment made Bud grin too. J.D. stayed in the kitchen to start dinner while the kids showed him around. The tour took an extraordinarily long time considering how small the apartment was. No doubt the younger ones were showing him each and every thing they could claim as their own. By the time they made it back to the kitchen, Noah and Gracie were acting as if they'd found their long-lost grandfather.

"Why don't you kids go watch a little television while I help J.D. with dinner?" Bud suggested, and they both ran off. He washed his hands, then located a knife and pitched in with peeling the potatoes. J.D. worked silently, waiting for the impressions that were sure to come.

"Interesting place."

"Hmm."

"Interesting life you've built for yourself here."

"Doesn't have much in common with Chicago, does it?"

"Nope. But neither do you. You look good."

You look good. As compliments went, it was on the bland side. People said it to co-workers, neighbors, folks they hardly knew. It was about as insignificant as Have a nice day. But it meant the world to J.D. because Bud had seen him at the lowest a man could go—weak, defeated, damn near destroyed. *You look good* was at the other end of the spectrum. "I feel good. Most of the time."

From down the hall came a burst of giggles that made his father smile. "Noah asked if he should call me Mr. Grayson, Mr. Bud, or maybe Grandpa Bud. I told him he could call me whatever he wanted."

"I'm impressed. It took them about a week to stop calling me 'the man.' As far as Caleb's concerned, I still have no name. I'm 'he' or 'him,' said in that particular tone of voice that kids do so well, of course." J.D. hesitated. "Would it bother you for them to call you Grandpa?"

For a moment the knife went still in Bud's hand. J.D. didn't risk a look at his face. He knew too well the sadness he would see there. Then, abruptly, the knife started again, shaving potato peels onto the counter. "No, not at all. They're young kids. I'm an old man. It seems pretty natural." Without a break in tempo he changed the subject. "I see you've got seven places set. Who's joining us tonight?"

"Kelsey Malone."

"With a name like that, she'd better have red hair, porcelain skin, and freckles."

"Brown curls, peaches-and-cream skin, and legs that could give a man sweet dreams."

"Ah."

J.D. rummaged through the cabinets until he found the pot he wanted, then began filling it with water. *"Ah?"* he echoed. "No, Dad, no *ah*. She's the kids' social worker, and she's coming to see you."

"Uh-huh. This might come as a surprise to you, son, but someday you're going to meet a woman, fall in love just like it was the first time, and get married and raise me a houseful of grandkids." Bud wagged his knife at him. "You know, man is not made to live alone."

It would come as a surprise to his father that J.D. was well aware of that fact. Maybe not love just like the first time, but definitely for the last time. He'd known it in his head for a long time. He was starting to feel it in his heart.

But there was no way he was telling Bud that. Even a son deserved a few secrets from time to time. "You're a fine one to talk. You've been alone a long time."

"That's different. I was with your mother for forty years. I'm too old to think about getting used to someone new."

"You're never too old, Dad," he disagreed as the door-bell rang. "Not as long as there's breath in your body."

After opening the door, he leaned one shoulder against the jamb and slowly smiled. Kelsey stood on the porch, wearing a summery dress with no sleeves, a rounded neck that dipped low over her breasts, and a hem that skimmed her thighs inches above her knees. Her hair was secured at her nape, but a few tendrils had managed to escape, curling gently around her face.

By doing nothing more than standing there, she'd proven his last point. There was breath in his body—and it was hot.

"Hi," she said, her smile tentative, a bit shy.

"Hi."

"Am I early?"

He didn't bother checking his watch. "No. You're right on time."

Her own smile faltered, then returned. "Then can I come in?"

He tore his gaze away from her as he moved back. "Where's your car?"

"It was such a pretty evening that I walked here."

He looked her over again, from head to flirty little yellow dress to toe, then murmured, "That's a sight I would've paid money to see."

She eased past him, careful not to touch, but leaving behind a hint of the fragrance he was certain he would recognize in his sleep. He breathed deeply, once of her, then once again. *Ah*, indeed.

Bud was waiting expectantly in the kitchen. "Well, well, well." He gave her the same sort of appreciative survey J.D. had just indulged in, then grinned. "You're everything my son said and more."

"Kelsey Malone, this is my father, Bud Grayson. He's a bit of a flirt and a charmer, so watch out for him."

"Don't believe a word he says," Bud admonished as he claimed her hand. "He just wants you for himself. Can't say as I blame him either. I raised a smart boy. Go see to the children, son. Kelsey will keep me company while I cook. We'll talk."

"That's what I'm worried about." J.D. stood to one side of the doorway and watched as Kelsey moved into the room. *Brown curls, peaches-and-cream skin, and legs that could give a man sweet dreams.* Oh, yeah, she was all that and more. She was the sort of woman who could keep a man warm at night, who could keep the shadows at bay and make him feel protected. Needed. Trusted. She was the sort of woman who would draw strength from her partner and give it back two, three times over. She was the sort of woman he wanted, needed.

And she was one hell of a kisser.

He started down the hall, then lingered for a moment, out of sight of the kitchen, to eavesdrop.

"What can I help you with, Mr. Grayson?"

"Well, for starters, you can call me Bud. And you could chop those tomatoes there for the salad."

Her next words came over the sound of running water. "You and your son share a preference for nicknames, Bud. You know, he won't even tell me what J.D. stands for. I don't suppose . . ."

Grinning, J.D. went down the hall, losing the rest of the conversation. In the living room he paused to check the kids, then he continued down the hall to their room. The door was half open. As he knocked, he pushed it all the way open.

Caleb sat cross-legged on his bunk, holding a picture frame in both hands. His eyes widened and his thin face flushed, as if he'd gotten caught redhanded doing something he'd been warned about.

J.D. recognized the frame in an instant, though he

hadn't seen it in nearly eighteen months. It had been a cold, snowy January night when he'd unpacked the office and set that frame on his desk. Dissatisfied with it there, he'd hung it on the wall, then moved it to a lower shelf, then a middle one, and finally to the top. Unable to bear it there either, he'd turned it facedown and pushed it back so far that he could almost pretend it wasn't there. For a long time he'd known it was, but at some point he'd started forgetting, probably hoping that at some point in his life he would start forgetting.

It hadn't happened yet.

He forced his fingers to uncurl from the doorknob, made his feet move from the spot where they'd begun to sink into the floor. He crossed the room, pulled the frame from Caleb's hands, and casually said, "I'd forgotten that was up there. Thanks." Holding the picture side of the frame against his leg, he started toward the door.

"I wasn't snooping or nothing," Caleb said belligerently. "It was just lying there on the shelf."

"It's okay. No problem. Listen, supper will be ready soon. Why don't you get the kids washed up?" Without looking at Caleb he left the room, went into his own room, and closed the door, then went to the closet. Though his hands trembled, he managed to take down the box in the darkest, remotest corner. He rested it on the edge of the dresser and unfolded the flaps, intending to deposit the frame inside, then put the box back in hiding. But when the last flap was opened, he didn't reach for the frame secured under his arm. For several raw moments he simply stared inside.

There were stacks of envelopes, each addressed in his own hand, each stamped and sent off to its destination, each bearing the same scrawled message for its trip back—Return to Sender. There were apologies given and rejected, gifts offered and refused, pleas put to paper but never mailed at all. This well-used, dusty box held the ragged remnants of his relationship with Trey, reminders too painful to keep accessible, too important to throw out.

His hand trembling, he picked up the top few letters. He could recognize the occasions from the postmarks— end of school, Easter, Christmas, with a big box under the bed to match. Thanksgiving, Halloween, birthdays. Every holiday, every special day, every nothing-special day—for months he'd remembered them all, until finally one day it had become too painful. The hope couldn't make up for the inevitable disappointment, and so he'd stopped.

But it still hurt.

He dropped the letters back into the box, laid the frame on top, and clumsily refolded the flaps before returning the box to its dark corner. Then he sagged against the wall, closed his eyes, and gasped for breath, for just one breath that didn't feel as if it might kill him. After a few noisy efforts that some might even call sobs, he found one, and soon he found another, and another.

He wasn't going to die, not without significant effort on his part. He'd learned that two years, three months, three weeks, and six days ago. He'd also learned that he lacked the courage to make that effort.

No, he wasn't going to die.

He just felt like it.

DINNER WITH THE GRAYSONS AND THE BROWNS was the most pleasant time Kelsey had spent in their company. Part of the credit went to Bud, who was as entertaining as he was charming, but a good deal of it went to J.D. and Caleb. J.D. was more relaxed. Caleb was less hostile. Maybe Monday's events had been the corner they'd needed to turn to get their relationship on track. Too bad they couldn't have accomplished it without split lips and wounded feelings. But *any* way they accomplished it was good in her book.

She swallowed the last of her ice cream, dropped her spoon into the bowl with a clang, then sighed. "I'd better head home."

A few steps above her, J.D. was leaning against the wall. Scattered down the steps below were the kids and Bud, eating their own ice cream. Bud looked up as he licked his spoon. "I'll get the kids ready for bed, son. You go with Kelsey."

"I don't need an escort," she said politely. "But thank you for offering."

Ignoring her, J.D. stacked his bowl with hers, then stood up and offered his hand. She let him pull her to her feet and, because her hand felt good in his, even let him lead her on a zigzag path down the steps. At the bottom, though, she tugged free and turned back. "Bud, it was a pleasure meeting you."

"The pleasure was all mine. Come back again."

"I will."

"How 'bout tomorrow?" Gracie asked. "Grandpa Bud is gonna make s'ketti, and not out of a can like Dr. J.D. does."

Ignoring the question, Kelsey brushed a hand over Gracie's hair. "Good night, kids, Caleb."

"You want to drive or walk?" J.D. asked, falling in step alongside her.

"I'm perfectly safe walking home by myself. Bethlehem doesn't have much of a mugging problem."

"We don't have *any* mugging problem. So . . . drive or walk?"

"You're suggesting that we drive only so I'd have to climb into your truck."

His gaze dropped to her too-short dress, and a devilish grin lit his face. "It's not my fault you dress to entice me."

"I don't—" With an amused sigh she broke off the protest. "It's a beautiful evening. Let's walk."

Dusk had settled and the streetlamps were on, casting pools of bright light that made the shadows seem shadowier. There were lights on in most of the houses they passed, and Kelsey easily imagined the families inside, eating a late dinner or sharing kitchen cleanup, as she, the Graysons, and the Browns just had.

But the Graysons and the Browns weren't a family, and even if they were, she wouldn't be a part of it.

The thought saddened her.

When she would have crossed Main Street, J.D. caught her hand and turned her to the right. Even after she'd obeyed his silent directions, he didn't let go. She didn't ask him to.

The downtown area was quiet, dim lights shining in shops closed for the night. Few cars passed, and there was no one on the streets but them. It was pleasant. Peaceful. Enticing.

"What are you thinking?"

She grabbed the first thought that came to mind. "Your dad's a nice man."

"He is."

"But he wouldn't tell me what J.D. stands for."

His laughter was soft, pleasant. "I warned you not to try to charm it out of him."

"I guess I wasn't charming enough."

"Oh, you're plenty charming. Trust me."

"Trust you? Your father told me not to believe a word you say."

"He was wrong."

"He also told me you were the best son a man could ask for."

"Well, not entirely wrong."

"So . . ." She fell back on the guessing game. "Is it Jonathan Drake?"

"Nope."

"Joe Don? Jethro Delbert?"

"Do I *look* like a Jethro? Or a Delbert?"

"No," she murmured without looking at him. She didn't need to notice how handsome he was or how the dim light changed the blue of his eyes, or the way his amusement softened his face. Tonight, when she felt vulnerable, she didn't need any reminders that he was exactly what she needed to feel whole.

"How about Justin Dwayne?" she asked as they strolled. "I could see you as a Justin. Or Julian Duncan."

"Nope, no Justin, no Julian. And no Juno or Jupiter or Jehoshaphat."

As they turned onto the street that led to her apartment, she finally risked looking at him. She opened her mouth, and words she would have sworn she hadn't even thought popped out. "Did *she* know?"

All traces of humor slowly disappeared from his face, but he didn't become sad or angry. Merely serious. "I was married to her. Of course she knew."

Twice before, they'd discussed his marriage. The first time he'd snapped a plastic fork in half and walked away. The second time he'd told her it was none of her business because they were just friends and nothing more. Did Saturday night's kiss make them something more? With business between them, could they even be something more?

Might as well hang a Hands Off sign around his neck, Mary Therese had advised. It hadn't been a warning—the woman believed Kelsey was too smart to get involved with a client—but it might as well have been. It was a warning she'd been giving herself since coming to Bethlehem.

It was a warning that was becoming increasingly harder to heed.

"What is it you want to know, Kelsey?"

She wanted to know that he wasn't still desperately in love with his ex-wife, that she wasn't making a major mistake. She wanted to know his past and her future, wanted promises, guarantees, reassurances. She wanted . . .

Him.

Nervously she pretended that crossing the street, then the apartment parking lot, required her utmost attention. Digging in her pocket, she pulled out her keys, then ran up the steps to the door.

"It scares you, doesn't it?" he asked quietly. "This thing between you and me."

The key was in the lock, but she didn't turn it. Instead, she looked at him, standing at the bottom of the steps, hands in his pockets, looking incredibly earnest.

"You want to pretend that we're just friends, but you know it's not true. I don't kiss my friends. I don't spend most of my days thinking about them. I don't spend most of my nights dreaming about them."

She stared, unable to move, to speak.

"Tell me you don't think about me, Kelsey." He moved up one step. "Tell me you don't miss me when I'm gone." Another step. "Tell me you're not interested in touching or kissing me." One more step. Now he was directly in front of her. "Tell me you don't want me."

Feeling hot, edgy, and in far more danger than she could survive, she tried to turn away, but he caught her arm. His fingers were gentle, his grip loose. She could pull free with no effort, but she didn't. She didn't want to.

Her fingers trembled as she lifted them to his face, hesitantly touching his cheek, his jaw, before withdrawing. "I could lose my job," she whispered.

"Or your heart. Which one scares you most?"

Both. She'd devoted her life to her career, to making up

to Steph for letting her down. Often the work was difficult, sometimes thankless, but it was her life. Or had been
so far.

But wasn't a job, even a career, worth sacrificing if it
meant getting someone to share her life in return? Wasn't
the opportunity to love worth the possibility of heartbreak? Wasn't it the risks that made the prize so worth-
while?

He climbed the final step and she took a matching step
back. He continued to advance, his movements slow, deliberate, threatening—no, not threatening. Promising.

She continued to retreat until the door was at her back.
"I'm not scared," she murmured.

"Of course not. You're just trembling for fun."

"It's cool."

"It's seventy-five degrees."

"I'm just—"

He touched his fingers to her mouth, and she stilled.
Such a small touch . . . but it sent heat through her
body. Tied her stomach in knots. Made her lungs impossible to fill. "Tell me, Kelsey."

She swallowed hard, brushed his fingers away, then
clung to them. "I don't think about you. I don't miss you.
I don't want to touch you or kiss you. I don't want you."
With each lie she pulled him closer, and as soon as the last
one faded from her lips, she touched her mouth to his, slid
her arms around his neck, brought her body into contact
with his.

It was a hungry, needy kiss, fueled by urgency, passion,
and heat. He held her tightly, thrust his tongue into her
mouth, stroked her, teased her, made her sizzle. His hands
glided over her hips, sending a throb through her as he
touched the bruise, but the pain was forgotten the instant
he lifted her bottom against him, rubbing his arousal
against her.

For a moment she tried to remember Mary Therese's advice, her own warning, but he tasted too good. She felt too good. She was past caring about consequences. There was always time to deal with them later.

Cupping her hands to his jaw, she pushed him away, ending the kiss even though he protested. For a long time she stared at him, and he stared back. It was easy to identify the desire in his eyes, but there was more, something that softened it, that intensified it, that made her feel . . . special.

She pressed one chaste kiss to his mouth, then turned, opened the door, and went inside. She left the door open in silent invitation, ignored the lights, and started through the darkened living room to the bedroom. She was halfway there when the door closed behind her. A moment later she heard her keys hit the dining table with a jangle.

And then he was in the bedroom.

Thin light came through the window. She moved to close the blinds, but his hoarse command stopped her. "Don't. There's nothing but woods out there. No one can see but me . . . and I want to see."

With a faint smile she turned back. He'd stopped just inside the door and was looking at her as if he liked what he saw. She folded her arms across her chest, noticed that it pulled the neckline of her dress lower, then dropped her arms to her sides. "You're the first man I've brought here."

"I'm going to be the only one."

"You're pretty sure of yourself."

He didn't respond but came closer, then moved around behind her. With strong, gentle fingers he unfastened the tortoiseshell clasp that restrained her hair, then let it fall over his hands. "I don't know about you or even myself, but I'm damn sure of *us*. I'm sure we belong together. I'm sure this is right. I'm sure." He brushed her hair to one side and touched his tongue to her ear, making her shiver, making her turn in his arms to face him.

He rationed his kisses—slow, sweet touches to her ear, her jaw, her chin, and finally her mouth. He coaxed her lips apart, eased his tongue inside, teasing, tasting, feeding her hunger. Leaving her mouth, he dusted a trail of kisses down her throat to the sensitive skin between her breasts, where her dress blocked his way. He returned his mouth to hers and let his hands explore further, stroking over the fabric, leaving heat and want and need everywhere they touched.

"Please," she whispered, but the word had no sound. It passed from her mouth to his, swallowed in his kiss, lost in the sweet ache he created.

She settled her hands at his waist, where her fingers tugged up the bottom of his shirt, where her palms flattened and rubbed across his belly, over his chest, across his nipples, making his breath catch, making him groan. Her hands took his shirt with them, worked the sleeves over his arms, pulled it over his head. They had to interrupt the kiss to discard the shirt, and she took advantage of the break to brush her mouth across the smooth, warm skin of his chest.

Though his muscles were taut and his breathing ragged, he didn't interrupt her slow exploration. He didn't hurry her along, didn't guide her to the kisses he wanted most, though she knew. The instant her teeth closed around his nipple, he gasped and his fingers, tangled in her hair, tightened their grip. When she sucked it, his muscles grew harder, and so did he. She felt the proof against her hip.

When her fingers dipped low over soft denim and hard flesh, he grabbed her wrist and pulled her hand away. He swept her dress over her head with one swift movement, kicked off his shoes, and, with her help, stripped off the rest of their clothes, then lifted her against him while he kissed her with fierce demand, fierce need. By the time they settled on the bed, he was inside her, stroking her hard, deeply, smoothly, kissing her the same way.

Release came quickly, bubbling up from deep inside, unbearably hot, unbearably intense. Crying out, she arched against him and heard his own hoarse groan, felt his own powerful completion. He took a moment, gave her a moment to breathe, to calm the tremors ricocheting through her, to regain her balance, but only a moment, and then he began the process all over again. Touching, kissing, stroking, caressing, sucking, thrusting, tormenting. Teasing, pleasing, easing.

Loving.

J.D. SAT ON THE SIDE OF THE BED, RAN HIS FIN-gers through his hair, yawned, then reached for one shoe. His shirt was around there somewhere, along with the other shoe, but damned if he cared where. Getting his jeans on had taken all his energy. He wasn't sure how he was going to make it home.

"I wish you could spend the night."

He glanced over his shoulder. Kelsey lay curled on her side, the sheet tucked over her breasts and under her arm, her hair spread out over the pillow. He wished he could spend the night too, but Bud was expecting him. So were the kids. "Don't tempt me, darlin'. I'd like nothing better."

He'd tied his shoelace and located the second shoe, half under the bed, when she spoke again.

"J.D.? I don't know how to act."

He turned to face her. "You act like you always do, except when we're alone. Now I have the right to touch you and kiss you as much as I want. Now you have the right to seduce me whenever you want."

The faint smile that touched her mouth was sad. "When we're alone," she echoed. "In secret, like it's something to be ashamed of. Like we've done something wrong."

"In private," he disagreed. "Like it's something very personal and very intimate, just between you and me. Isn't that how most relationships start out?"

With a shrug she tugged the sheet higher, up to her chin, and curled into a tighter ball. "It *is* wrong. It's a breach of professional ethics. A serious issue of impropriety. Grounds for losing my job."

Laying his shoe aside, he grabbed a fistful of sheet and pulled on it. She had only two choices—come with the sheet, or lie exposed in front of him. She came with it. "I don't like being considered unethical or improper," he growled, his mouth only a breath from hers. "What we did wasn't wrong. It was incredible, and I would be more than happy to adjust the opinion of anyone who thinks otherwise, starting with you."

He gave her a hard, greedy kiss, one that made her sink against him, that almost persuaded him to shuck his clothes, crawl back in bed with her, and stay there forever. Instead, he ended the kiss, tangled his fingers in her hair, and gave her a crooked grin. "You're a hard woman to walk away from."

"So stay."

He wanted to, because he knew when the door closed behind him, the doubts would start. In the time it took him to get back home, she could talk herself into never speaking to him again. But he couldn't be with her every minute of every day. Better that she should deal with the doubts up front, because they might get in the way when he asked her to marry him.

And he *was* going to ask her to marry him. Somewhere

inside, he'd known it for a while, but he would bet she didn't have a clue. It was about time he gave her one.

"I'll miss you."

She smiled that faint smile again. "I'll miss you too."

He finished dressing and walked to the door, then looked back. "Kelsey. What happened between us . . ." His gesture covered the space between them and took in the bed. "This is as right as it ever gets. Trust me."

This time there was more confidence in the smile. "I do. Be careful on your way home."

Once more he turned to go. Once more he stopped. "You know I'm falling in love with you, don't you?" He said it more as statement than question, an obvious fact that she couldn't possibly have overlooked. "I just wanted to be sure."

Grinning at the surprise on her face, he took his leave then. He locked the door behind him, took the steps in one bound, and headed for home. The blocks passed too quickly. Before he was ready for it, his apartment was one short flight of stairs away.

He let himself in quietly, locked up—and turned to find his father watching him from the kitchen while he stirred honey into a cup of steaming tea.

"I wasn't aware Bethlehem was so big that it could take this long to walk a girl home," Bud said in greeting, sounding as innocent as the kids asleep down the hall.

J.D. bounced his keys on his palm a couple of times before tossing them onto the counter. "Sometimes it takes a while to say good night."

"Reckon a man ought to have sweet dreams after a good-night like that."

"Reckon he should," J.D. agreed. Though they would have been sweeter if he'd been able to stay in Kelsey's bed. Aw, hell, if he'd stayed in Kelsey's bed, he wouldn't have slept long enough to have dreams. He would have made love to her the whole night long.

"So maybe I'll get those grandkids sooner than I expected."

"Maybe you will." Turning serious, J.D. leaned against the counter. "Would that bother you?"

"Why should it?"

"She's not—" He broke off, feeling as if he were about to betray Kelsey, as if he were somehow assigning fault to her when there was none. In spite of the discomfort, he took a deep breath and finished. "She's not Carol Ann."

"No, she's not. She's Kelsey Malone, and she's a fine woman in her own right." Bud sighed. "Son, you know I loved Carol Ann dearly. *You* loved her dearly. But she's not here. And if you think you might love Kelsey, well, that's enough for me to love her too."

"I think I might," he admitted.

"Good." Bud started to walk out, but he stopped in the doorway. "I have just one comment to make. If I were you, and I'd just discovered I was in love with a girl like Kelsey, I wouldn't be back here talking to me. I'd be over there with her, making sweet memories to keep us company through our old age." He grinned. "But, of course, that's just me. Good night, son. See you in the morning."

"Good night, Dad." J.D. turned off the lights and went down the hall. He bypassed his room for the open door to the guest—the kids' room—where he silently slipped inside.

Gracie lay sprawled on her back, her hair tangled about her head, her covers more off the bed than on. Noah, his pajamas on backward, cuddled the stuffed alligator, and Jacob was using a stuffed bear for a pillow and had a snore to match. Caleb was the only one without a security blanket, but then, the kids were his security. As long as they were all right, he was all right.

After straightening Gracie's covers, he went to his room and closed the door. As he settled into bed, he admitted that Bud was right. He should have stayed with Kelsey. His bed was too big and too empty, and the smells of her that clung to his skin were too enticing.

Finding the phone in the dark, he dialed her number. She answered on the second ring. "Can I see you tomorrow?" he asked without preamble.

"I've got home visits that will last into the evening."

"When you're finished?"

"All right. J.D.—"

"No regrets," he said quickly. "You'd break my heart if you regretted making love with me." Though he said it lightly, he wasn't kidding. He would be more disappointed than words could express if she was sorry.

"No, no regrets. I'll see you tomorrow."

"Hey, what were you going to say?"

She hesitated, then murmured, "I didn't know."

His forehead wrinkled into a puzzled frown, then he remembered his last words before leaving her apartment. *You know I'm falling in love with you, don't you? I just wanted to be sure.* "Well . . . now you do. Have you had time to consider whether it's good news or bad?"

"If you'd stayed, I would have shown you. Now you'll have to wait until tomorrow."

"Promises, promises. I'll hold you to it." His smile faded. "Good night, Kelsey."

She said good night, then hung up. A moment later he hung up, too, and settled down in bed for sleep and sweet dreams.

Chapter Thirteen

IT WAS TURNING OUT TO BE A LOUSY SUMMER, Caleb decided Thursday afternoon. At least if he were home, he could go off in the woods or go hunting or fishing or do whatever he wanted. But not here. He had to be baby-sat, as if he were a kid, and was never left alone except when he was in his room, and sometimes not even then.

And today was the lousiest day of all, because Grayson had picked up all three kids and taken them to the old folks' home with him and the dog, and Caleb was all alone with Bud and nothin' to do. The shrink had asked Caleb to go with them, and even though he kind of wanted to, he'd said no. He spent enough time with old folks as it was. He wasn't goin' lookin' for more.

Grayson had looked at his old man, sitting right there, but Bud had just laughed and said he was right. He should spend the afternoon with kids his own age. Trouble was, he didn't know any. Least, not any that he'd want to be with, who would want to be with him.

Except maybe Alanna.

He hadn't seen her since the trouble at church Monday and hadn't heard any more about that. Stupid Kenny hadn't died of his bloody nose or black eye even though he'd acted like he would, and so his parents hadn't done anything to get Caleb into any more trouble. Of course, it wasn't Sunday yet. Maybe they wouldn't let Caleb in church on Sunday. Maybe they'd be waiting at the door, pointing fingers, and saying, "That boy shouldn't be here," as if he weren't fit to be around normal people.

Maybe they'd be right.

He sighed loud and made Bud look at him. "Can I go somewhere?"

"Where do you want to go?"

"I don't know. Maybe for a walk." Maybe by Alanna's house, just to see if she was around.

"I suppose it'd be all right. Don't go far," Bud added as Caleb jumped to his feet. "And don't stay gone too long."

"I won't." He went out the door, then took the stairs two at a time. He hadn't been out by himself, really by himself, in a long time, and it felt good. Not that he had anywhere to go, or anything to do. But at least Bud trusted him enough to let him go.

He didn't head toward Alanna's right away. Instead, he walked all the way to the end of Sixth Street. He liked living in the country, but it was nice living in town too. At least in town, going places was no big deal. There wasn't anywhere in Bethlehem that he couldn't walk in less'n half the time it took him to walk from his house to the edge of town. If he had any reason to go to the store and the money to spend there, he could go and be back in no time. If the kids wanted to go to the library, he could take 'em without having to wait for a grown-up, and if he had any friends . . .

Make 'em, the welfare lady said as if it were the easiest

thing in the world. Maybe it was for her. She was pretty and smart, and her family couldn't have been poor if they'd gone to the beach every summer. But he didn't know how to make friends. He didn't even know where to start. Besides, kids didn't want to be friends with him, and he'd rather not even try than have 'em say so again.

It hurt too much.

Wiping his eyes, he turned left and walked two blocks to Fourth, then turned left again. As he walked, he saw some kids playing outside their houses, but mostly they were little kids, Noah's and Gracie's age. He didn't see anyone his age and figured they were all inside watching TV or playing video games or doing stuff on their computers, or they were off on vacation somewhere, maybe at the beach. He wouldn't mind a trip to the beach. Maybe, if his dad ever come back, he'd take them.

Hearing his own words echo in his head, he stopped right where he was. *If* his dad ever come back? Of course he would. He'd promised! He'd come, and he would know that everybody else had doubted him except Caleb. He'd know that Caleb had always believed in him—*always*.

A honk from a car's horn made him jump, then someone yelled, "Caleb Brown, get out of the street!"

Startled, he noticed the car that had stopped for him to cross the street, then he realized he was right by the Winchesters' house. Right where he'd wanted to come. It was Alanna who yelled at him, and he looked like an idiot. As usual.

The lady in the car waved for him to go on, and his feet obeyed without his mind telling them to. He stepped onto the curb and faced Alanna, standing at the edge of the yard, holding a baby on one hip.

"Are you trying to get killed or something?" she asked, sounding like she did whenever she bossed around Josie or Brendan.

"I was thinking," he said defensively.

"About getting hit by a car?"

Shoving his hands in his pockets, he scowled at her. For a moment she scowled back, then slowly she began to smile.

"Come sit down." She sat at one end of the glider, with him at the other. There was a baby bottle and a cloth diaper for wiping the baby's mouth in the middle. "I was hoping someone would come by. Miss Agatha took the kids to the library for story hour, and it gets awful quiet when they're not around."

"Why didn't you go with them?"

"It's for little kids." She shrugged. "I saw Gracie and your brothers with Dr. J.D. when he picked up Buddy to go to the nursing home. Why didn't you go with them?"

"Didn't want to."

She looked at him, and he could feel that she was staring at his mouth. Even though it was still sore, he pressed his lips together and looked away.

"Did you get in bad trouble over what happened at the church?"

"Not really."

"I told Dr. J.D. it wasn't your fault."

Still staring away, Caleb shrugged. "He didn't care whose fault it was. He didn't care at all."

"He was worried," she said softly, and he looked at her again.

"Not about me."

She looked as though she were gonna argue with him, but she didn't. Instead, she started bouncing the baby on her lap. The baby looked like Gracie and Noah did when they were babies, with brown hair and great big eyes, and chewing on things and drooling all over. "What's his name?"

"Mike. Well, that's what Uncle Nathan and I call him.

Aunt Emilie calls him Michael, and Josie and Brendan call him Mikey. It doesn't matter. He doesn't answer to any of them, do you, Mike?"

He reached across the bench, and the baby latched on to his finger, curling his fingers around it while chewing on his other hand. "I used to take care of Noah and Gracie when they were this little, changed their diapers, fed 'em, rocked 'em to sleep."

"What did your mom do?"

"Not much. She used to say she wasn't the motherly type."

"Do you remember much about her?"

Caleb thought about it a moment. He mostly remembered the fights she'd started with his dad. She'd always wanted to go somewhere, do something, spend money. She'd blamed his dad for them being poor, but she hadn't worked. She'd always said she couldn't have a job because of the brats—that was what she'd usually called them—but what work was done around the house and with the kids was mostly done by Caleb and his dad.

The truth was, his mom had been lazy, selfish, and mean. There wasn't much nice to remember about her, but he didn't tell Alanna that. He just shook his head. "I don't remember a lot about her. But I know everything about my dad."

"Except where he is now," Alanna said. Right away her face turned red, as though she hadn't meant to say it out loud.

"He's coming back," he said fiercely.

"I hope he does," she said, then asked, "How long has he been gone?"

He didn't want to answer, because he knew what she'd say, but he did anyway. "Fifty-eight days."

"Wow. That's almost two months. That's a long time, Caleb."

"But he's coming back." He said each word with as much confidence as he could find.

"If he doesn't—"

"He *will!*"

"But if something happens that he doesn't . . ." She shrugged. "At least you got Dr. J.D. You got a nice place to live with someone who'll take good care of you."

"We're not staying with him. This is just temporary."

"Maybe. But I heard the grown-ups talking and they said you'd probably live with Dr. J.D. for a long time. Maybe till you were grown-up."

Caleb snatched his hand back, making the baby screw up his face, and jumped to his feet. "We're not staying with him! He don't like us, and we don't like him."

"Everyone likes him but you," she said, lifting Mike to her shoulder and patting his back to keep him quiet. "Gracie does, and Noah, and even Jacob. They already call his dad Grandpa. Before long they'll be wanting to call him Dad."

"You don't know what you're talking about! They'll *never* call him that, not ever! And we won't stay with him! Anyplace would be better than with him! Living alone in the woods and going hungry would be better than with him, and if you weren't so stupid, you'd know that!"

She gave him that really-mad look that meant he'd gone too far. "*I'm* not stupid. *I'm* not the one who got held back a grade because he wasn't smart enough to go on to the next one. Why don't you go live alone in the woods and be hungry? Why don't you just go back to your little old house and sneak into town to steal food from other people, or just go hungry till you die? Nobody'd care. But Jacob and Noah and Gracie won't go with you, 'cause they *like* being clean and having food and nice clothes and a nice house and a nice father who doesn't go off and abandon them, like *your* father did."

Breathing hard and clenching his fists, Caleb stared at her. He wanted to hit— Not her. His dad had told him that boys don't ever hit girls, no matter what. But he wanted to hit *something,* wanted to hit and hit until he couldn't hit anymore. But since there was nothing around to punch, he settled instead for the meanest voice he could manage. "I hate you."

She blinked, then held Mike closer. When she answered, her voice wasn't mean at all. It was just sad. "I feel sorry for you, Caleb."

"You're not my friend!" he accused Alanna.

"No," she agreed. "I'm not." And then she stood up and took the baby inside. She didn't even look back at him, not once.

When the screen door closed, Caleb stomped off down the sidewalk. He crossed Fifth Street, then Sixth, and kept on going, hands in his pockets, head ducked down. At first he was just *real* mad because she was stupid and said such stupid things. But finally he admitted that what he really was was afraid. He was afraid Alanna was right, afraid that the kids would want Grayson to be their new dad, that his dad really might not come back, that nobody *would* care if he went off by himself, that she really wasn't his friend. He was afraid that everybody was right and his dad had just decided he didn't want them anymore. There was no law that said moms and dads had to love their kids or want them or live with them. Their mom had stopped loving them and left more than two years ago. Maybe their dad had too.

"Hey, look," a voice called out. "It's dumb Caleb Brown."

Raising his head, he realized that he'd passed the edge of town. The nearest house was a hundred feet behind him. The street went another fifty feet ahead, then ended at a pile of dirt and a wood fence. Between him and that pile of dirt was Kenny Howard and Garth, and their friends were circling around behind him.

He could probably outrun all of them, but he didn't feel like running. He felt like hitting something, like making something hurt as bad as *he* did. He felt like causing trouble—for himself, for Kenny and Garth.

And especially for Grayson.

"I'M SORRY, SON."

J.D. stood on the porch, hands in his hip pockets, and stared down the driveway. "He's been gone only two and a half hours. That's not so long for a kid his age."

Bud sighed heavily. "I thought—"

"You thought he could be trusted. It's not your fault. If I'd been here, I would have let him go too."

"Does he have any friends he might visit?"

"No. Just Alanna, and I saw her when I took Buddy home. He wasn't with her."

"Do you think he might go back to his house?"

"Maybe. Why don't you wait with the kids in case he comes back, and I'll check out there." He offered his father a smile that wasn't nearly as reassuring as he'd intended, then headed down the stairs.

Leave it to Caleb to cap off with his disappearing act what had been a surprisingly pleasant afternoon. The kids had had a great time at the nursing home, entertained more than a few of his patients, and reveled in all the attention paid them. J.D. had been proud of the way they'd behaved themselves, and he'd come home in a good mood, looking forward to dinner with the whole bunch, looking forward even more to seeing Kelsey, only to walk into the apartment and find Caleb gone and Bud pacing the floor.

He climbed into his truck and drove to the end of the

drive. There, movement in the rearview mirror caught his attention—Caleb, cutting across Mrs. Larrabee's yard. He backed into his parking space, then jumped out, reaching the bottom of the stairs just as the door slammed at the top.

The house was unnaturally silent when J.D. got inside. Bud and the younger kids were spaced along the hallway— one in the kitchen, one in the dining room, and two in the living room. With a nod Bud gestured toward the kids' room, and J.D. started in that direction. Before he got there, the door opened and Caleb came out, carrying clean clothes. His hair was disheveled, his face red and damp with sweat.

J.D. blocked his way. "Where have you been?"

"Out."

"Where?"

"I don't have to answer to you," Caleb said with a sneer.

"As long as you live in my house, you most certainly do. What have you been up to, Caleb?"

The boy fixed his gaze somewhere around J.D.'s feet. "Nothing."

"What happened to your shirt? How'd you get so dirty?"

He stuck out his lower lip and didn't answer.

"Don't play games with me, Caleb. I can outlast you anytime. I'll stand here all night if necessary."

"You do whatever the hell you want." Caleb spun around, intending to return to his room, but J.D. grabbed his shoulder. The kid spun around again, dropped his clothes, and hit J.D. square in the chest with both hands, shoving him against the wall. "Leave me alone! And don't touch me!" he shrieked. "You aren't my boss! You're no-body! Just leave me alone!" Then he ran into his room, slamming the door hard enough to vibrate the wall against J.D.'s back.

"Leave him be," Bud advised, but J.D. ignored his father. He followed Caleb into the bedroom, giving the door a good slam.

"Listen up, Caleb," he said angrily, facing the boy from across the room. "You're pissed off because your father's gone. We all know that. We've all made allowances for you because of that. But I've had enough. You can be as angry as you damn well please, but you won't behave like that in my house. You won't talk to me like that in my house. Because if you do, if you continue your poor-little-Caleb act, you're going to find yourself doing it someplace else, without your brothers or your sister or me for an audience. Do you understand?"

Caleb stared at him, his face white, his eyes filled with rage. "You can't tell me what to do!" he screamed. "You're not my dad and you never will be! I hate you! I hate you, and I wish you were dead!"

The words, the hatred, reverberated in the air, twisting around and through J.D. He'd heard them before, at a time when he'd been too devastated to endure them. That time they had almost destroyed him. This time they brought back all that pain, all that bleak hopelessness he'd foolishly thought he had escaped.

After a moment of utter stillness he took a breath. When nothing shattered, he took one more, then another, until he trusted that he could speak, could move, could function in spite of the ache inside. "You'll spend the rest of the evening in this room," he said quietly. "You'll eat your dinner here, and then you'll go to bed. I don't want to hear you or see you or even know you're here before tomorrow morning." Then he walked out of the room, closed the door quietly, and simply stood there a moment.

Down the hall, Gracie whimpered and Jacob, on his

knees with his arms around her, harshly told her to hush. Noah stood motionless and afraid. Bud stood behind him, hands on his shoulders, and also looked afraid.

I hate you, and I wish you were dead! With the raw, ugly hurt of the words clawing through him, J.D. started down the hall.

"Son—"

He raised one trembling hand. "It's okay, Dad. Listen, I'm going out for a while. Can you feed the kids and make sure they get to bed on time?"

"Of course I can. But, son—"

"Caleb's grounded. I don't want him out of his room for any reason but going to the bathroom. I won't be gone long. Don't worry."

"J.D.—"

Forcing a smile that was as unsteady as he was, he walked out the door and down the stairs to the truck. He didn't open the door though, didn't climb inside and start the powerful engine. Behind the wheel of a car was no place to be when you were less than a hundred percent in control. He'd learned that lesson in Chicago.

Instead, he started walking. He had no destination in mind other than away. That had been his goal with Trey too, and he'd run all the way here. To Bethlehem, where Caleb Brown had been just waiting for the chance to echo Trey's words, his anger, his hatred.

You're not my dad and you never will be! I hate you, and I wish you were dead!

They were just words from a twelve-year-old boy. He was angry. He didn't mean them.

But words were never just words. They were the most powerful tools people had at their disposal. They could hurt, heal, destroy, or save. Once spoken, they could be forgiven, maybe even forgotten, but they could never be taken back. They were always there, always waiting for a weak moment to ease back into your mind, or for an angry moment to flood back with all their power, all their hurt, intact.

Those words had broken his heart once. They threatened to do it again.

And he didn't even know why. Caleb meant little to him. He was an obligation, a responsibility J.D. had taken on for a while. He was a royal pain in the butt, nothing but trouble, and he wasn't *special,* not the way Trey was. Caleb was just somebody he'd thought he could help, but obviously he'd been wrong. He didn't even like the kid, and he wouldn't be sorry to see the last of him.

And if he told himself that another dozen or so times, he admitted with a sigh, he might begin to believe it. Caleb *was* special. Not the way Trey was, granted, but there would never be another Trey.

But there was something about Caleb . . . His devotion to his brothers and sister. His unwavering faith in his father. The vulnerable young boy inside who was so hungry for love and acceptance, and the belligerent, hostile youth outside that protected him from admitting just how fierce that hunger was.

Caleb was worth saving, worth loving, but maybe J.D. wasn't the one meant to do it. Maybe, as with Trey, he was doing more harm than good. Maybe the best thing he could do for the boy was admit that, turn him back over to the state, and keep his distance.

Maybe.

After a time he realized that he'd stopped walking and took a look around. He was on the south edge of town, in front of one of Bethlehem's three bars. One was quite respectable, one quite disreputable. This one was in between.

A slight breeze blew from behind the building, bringing with it the aromas of fried food, cigarette smoke, and, barely noticeable under the stronger odors, the faint scent of alcohol. The place had a reputation for serving cold beer, greasy burgers, and the best onion rings in town, but J.D. couldn't vouch for it. He'd never set foot inside.

Tonight he was tempted.

He measured the distance from where he stood to the front door. Twenty feet, five or six strides, a couple of seconds.

And the distance back? Immeasurable. Impossible.

A soothing feminine voice came from behind him. "If you're looking for dinner, you can do better than the grease-laden junk this place serves. And if you're looking for a friend or a little peace from your troubles, you won't find either in there. All that waits for you through that door is heartache."

He scanned the twenty feet once more before turning to face her. She leaned against the streetlamp, looking as out of place as he felt. The early evening light gave her hair a silvery tinge, her smile an ethereal gleam.

The mysterious Noelle, who was responsible for getting him into this mess.

He moved a couple of steps toward her. "You lied to me."

"About what?"

"You told me that taking in those kids was the right thing to do. You told me I could help Caleb. That he needed me, not someone, not a father figure, but *me*."

"Those weren't lies, Dr. Grayson. Caleb does need you, and you *can* help him, once you get past your guilt. Once Caleb gets over his hurt."

"Oh, well, I guess those two small prerequisites just slipped your mind," he said sarcastically.

She moved away from the lamppost. "Walk with me. The smells from this place foul the air."

J.D. looked once more at the bar. He thought about

walking those twenty feet, opening the door, stepping inside. Walking to the bar. Ordering. Lifting the glass to his lips. Tilting back his head, tipping up the glass—

Swallowing hard, he joined Noelle, and they walked away in silence. When they'd gone a block, he breathed deeply and smelled only summer flowers and faint perfume. They smelled sweet, clean, pure, and reminded him of Kelsey. Kelsey, whom he would see that night, who would make him feel immensely better by simply showing up, by smiling, by existing.

"I didn't lie, Dr. Grayson," Noelle pointed out. "I didn't say it would be easy. I didn't think a man with your experience would expect it to be."

"You also didn't say it would be this hard."

"A man with your ex—"

"I have no experience with four children."

"Three of them aren't the problem. And you *do* have experience dealing with one troubled child."

And that was the problem, he admitted. He would give anything in the world to have another chance with Trey. Instead, he'd been given a chance with Caleb, whom he insisted on seeing as a poor substitute for what he really wanted.

But Caleb wasn't a substitute for anything. He was an individual, a real, live, breathing, hurting child who deserved so much more than he'd gotten—from life, from his parents, from J.D. himself. He deserved to be wanted for himself, loved for himself, and not disliked merely for reminding J.D. of someone gone from his life.

"Sometimes loving a child can be as easy as breathing," Noelle remarked. "Take Gracie, for example. She's charming, even-tempered, eager to please, and she's got the face of an angel. There's not a heart around that could resist her. Caleb, on the other hand . . . he's so afraid, and he tries to be strong and hide his fear, but he doesn't know how, and so he becomes defensive and antagonistic."

Those were the usual defense mechanisms, J.D. acknowledged, which he could easily deal with if his own defense mechanisms weren't so firmly in place. The simple truth was he was afraid too, afraid of failing again. Of damaging another child. Of caring again and losing again. Of finding out beyond a doubt that yet another boy would have been so much better off if J.D. had never come into his life.

He was afraid of facing his past. Of dealing with Trey and all the ways he'd let him down. Of examining his shortcomings, his mistakes, and thereby undoing the life he'd saved for himself in the last two years.

He was so damn afraid.

"It's been more than two weeks," he said quietly. "If anything, Caleb is angrier, more antagonistic, than ever."

"Sometimes situations have to get worse before they get better."

"And some situations never get better."

She gave him a sidelong look. "Do you believe Caleb is one of those situations? That the two of you aren't capable of the sort of relationship you share with his brothers? Do you honestly believe that Caleb is a lost cause?"

With Caleb's angry words still echoing in his head, he wanted to say yes. He wanted to insist that he would always resent Caleb, that Caleb would always hate him. He wanted to say whatever it would take to get himself to a place where Caleb couldn't hurt him.

But it was already too late for that. If such a place had existed, it had disappeared the day he'd stood in front of the church and looked at the photograph of that thin, needy boy and said, *All right. I'll take them.*

"No. He's not a lost cause," he admitted grudgingly. Then, because he felt trapped, by himself and his own ambivalence, he ill-naturedly added, "I just don't know why he has to be *my* cause."

Noelle stopped on the corner where the street intersected Main and looked up at him. "Because, Dr. Grayson, you need him as much as he needs you. You two are going to save each other. You didn't think it was all one way, did you?" She flashed him a smile. "Give and you shall receive. Help Caleb, and you'll be helped too."

His only response was a scowl that made her chuckle. "You get cranky when you haven't eaten, just like a child. Go on down to Harry's. Tonight's special is roast beef with all the trimmings, and it's unusually good. And who knows? You might even find somebody there to cheer you up."

He glanced down the block, where Harry's Diner was the only business open. Dinner did sound good, and Maeve and Harry were always good company. "Thanks for the—" He looked back and saw that Noelle was already stepping up on the curb on the opposite side. "Hey, where are you going?"

"I'm just in town for a short visit," she called as she walked briskly along in the same direction he was heading. "My schedule's pretty tight these days. But you'll see me again. I'm always popping in and out."

She reached the street that formed one border of the square and turned with a jaunty wave. J.D. walked a few more yards, opened the door to Harry's, then glanced back. She was already out of sight.

WITH A WEARY SIGH KELSEY LAID HER BRIEFcase on the passenger seat, then glanced at her watch. Her long day was finally over. She'd put in a full twelve hours—the usual office routine, plus a round of home visits with her clients, both young and old. She'd also placed a number of calls to Howland, trying to catch Mary Therese in the office. That was why she'd stopped by her office one last time, to check the answering machine for messages. There'd been one from Mary Therese saying they would talk tomorrow, and another from J.D., just a quick lunchtime gee-I-miss-you call.

She'd listened to it a couple of times, but it wasn't the message she heard. Instead, her mind kept substituting the words he'd said last night. *You know I'm falling in love with you.* It wasn't as good as an outright declaration, but it was close. It was enough to make her feel giddy, enough to almost make her not care that she'd broken every rule in the book last night.

It was also the reason she'd tried repeatedly to reach her boss. She was going to tell Mary Therese that she could no longer be the Browns' caseworker. Of course, Mary Therese would want to know why. Kelsey hadn't decided yet exactly how to phrase her answer. Because she was having an affair with her client? Because she was involved with him? Because she had slept with him?

All three were accurate, to a point. But an affair sounded sleazy, *involved* seemed evasive, and there'd been so much more to last night than just sex.

She could say they shared a relationship. That she had feelings for him. Or she could just get straight to the point and say that she was in love with him.

But when she hadn't yet acknowledged it to herself, much less J.D., was it fair to tell anyone else?

Putting the subject out of her mind in favor of a shiver of anticipation, she turned into J.D.'s driveway. She parked beside his truck, brushed her fingers over her hair, and checked her makeup before she got out and climbed the long stairs. She'd waited all day for this visit, had been distracted by it, impatient for it. Now that it was time, though, she was nervous. She wasn't sure what to say, how to act, or even how to greet him. With a simple hello? A smile? A chaste kiss?

Bud answered the door and greeted her with a big smile. "Aren't you a sight for sore eyes," he said, taking her hand and drawing her inside. "Can I get you something to eat? I've got leftovers from my super-duper special cooks-all-day spaghetti."

"No, thanks. I've eaten."

"Maybe a cup of coffee and a little dessert?"

"No, thanks, Bud." She looked past him. A light was on in the kitchen, but only the hall light illuminated the dining room. From down the hall came the sound of the television. "Is J.D. here?"

Bud's smile faded. "No, darlin', he's gone out for a bit. But I expect him back any minute now. We'd be pleased to have you wait." He grinned and gave her a wink. "I know it would please my boy to find you here when he returns."

"I can wait awhile," she said, hoping her smile hid her disappointment. "Are the kids busy?"

"Three of them are in the living room. Caleb's in their bedroom. Go on in and say hello."

The kids were in their pajamas and sprawled together on the couch, one big blob with multiple limbs and heads. When she sat down near them, Jacob used the remote to stop the video they were watching, and Gracie separated from the others to scoot over beside her. "Hi," she said, resting her hand on Kelsey's knee. "Caleb's in trouble."

"He is?"

"Yeah, big-time," Noah replied. "Ya wanna know what he did?"

Was that why J.D. had gone out and why Bud's smile had dimmed when he'd told her so? Because J.D. and Caleb had had another go-round? She tried to not get involved with the minor skirmishes that were a daily part of practically every foster parent's life. The parent had to have the authority to manage the child—within reason, of course—or the foster system would cease to function. Generally she stepped in only when someone else was involved, the misbehavior was escalating, or the child's punishment wasn't appropriate to his crime. She was sure none of those applied to this situation.

"Caleb said a bad word," Gracie said in a hushed voice. "Our daddy said don't ever say bad words, no matter what, but Caleb did, and so did Dr. J.D. And he slammed the door real hard, and the whole house shaked and then he cried."

"Caleb slammed the door?" Kelsey asked.

Gracie nodded vigorously enough to make her hair bounce. "They both did. And then Dr. J.D., he lefted, and Caleb can't come out for nothin'."

Noah scooted over, too, and fixed his big brown gaze on Kelsey. "We were scared, weren't we, Gracie?"

Nodding again, she shifted even closer to Kelsey.

"There's nothing to be afraid of," Kelsey said, sliding her arm around two sets of narrow shoulders. "Sometimes grown-ups and children argue. Didn't Caleb argue sometimes with your dad?"

"Never," Jacob replied from the other end of the sofa. "Caleb loved our dad. He hates Dr. J.D."

"He doesn't really—"

"Yes, he does," Jacob interrupted. "And sometimes he gets mad because we don't hate him too."

Feeling a little queasy, Kelsey managed to smile and change the subject. "What movie are you watching?"

"Oh, it's wonderful," Gracie said with a bright smile. "It's about a mermaid in the ocean, and she's beautiful. D'ya think I could be a mermaid when I grow up?"

"Gracie." Noah rolled his eyes. "Grandpa Bud and Jacob and I told you and told you there's no such thing as a mermaid. That's just TV."

She tossed her head in a determined-female manner that made Kelsey smile. "Well, then, I could be a mermaid on TV. Couldn't I, Kelsey?"

"Maybe so. Listen, you guys get back to your movie, and I'm going to say hello to Caleb."

"He can't come out of the bedroom," Noah reminded her as she crossed the room. "He'll be in big trouble if he does."

"He's already in big trouble," Jacob reminded him.

Before heading for the bedroom, she backtracked to the kitchen, where Bud was washing a pot at the sink. It couldn't hurt to get an adult's take on the argument before she heard from Caleb. "The kids tell me there was a problem tonight."

He sighed heavily. "I let Caleb go off for a walk by himself. He stayed out longer than he was supposed to and came back upset and filthy. When J.D. tried to deal with him, the boy exploded. Said he doesn't have to answer to J.D., that he's not his father, that he hates him." He offered a thin smile. "You know. The usual angry-teenager stuff."

"I bet J.D. never tried the 'usual angry-teenager stuff' with you."

"No, ma'am, he didn't. And I'd wager that you never pulled it on your parents."

She shook her head. "Oh, I got mad, but blowing up was not an option, not in my house. Of course, J.D. and I were never in Caleb's position."

"If the boy would just let go of that anger . . ." Bud put a storage container of spaghetti sauce in the refrigerator, then leaned against the counter. "When he called me in Philadelphia, J.D. told me those kids would break your heart. That's not a problem for me. My heart's been broken before, and I survived, but J.D. . . ."

She patted his arm. "J.D.'s a rock."

The look he gave her was filled with concern. "Even rocks crumble, Kelsey."

J.D. crumbling was an event she couldn't imagine. Instead, she gave Bud one last pat. "I'm going to talk to Caleb, then I'll get out of your hair."

"You're not in the way. Stay as long as you want. I know J.D.'s looking forward to seeing you."

Smiling faintly, she went down the hall to the last room and knocked. When no invitation was forthcoming, she let herself in.

Caleb stood at the window, staring out. "You can't come in here," he said flatly, his voice devoid of emotion.

"No, Caleb, I can go just about anywhere I want. You're the one who's grounded." She glanced at his dinner, untouched on the dresser, then moved to the other end and leaned against it. "Want to tell me about it?"

"Why? You'll just take *his* side."

"Why do you say that?"

"Because that's what grown-ups do."

"I'm not here to take sides, Caleb. I'd just like to hear what happened."

"He's *not* my boss."

"You know what? All our lives we've got somebody telling us what to do. When we're kids, it's our parents and our teachers. When we grow up, it's our bosses and supervisors, our legislators, our husbands and wives. There's not a person in the world who doesn't have to answer to someone. In your case, right now that person is J.D."

"He's not my dad."

"No, he's not. But he's here, and your dad's not."

"He's coming back." His whisper was a sad change

from the vehemence with which he normally made that statement. Was he beginning to have his doubts? Was he starting to accept that his father had left them for good?

"I hope he does, Caleb. I really do. But until that happens, you've got to adjust to living with someone else, to answering to someone else."

"Not *him*. I'll never answer to him. I'd rather die."

"Caleb . . ." She crossed the room to him and laid her hand on his shoulder. His reaction was immediate—a wince, a shrug away. Curious, she moved closer and tugged at the neck of his T-shirt. He winced again.

"Quit," he grumbled, spinning away and going to the opposite end of the window. "Leave me alone."

"Take off your shirt, Caleb."

"No."

"You acted like it hurt when I touched you. I want to see. Take off your shirt."

"Nothin' hurts. I just don't want to be touched."

"Caleb." When she started toward him, he backed away, but the corner was only a few feet behind him. He couldn't go any farther.

Taking hold of the bottom, she pulled his shirt up and over his head before he could stop her, and she stared. There were bruises on his shoulders and both upper arms, the pattern typical of a grabbing-type injury, and there were other bruises, a large one on his ribs, another across his stomach.

She drew a deep, calming breath. "How did this happen?"

He stared at the floor.

"Caleb?" She lifted his chin, but he still refused to meet her gaze. "How did you get these bruises?"

His lips, still bearing the mark from Monday's fight, barely moved. "He said not to tell."

"Who said?"

His jaw worked as if he wanted to blurt out the answer yet hold it in. After a moment he jerked away from her, grabbed his shirt, wadded it in a ball, then went to climb with a grimace onto his bunk.

"Who did it, Caleb?"

"*He* did," he said at last, and the words came out as if a dam had burst. "He grabbed me in the hall, and when I came in here, he came too, and he slammed the door. He said he'd had enough, that if I wouldn't behave, then he'd make me, and he said if I told anyone, he'd send me away and he'd keep the kids and I'd never see them again."

Feeling sick inside, Kelsey went to stand beside the bed. She had to tilt her head back to see him. He looked angry and ashamed and about to cry. She would be, too, if she were lying the way he was. "Caleb, you and I both know J.D. didn't cause those bruises."

"He did too! See! I told you you'd take his side!"

"Caleb," she said sternly. "Look." She gently placed her fingertips over the bruises on his left arm. "The fingers that left these bruises are smaller than mine. J.D.'s aren't."

He burst into tears, great, heaving sobs. "It *was* him! It was, I swear! Why won't you believe me?"

She bowed her head, resting her forehead against the smooth wood of the bed. She knew he was lying, knew J.D. wasn't capable of causing physical harm to any child. But at this point, truth didn't affect what she had to do next.

Oh, God, she'd taken part in so many of these investigations. She'd seen firsthand the damage caused by such lies. No matter how much evidence they found to exonerate the parent, no matter if the child recanted his own accusations, that damage always remained. There were always some who believed the parent was guilty, always some who wondered. The loss of trust, the suspicion, the wariness—they could never be undone.

Raising her head, she met his gaze once more. "Caleb, last chance. Tell me the truth. Who caused those bruises?"

His glare was fierce. "*He* did. Grayson. The shrink."

She sighed heavily. "Get your shirt and shoes on."

"Why?"

"I have to take you to the hospital and report this to the police."

"But—"

"And then I have to find a new home for you and the children until we can schedule a hearing."

He studied her. "You'll move us out tonight?"

She nodded.

"All four of us? Together?"

She nodded again. "When you're ready, come on out. I'm going to tell Bud." As he climbed down from the bed, she let herself out of the room. God help her, she didn't want to do this. She didn't want to walk down the hall and tell that kindly old man that the boy he was worrying about had accused the son he was worrying about of abusing him.

The only thing she wanted less was to give J.D. the same news.

Bud had just poured himself a cup of coffee when she walked into the room. With a smile he offered it to her, but the sickness she felt inside must have shown on her face, because his smile slipped away.

"Bud, I'm sorry, but I've got to take Caleb with me. He's bruised pretty badly, and he says—" She squeezed her eyes shut for a moment, then looked at him once more. "He says J.D. did it."

Bud simply stared at her, then his hand began to tremble, sloshing coffee over the rim before the cup slipped to the floor. It shattered there, and the milky brew seeped out in an ever-widening circle.

From down the hall came the children's voices. "Caleb,

you're gonna get in trouble! You're not s'posed to be out of our room! Grandpa Bud! Caleb's outta the room!"

Caleb came to stand beside her, and Bud's stunned gaze moved to him. "How can you do that, son?" he asked, his voice as unsteady as his hands. "How can you lie like that?"

Caleb stared mutely at the floor.

Kelsey looked from him to Bud. "When J.D. comes back, tell him we're at Bethlehem Memorial. I'll have to come back for the other kids. Could you have them ready?"

"But, Kelsey, you can't—"

"I have to, Bud. It's policy." She gestured for Caleb to leave, then turned back. "I'm sorry. I'm so sorry."

The drive to the hospital passed in silence. Kelsey parked near the emergency room entrance, then went inside to the admissions desk. By the time she finished filling out the forms, a nurse was waiting to escort them to an exam room. She left Caleb in the doctor's care, then returned to the desk to make two phone calls, one to Mary Therese, one to the Bethlehem Police Department.

She requested to see an officer and got the chief of police. It wasn't ten minutes before Mitch Walker came through the sliding doors, and J.D. wasn't more than a minute behind him. His hair stood on end, and he looked frantic.

So much for worrying how to greet him. There were no hellos, no smiles, no kisses. Just J.D.'s worried demand. "Is Caleb all right? Dad said you brought him here. Is he hurt? What—"

"He's okay. He's with the doctor now."

He dragged a hand through his hair, paced a few steps away, then came back. "Kelsey, what the hell's going on?"

She drew an unsteady breath. "Caleb has bruises on

both arms, his stomach, and his ribs. He says . . . J.D., he says you caused them."

He stared at her. "No. No, he wouldn't— I would never— You can't possibly believe—"

"Of course, I don't."

"Then why are we here? Why is Dad home packing the kids' clothes? Why the hell did you call Mitch?"

Mitch laid his hand on J.D.'s arm. "J.D., come on. The kid's been hurt, and he's pointing his finger at you. We've got to get to the bottom of it."

"He's lying, Mitch."

"I know, buddy."

"He's *lying*. I never laid a—" J.D. broke off and rubbed his eyes. Kelsey recognized the guilt stealing over his face and felt the sickness return.

"I did grab him," he said, appalled by his own admission, by the implications. "I was talking to him, he started to walk away, and I grabbed his shoulder and pulled him back. But I didn't grab him hard enough to bruise." An anxious note entered his voice. "I know how much force it takes to leave a bruise, and there's no way, I swear, there's *no way* I grabbed him that hard."

Kelsey wrapped her fingers tightly around his. "The marks on his arms were made by hands smaller than mine. If you'd caused them, they'd be twice that size. He's obviously lying, J.D., to get back at you because you grounded him, because the kids like you, because he sees you taking his father's place with them, because he wants to remove you from their lives."

"And you're going to do that, aren't you?" Accusation was as dark in his eyes as in his voice. "You're going to take them. You know he's lying, and yet you're going to give him what he's lying to get."

She swallowed hard. "I have no choice."

"You always have a choice, Kelsey. You're just making

the wrong one." Slowly the emotion faded from his eyes, leaving them flat and dull, and he pulled his hand from hers as if he could no longer bear the contact. "Apparently so did I."

The words hurt more than any blow could have. In spite of his concern that she would regret last night, instead, he did. He was sorry he'd made love to her, sorry he'd kissed her, trusted her, told her that he was falling in love with her. He regretted it all, and that was enough to break her heart.

He turned to Mitch, effectively dismissing her. "Can I see him? With you or the doctor or whoever?"

Mitch looked to Kelsey, and she nodded numbly. "Sure, come on."

As they walked away, she sagged against the counter. He was wrong. She *didn't* have a choice, not when it came to the kids. Anytime there was an accusation of abuse, the child—in this case, children—*must* be removed from the home until an investigation was completed. Even if there was evidence that the accusation was a lie, she had to follow procedure, for the kids' safety and for her own peace of mind. If Steph's social worker had done so twenty years ago, she wouldn't have been dead a few weeks later. That wasn't a result Kelsey was willing to risk.

But she did have a choice when it came to him. She could protect herself from him, could avoid him at all costs and keep herself safe. Keep her heart safe.

If it wasn't too late.

Chapter Fourteen

J.D. STOOD IN THE HALLWAY, HANDS KNOTTED in impotent fists at his sides, and watched as Mitch carried a wailing Gracie out the door, followed by Bud with Noah sobbing against his shoulder. His arms filled with bags of clothing, Jacob stopped on the porch and looked back. "I'm sorry," he whispered.

"It's not your fault, Jacob." It was *his* for ever agreeing to take the kids in. For not expecting Caleb's lies. For being so arrogant as to think that he could help Caleb.

"We 'preciate everything you done. We—we liked being here. 'Least, me and Gracie and Noah did."

J.D. swallowed hard. "I liked having you here."

Jacob's eyes appeared twice their normal size and were swimming with tears. "We're real sorry Caleb lied. It was nice bein' a family with you. We wish—" The first tear slipped free, and he turned and raced down the stairs.

Kelsey stepped into the doorway, then looked back. "I'm sorry about this."

How could the woman he'd made love to just last night

sound so cold tonight? Surely she didn't believe— She'd sworn she didn't believe Caleb's lies, but maybe *she* had lied. Maybe she did believe him capable of hurting a child. Maybe she knew so damned little about him, thought so damned little of him. Maybe last night had meant nothing to her . . . when it had meant the world to him.

He didn't look at her. He couldn't bear to see what was on her face, what was in her eyes. "Don't do this, Kelsey." His voice came out low and choked, but it was the best he could manage. "They belong here. They belong with me. Please . . . *please* don't take them."

"I can't leave them. You know that."

No, she couldn't. Especially not with Stephanie and the utter senselessness of her death guiding her.

"Where are you taking them?"

"I—I can't tell you that." At least she had the grace to sound embarrassed about it. "J.D.—" But she thought better of what she was about to say, closed her mouth, and walked out.

He heard the engines start, heard the cars drive away, followed by his father's slow, disheartened steps on the stairs. At last he reached the top and came inside, closing the door. Bud walked straight to J.D., put his arms around him, and held him tightly. "It'll be okay, son. Everything will be okay."

There had been a time in his life when his father's word was gospel. If Bud said everything would be fine, then, by God, it *would* be fine. But that time was long gone, and this was never going to be okay, and if he ever considered caring about someone again, he'd just shoot himself and avoid the heartache.

After a long time J.D. let his fingers relax, then lifted his arms to hug his father. "It's been a long day, Dad," he said wearily. "If you're getting tired of the sofa, I've got four beds avail—" He couldn't finish the word, couldn't say anything else at all.

They stood there a long time, then Bud turned away and wiped his eyes, blew his nose. "I don't mind the sofa. Let's get some rest, son."

They walked down the hall together, then separated at the living room. J.D. flipped on the hall light as he passed, got to his bedroom door, then returned and shut off the light. The kids were gone. There was no need for the night-light.

He didn't undress. He just lay atop the covers and stared at the ceiling. The living room light went off. The sofa creaked as Bud settled in. A car passed by on the side street. His heart pounded.

He'd gotten what he wanted in the beginning—the kids were gone. Unfortunately now he knew he'd only *thought* that was what he wanted. Now that they were gone, he wanted them back. He *needed* them back. He needed to know that they were asleep in the next room, that Gracie had her stuffed animals, that Noah hadn't put his pajamas on backward, that a light was left on for whichever one was afraid of the dark.

Damn Noelle for giving him the kids, and damn Kelsey for taking them away.

And he could damn himself for not trying harder with Caleb. For not heading off this problem before it occurred. He'd known Caleb resented his closeness to the other kids, had known he'd look for some way to get J.D. out of their lives. Any kid who watched TV, heard the news, or talked to other kids knew that an accusation of abuse was quick, easy, and effective. He should have been prepared for it.

But it still threatened to break his heart.

And Kelsey was likely to finish the job.

Turning onto his side, he picked up the phone and

dialed her number. She answered on the third ring, sounding wary, suspicious.

He knew all the things he wanted to say. *Tell me you'll let the kids come home again. Promise you'll help me get Caleb back. Tell me you believe me. Tell me you know me better than that. Show me that last night meant something to you.*

But he couldn't find the right words to give voice to one request—to one plea—and so he said nothing. He lay there, listening to the hum on the line and the soft sound of her breathing, and his fingers tightened till his knuckles turned white, and he said nothing.

She didn't say anything either, not after that first hello. After a full minute, maybe two, she hung up. She'd known it was him, and she'd had nothing to say.

Wearily he hung up too.

He dozed fitfully through the early morning hours. After his run he showered and ate the breakfast Bud had cooked, then went to the phone. Mitch Walker had filled him in on what to expect. The police department would conduct an investigation, then make a report to the district attorney. If there was no finding of abuse, that would be the end of it for J.D. There would be no charges filed— but there would also be no children. He would be removed from the foster parents roll, which meant he wouldn't be eligible to take the kids when their current emergency placement ended.

If there *was* a finding of abuse, charges would be filed and there would be a hearing. He would still lose the kids, and maybe a whole lot more.

Either way, Mitch had recommended that he hire an attorney first thing that morning. J.D. had protested that he hadn't done anything wrong. He was *innocent.* But sometimes, Mitch had pointed out, when a case involved kids, innocence was no defense.

There were only two lawyers in Bethlehem. Since Alex

Thomas was the kids' court-appointed lawyer, that left Jillian Freeman. He called her office, arranged to meet her at nine, then hung up to face his father's scowl.

"You shouldn't have to do this," Bud said vehemently. "You tried to help that boy, and they're punishing you for it. Any fool can see he's lying."

Though J.D. fervently hoped so, his shrug was casual. "He's a kid. You can't be too careful when a kid's safety is at stake."

"Anyone who knows you knows you'd never do something like that."

Again J.D. hoped so—but he wasn't sure. He couldn't swear that Kelsey knew.

After finishing his coffee, he drove downtown. Jillian's office was across the street from the courthouse in a Victorian house that had been converted to a quilt shop on the first floor, offices on the second. He climbed out of his truck and glanced across the street, his gaze automatically going to the third floor windows that looked in on Kelsey's office. Was she there at her desk, swept up in plans to tarnish his reputation and quite possibly destroy his life?

Actually, no. She was standing in front of the courthouse. Her hair was down except for a few strands on either side, gathered and pinned in back, and her frilly, feminine dress was made from fabric that resembled a Monet watercolor. She paced back and forth, clearly waiting for someone. Mitch? The D.A.? Judge McKechnie?

As if she'd felt his gaze, abruptly she turned and looked straight at him. Even with the street between them, he could see the color rise in her cheeks—could see the softness disappear and the defenses go up. When she slowly, deliberately, turned her back to him, it was apparent whose side she'd taken in this ugly mess.

He felt as if he'd been betrayed.

Jillian was waiting in her office. She was a few years

older than him, divorced with three kids, and one tough lawyer. Like him, she'd come to Bethlehem from somewhere else—like him, for a reason. He didn't know what it was and didn't care.

She invited him to sit. He chose to pace. As he walked the length of the office, he sketched out the bare bones of the case. He finished his story and the pacing at the window, watching as Kelsey shook hands with Mary Therese, then led the way inside the courthouse.

"So you admit to grabbing the boy," Jillian said at last.

"Once. Only once."

"Which shoulder?"

He stopped to think. "Right."

"And this was in the hallway. When you went into the bedroom with him, did you touch him?"

He closed his eyes. The question made him feel sick. He had asked other people questions of that nature before, but he'd never dreamed that someday he would be on the receiving end of the suspicion. "No, I didn't. We stood on opposite sides of the room. I was never closer to him than ten feet."

She asked a few more questions, then swiveled her chair around to face him. "You came here about a year and a half ago from Chicago, didn't you?"

He nodded.

"Is there anything in your past that might count against you if there's a hearing? Any legal trouble, disciplinary problems with your job, personal problems?" She cleared her throat. "I'm not trying to pry, J.D., but I can guarantee you that if there's a hearing, the state's going to find out everything there is to know about you. I don't like surprises in court. I want to be prepared. *Is* there anything?"

He stared out the window for a long time, vaguely

aware of the grim reflection looking back, then finally replied, "Yeah. There is."

He drew a deep breath, but the ache in his chest didn't ease. It wouldn't, not until he was finished, not until this whole mess was finished.

Maybe not even then.

HUFFING FROM THE EXERTION OF CLIMBING THE stairs, Mary Therese followed Kelsey into the office, set her briefcase and handbag on the desk, then plopped into the orange chair before fixing her gaze on Kelsey and saying, "Run that past me again, will you? I think my heart was pounding so loud that it played tricks with my hearing."

Kelsey sat down behind her desk, folded her hands on the desktop, then lowered them to her lap. "I want to be removed from this case."

"That's what I thought you said. Why?"

"I can't take part in an investigation where I *know* the person being investigated is innocent."

"Seems to me like that's one you would most particularly like to be involved in." Mary Therese's gaze narrowed. "How do you *know*?"

"I know J.D. He wouldn't do what Caleb's accused him of."

"I know J.D. too—known him a lot longer than you have. But I'm not so sure he wouldn't do it. People surprise you, Kelsey. You learned that your first year in this business, or should have." Mary Therese made an impatient gesture. "I'm shorthanded already. If I remove you from this case, then that means *I* have to take it over. Give me a reason to do that."

Kelsey knotted her fingers together, exhaled loudly,

and, with heat rushing into her face, blurted out, "I like J.D."

"Honey, I'd wager there's not a woman in this county who hasn't fancied herself half in love with the man. Heavens, look at him. He's handsome, funny, smart, a doctor, and he's got a body to die for, and money to boot."

Kelsey cleared her throat, forced her fingers to relax, forced her gaze to remain steady on her boss. "Well, I'd wager there's not another woman in this county whom he's fancied himself half in love with." Unless he'd lied.

Mary Therese's expression turned serious as death. She got up, closed the outer door, then Kelsey's door, then returned to rest her palms on the desk. "He's told you that?"

Kelsey nodded miserably.

"A man doesn't generally say things like that without having a reasonable expectation that his feelings are returned. Are they?"

Her nod this time was slighter, less noticeable.

Mary Therese paced to the opposite end of the office. For a moment she stood in front of the file cabinets, her head bent. When she turned again, she looked angry, but the anger was under tight control. "How far has this gone?"

"We . . . um . . ." Kelsey wet her lips. This wasn't right. The private details of her life were supposed to remain private. They weren't meant to be laid open for examination by others, to be judged and condemned by others.

But when she'd chosen to have an affair with one of her clients, she'd given up the right to privacy. She'd opened herself up to examination, judgment, and condemnation.

"You slept with him, didn't you?" Mary Therese was tight-lipped. Disappointed.

Kelsey nodded once. "I never meant for it to happen. I've been doing this job for twelve years, and I've never been the least bit interested in any client, but with J.D., it was just . . . so right, and—"

"It was just so *wrong*. You can't do that, Kelsey! You just can't—" Mary Therese came back and sat down. "Well, hell. Are you going to marry him?"

"I—" Alone in her bed Wednesday night, Kelsey had dared such dreams of the future. After the scene in the hospital corridor the night before, she couldn't even convince herself that they shared a future. "I don't know what's going to happen."

"I hope something comes of it. I hope you didn't risk your career for a short-term fling."

Oh, God, she hoped so too.

Her boss sat silent for a time, then reached a decision. "I'll tell you what, Kelsey, because I *am* so shorthanded, I'm going to keep you on this. We'll handle it together, because everyone deserves someone who believes them on their side. When it's over and all this is settled, then we'll look at the matter of your . . . relationship. Of course, until this is settled, I expect you to keep your distance from J.D. Fair enough?"

More than fair. Kelsey was relieved to accept the offer.

"Now, get me those files—oh, here they are." Mary Therese picked up the records Kelsey had taken home with her last night and brought back again that morning. "J. D. Grayson. Did you find out what the J.D. stands for?"

The innocent question freshened the pain Kelsey thought might never go away. "No, I didn't."

"Probably something simple like John David or Jimmy Dean. Or maybe"—looking up, Mary Therese grinned— "his father was named Jay and his mother was named Dee."

"His father's name is Bud," Kelsey said. "At least, his nickname is." She didn't add that he was a very nice man who'd made her feel welcome—at least until last night, when he'd looked at her with such disappointment as he'd carried Noah to her car. He hadn't spoken to her, hadn't asked how she could do this to his son, but she'd read the accusation in his eyes. She'd felt the disapproval in his silence.

It seemed she was disappointing everyone lately.

Including herself.

"What time is Caleb's appointment with the detective?" Mary Therese asked without glancing up from the folder she was reading.

"Ten. We should leave in a few minutes."

"The background material here on J.D. is a little sketchy. It covers only the time he's been in Bethlehem, which means none of it's more than eighteen months old. There's nothing about his life before he came here."

"He came from Chicago," Kelsey said quietly. She wasn't betraying a confidence. Everyone in town knew where he'd lived. Still, she felt . . . underhanded. As if she were telling secrets.

"Slide that phone over here, would you?" As soon as she did, Mary Therese began punching in a number. "A girl I worked with just out of college was from Chicago. She went back there when she got married. I'll see if she can help us out."

Five minutes later she hung up, smiling. "She'll get what she can and fax it to us. Now, I believe you and I have an interview to attend to."

CALEB WAS SCARED—MORE SCARED THAN HE'D ever been in his life. His dad had always told him it was wrong to lie, and now he knew why. That one little lie he'd told the welfare lady had gotten bigger and bigger, and now it was causing trouble for everyone, especially Grayson, but he didn't know how to stop it. He couldn't tell the truth, not with the police a part of it now, and the welfare lady's boss and the doctor at the hospital. If he tried to tell the truth, they'd arrest him and send him away and he'd never see the kids again.

If he didn't tell the truth, they might arrest Grayson and send *him* away.

He sat at the dining table in the house where they'd spent last night. It was bigger than Grayson's house and the lady—Mrs. Thomas—was real sweet and pretty, but she fussed over them. He liked not being fussed over, like the doc did.

Kelsey said last night that the woman's husband, Mr. Thomas, was their lawyer, and that had scared Caleb. He didn't need a lawyer, he'd insisted. He hadn't done anythin' wrong—another lie. She'd said they had a lawyer to look after their rights 'cause they were kids and wards of the state. She hadn't said anythin' about him doing anything wrong, because she knew he had. She knew he'd lied, and she hated him for it. Grayson hated him for it. Even the kids hated him for it.

There were other people sitting at the table. Kelsey and her boss, and Mr. Thomas, and a policeman. He was a detective, so he didn't wear a uniform, but he had a badge and a gun. Caleb had seen them when he came in. He could arrest Caleb and take him away if he said one thing that was different from what he said before.

It would break his dad's heart if he came back and found out Caleb had told lies to the police.

But it would break even more if he came back and Caleb was gone and no one was there to take care of the kids.

Mary Therese Carpenter laid her hand over his. Hers

was warm. His was sweaty and cold. "Caleb, we're going to ask you some questions, all right? There's nothing to be afraid of. All you have to do is answer them. Do you understand?"

He nodded, then tugged at the neck of his shirt. That made his bruises hurt and made him wiggle in his chair. He wanted more than anything in the world to jump up and run out of the house and just run and run until he couldn't go no farther. But they'd come after him. The policeman would catch him and know he'd lied and take him away.

The policeman introduced himself, but his name went in and out of Caleb's head. He'd never met a policeman that didn't scare him, except maybe Alanna's uncle. But even her uncle would be mad at him now, and Alanna would hate him because she loved the doc and she would never forgive Caleb for lying about him. She would never be his friend again.

"Where did you get the bruises, Caleb?"

He swallowed hard. Truth or lie? One would get Grayson in trouble. The other would get *him* in trouble. One would keep Grayson away from the kids. The other would keep *him* away. He'd promised his dad he would look out for the kids, would protect them and keep them safe. They weren't safe with Grayson, 'cause they were starting to love him. They were starting to think of him like he was their dad, and he wasn't, and that would break their real dad's heart.

He couldn't let anyone break his dad's heart.

He stopped squirming in his chair and looked right at the policeman. "*He* did it. Dr. Grayson."

He lied.

Again.

And nobody was ever gonna forgive him.

•   •   •

WHEN HE LEFT HIS HOUSE SATURDAY MORNING, J.D. pretended that he was going for a run, just as he did every morning. He went early, long before the sun was up, because he wasn't sleeping well and might as well be up and accomplishing something, not because he wanted to avoid all the offers of sympathy and support. He headed for the south side of town because he'd run everywhere but there in the last few days, not because Kelsey's apartment was over there.

But he gave up his pretenses as he approached the apartment complex. He turned into the dimly lit lot, slowed to a walk at the sidewalk that led to number three. He didn't ring the doorbell though. He simply sat down on the top step and waited. He figured she usually headed out around six. That gave him an hour to figure out what the hell he was going to say. He didn't have a clue as he leaned against the wall.

How had the ugliness that had dogged him in Chicago found him in Bethlehem? He'd thought he was safe here. He'd thought he could live the rest of his life here, as happy and contented as a man with his past was ever going to be. He had friends—a lot, he'd discovered in the last thirty-six hours—and a job he liked and a woman to ease his occasional loneliness. He could have lived the next fifty years like that and been satisfied.

But, no, he'd gotten cocky. He'd had to take in those kids and try to be a parent to them even though he'd known the risks. He'd had to get involved with Kelsey even though he'd known the dangers. And what had he gotten in return? A little pleasure, a whole lot of pain, and a life that was never going to be the same.

If he could go back to that Sunday after church . . . He would tell Noelle no, would run the other way, not only from the kids but from Kelsey too. He would quit being a sucker for others and would put himself first . . . even though putting his own needs first back in Chicago had started this whole mess.

He would have peace.

There was a sound behind him, then the door opened and Kelsey stepped out. She stopped immediately, as if she wanted to go back inside, then locked the door and faced him.

She was wearing old, faded running clothes and still looked damn beautiful. The tank top revealed more of her multicolored bra than it concealed, and her shorts were so short that her legs seemed to go on forever. It had seemed that way three nights ago too, when they were wrapped around him, holding him inside her—not that he'd had any desire to be anywhere else.

His first impulse was to smile, his second to reach for her, his third to pull her down to him, on top of him, underneath him. Instead, he swallowed hard and knotted his hands into fists and satisfied himself with simply looking at her.

It was a sorry substitute.

After a while she walked past him and down the steps.

"Can't you even speak to me, Kelsey?" His voice was hoarse, ragged.

She stopped, then slowly pivoted to face him. There was no warmth in her eyes, no affection, certainly no love. Not even a hint of it. "Actually, no. I'm under orders not to."

For a moment her words confused him. Then understanding dawned. He got to his feet, feeling achy in every joint. "You told Mary Therese."

"I had no choice."

"You always have choices, Kelsey."

His response made her flinch, made anger flare in her

eyes. "So do you. Forgetting about the mistake you made with me is one of them."

"What mistake? I don't know what you're talking about." His only mistake was in leaving her bed, in not staying there all night Wednesday, all day Thursday, and all that night too. Then Caleb could have made all the accusations in the world, and it wouldn't matter, because she would have had irrefutable proof—the sweet aches in her own body—that he was innocent.

So stiff with tension that she practically vibrated, she parroted back words he'd said to her in the emergency room. " 'You always have a choice, Kelsey. You're just making the wrong one. Apparently so did I.' " The words were underlaid with sarcasm and anger and, hidden deep within, hurt.

Bleakly he shook his head. "I wasn't talking about you. Making love with you—falling in love with you—wasn't a choice. It just happened, because it was right. It was meant to be. It was—you are—the best thing that's happened to me in a long time." He reached out a trembling hand to her but drew back when she stiffened even more. "God, Kelsey, I never meant to hurt you."

For a long while she looked at him, her expression unreadable. He half expected her to walk away and leave him alone. Instead, she hesitantly, reluctantly, asked, "Then what was your wrong choice?"

He curled his fingers at his sides. "The kids. I thought I could have them in my house, in my life, for a few weeks, maybe a month or so, and everything would be fine. They'd be better off for having known me, and I—I would remain untouched. But I was wrong." His voice quavered. "I want them back. And I want you back. Kelsey, I lo—"

She stumbled a few steps back. "I can't talk to you," she said frantically. "I can't see you. I'm sorry." Spinning on one heel, she started away, breaking into a run before she'd gone ten feet. Within moments she'd disappeared into the darkness.

J.D. leaned against the wall for support. The night they'd made love, she'd stood here on this porch, touching him so gently as she gave her one argument against what they were about to do. I could lose my job, she'd whispered.

Or your heart, he'd replied. He'd thought that her concerns for her job were an excuse—a valid one, but still an excuse. He'd thought her real reason for holding back was fear of commitment, of falling in love, of risking her heart.

Apparently he was wrong again.

Chapter Fifteen

A LANNA DALTON PUSHED HER BIKE ACROSS the intersection, then hopped on to pedal the last half block. She'd told her aunt Emilie that she was going to Susan's house, and just so she wouldn't make a liar of herself, she intended to go there, but first she had to make one stop. She had to see Caleb.

It was supposed to be some sort of secret where Caleb, his brothers, and Gracie were staying now that they'd left Dr. J.D.'s, but Bethlehem was a little place. Everyone talked about everyone else, and her friend Nelia, who lived across the street from the Thomases, said the Browns were there. She'd seen them from her bedroom window when Miss Kelsey and Chief Walker brought them over Thursday night and had seen Miss Kelsey and another lady and one of the detectives who worked with Uncle Nathan come back Friday, and she'd called Alanna and told her all about it.

Alanna rode her bike into the Thomases' yard, then let it fall as she climbed the steps to the porch. For just a second she hesitated, then pushed the doorbell and waited. It took only a minute for Miss Melissa to answer the door. She smiled widely, as she always did. "Hi, Alanna. What are you doing so far from home?"

Alanna brushed back her hair. "It's not so far," she said nervously, because it was farther than Aunt Emilie let her go by herself. "And I rode my bike, so it seemed even shorter. Is Caleb here?"

"Yes, he is."

"Can I see him, please?"

"Sure." Miss Melissa stepped back and let her in, then pointed upstairs. "He's in his room—turn right at the top, last door on the left. Would you like some lemonade and cookies? I just served the younger kids, but Caleb said he didn't want any."

"No, thank you. I just want to see Caleb." She climbed the stairs quickly, then went down the hall to the right. There were two rooms there, both with doors open. In the room on the right were two beds covered with Gracie's and Noah's stuffed animals, and there were toys and clothes scattered around. In the room on the left, there was just one bed and nothing scattered around. Caleb sat on the bed, his knees drawn up, his face hidden in his arms.

"Hey, Caleb," she said uneasily as she walked in.

"Go 'way."

"What's wrong?"

"Everything's wrong." He raised his head then, and she wished he hadn't. He'd been crying, and he looked miserable, as if he just wanted to curl up and die. She knew other kids cried sometimes—so did she once in a while—but she'd never thought about Caleb crying. No matter how mean kids were to him at school, he never cried. He just got madder and quieter. He must be hurting really, really bad to cry now, and that made a lump form in her own throat.

She sat down on the edge of the bed. "Why're you in here by yourself? Why aren't you downstairs having lemonade and cookies with the others?"

At first she thought he was going to yell at her and maybe call her stupid. But he didn't. He just looked like he might cry again.

"They don't want me down there, or sharing their room or nothin'. They don't even want me bein' their brother no more. They said I ruined everything."

Alanna felt her face turn red. She thought he'd ruined everything too. They'd had it good at Dr. J.D.'s. He would've been a good father if Caleb had just given him a chance and if he hadn't lied about Dr. J.D. hurting him. "Who hit you?"

The look he gave her was mean and scary and made her scoot back a bit. "Did *he* tell you to ask that? Did you come here 'cause of *him*?"

"No. I came because . . . well, yes, because of him. Because you're lying and hurting everybody. If you'd just tell the truth, Caleb, it's not too late. Everything can be fixed, and you guys can go back to Dr. J.D.'s house, and we can all still play together, and—and everyone would be all right. But you have to tell the truth."

He rolled off the other side of the bed and went to the window. "If I told—if I changed my story, they wouldn't let me go back. They'd arrest me and send me away. 'Sides, even if they did let me go back, *he* wouldn't. He don't want me. He never did."

"I don't think they'd arrest you," she said hesitantly. "You're just a kid, and I don't think they arrest kids, not just for telling lies, not even big lies like this. I can ask Uncle Nathan if you want."

For a moment he looked at her as if he were thinking about it. She held her breath. If he would tell the truth, then everything could go back to the way it was. She could see him practically every day. They could be friends again.

Then he shook his head. "Even if they didn't arrest me, he wouldn't take me back. He'd keep the kids and send me away, and I'd never see them."

"Dr. J.D. wouldn't do that."

"He told me so." He looked sadder and sorrier than anyone she'd ever seen. "I wish I could just go away and everyone would forget what I said and the kids could go back and be a family the way they want to."

"Yeah, but then what would happen to you?"

"It don't matter," he said quietly.

Alanna left the bed and walked over to stand beside him. "It matters to me, Caleb."

When he looked at her, there was hope in his eyes, like he just might believe her, but too soon it was gone. He shook his head again and turned back to the window.

"I guess I'd better go. Aunt Emilie thinks I'm over at Susan's."

He didn't say anything.

She walked to the door, then faced him one more time. "Think about telling the truth, Caleb. If you don't, they're gonna make you go to court and swear to God that you'll tell the whole truth and nothing but the truth, and you're gonna have to sit in this big chair and tell those stories and . . ." Her voice dropped to a whisper. "You might really ruin everything then. Forever and always."

He shook his head slowly back and forth, then leaned his chin in both hands. "It's too late. I just want to go away."

THE THIRD FLOOR OF THE COURTHOUSE WAS EErily quiet late on a Saturday afternoon. If she had a radio, Kelsey would turn it on just to provide herself with some distraction, but she didn't. All she had was the paper-work from the Brown/Grayson case in front of her, and it was depressing as hell.

The phone in the outer office rang, the shrillness making her jump. The fax machine picked up before the first ring ended. By the time it started printing, she was standing in front of it.

The fax was from Mary Therese's friend in Chicago. The first page was a handwritten note. *Found lots of professional stuff, but this was the only personal. Will follow up further on Monday.* "This" was a newspaper article—grainy, enlarged to make up for the poor quality. *Two Killed in Traffic Accident*, the headline read. She started reading on her way back to her desk.

> Two area residents died Wednesday evening in a two-car accident in downtown Chicago, police said. Pete Jones, 52, of Crystal Lake, was driving west on Jackson Drive just after 9 p.m., when he failed to stop for a red light and struck a vehicle northbound on Michigan Avenue. Witnesses said Jones's truck was traveling at a high rate of speed when it entered the intersection and collided with the second vehicle, driven by J. D. Grayson, 34, of Chicago. Jones died en route to Cook County Hospital. A passenger in the second vehicle—

A rap at the hall door echoed faintly, but Kelsey didn't look up. She couldn't. "Come in," she called while continuing to read.

> A passenger in the second vehicle, Carol Ann Grayson, was pronounced dead at the scene.

Her husband was treated for minor injuries and released.

"Kelsey? I thought I saw your car in the parking lot." Mitch Walker came as far as the inner doorway. "We just got a call—are you okay?"

She gave him a blank look.

"Bad news?"

Slowly she lowered her gaze to the fax, but she couldn't focus on it. Her hands were trembling too badly. She turned it facedown on the desk, then clasped her fingers together to stop their shaking. "I, uh, no, just—" She drew a deep breath. "What can I do for you, Mitch?"

His expression shifted from friendly concern to grim worry. "We just got a call from Alex Thomas. Caleb's disappeared."

T HE SCENE AT THE THOMASES' HOUSE WAS CON- trolled chaos. Most of the Bethlehem Police Depart- ment, including all the off-duty officers, and half the sheriff's department, had gathered. Within minutes after arriving, Mitch was huddled with Sheriff Ingles to deter- mine the best way to proceed with a search.

Kelsey listened in for a few minutes, then sought out Melissa Thomas, sitting on the couch with the younger three kids. "I'm so sorry, Kelsey," Melissa said, looking as miserable as she sounded.

"What happened?"

"After lunch he said he was going out in the backyard. There's a swing out there. He sat down and . . . he just looked so alone. I didn't want to disturb him, but I checked on him while I was doing dishes and when I went upstairs to make the beds. He was fine, just sitting there.

Then, the next time I checked, he was gone, and I couldn't find him anywhere. I am so sorry!"

"It's okay. It's not your fault. If he wanted to leave, he would have found a way no matter what."

"I know where he went," Noah piped up.

"Where, Noah?"

"Away. Just like Daddy. And Mama."

"But he'll be back," Kelsey said, giving him a reassuring pat on the knee. "We'll find him."

"Nope." He shook his head confidently. "When people leave, they don't come back. It was just Caleb's turn to go. Pretty soon it'll be Jacob's turn, and then mine, and then we'll all be alone. We'll never see each other again."

"It wasn't Caleb's turn to go," Jacob said angrily. "He left 'cause we were mean to him. 'Cause we told him we'd rather live with Dr. J.D. than with him and we didn't want him to be our brother anymore."

"*I* didn't tell him that," Noah protested. "You did, and Gracie, but not me."

Jacob poked his brother with an elbow, then turned a tearful gaze on Kelsey. "We didn't mean it. We was just mad 'cause he's causing so much trouble and we just wanna go back home and we can't long as he's tellin' lies. We just wanted to make him tell the truth 'bout how he got hurt so's we could go home."

"Do you know how he got hurt, Jacob?"

He shook his head. "But Dr. J.D. didn't do it. He's sort of like our daddy, and daddies don't hurt their kids."

That naive faith said a lot for Ezra Brown's fathering skills, Kelsey thought with a faint smile. "Where would Caleb go if he was angry or scared?"

"Away," Noah replied. "Like our mama and our daddy."

This time Gracie poked him. "He liked to sit on the glider at Miss C'rinna's. And on his bed at Dr. J.D.'s."

"What about at home—at your other home?"

All three kids looked blank, then Jacob shrugged. "He never had time for being angry or scared. He always had things to do, like takin' care of us."

Gracie's plump lower lip began to tremble. "Who's gonna take care of us now?"

"Don't worry," Kelsey said with more confidence than she felt. "We'll find Caleb. Until we do, Melissa's going to take care of you, okay?"

She waited until each of the kids nodded before getting to her feet and joining Mitch in the doorway. "Has anyone talked to J.D.?"

"Not that I know of."

"I'm going to see if I can track him down. Maybe Caleb went looking for him."

Mitch nodded, then laid his hand on her arm. "I don't know if you've heard yet, but . . . the D.A.'s scheduled a hearing for Monday morning. Mary Therese said she would let you know."

A chill swept through Kelsey. So Caleb's claim of abuse was considered founded. Of course, how could it not be? He and J.D. had argued. J.D. admitted to grabbing him, and Caleb had the bruises to prove it. How he really got those bruises was anyone's guess, but until he decided to tell the truth, the investigating officer had been left with little choice.

Oh, God, she wished she had stayed in New York City! She wished she'd never come to Bethlehem, never met these people, these kids, J.D. But that wasn't true. Not for a minute.

"You think the kid ran away because he finally realized how much trouble his lies were going to cause?" Mitch asked.

"I think so."

The police chief shook his head. "What a mess."

She gave him a tight, grim smile of agreement before leaving.

J.D.'s truck wasn't in its usual space outside his apartment. She didn't bother checking to see if Bud was home. She didn't want to see how he would look at her. It was Saturday, and before the kids, J.D. had spent most Saturdays working on his house. It was logical to assume that after the kids he would go back there again.

She headed out of town, practically missing the turn off the highway. She drove slower than necessary along the narrow road, delaying the moment when she would have to face him. She'd brought enough bad news in the last few days. Couldn't she be spared having to tell him that Caleb had disappeared? Couldn't she be spared facing him so soon after discovering the truth about how his marriage ended?

She hadn't even had time to take it in, to process it and come to all the logical conclusions—like the fact that for his wife's death to still hold such power over him nearly two and a half years later, he must have loved her dearly. Or the fact that he'd come to Bethlehem to deal with his grief over losing her, not to replace her. Or the fact that he'd kept her life and death such a secret because it was the most precious, most private part of himself, too precious to share with anyone else.

Even her.

Apparently she wasn't going to be spared anything. The clearing came into view ahead, and his truck was parked right in the middle. She pulled in beside it, shut off the engine, and climbed out. The place was quiet, with only the standard forest noises. There was no whine of a drill to interrupt the birds' song, no hammering steady and strong enough to make a woodpecker envious. Just quiet.

But not peace.

She climbed the steps to the porch, tried the front door,

and found it locked. Circling the house, she paused before the last corner, breathing deeply, trying to prepare herself for the next few minutes. But she could stand there and breathe until she keeled over from hyperventilating, and she would never be prepared, and so she simply forced herself to turn the corner.

J.D. sat at the table at the far end of the deck. He wore shorts and a T-shirt—work clothes—and his jaw was unshaven. From this angle, at this distance, he looked slightly disreputable and entirely handsome. But then he looked at her, and she saw the haunted, helpless look in his eyes. Even rocks crumble, Bud had told her two nights before. She'd patted his arm patronizingly and dismissed his warning, but she knew from that look that Bud had been right. Rocks did crumble, and J.D. was on the verge.

Just as slowly as he'd looked at her, he turned away, redirecting his gaze to the tabletop. Two empty beer cartons had been cast aside, and twelve bottles were neatly lined up in an arc in front of him, their caps all intact. Something about the bottles' placement bothered her— too much attention paid to it, she supposed, as if each bottle were of utmost importance.

Finally she left the safety of the distant corner and approached him. She wanted nothing more than to sit down beside him, to wrap her arms around him and hold him close, comfort him, tell him that everything would be all right, that together they could make it all right. But she did none of that. Too cowardly, too afraid that nothing would be all right, she slid onto the bench opposite him.

"Does Mary Therese know you're here?" His voice sounded raw, weary, undone. She wondered how he was sleeping, then silently chastised herself. Hadn't she found him on her porch at five o'clock that morning? And hadn't she foolishly turned him away?

"No, I don't suppose she does."

"Then you'd better run back home before she finds out that you're fraternizing with the enemy." He picked up one of the bottles, cradling it in both hands. "I suppose you've heard the news. On Monday morning, at eleven o'clock I have to appear in court to be formally accused in front of my friends and neighbors of physically abusing a child in my care."

"I'm sorry, J.D."

He pointed the neck of the bottle at her. "Tell that to the people who will believe I'm guilty. Tell it to the kids who have come to think of me as their friend. Tell it to everyone whose faith in me is tarnished or weakened or destroyed altogether by this."

"No one will believe you're guilty."

His laugh was cold and bitter. "Well, hell, honey, *somebody* believes it, or they wouldn't be hauling me into court to try to prove it." Just as quickly as the black humor appeared, it disappeared. "All my life I've tried to be the best man I could be, a man my father and mother would be proud of. Sometimes I've failed. In Chicago I failed miserably, but here . . . I had begun to believe that this was the person I was meant to be. But is this what those failures were leading up to? *This?* A man accused of hitting a little boy?"

He continued to toy with the bottle—twisting the cap, breaking its seal, taking it off, then immediately screwing it back on tight. She watched him caress the glass, watched him swallow hard, as if the longing were almost too much to resist. He put the bottle down, returned it to its place in the arc, and his hand trembled as he drew back.

Why don't you drink? she had asked him at the carnival, and he had given her several reasons—he was on call all the time, he couldn't attend to patients with his senses impaired, he cared too much for his health.

But he hadn't told her the biggest reason of all.

He looked up at her, and the bitter smile returned. "You look appalled. I guess my secret's out—one of 'em, at least. Did you guess? Or did you snoop around under the guise of doing your job and find out that way?"

She could hardly breathe. Her lungs were tight, and her heart felt as if it just might shatter. "You're an—"

"You can say the word. It won't taint you." His movements jerky and angry, he stood up as if at a podium in front of a crowd and intoned in a strong voice, "My name is J.D., and I'm an alcoholic." Then he slumped onto the bench again. "God, I thought I'd said that for the last time."

She was stunned. She didn't know what to do, what to say. She couldn't even think, couldn't wrap her mind around the fact that J. D. Grayson, the steadiest, calmest, most stable person she knew, was an alcoholic. J.D., who was strong for everyone else, who healed everyone else, had a weakness of the most vicious kind.

"And that's not even the worst of it," he went on.

"I know about Carol Ann."

Abruptly he turned cold. "You know nothing about Carol Ann."

"I know that she was your wife. I know that she died in a car crash over two years ago."

"Do you know that she had dark hair and dark eyes and looked as innocent as Gracie? That she studied ballet for nineteen years and gave up her chance at a career to marry me? That she loved children and old movies and romance novels and dogs? Do you know that she was ticklish and spoke fluent French and was self-conscious about the way she laughed, because she was so delicate and graceful and her laugh was so big and full-bodied? That she talked in her sleep and never met a stranger and was fascinated by archaeology and astronomy and movie special effects?" He broke off for a breath, a deep, ragged sob that made Kelsey ache. "Do you know that she was the worst cook in the entire world and that she always believed the absolute best of everyone, including me?"

He closed his eyes, covered his face with his hands, muffling his next words. "Do you know that it's my fault she's dead?"

"That's not true," she protested, her voice unsteady, her throat tight. "The other driver was speeding. He ran a red light."

So slowly, as if the action hurt, he removed his hands from his face, then shook his head from side to side. "It's my fault. She loved me more than anyone has ever loved me. She had faith in me. She *trusted* me. And she paid for that trust with her life. And I get to live with that knowledge. That's my punishment."

Once more he gave her a heartrending look. "And that's not all. Carol Ann and I had a son. He lives in Chicago with her parents and wants nothing to do with me. I've been judged an unfit parent. I can't have custody of my own child. And that—" He looked longingly at the beer. "That's also my punishment."

THE WIND THAT BLEW ACROSS THE DECK WAS gentle, not even enough to stir the curls that hung loose down Kelsey's back, certainly not enough to blow that stunned look off her face. Though he'd thought he was fresh out of courage, J.D. watched her. This would make or break them. Either she would stand by him, or she would damn him the way he'd damned himself for so long. It wasn't fair to hope for a better reaction from her than he was capable of himself—after all, they were his own sins—but he was hoping.

Right now hope was about all he had left.

"Trey," she whispered softly. "Trey wasn't your patient. He's your son."

He nodded.

"You were named after your father. And your—your son—" She frowned, shook her head, then repeated the words to herself. "Your son is named after you. Senior, junior, the third. Trey." She raised a hand to rub her forehead, then let it drop limply to her lap. "My God, J.D."

He wondered what that meant. *My God, I'm sorry. My God, what you've been through. My God, what you've done.* Was she pitying him or damning him? He wasn't sure he could bear either one.

"Tell me . . ."

His throat was dry, and he wished for something to make the words easier. The beer would do the job, but he knew too well that if he started drinking now, he would never stop. His two years, four months, and three days of sobriety would be lost. *He* would be lost, and not even Kelsey would be able to save him.

He wasn't sure exactly what she wanted to know, and so he told her everything. He began at the beginning, and he would end at the end. The end for him and Carol Ann, the end for him and Trey. Would it also be the end for him and Kelsey?

"Carol Ann and I got married in college, and Trey was born while I was in med school. It was her idea to name him after me. She thought it would please my dad, even though neither of us had ever used our given name, and she was right. It did please him."

Bud had been thrilled with his only grandchild. He'd doted on Trey, and it had almost broken his heart when J.D. had moved the family to Chicago after medical school. They'd remained close, though, until two years ago. When Trey had cut J.D. out of his life, he'd also turned his back on his grandfather.

"I was ambitious. I liked psychiatry. I was good at it, and I intended to be the best. But you don't get to be the best at anything without long hours and hard work. I devoted myself to that while Carol Ann took care of everything else. She ran the house, managed our social lives, played both mother and father to our son. As far as Trey was concerned, I was this person who passed through the house from time to time, who never made it to his soccer games, who didn't show up at his school programs. Sometimes I don't think he even saw me as part of the family. I was just someone who paid the bills and took his mother's attention away from him."

He risked a look at Kelsey. She was sitting very still, barely breathing. Her gaze was directed down, as if the boards that made up the tabletop greatly interested her. He wished she would look at him so he could try to judge the emotion in her eyes. At the same time, he was glad she was avoiding him. If he was going to lose her, he'd rather not see the proof just yet.

"I saw patients, read, studied, researched, wrote papers. I built a reputation, made a name for myself. I took the toughest cases—the kids who had been abandoned, abused, neglected—and I achieved remarkable success. And it depressed the hell out of me."

Picking up the nearest bottle of beer, he unscrewed the cap and thought about how easy it would be to drink it. In the months after Carol Ann's death, he would have sold his soul for just one drink. Hell, he would have sold *her* soul. There were times when he would have rather been dead than alive and not drinking, times when *nothing*—not sobriety, not self-respect, not even his son—had been worth the hell he was going through. He'd had no pride, no dignity, nothing but the raw, jagged, bone-deep *need* for alcohol and the peace it could give him.

His mouth watered at the thought of taking a drink. His stomach roiled. He started to tip the bottle over, to let the beer run over the planks and spill through the cracks to drip on the floor below. Instead, he screwed the cap back on, then clasped both hands around the bottle neck and returned to his story.

"I began having problems separating myself from my job. I spent my life listening to firsthand accounts of the most terrible atrocities one human being could do to another—to innocent, helpless children—and I was expected to just leave it in the office when I walked out the door. I couldn't do it. No matter what I did, I couldn't get away from it. There was so much sickness out there, so much depravity and pure evil, and I felt contaminated by it. Finally I discovered that a drink helped me relax. If one drink helped, then two would help more, and four would make life bearable, and after eight or ten or twelve, I could actually find a little peace."

Of their own will, his fingers began twisting the bottle cap again. He forced them to stop.

"My family and friends never suspected a thing. They knew I drank a lot, but they never saw me drunk. I never staggered, slurred my speech, or appeared hung over, so they assumed I had it under control. The truth was, I drank so heavily that what would normally make a man of my size appear profoundly intoxicated barely touched me."

Feeling anxious and edgy, as if he couldn't possibly sit still any longer, he set the bottle aside and stood up. He paced to one end of the deck, then the other. Finally he settled at the railing, staring out into the woods, his hands tightly gripping the curved rail cap. "One evening Carol Ann and I had dinner plans with friends. I had a few drinks before we left the house, and I had quite a few more through the meal. She wanted to drive home from the restaurant. She said I'd had too much to drink, and I blew up at her. It was the first time she'd ever commented on my drinking, and it scared me. I was this hotshot psychiatrist, the best damn head doctor in the city, one of the top shrinks in the country. My ego—my arrogance—couldn't let anyone know that I couldn't handle it, that I needed a crutch to survive the day, that without the booze I would be as dysfunctional as my patients."

Before long the sun would set. He wished he could hurry it up, could bring on the shadows and hide in them forever. He wished this hellish day would end so he would never have to relive it again.

Behind him a floorboard creaked, and he sensed Kelsey's approach. She hesitated near him, then moved to stand a few feet away. He saw her from the corner of his eye, but he didn't look at her, didn't reach for her though his fingers ached to.

"I got in the car and told Carol Ann that she could come with me or find her own way home. I didn't care. She chose to come with me. Four blocks later I stopped at a red light, and when it turned green, I pulled into the intersection in front of a speeding truck. The impact knocked our car halfway down the block. I remember the sirens of the police cars, a fire engine, the ambulances, someone screaming. . . . It was me. The other driver was dying, and Carol Ann was dead, and I . . . I walked away. I lived to go home and tell our twelve-year-old son that his mother was dead, and he didn't even need to smell the liquor to know. . . ."

He made a sound that might have been a dry laugh or the start of a strangled sob. "I worked every day with doctors, nurses, social workers, substance-abuse counselors, and none of them suspected a thing. But my twelve-year-old son had known for months that his father was a drunk. Not surprisingly he blamed me for Carol Ann's death. He said that if I had been sober, I would have been more careful. I would have looked to make sure the cars on the other street were stopping. I would have waited a few lousy seconds . . . and she would still be alive. And he was right."

The silence that settled when he stopped talking was deafening. He could hear his own heart thudding painfully in his chest, could hear the uneven tenor of his breathing, but there was nothing else. No sympathy from Kelsey. No comfort. No assurances that he wasn't responsible, that he didn't contribute to the death of the woman who'd loved him more than anyone deserved to be loved. Just that terrible, damning silence.

His breath caught in his chest as he forced himself to finish. "Trey went to her funeral with me. He stood beside me, said the prayers with me, but when it was over, he refused to go home with me. He very calmly told me that he wished I had died instead of his mother, that he would never forgive me for what I'd done, and that he was moving in with her parents. I let him go. I thought he was upset. He was grieving, in shock. I was going away for treatment, and he needed someplace to stay anyway. I thought that when I came back would be the time to resolve things with him.

"So I went to a rehab facility. I started therapy, got sober, learned how to handle my problems, went home to pick up the pieces, and my in-laws slapped me with notice that they were suing for custody of Trey. He hated me. They hated me. Hell, I hated myself. So I saved them the trouble of going to court. I relinquished my parental rights, and I came here to start over again." His scorn was painful. "*Relinquished my parental rights.* It sounds so much better that way, so much less contemptible. The plain and simple truth is, I gave away my son. Like a piece of property I no longer needed, no longer wanted, I gave away my own child, and I haven't had any contact with him since. I've written him, sent him gifts, tried calling him, but he wants nothing to do with me. I no longer exist for him."

Again the silence settled. This time he had nothing further to say. If she didn't, then they truly were finished.

Kelsey held on to the rail for support. It wasn't often that she found herself at a loss for words, but she had no idea what to say or how to say it. She wasn't sure she wanted to say anything at all.

And so she didn't. She moved away from the rail, walked right up to J.D., said a quick prayer that he wouldn't reject her, and wrapped her arms tightly around him. For one moment he held himself stiff, then in a flash the tension fled his body and he sagged against her. He held on to her, buried his face in her hair, shuddered against her.

She didn't know how long they stood that way. Long enough for his shudders to pass. Long enough for her to find her voice, even though it was husky with unshed tears. "You didn't kill your wife, J.D. A speeding driver did. You didn't make your son hate you. Grief did that. And you didn't give him away. You put him in the custody of people who wanted to give him a loving home."

Slowly he lifted his head from her shoulder, but he didn't step away. He didn't loosen his grip on her. "And what can I blame for my drinking? Because the fact remains that if I hadn't been drinking that night—"

"If you hadn't been drinking, and the accident still happened, if the other driver still chose to speed, still chose to run that red light, and Carol Ann still died, then what? On what grounds would you blame yourself?" She shook her head. "J.D., there are hundreds, maybe thousands, of ifs. If you hadn't turned onto that street, if you hadn't gone to that restaurant, if you hadn't become friends with those people, if you hadn't moved to Chicago, if you hadn't married Carol Ann, if you hadn't ever been born . . . If you look hard enough, you can find a way to accept responsibility for everything that ever went wrong. But accepting it doesn't *make* you responsible. Bad things happen. Sometimes we know why. Sometimes we don't."

He raised one hand to gently touch her face. "It should have been so easy. She was beautiful, and I was smart. She had a capacity for loving, and I had a talent for healing. She was great at home. I was great at work. She loved me, and I loved her. Oh, God, how I loved her. Our lives should have been perfect."

Kelsey felt a twinge of pain at hearing him talk about such love for another woman. It made her feel like second best in a contest where only first place counted. Carol Ann was the great love of his life, and she was the consolation prize who could take the other woman's place but could never replace her.

Then guilt swept away the pain. She had no right to feel sorry for herself. J.D. was the one facing legal charges, a court hearing, damage to his reputation, and loss of the kids, to say nothing of the temptation awaiting him on the table.

She wished she could slip out of his arms and across the deck, gather the beer, and empty it in the dirt. But that couldn't be her choice. She couldn't say no for him. If she tried, how difficult would it be for him to go back to the store and simply buy more? He had to want it for himself, had to want to hold on to the sobriety he'd fought so hard for for himself and no one else.

He smoothed back her hair, then cradled her face gently. "I love you, Kelsey."

For the first time in two days her smile felt real. It wasn't *Oh, God, how I love you*, but it was a start. Maybe after ten or twelve years he would feel that sort of passion for her. And if he didn't, if Carol Ann always remained first in his heart . . . well, she could live with being last.

After a moment he eased his hold on her, then put a little distance between them. He still held her hand, though, his fingers twined with hers. "Why did you come out here? You were the last person I expected to see today."

"Oh, my God, Caleb!" Stricken, she squeezed her eyes shut. How could she have forgotten? All this time, all this talk, and she'd forgotten the one thing she should have said first.

Apprehension swept over him, as visible as the shudders that had earlier rocked through him. "What about Caleb?" he asked quietly, cautiously.

"The Thomases called Mitch this afternoon to say that Caleb had disappeared. Apparently he's run away."

His fingers tightened until hers throbbed, then abruptly he dropped her hand and paced away. When he turned back, his gaze was filled with regret and sharp-edged despair. "My God, Kelsey, what have we done?"

Chapter Sixteen

SUNDAY MORNING'S CHURCH SERVICE WAS A somber one. Corinna had tried to pay attention to the sermon, but the reverend's words were difficult to concentrate on when little Jacob, Noah, and Gracie Brown sat in the pew in front of her, looking so lost without their older brother. They were worried sick—and who wasn't? Regardless of how mature he seemed, Caleb was really just a young boy, and he was in no shape to be on his own. Of course he was more or less safe in Bethlehem, but once he left the valley, why, anything could happen. He must be frightened, hungry and sick at heart.

She was heartsick.

Once the sermon ended, no one stood around chatting the way they normally did. Some went home to get a quick dinner on the table before joining the search parties. Others went to prepare meals for those who'd worked all morning and all through the previous night. Unable to sleep, she and Agatha had begun cooking before dawn.

They'd dropped off baskets of food at the police department on their way to church and would go home to prepare more.

And, as they'd done in church that morning, they would pray.

"Miss Corinna?"

The timid voice came from behind the nearest tree. She stepped off the sidewalk and peered around to see Garth Nichols all but hugging the bark off. "Yes, Garth, what do you need?"

"Can I . . . talk to you?"

"Yes, you may." She folded her hands over the edge of her Bible and waited, but all he seemed interested in doing was digging at the ground with the toe of his good Sunday shoe. "Yes?" she prompted. "What is it?"

"My mom said I can walk home," he blurted out. "Can I walk with you?"

"I live in the opposite direction, Garth. You know that." After studying him a moment, she said, "Wait here. I'll be back." She crossed the street to the car, where Agatha waited, distractedly tapping one finger on the steering wheel. "Go ahead without me," she said. "I'll be along shortly."

"But where are you—what are you—" Agatha saw Garth, half hidden behind the tree again, and said, "Oh."

Corinna smiled. Garth Nichols was an *oh* sort of boy. After handing her Bible and handbag through the open window, she returned to the boy. "Are you ready?"

"Yeah." Then he quickly corrected himself. "Yes, ma'am."

They walked the first block in silence. At the end of the block, she looked at Garth. "If it's just my company you're wanting, I'm flattered. But if it's talking you want, then you're going to have to open your mouth."

He flushed and tugged at the open collar of his dress

shirt. "It's—it's about—" His Adam's apple bobbed when he swallowed vigorously, then he fell silent again.

He'd been in her Sunday school class for two years, and while he was one of the rowdier of her students, he wasn't a bad boy. He simply didn't get the guidance he needed at home. Nora Nichols had her hands full with work, the house, and one sickly child. Garth's father wasn't of much help. His job driving a truck took him away from home for weeks at a time. While the money he earned was needed, Corinna thought quite frankly that the entire family could use less of his money and more of his company.

"Garth," she prodded again.

He gulped a deep breath, then blurted out, "It's about Caleb. Dr. J.D. didn't give him those bruises. We did, Kenny and me and Tim and Rob and Matt. We saw him that afternoon, that Thursday. He was by himself, off at the end of Hawthorne, past the Mickelsons' house, and we—we decided to pay 'im back for gettin' Kenny and me in trouble at the church and for givin' Kenny that black eye and bloody nose, and so—and so we did."

Calling upon forty years of teaching school to hide her anger, Corinna quietly, calmly, asked, "You did what?"

"Paid 'im back."

"How?"

"We—we jumped 'im."

"Five of you. Against one. And when you'd heard that Caleb had blamed Dr. J.D., you chose to keep your silence."

The boy squirmed. "We hadn't meant to hurt him, not really, and—and when we heard about Dr. J.D., we thought, well, we thought—"

"Why come forward when someone else was already getting the blame."

"Yeah." He rubbed his nose with one hand. "But it ain't right. It ain't—"

"It isn't."

He accepted her correction without a blink. "It isn't right that someone else gets in trouble for what we done—what we did. I don't know why Caleb lied about it, but . . . I have to tell someone."

"You just did, Garth, and I'm proud of you for coming forward." She stopped at the next intersection. Her house was a few blocks to the left, the police station a few blocks to the right. She patted the boy's shoulder before steering him to the right. "Now you have to tell someone else."

"You mean—" His eyes widened. "But couldn't you tell 'em for me? Couldn't you just say you heard it from someone?"

"I could, but it would hardly have the same impact as you telling them. After all, you were there."

"But . . . my mom's expectin' me home soon. She'll be real worried if I don't show up pretty quick."

"I'll call her from the police station." She squeezed his hand reassuringly. "It won't be so difficult, Garth. I'll be with you. And believe me, you'll feel better when it's over."

It wasn't a complete untruth, she assured herself. Once he'd taken his punishment, dealt with the friends he'd told on, and faced up to the people he'd harmed with his silence, he truly would feel better.

Eventually.

A FTER LISTENING TO THE NICHOLS BOY'S CON-fession, J.D. left the courthouse for the square, where he took a seat on the bandstand steps, closed his eyes, and, for what felt like the first time in a very long time, took a deep breath. On any normal summer Sunday the square would be host to any number of families enjoying the weather. But this was no normal day, because Caleb Brown—whom most people hadn't even heard of four weeks before—had run away.

Please, God, don't let it be anything more sinister than that.

"You look like a man who could use about twenty-four hours of sleep."

He looked at Kelsey, standing at the bottom of the steps. She'd spent last night with him at the police station, waiting for news, but she didn't look as wrung out as he felt. In fact, in her pale blue vest and pastel-hued skirt, she looked as fresh as a field of spring flowers.

She looked beautiful.

"I'm under orders to take you home," she said, offering her hand.

He didn't hesitate to take it. It was the first time he'd touched her in too long. "Whose orders?"

"Mitch's. Your dad's. Miss Corinna's." She smiled faintly as she helped him to his feet. "While I might ignore the men, I've learned that one doesn't say no to Miss Corinna."

"No, ma'am, one doesn't."

Once he was on his feet, she let go of his hand. He wondered if it was because they were in public, or because Mary Therese was a few yards away in the police station, or because she simply didn't want to hold his hand. He'd told her yesterday he loved her, and she'd told him . . . nothing. She'd smiled that sweet, sweet smile, but she hadn't said I love you or I like you or I like having sex with you or go to hell. She'd said nothing.

Maybe because she felt nothing.

He settled in the passenger seat for the drive home, tilted his head back, and closed his eyes. It was good to have five minutes with nothing to think about except Kelsey, with nothing to do but be with her. Just knowing she was close enough to touch made everything a little more bearable.

"Here we are."

He opened his eyes, gazed at the empty apartment, then at her. "Come in with me," he said quietly.

It was more than a simple invitation, and she knew it. He could see it in the way her eyes darkened, in the desire that flared. She gazed off into the distance for a long time, then looked at him and offered the faintest of smiles, so faint that he might have imagined it.

They climbed the stairs together. He opened the door, then stepped back for her to enter first. She waited in the hallway, and after locking up again, he led the way to his bedroom.

The only light came through the windows and served to shadow more than it illuminated. He didn't need much light though. Just enough to see her.

Standing in front of her, he fingered the soft cotton of her vest. "You are so beautiful. Off and on through the night, I'd look at you and think how soft and lovely you looked and wonder what you were wearing underneath this. Under the circumstances it seemed inappropriate to care. Now it's only fair . . ." He slid his index finger under the fabric where it draped over her shoulder. There was no bra strap underneath, just warm, silky skin. Just as he'd thought.

Settling his hands at her narrow waist, he pulled her close for a kiss—a slow, lazy nuzzling that took its sweet time to travel from her jaw to her throat to her mouth. When he got there, she was ready, opening to him, welcoming him. His tongue stroked hers, searched here and there, tasted, savored, fed, and she responded so sweetly, with her breath growing uneven, her fingers curling over the waistband of his shorts, her body rubbing sensuously against his.

He trailed his kisses to her jaw, down her throat, following bare skin to the V of the vest. Fumbling, teasing, tormenting, he worked the first button free, then kissed the skin revealed while repeating the process with the next button. By the time the vest hung open, exposing her, he was hard and she was weak. Her head hung back, presenting him with a long, tantalizing expanse, from chin to waist, of pale, warm skin, full breasts, swollen nipples. The sight was beautiful, enticing, erotic.

He slid the vest off her shoulders, then lowered her onto the bed. Her hair spread across his pillows, wild curls in pure, rich brown, and tempted him to bury his hands, to bury his face, and cling to her forever. Instead, he sucked first one breast, then the other, while his hands eased her skirt and panties over her hips, down strong-muscled thighs and runner's calves. Wriggling and kicking, she helped him strip away the clothing, then stretched out, head to toe, under his exploratory caresses.

When his fingers stroked between her thighs, she gave a low, shuddering groan, then opened her eyes. "I'm lying here completely naked, and you're fully dressed," she said in a throaty voice. "What's wrong with this picture?"

Leaning on one elbow, he gave her a long, leisurely look. "Not a damn thing. You are a beautiful woman, Kelsey." He dropped a kiss on her lips, then drew back to work his own clothes off. "You're strong and powerful and capable, and you know that there's not good in everyone, but you still have faith, and you're exactly what I need, exactly what I want." Finally naked, he moved between her thighs and slowly eased inside her. When he'd filled her, when her body held him tightly, completely, he closed his eyes for one moment to capture the feeling—the rightness. The belonging. The peace. *Home*.

"I love you, Kelsey Colleen Malone," he said, and then she wrapped her long legs around his hips, and her strong arms around his neck, and kissed him, and for a long time neither of them said anything.

At least, not with words. Their actions, on the other hand, spoke volumes and left him breathless. Helpless. And hopeful.

Very, very hopeful.

TURNING ONTO HER SIDE IN THE CIRCLE OF J.D.'s arms, Kelsey pressed a kiss to his chest. She couldn't remember ever feeling this good in her entire life. Her whole body seemed to vibrate with the most peaceful, soothing sensations she'd ever experienced, and she thought she would be content to lie there with J.D. forever. Who needed food, clothing, a life, when they had *this*?

But they had a life, and it was just waiting to encroach on them again. In fact, however reluctantly, she opened the door for it. "I guess tomorrow's hearing is cancelled."

Beside her, J.D. tensed. "I talked to the D.A. after Garth Nichols came clean. He said he would cancel the hearing. I told him no."

"But the question of abuse has been settled."

"The question of custody hasn't." He turned onto his side, too, so that they were face-to-face, practically nose to nose. "I want those kids, Kelsey. They deserve a stable home with someone who loves them, where they know they'll be welcome—all four of them together—next week and next month and next year. They shouldn't be bounced around from place to place, never really belonging, always fearing that they'll lose each other in the next move. Caleb shouldn't think that he has to run away to solve his problems."

"Noah shouldn't think that leaving is what people do," she murmured.

"I know I'm not a good candidate for this. Mary Therese will take one look at the fact that I'm an alcoholic who doesn't have custody of my own son and will automatically assume I shouldn't have custody of anyone else's. But—" The bleak sorrow at the mention of Trey faded from his eyes and was replaced by determination. "I love those kids, Kelsey, and I'm willing to fight for them."

And that was something the Brown children desperately needed.

"I also know that this makes things more difficult for you and me," he said quietly. "But I'm willing to fight for you too."

"I'll do what I can to help you," she said quietly. "I can't promise much, but . . . whatever I can."

"That means a lot, Kelsey." He yawned, then resettled on his back. "I think I'm going to take that nap now. Stay with me."

"I will."

"If there's any news about Caleb . . ."

"I'll let you know."

She leaned on one arm and watched as his eyes drifted shut. His breathing evened and slowed, and, like that, he was asleep. He'd been exhausted for too long, running on pure stress. She could use a few hours' rest too, but she wasn't ready yet.

One day soon, she thought, he was going to ask her to marry him. Saying yes, especially if he got custody of the kids, could mean big changes in her job. Provided she even had a job once Mary Therese was finished with her. She could be forced to quit for the improprieties she'd already committed, and that didn't include that afternoon's interlude.

Quitting the job that meant so much to her—that was a staggering thought. For twenty years, first becoming, then being, a social worker had been her life, and now she might have to walk away from it. But if she had to leave the job, she couldn't do it for a better reason than J.D. The job meant a lot, but he meant more. He was her future. If Mary Therese and everyone above her thought Kelsey wasn't fit to be a social worker any longer, then she would be happy to tell them good-bye. She would be thrilled to spend the next forty years as a wife and mother.

She thought Steph would approve.

After a time, she eased away from J.D. His arm tightened around her and he murmured her name, but almost immediately he relaxed back into a deep sleep. For a moment she stayed there, her eyes damp with tears. Even in sleep he'd known it was she beside him. Even in sleep he hadn't mistaken her for Carol Ann, and that made her happier than she could express.

After getting dressed, she took a soda from the refrigerator, then went outside to sit on the steps. The midafternoon sun was still high in the sky, but inevitably it would disappear and night would set in. Where would Caleb be when that happened? Was he scared? Was he safe? Would they ever know?

If only there were some way to tell him that Garth had come forward, that the truth about his injuries had come out. Maybe, with the criminal charges against J.D. out of the way, Caleb could find the courage to come back. Maybe he could deal with his anger over his father's abandonment and could help J.D. gain custody of the kids. It was going to be an uphill battle, and the support of the eldest child could count for a lot.

"Hi."

Looking up, Kelsey focused her gaze on the woman at the bottom of the stairs. She'd certainly been quiet in her approach. Even Gracie's small feet crunched over the gravel that lined the driveway and led right to where the woman stood.

It was the woman from the church, the one who'd been in the courthouse Monday afternoon. "You look like you could use a sympathetic ear."

Not really, Kelsey thought uncharitably. She needed a crystal ball. A miracle.

"It's not a bad idea," the woman said as she climbed halfway up the stairs to lean against the rail.

"What isn't?"

"The support of the eldest child. To help J.D. get custody of the Brown children."

Kelsey stared at her. That had been her last thought before she noticed the woman standing below. How had she—"What? Was I talking out loud?"

"No. But I think you have the wrong child in mind."

"Caleb *is* the oldest Brown."

"Yes, but Trey's support could count for a lot."

Stunned, Kelsey opened her mouth, closed it, then blurted out, "How do you know about Trey? *What* do you know about Trey?"

"I know he's missed his father. And I know he's in Chicago. And I think a little trip to Bethlehem in the middle of a boring summer might do him some good." She reached into her pocket and drew out a slip of paper. "Twenty-eight months can calm a lot of anger and ease a lot of hurt. It can make a child see that hating his father won't bring back his mother. It only costs him his father."

When Kelsey didn't move, the woman waved the paper so its edges fluttered. "Go see him. For J.D.'s sake. For Trey's and Caleb's. For your own."

Slowly she laid her soda aside, stood up, walked down the steps that separated them, and took the paper. As she climbed back to the top, she looked at the name and address written in graceful script. Trey Grayson. J.D.'s son. A child who might look like his father or not, who had J.D.'s blood flowing through his veins.

When she reached the landing, she turned back to speak to the woman, to demand to know how she knew of Trey's existence, how she knew Kelsey's own thoughts.

The driveway was empty. So was Mrs. Larrabee's yard. There was no sign of the woman anywhere.

She was gone.

Her heart pounding, Kelsey looked at the paper again. Chicago wasn't so far. A short drive to Howland, a commuter flight to Syracuse, and she would be in Chicago in no time.

She went inside and to the bedroom, where J.D. still slept. He would probably argue her plan. She couldn't get his hopes up. Instead, she kissed him, then leaned close to his ear and whispered, "I love you, J.D. I swear I do."

After leaving a brief note propped on the dining table, she left his apartment and headed for her own.

THE CHICAGO AIRPORT WAS BUSY WHEN KELSEY arrived. She slung her carry-on bag over her shoulder and rented a car. It looked like a turtle on wheels, but she didn't care. It came with the only thing that mattered—detailed directions to her destination.

The neighborhood was old, nicely middle-class. Each house had its own distinctive personality, none more so than the white two-story that matched the numbers on her mysterious benefactor's note. The yard was lushly green and edged around the borders, and the flowers that filled the beds would fit nicely in any master gardener's planting. Two nice, middle-class sedans were parked in the driveway, and two nice, middle-class adults were sitting on the porch.

Kelsey parked across the street and for a moment studied the couple. They looked about the age of her own parents, though where her mother was still winning the battle over gray hair, the woman on the porch had surrendered to it. She was attractive and her husband was handsome, not that Kelsey expected any less of the parents who had produced the beautiful, delicate, perfect Carol Ann.

Kelsey grabbed her purse and climbed out. She didn't immediately cross the street, but instead wondered if she was doing the right thing. These people whose names she didn't even know blamed J.D. for their daughter's death. They thought he wasn't fit to care for his own child. How eager would they be to help him gain custody of someone else's children? They were probably far more likely to side with the state in keeping the kids from him.

But she'd come all this way. What was the worst that could happen? They'd turn her down. J.D. would never have to know.

Displaying more confidence than she felt, she crossed the street and followed the sidewalk to the porch. By the time she reached the steps, J.D.'s father-in-law was on his feet. "Can I help you?"

"I hope so." She offered a business card first to him, then to his wife. "My name is Kelsey Malone. I'm a social worker in Bethlehem, New York. I'm looking for Trey Grayson."

At the mention of Bethlehem, the friendliness disappeared from their faces. They exchanged glances, then the man took the card back from his wife and returned them both to her. "What do you want with my grandson?"

Her palms grew sweaty as the hope that had brought her this far began shrinking. Still, she pressed on. "I'd like to talk to him about his father."

"He doesn't want to hear what you have to say."

"I can certainly understand that, if that's the case, but I'd like to hear it from him."

"Did J.D. send you?"

"No," she answered, relieved she could say it truthfully.

"He has no idea that I'm here. This is official business, Mr.—?"

"Whittaker." He offered a handshake, callused and strong. "Earl Whittaker. This is my wife Bev."

Kelsey acknowledged the introductions with a nod before Mrs. Whittaker asked, "What kind of official social services business involves our grandson, Ms. Malone?"

"A custody hearing."

Mr. Whittaker staggered back, and his hand came to rest on his wife's shoulder. She clutched it tightly in hers. "He's suing for custody of Trey?"

"No, ma'am." Though, in her opinion, it might not be a bad thing. "He's seeking custody of the foster children he's been caring for."

Scorn quickly replaced alarm in Bev Whittaker's expression. "J. D. Grayson? Taking in foster kids? What fool in their right mind would allow such a thing?"

A flush warmed Kelsey's cheeks as she moved to lean against the railing in front of Mrs. Whittaker's rocker. "I'm one of the fools. I'm the children's caseworker. You've had no contact with J.D. since your daughter's death other than what was necessary to gain custody of Trey. Is that right?"

"And we don't *want* any contact with him," Mr. Whittaker replied. "And we don't want any part of this custody hearing, and we don't want you bothering our grandson. So you can go now, Ms. Malone, and don't come—"

One quiet word from inside the house interrupted him and drew Kelsey's attention to the door. "Wait." The figure in the doorway was little more than shadow at first, but under their watchful gazes he came into sharp focus as he stepped outside. Like his grandparents, she simply stared. Trey Grayson was taller than her by several inches. His hair was dark, as were his eyes—like his mother—but she could see hints of his father in his face—his bones, the shape of his eyes, the well-defined calves revealed by his shorts. He was unbearably handsome—like his father— and too composed for a fourteen-year-old, and the desire to gather him into her arms for a heartfelt embrace was almost too strong for her to ignore.

He came to her but didn't offer his hand. Instead, he stuck both hands, palms out, in his hip pockets. "You're here about—about my father?"

"You don't have to talk to her," Mr. Whittaker said sharply. "You don't have to listen to anything she says."

"He's right. You don't," Kelsey agreed, though she didn't want to.

Mrs. Whittaker laid a hand on Trey's arm. "Nothing she says matters. Nothing about *him* matters. We'll send her away now."

Trey looked from his grandmother to his grandfather, then to Kelsey. The expression in his eyes was troubled and torn, and for one sinking moment she thought he was going to agree. Then he gave his grandparents a shaky smile and said, "I can't know if it matters until I hear it. I—I want to hear it."

"Trey—"

He brushed off his grandmother's plea and gestured toward the steps. "Want to walk and talk?"

Well aware of the Whittakers' glares burning into her back, she preceded Trey down the steps to the sidewalk that cut across the lawn. They were in front of the next-door neighbor's house before she spoke. "I'm Kelsey Malone."

"J. D. Grayson the third. Everyone calls me Trey."

She glanced at him. "I don't imagine you'd tell me what the J.D. in your name stands for."

His grin was wry. "It's a family secret." Immediately, at the mention of *family,* the grin faded. The name—and the secret—was the only thing he still shared with that family,

Kelsey thought sadly. That and, of course, a great love and sorrow for his mother.

"You know my dad?"

"Yes."

He sighed heavily. "I don't."

"It's hard to get to know someone when you've cut him out of your life."

He gave her a long, steady look that reminded her of J.D. "He wasn't *ever* a part of my life, not only after my mom died."

After my mom died. Not *After he killed my mom.* That was a good sign, she thought. "No. I understand he was working long hours."

"And drinking gallons of booze. And caring more about total strangers than he did his own family."

He spoke in the same tone Caleb had used after the run-in with Kenny Howard at the church. *He didn't even ask if it hurt . . . if it'd been Gracie or Noah or Jacob, he'd've asked.* "It may have seemed that way, Trey, but he loved you and your mother very much. He just didn't do a very good job of showing you." Though she had no doubt that Carol Ann had known.

"So . . . is he still sober?"

She nodded. "He has been since your mother's death."

"Good for him." But he didn't sound very sincere. In fact, he sounded as if the next logical comment would be a question—why couldn't he have gotten sober and stayed that way *before* she died? Why did he find the strength to stay sober now, when the family had already been destroyed, instead of two and a half years ago, when they could have been saved?

She wished, for J.D.'s sake, for Trey's and his grandparents', that J.D. had found sobriety earlier than two and a half years ago. But if he had, he would be living happily here in Chicago with the woman he'd loved dearly. He wouldn't be a part of Kelsey's life, and yes, it was selfish, but she *wanted* him in her life. She *needed* him.

"What's he doing?"

"He's still a psychiatrist. He works at the hospital in Bethlehem, and he also sees patients at the schools and the nursing home."

As they'd walked, the houses had gradually given way to businesses. Now they stood at an intersection with shops on all four corners. Trey gestured toward the McDonald's across the street. "Want a Coke?"

"Sure."

He was the one who paid for a hamburger and two Cokes. He polished off half the burger in two bites before asking, "Why'd you come here?"

"J.D.—your father—"

"You can call him J.D."

She nodded with a tinge of regret. "He's had temporary custody of four foster children—three boys and a girl, ages five to twelve. He wants to keep them. My boss found out that he's a recovering alcoholic who lost custody of his own son, and she wants the kids placed elsewhere."

"He didn't *lose* custody of me. He gave it up."

"He thought it was best for you. He thought it was what you wanted." She folded her hands together to stop her fingers from knotting. "He tried to keep in touch with you. He called and wrote you letters."

"I know. In the beginning I didn't want to talk to him or read his letters, and Grandma and Granddad said I didn't have to, so I didn't. But once"—a sheepish look came onto his face—"I hid one of the letters from them, and after they went to bed, I steamed it open and read it, and I felt—really weird. Kinda bad for him and—and kinda bad for me too, like *I'd* done something wrong. But I didn't. *He* was the alcoholic. *He* was the one driving drunk when Mom died."

Kelsey watched as he finished off the burger, then crumpled the wrapper with great attention to detail. She was always amazed by the capacity for forgiveness shown by the abused and neglected children in the state's care, always wondered where that kind of love came from and often wished it would go away. Abuse and neglect were easier to deal with if you didn't dearly love the person guilty of them. Rejection and abandonment didn't hurt so deeply when the person rejecting and abandoning you wasn't of utmost importance in your life.

Now, though, she found herself wishing that Trey Grayson possessed just a little of that forgiveness and love those other kids had, that he wasn't so aware that he had good reason to hate his father.

"You're absolutely justified in breaking off contact with J.D.," she said quietly. "He made a lot of mistakes, mistakes that hurt you, and he'll be the first to admit it. But he's worked very hard to get where he is today. He's struggled to rebuild his life, to rebuild himself. He's not the same man you used to know. He's a very kind, generous man who's admired, respected, and loved by everyone in Bethlehem, including those foster kids."

He gave her another of those long, steady J.D. looks but said nothing.

"The custody hearing is tomorrow. It would mean a lot if you would testify on his behalf."

"He never had time to be a father to me, never even tried to get custody of me, and you want me to go to court and say that I think he'd be a good father for those other kids?"

She smiled faintly. "When you put it that way, it does sound a bit ridiculous, doesn't it? To even consider that, you would have to have some feeling for him besides hatred."

"I don't hate him exactly," he admitted grudgingly.

"Sometimes I wonder, you know, what he's like, how he's doing. Sometimes I wonder if he's sorry, if he still misses Mom, if he—if he misses me. Sometimes I think he's forgotten all about me. He never really cared much in the first place, or he wouldn't have always been working and he wouldn't have just let Grandma and Granddad have me, but sometimes . . ." His voice trailed away until it was barely audible. "Sometimes I wonder."

She laid her hand over his. "He's very sorry, Trey. You and your mother are the biggest sorrows, the biggest regrets in his life. But you don't have to take my word for it. Go back with me tomorrow, and he'll be more than willing to tell you himself."

His expression took on that troubled look again. After a moment, without answering, he slid out of the booth and picked up his trash. "We'd better go home. Grandma and Granddad will be worried."

Reluctantly Kelsey followed him outside. They made the return trip more or less in silence, their only conversation meaningless remarks about summer and weather. When they got to the Whittaker house, she handed him a card with the number of her hotel and her departing flight information on the back. "Call me."

He looked at it, then glanced over his shoulder at his grandparents. "I don't know."

"Your dad wasn't there for you when you needed him—I understand that. But if you find it in your heart to give him another chance, I promise he'll never let you down like that again."

"Granddad says Mom gave him too many chances and it got her killed."

"And what would your mom say to that?"

He shrugged awkwardly.

"Think about it." She closed his fingers over the card, then wrapped her own fingers around his. "Think about what your mom would want you to do. Think about what *you* want to do. Will you do that?"

After another look at his grandparents, he nodded.

She couldn't ask for anything more. "Thank you for your time. I hope to hear from you." She started across the street, then, after a few steps, turned back. "Trey? It was an honor meeting you."

His cheeks colored and he mumbled some response before turning to run up the sidewalk.

She'd done all she could. Now she could only wait . . . and pray.

K ELSEY'S NOTE TO J.D. WAS SHORT—*I'LL BE back*—but waiting for her to return was taking forever.

People got swept away in the heat of a moment. Spurred on by passion, people said and did things that they later regretted. Maybe she was off somewhere, regretting that afternoon. Maybe she was trying to figure out how to deal with it, how to let him down without risking the delicate balance he'd finally regained.

But she loved him, had told him so while he slept. He knew in his soul it hadn't been a dream. She believed in him, and the least he could do was return the favor.

That didn't stop him from worrying though.

He waited through the night, dialing numbers by instinct, leaving messages that edged into pleading. He lay in his bed, where the smells of her clung to the sheets, listened to Bud's snores down the hall, and waited.

He'd finally dozed off when the phone rang. Instantly awake, he grabbed it, but it wasn't Kelsey. It was Mitch Walker.

"Good news, J.D. We just got a call from the Binghamton P.D. They picked up Caleb tonight. Other than being scared and hungry, he appears to be in good shape. They

said he wants you to come pick him up. He was insistent
about that." Mitch stopped to yawn. "I can't get hold of
Kelsey. She isn't with you, by chance, is she?"

"No. I've been trying to reach her too."

"I told them you'd be there in a couple or three hours.
That a problem?"

"No. I'll leave now."

Mitch yawned again. "Talk to Detective Mendez. He's
expecting you."

"Thanks, Mitch. Thanks a lot." His hand trembling,
J.D. hung up, then closed his eyes. Thank God, Caleb was
safe. If he only knew the same about Kelsey . . .

It was a long drive to Binghamton. By the time J.D.
parked in front of the police station, the sun was up and his
stomach was growling. He spoke to the detective who'd
found Caleb, showed his identification, and signed endless
forms before the kid was finally brought out to him.

Caleb shuffled along beside the officer, his gaze cast
down, looking as bereft as anyone J.D. had ever seen.
When he stopped a few feet away, J.D. cupped his chin,
pushed his head back. There were no new marks on his
face, just a few dirty streaks across one cheek. His bottom
lip was trembling though, and his eyes were so full of tears
that one blink was going to wash them over.

"Are you all right?"

Caleb nodded mutely.

"You are grounded forever." Then, wrapping his hand
around Caleb's neck, J.D. pulled the boy to him in a fierce
hug. "My God, Caleb, I was so scared—"

Pressing his face against J.D.'s shirt, Caleb burst into
sobs that racked his thin body. "I'm sorry, doc! I'm so
sorry! I thought—I thought you didn't want me and
ever'one would be happier if I was gone, but I didn't have
no place to go and I was scared and—" He pushed back to

look up at J.D. with anguish. "My dad's never comin' back, and I—I want to go home."

J.D. held him until he was all cried out, until he'd cried a few tears of his own, then dried Caleb's face with the bottom of his T-shirt. "I thought I didn't want you too," he admitted, "but I was wrong. I *do* want you, Caleb. I want you and the others to stay with me forever. But first . . ." He took a deep, steadying breath. "Let's talk about your dad, and let me tell you about my son."

THE HEARING WAS SET FOR ELEVEN O'CLOCK. IT was half past when J.D. parked his truck down the block and he and Caleb hurried to the courthouse. Half the town, it seemed, was gathered outside. Some were there, no doubt, to testify on his behalf. Others waited to wish him well and to welcome Caleb back. He saw all the people who had come to mean so much to him in the last year and a half—everyone but the kids.

And Kelsey.

They made their way inside the courtroom, and the hope he'd been harboring all the way to Binghamton and back died. She wasn't there. Judge McKechnie was on the bench, the court reporter at her seat in front of him. Bill Robbins, the district attorney, was chatting at the defense table with Jillian Freeman. Mary Therese sat on the first row in the gallery, along with one of the intake workers from her Howland office, a young woman named Lisa, and Jacob, Noah, and Gracie were beside them—at least, until they saw Caleb.

With excited cries they surrounded him, Gracie and Noah climbing into his arms. While the four of them huddled together, J.D. approached Mary Therese. "Where is Kelsey?"

Her only response was a grim shake of her head.

"I thought . . ." He sighed dejectedly. "I thought maybe she was working. Doing something for you." Or something for him, for them. I'll do what I can to help you, she'd promised. Never in his wildest dreams had he thought that might be running away.

No. He believed in her. Wherever she was, whatever she was doing, she hadn't run away.

"I don't know where she is." Mary Therese shifted uncomfortably. "J.D., I'm sorry for what's going to happen here. I believe you're a good man, but—with your history . . . We have to be so careful. I'm sorry."

Looking up from the papers in front of him, Judge McKechnie cleared his throat. "Now that Dr. Grayson and young Caleb have decided to grace us with their presence, shall we get this show under way?" He gave them a moment to take their seats. "Now, as I understand, the allegation of abuse has been dropped. Caleb, Garth Nichols says you got those injuries in a fight with him and some other boys. Is that correct?"

The judge easily intimidated grown men, but Caleb got to his feet and unflinchingly met his gaze. "Yes, sir."

"We'll discuss your lies later, young man. Right now we're going to skip on to the issue of custody. You children will wait next door with—what's your name? Lisa. Just take them through that door." He waited until they were gone, then turned to the D.A. "Bill?"

Robbins called Mary Therese to the stand. She hit—and hit hard—on everything—his alcoholism, Carol Ann's death, and, most especially, the fact that he'd given up custody of Trey. She was apologetic, but she was also unswerving in her belief that in light of this recently uncovered information, he was *not* a good candidate to take custody of four young children.

Mary Therese was the D.A.'s only witness. Jillian called each of the kids, who said yes, they wanted to stay with

J.D. Next she called an interesting mix of character witnesses—Bud, Miss Corinna, Mitch Walker, and Alanna Dalton among them. Everyone said what a nice guy he was, how much they liked and respected him, how they couldn't imagine anyone better to take care of the Brown children.

It was heartwarming, J.D. thought sadly as the last witness left the stand, but it wasn't enough. If he'd been called as an expert witness, there strictly as a psychiatrist to determine whether an alcoholic—even one who hadn't had a drink in two years, four months, and counting—whose own son refused to live with him should have custody of four children not his own, he would side with Mary Therese.

If he was going to get the kids back, it would depend on his testimony. He would need the most eloquent, most persuasive arguments he could come up with, but his mind was blank. All he could think was that he was losing the kids and he might have already lost Kelsey, and then what would he have?

He was staring bleakly at the scarred oak table when the bailiff came in and handed a note to Jillian. She scanned it, spoke to the man, then faced the judge. "Your Honor, for my next witness I'd like to call J. D. Grayson." When he started to stand, she laid a hand on his shoulder, pushing him back. "The third."

J.D. jerked around in his chair as the door at the back of the courtroom opened. Earl and Bev Whittaker came in first, followed by Kelsey—beautiful Kelsey, who hadn't let him down at all—and, beside her, a tall, slender, dark-haired young man. He was the most incredible person J.D. had seen in his life.

As Trey approached the front, his gaze met J.D.'s and the faintest of smiles touched his mouth. J.D. slumped back in his chair, barely noticing when Kelsey sat down behind him, when she laid her hand reassuringly on his shoulder.

His *son*. She'd brought him his son.

Jillian approached the witness stand. "Your name is J. D. Grayson the third. What do you prefer to be called?"

"I go by Trey." His voice was deeper than before and sounded remarkably grown-up. His little boy *had* grown up, J.D. thought with a bittersweet ache, and he'd missed it. All of it.

"What is your relationship to Dr. Grayson?"

Trey glanced his way again. "He's my father."

"But you don't live with him, do you?"

"No, ma'am."

"Why not?"

"When my mother died, I blamed him. She was killed in a car wreck, and he was driving, and I thought it was his fault because"—he nervously glanced J.D.'s way, then turned his attention back to Jillian—"because he was drunk. After that he had to go away, to get help for his drinking, and I stayed with my mom's parents. I still live with them."

"And do you still blame your father for your mother's death?"

Trey looked at him then, really looked. J.D. felt as if his answer could make or break his life. Then the boy returned his attention to Jillian. "No."

"Why not? What's changed?"

He shrugged. "Everything, I guess. Me. Him. I'm not still mad. He's not still drinking. I've grown up. I think maybe he's not so grown-up."

"And is that a good thing?"

Trey chuckled. It was an amazing sight. "Oh, yeah. You don't know what he was like before."

"Tell us."

"He worked all the time. He wanted to be the best at

any cost. People respected him, but not a lot of people liked him. Now"—he gestured toward the door—"there's a whole town out there waiting because of him. People who respect him *and* like him. People who are willing to like *me* just for being his son. He's got friends. He's got a life. He's changed. And that's real good."

Jillian asked one last question. "Do you think he's changed enough to be a good father?"

"I don't know," Trey replied, his honesty seeming as painful for him as it was for J.D. "But I'd like the chance to find out."

"Thank you, Trey. I have no further questions."

As Trey left the witness stand, Judge McKechnie stood up. "Wait here," he commanded. "I'll be back." With his black robes trailing behind him, he went into his chambers and closed the door.

With an exhausted sigh Kelsey pulled an envelope from her purse, then crossed the aisle to sit beside Mary Therese.

"That had better not be a letter of resignation," her boss said.

"I just don't know if I can do this job anymore."

Mary Therese looked from her to J.D., then back. "Go ahead. Jump at the first better offer that comes along."

"He hasn't offered yet."

"But if he does, you're gonna grab hold with both hands. You're no fool. That's one of the things I like about you." Mary Therese tapped the envelope. "Hold on to that for a while. You can always turn it in later if you decide you have to."

Kelsey nodded, then started back to her seat. She was halfway there when J.D. caught her hand and guided her around the knee wall to join him as Trey and the Whittakers approached. "I cannot believe you brought me my son," he murmured.

"He wanted to come. He just needed the invitation."

For a long while Earl and Bev simply stood there, looking, and so did J.D. Finally Earl offered his hand. "J.D."

"Earl." J.D. accepted his handshake. "Thank you for letting Trey come."

His father-in-law shrugged. "It was his decision. He wanted—"

When he didn't go on, Bev did. "He wanted to come, J.D. He wanted to see you." She curled her fingers gently around his. "You look real good."

"I've been working at it."

"I know. We should have been there to help, but—" Breaking off, she blinked back a tear or two, then caught Trey by the arm and pulled him close. "Come on up here and say hello. You've waited a long time for this."

Looking supremely awkward, Trey shoved his hands in his pockets, flashed a grin that mirrored his father's, then shrugged. "Hi."

"Hi." J.D. stared at him for a moment as if he were hungry for the sight. "You've changed."

"So have you." Trey shrugged again. "You look real good." After another long, stiff silence, he said, "I—I don't know if—what I said made any difference—"

"Oh, yeah. It made all the difference in the world."

For an instant Kelsey thought J.D. was going to let go of her and reach for his son. She silently urged him to, but instead his fingers curled even more tightly around hers. "God, Trey, I've missed you."

"I've missed you too. I, uh—I understand you're building a house." Trey cleared his throat, shifted from foot to foot. "Granddad's taught me how to use his tools, and I—I have some time before school starts if—if you're—interested."

"I would love that," J.D. replied.

"Better be a big house. Four kids, Grandpa, Kelsey."

Trey swallowed hard, pulled his hands from his pockets, then shoved them back. "Are you sure there's room for one more?"

"Aw, hell." J.D. dropped Kelsey's hand and reached for Trey. The boy went willingly, gratefully, into his embrace. "There's always room for you. You're my *son.*"

Kelsey closed her eyes and breathed deeply. She was more tired than she'd ever been in her life, more emotionally raw—and she couldn't be any happier. Well, unless the judge would come back right then and give J.D. custody of the Brown kids. She liked the idea of an immediate family. Marry one and become mother to five. It would thrill her grandchild-hungry mother no end.

Across the room the door to the judge's chambers opened, and he returned to the bench. "Sit down, sit down, wherever you are."

Trey took the empty chair next to J.D.'s. Kelsey returned to her own seat a few feet behind.

"On paper, I admit, J.D. doesn't look like much of a father—a recovering alcoholic whose own child chooses to live elsewhere. But we don't live our lives on paper. What's in our past is important in that it makes us what we are in the present. And what J. D. Grayson is in the present is a part of this community. He's respected—and well liked," he said with a nod to Trey. "He's a good friend and neighbor. He's responsible, a hard worker, and a generous man. In the year and a half he's lived here, he's remained so sober that not one of us suspected he had a problem.

"Now, Mary Therese, I know your motto is better safe than sorry when it comes to the children in your care. But sometimes being safe also means being sorry. Did J.D. have problems in the past? Undoubtedly. Is he having problems now? No. Is he likely to have problems in the future? That's something only the good Lord knows for sure, but I'd be willing to wager that the answer is no. As his son pointed out, he's a changed man. He's got his priorities straight, and if he ever needs a gentle reminder, he's got plenty of people to give him one—the whole darn town, in fact.

"Maybe you could find someone else who wants those kids as much as he does, but I doubt it. You and I both know that there are a lot more people leaving their kids than there are other people wanting to take them in. And maybe you could find someone that those kids want more than him, but I doubt that too. Our sheriff's department has been looking for a family relation for more than a month without success. The way I see it, we've got two sides that want the same thing, and I see no reason to stand between them. I hereby order custody of Caleb, Jacob, Noah, and Gracie Brown returned to J. D. Grayson, effective immediately."

I T WAS A QUIET, STILL EVENING. ACROSS TOWN the younger three kids were tucked in their bunks, and Caleb and Trey were keeping Bud company. In her apartment, tucked in her own bed, Kelsey was keeping J.D. company. They'd made sweet love, and now she lay cradled in his arms, more asleep than awake as the last four days finally caught up with her.

She was about to doze off, when he matter-of-factly spoke. "When you marry me, we'll be able to share a bed in the same house. No more sneaking across town to make love. I might miss it."

She woke up enough to give him a haughty look. "*When* I marry you? Awfully sure of yourself, aren't you?"

After a moment's thought he smugly grinned. "Well . . . yes, as a matter of fact, I am."

"You haven't even asked."

He rolled over, then held himself above her, his hands bearing his weight on either side of her head. "Kelsey Colleen Malone, I love you dearly and can think of nothing that would make me happier than to call you my wife. Will you marry me?"

She pretended to consider it, then said, "Yes . . . on one condition."

"I'll love you forever."

"That's not the condition."

"I'll devote myself to keeping you happy."

"That's not it either."

"I'll rub your back when you're pregnant and your front when you're not. I'll buy you ice cream and plant you flowers. I'll keep your feet warm in winter and scrape the ice off your car windows and share the household chores. I'll buy you a puppy and take you to the beach once every summer and tell everyone I meet that I'm the luckiest man in the entire world for having you." Suddenly he grinned, and the gleam in his eye turned devilish. "I'll tell you what J.D. stands for."

Her smile spread from ear to ear. "It's only fair. After all, you call me by my full name. When I tell you that I love you with a passion and would be honored to become your wife, I can do it with your full name."

Leaning lower, he brushed his mouth over her ear, sending a delicate shudder through her, and he whispered the words. Her first impulse was to laugh, but he chose that moment to lower himself to her, to slide easily inside her, and she gave a heavenly sigh instead. "I love you, J. D. Grayson, and I would be honored to become your wife. But I will be damned—"

Her body arched and her breath caught as he did such wickedly enticing things to her.

"—if I will ever call you—"

He stroked her with his fingers, sending shivers rippling through her.

She whispered the name on a gasp that swiftly became a moan of pure need.

"I don't care what you call me," he murmured as his body stiffened, as hers went taut with pleasure. "Just as long as you call me."

Epilogue

THE COOLER WEATHER OF FALL BROUGHT changing leaves and hunters to the mountains. It was the latter who discovered the rusted-out pickup truck deep in a ravine off one of the valley's most isolated roads. They reported their find to the sheriff, who took no pleasure in passing along the news to J.D.

Ezra Brown had been found.

The church had been crowded with mourners who'd never met the man, who wouldn't have recognized him if he'd walked in and sat down among them. They'd come out of respect to his children, for which J.D. was grateful. A lonely funeral on a chilly fall day was no place for children.

Now all the visitors who'd brought food and condolences had gone. The younger children were tucked in their beds in the room they shared. Caleb, who had, predictably, taken his father's death the hardest, had changed from his suit and gone for a walk in the woods. Though dusk was settling and he hadn't yet come back, J.D. wasn't worried. Trey was with him. He would look out for him.

The French door behind him opened with a creak, then closed again. A moment later Kelsey wrapped her arms around him from behind. "Are you okay?"

He clasped her hands. "I was pretty sure from the beginning that he wasn't coming back, but . . . I had hoped. For the kids' sake."

"I know." She sighed, and he felt her breasts shift against his back. "But at least they know."

Yes, they knew. For whatever comfort that provided.

The license tag on Ezra's truck had been expired, and there'd been no money to get a new one. The insurance had also expired, and Caleb had explained that that was why he'd taken the back roads when he'd started his search for work. He'd hoped to avoid the scrutiny that might bring him fines he couldn't pay.

His plan had worked all too well.

There was no way to tell what had caused him to veer off the road, no way to know whether his injuries had killed him immediately or if death had come slowly. For the kids' sake, J.D. had chosen the first theory, and because he was a doctor—because he was their new father—they'd believed him.

Rustling in the woods beyond the deck caught his attention, and he watched as Trey and Caleb came into the clearing. Kids were so adaptable. Lose your parents, get new parents, move in with new brothers and a sister, make a family out of so many different parts . . . They were nothing less than miraculous.

"You guys going to bed?" he asked as they came up the steps together.

"It's not even nine o'clock."

He couldn't tell which of them had spoken. They acted

alike, moved alike, were even beginning to sound alike. Miraculous.

"He just wants us to go to bed so he can be alone with Kelsey," the other said, and now he could see that it was Trey. "You'd think they weren't married, the way he carries on with her."

"Hey, I'm standing right here," Kelsey protested as she stepped out from behind J.D. "Did you not notice?"

"Kinda hard not to notice." Trey patted her belly as he passed. "You gonna have twins or something?"

"Maybe triplets," Caleb said, mimicking his actions.

Trey started to open the door, then came back to kiss them both. "Good night, Dad. Good night, Kelse."

When he went inside, Caleb hesitated, then came back too. "My father was a good dad."

J.D. slid his arm around the boy's shoulders. "I know he was. He did a fine job with you."

"I don't think he would mind . . ." He looked away, then dragged his hand across his nose. "I don't think he'd care if you were my new dad, and if you were my new mom."

"I don't think he would either," Kelsey murmured.

"So . . . good night, Dad. Good night, Mom." As soon as the words were out, he raced across the deck and inside the house.

J.D. sighed as he sat down on the bench. "Kids. They'll break your heart." Then he gave an aggrieved yelp as Kelsey sat on his lap. "What *are* you carrying? Quints?"

She wrapped her arms around his neck and rested her head on his shoulder. "Wouldn't that be something? One night of pleasure, and bam, you go from five kids to ten."

"Oh, darlin', I've gotten a whole lot more than one night of pleasure from you. You've made my life whole. You've healed me. I love you, Kelsey Colleen Grayson."

She gave him a kiss and a sly, smug grin. "I love you too, J.D."

About the Author

KNOWN FOR HER INTENSELY EMOTIONAL STORIES, Marilyn Pappano is the author of nearly forty books with more than four million copies in print. She has made regular appearances on bestseller lists and has received recognition for her work with numerous awards. Though her husband's Navy career took them across the United States, they now live in Oklahoma, high on a hill that overlooks her hometown. They have one son.

Look for

Marilyn Pappano's new novel

FIRST KISS

Available from Bantam Books

Late summer 2000

**Holly McBride wants a fling.
Tom Flynn wants a wedding.
And everybody else in Bethlehem
just wants to stay out of the way.
There's big trouble brewing...unless
Holly and Tom realize what they
really want is each other.**

Deborah Smith

*"A uniquely significant voice
in contemporary fiction."*

—Romantic Times

Silk and Stone ___29689-2 $6.50/$9.99 in Canada

Blue Willow ___29690-6 $6.50/$9.99

Miracle ___29107-6 $6.99/$9.99

A Place to Call Home ___57813-8 $6.50/$8.99

When Venus Fell ___11143-4 $23.95/$29.95

Ask for these books at your local bookstore or use this page to order.

Please send me the books I have checked above. I am enclosing $____ (add $2.50 to cover postage and handling). Send check or money order, no cash or C.O.D.'s, please.

Name _____

Address _____

City/State/Zip _____

Send order to: Bantam Books, Dept. FN72, 2451 S. Wolf Rd., Des Plaines, IL 60018
Allow four to six weeks for delivery.
Prices and availability subject to change without notice.   FN 72 1/99